The Murder at Redmire Hall

The Murder at Redmire Hall

A YORKSHIRE MURDER MYSTERY

J.R. ELLIS

THOMAS & MERCER

Text copyright © 2018 by J. R. Ellis
All rights reserved.

Published by Thomas & Mercer, Seattle

www.apub.com

Amazon, the Amazon logo, and Thomas & Mercer are trademarks of Amazon.com, Inc., or its affiliates.

ISBN-13: 9781503904941
ISBN-10: 1503904946

Cover design by @blacksheep-uk.com

Printed in the United States of America

To Colin

Prologue

Redmire Hall, June 1980

At Redmire Hall, set in the countryside around Ripon in Yorkshire, there was a tangible sense of excitement as the wealthy guests assembled for a weekend party. It was a warm June evening. Bentleys and Rollers swept up the long drive through the grounds. Their host, Vivian Carstairs, Lord Redmire, had promised something extraordinary. His guests knew that that phrase usually meant it was worth travelling hundreds of miles to the home of the eccentric lord.

Redmire Hall was a Regency-style house, built in a beautifully weathered rosy-red brick. It had extensive gardens, laid out by the present lord's father in the 1930s, that were still lovingly maintained by a team of devoted gardeners. There were, however, rumours that Lord Redmire would soon be forced to open the doors of his grandiose pile to the paying public in order to make ends meet. Monetising one's property, along with covenanting it to the National Trust, had become a growing trend among the aristocracy in order to avoid the crippling death duties introduced by 'disgraceful' Labour governments.

Couples sipped champagne at the reception party held on the manicured lawn near the house, looking over the double herbaceous borders leading down to the River Ure, and remarking how dreadful it would be if all manner of Tom, Dick and Harry types were allowed to tramp around the lovely rose gardens, the white garden, the rockeries and the wisteria walk.

An excellent dinner was served in the long dining room and anticipation grew as the guests reminisced about other stunts and remarkable experiences their host had organised in the past. Such as the time they'd had dinner floating down the river, seated at a table that stood on lashed-together wooden rafts being steered by servants with long poles, like something going down the Amazon. When the wine had run out, Redmire had dived into the water and swum to the bank to collect some more from other servants waiting with bottles.

Or the time he'd purchased some lions from a circus, and turned them loose in the grounds for his guests to pursue with rifles. Tales of that particular stunt had got to the animal-rights people and the police, but Redmire had fobbed them off with his usual charm and apologetic self-deprecation.

At last, the host rose at the head of the table to speak. Lord Redmire – a handsome but rather outlandish figure in a sequinned red tuxedo – beamed at his guests. He was a bumptious, Mr Toad-like character, extrovert, gregarious, given to extravagant gestures of all types, and would constantly switch his attention from one all-consuming obsessive interest to another.

His latest craze was altogether more mysterious and secretive: magic. He was fascinated by the world of the illusionists, those mysterious men who could apparently make objects and people disappear in front of astonished audiences. After cultivating the acquaintance of some prominent British practitioners of these arts, he'd spent several months in Italy at the sumptuous palace home of Count Mazarini, who was, like him, a wealthy socialite, but also an accomplished illusionist who'd dazzled audiences all over Europe. When His Lordship had returned to Redmire, there were rumours of strange goings-on at the Hall. He was said to be working on an illusion of his own, helped by people sworn to secrecy.

And now, it seemed, he was ready for a performance before this specially invited audience.

'Ladies and gentlemen,' he announced in his rich baritone voice, with its aristocratic drawl. (There was no hint of a Yorkshire accent.) 'Tonight I crave your indulgence. You know me and my little hobbies.' Here, there was some knowing laughter. 'It is my special pleasure to present myself to you transformed. I am no longer merely Vivian Carstairs, Lord Redmire, but the great illusionist Carzini!'

There was a chorus of facetious 'ooh's and 'aah's from the guests, who were now well lubricated with alcohol and ready for some entertainment. Redmire's face assumed a self-satisfied smile and he held up his arms for quiet.

'I understand you will find it hard to take me seriously, as so many of you have humoured me in the past in my many other transient manifestations, but this . . .' He paused for emphasis and held up his hand. '. . . is the real thing.'

'Ladies and gentlemen, I have perfected what I believe to be a truly remarkable magic trick.' He paused once more. When he spoke again his voice was bolder, emphasising each phrase. 'You will see me disappear completely from a locked room, which you may examine before and after my disappearance. I will then reappear in the same room. And then, ladies and gentlemen, I will disappear from the room for a second time and materialise *outside* this same room.'

This extraordinary announcement silenced his guests. It sounded so preposterous that they were unsure whether or not it was a joke. Redmire was famous for his practical jokes. There were one or two stifled giggles among some of the slightly tipsy women.

'Is this one of your jokes, Viv?' asked a louche-looking character lounging back in a chair and smoking a cigar.

Redmire turned to him. 'Certainly not, Roger; I promise you this is real.' He turned back to the table. 'However, I sense scepticism, so without any further ado let us proceed to the locked room. Please follow me.'

With that he strode off down the dining room and out of the door, followed by his guests. They exchanged many questioning gestures and glances, but were prepared to humour their host. Redmire took them through the large entrance hall and then to the back of the house, which had formerly been part of the servants' quarters. A section had been opened out to form a lobby area, freshly decorated and carpeted but empty of furniture except for lines of chairs facing a door in the wall. Standing by the door was a glamorous young woman dressed in a sparkly, skintight costume. Redmire stood next to her as his guests took their seats.

'This is my assistant, Esmeralda.' The girl flashed a smile and bowed. 'Now, the next part will take some time and preparation because I want you all to examine the room into which I will enter and from which I will disappear. Please come forward.'

Redmire opened the door to reveal a small room, about twelve feet square, furnished like a study, with a chair, a wooden desk and bookshelves. There was a patterned rug on the bare floorboards, and a small window with a view of an area to the rear of the house.

'Please examine everything. You will find no secret panels or passages. There is a trapdoor here.' He indicated a small door cut into the wooden floor, with a brass handle that folded into a recess so that it was flush with the boards. 'But that is only for access to the wiring. A man can get down into it, but no further. And you will not find me hiding there when I have disappeared.'

This trapdoor was duly investigated, and found to lead, as Redmire had said, to a small cavity where there were wires and junction boxes attached to the floorboards. There was just about room for a person to fit into the space, but the base and walls were solid concrete, and there was no way of exiting other than back into the room.

The guests were now entering into the spirit and prodded, poked and examined everything. But they were all thwarted. They checked the floors and ceiling, the door, the window and the furniture. In the end they all agreed: there was no way out of the room other than by the door through which they'd entered.

Redmire watched their exploration with a self-satisfied smirk on his face. He then drew attention to the door.

'Before we start, ladies and gentlemen, please have another look at this door.'

He showed them the lock with the key in place and the two large bolts that secured the door firmly from the outside.

'You may have heard of illusions where locks are false and can be opened using wires and other tricks; but, as you can see, this lock and these bolts are ordinary and there is no way they can be opened from the inside. In any case, if I came out of the door you would see me straight away – and you won't.'

The lock and bolts were tried and pronounced sound.

'So now, ladies and gentlemen, lock me in.'

He sat in the chair, all the guests filed out, and two of the guests locked and bolted the door.

'Are you still in there, Viv?' one of them called out.

'Yes.' Redmire's voice was clearly heard coming from inside the room.

When everyone had assumed their seats, Esmeralda, in a theatrical manner, twirled around and pulled a curtain across the door. Suddenly, loud music – Wagner – filled the room for about fifteen seconds. When it stopped, Esmeralda pulled back the curtain to reveal the bolts still in place on the door. These were shot back, the key turned in the lock and the door flung open. The room was empty; Lord Redmire had vanished. There were exclamations among the guests.

'Good Lord!'

'Where on earth is he?'

With some caution and incredulity the room was examined again, including the space under the trapdoor; even a little girl popped her head through the door and seemed to be looking for something before her mother called her away. There was no sign of Lord Redmire anywhere.

'Lord Redmire will now reappear,' said Esmeralda, in a foreign accent that sounded rather fake. 'Please come out of the locked room.'

Obediently, everyone went back to sit on the chairs. The atmosphere was now more serious. It looked as if the beggar was going to pull it off! Esmeralda drew the curtain; the music was heard again, after which the curtain was drawn back and the lock and bolts reopened to reveal Lord Redmire, sitting in the chair and beaming! This time there were loud gasps from the guests and the curious little girl looked into the room once more.

'I say, Viv, jolly good show! How on earth did you do that?'

Redmire laughed and there was applause from the guests.

'It's not over yet. Shut me in again.'

The whole procedure was repeated and Redmire was discovered to have disappeared again; but now, when the door was opened for the second time, he still wasn't there. As his audience made another search of the room, they heard a voice.

'No point looking in there.'

It was Redmire, sitting in a chair behind them. Everyone was stunned, amazed and full of admiration.

'What the devil!'

'Good Lord, but that's incredible!'

'Bravo, old boy!'

The whole party burst into applause. Redmire, grinning from ear to ear, lapped it up.

The rest of the weekend passed somewhat anticlimactically, without further excitement. Despite the strenuous efforts of many to persuade him, Redmire would not perform the trick again and would say nothing further about his methods. He was clearly enjoying the tantalising mystery and speculation into which he'd plunged his guests. There was much intense discussion about how Redmire could have performed his feat, but it came to nothing. The trick was never explained.

True to form, and despite what he'd said, Redmire soon lost interest in magic. He became fascinated instead by the military campaigns of Julius Caesar. As expected, Redmire Hall underwent some interior refurbishment and was then opened to the public, bringing in much-needed revenue for its eccentric, spendthrift owner. There were tours around the Hall, but only of the big formal rooms with their sumptuous furniture and decorations. The gardens gained a nationwide reputation for their excellence.

The door to the locked room remained locked and bolted, and the key soon went missing. Redmire moved on but remained proud of the trick and would never divulge the details. The evening became legendary to those who'd been there; but, in the course of time, most of them died, including Redmire himself. The story faded and the locked room seemed to be forgotten. Until one day someone saw its potential for something more sinister than entertainment.

One

Frederick Carstairs, the latest Lord Redmire, sat at the desk in his study overlooking the famous double herbaceous borders of Redmire Hall, which stretched down from the house to the River Ure in a glorious sweep of colour. They were looking particularly fine on this July day and Redmire couldn't help admiring them, although he had no great regard for the wonderful gardens of his ancestral home except in so far as they earned revenue from visitors. These gardens had been bequeathed to him by his father along with the house and a debt that he'd never got under control.

He had never been quite sure how he felt about his father. He admired him for being a brilliant eccentric. While Frederick was growing up there had never been a dull moment, as the cliché went. He'd been on expeditions with his father to South America in search of undiscovered Inca cities; helped maintain a fleet of early Rolls-Royce cars; and dived for sunken treasure off the coast of Spain. The late Vivian Carstairs had involved his sons in some of his obsessional pursuits and Frederick's memories of those years were vivid. On the other hand, he realised how his father's reckless spending – albeit on fascinating and exciting endeavours – had almost ruined the estate and placed enormous stress on his mother, who was usually left at home to manage things.

However, it would have been unfair to place the entire blame for the estate's financial problems on his father; the new Lord Redmire had not been exactly careful with money either. His tastes when he was younger had been more conventional than those of Vivian Carstairs: fast cars, partying and womanising. He was now in his sixties and, although the more energetic of his pursuits had diminished, his increasingly costly gambling – mostly card games online, but also at various private clubs when he was in London – meant that money seemed to melt away almost as soon as it was generated.

There was a knock at the door and Andrea Jenkinson, his PA, came into the room with a coffee tray. She was in her late thirties and smartly dressed in a formal style. She placed the tray on Frederick's large mahogany desk.

'Cheers, Andrea. Have you and Richard double-checked everything for this evening?'

She gazed out at the stunning view. 'Yes. It's all in order; there's nothing to worry about.'

'I never do when you're in charge, my dear.' Frederick sat back in his chair and smiled at her. His face was somewhat wrinkled and haggard after a lifetime of decadence, but the outlines of his handsome features were still there. 'What's the running order?'

'The television people set up yesterday; they'll be back soon to check everything. Paying guests are allowed in at seven; family, friends and special guests need to be in position by seven thirty, and we go live at seven forty-five.'

'Good,' replied Frederick. 'We're all set, then.'

As Andrea left the room, Frederick smiled as he thought of the truly astonishing trick he was going to recreate later that day. Secrecy was of the utmost importance in all magic tricks. He remembered being a young man and witnessing his father perform the locked-room illusion to a private audience. Nothing would persuade Vivian Carstairs to repeat the trick or divulge any of its secrets – even to members of his own family, including Frederick. He'd thought the secret had died with his father but he was wrong: he'd recently rediscovered the locked room and learned how it worked. And he'd seen its potential to make him some money.

His father's performance had certainly impressed those who saw it. People wrote about it later in their memoirs. Articles had appeared in newspapers and magazines over the years, recalling the famous occasion and speculating about how it might have been done. The incident fitted beautifully into the wider legend of Vivian Carstairs and his fascinating eccentricity.

But now his son intended to take matters to a daring new level. Frederick had called in the media and was going to replicate his father's trick live on television. The benefit to the estate would be immense: afterwards people would flock to see the famous locked room. He intended to open it to the public as a kind of challenge: examine the room and explain the trick. He was even considering the offer of a substantial prize to anyone who could solve it, being very confident that nobody would. And, to further ensure the trick's credibility, he had persuaded a prominent member of the Harrogate Division of the West Riding Police to be present when it was performed.

From his study, Frederick was able to see the long road through the deer park up to the house and the steps up from the gravel drive past the fountain to the large front door. He watched with satisfaction as a succession of people arrived. Redmire had other, more personal matters to deal with, and inviting family and friends to this event was a good excuse to get them together.

First his brother, Dominic, and Dominic's wife, Mary, drove up in a Mercedes. He'd got on well with his sibling when they were both children and in awe of their father, but Dominic had turned into a huge bore when he reached adulthood. He was much more sensible and practical than his elder brother and ran a recruitment consultancy in York. Frederick knew that Dominic resented his lot as the second son, not inheriting the estate and the title and having to work for a living. He also knew that Dominic regarded him as a wastrel who had squandered the wealth of the estate.

Although he was forced to confess that there was some truth in that, he could never convince his pragmatic brother that the estate actually possessed far fewer financial resources than he thought. Frederick watched unseen as Dominic got out of the car wearing a tweed sports jacket, brown trousers and a tie. God! How suffocatingly old-fashioned the man was. Dominic turned towards the house, frowned and went round to help his wife out of the car. Mary was wearing a shortish skirt with an expensive-looking cashmere cardigan, a silk scarf around her neck and dark glasses. She was very attractive and far too good for his dull brother. She looked up in the direction of the study, as if she knew Frederick would be watching, and smiled. Could it be that on this visit they might . . . ?

The next to arrive was Redmire's daughter, Poppy, and her boyfriend, Tristram Benington, in a sporty Mini. Redmire had spent a fortune on his daughter's education at expensive private schools, but to no avail. She'd left without gaining any qualifications, and now swanned around in London, supposedly working as a photographer. But she never seemed to earn anything, despite the fact that he'd shelled out for some very expensive equipment. She was currently living with Tristram, a male model, in a ridiculously expensive flat in Chelsea – and guess who was helping her with her share of the rent? Frederick smiled sardonically to himself as he watched them get out of the car. They were both wearing designer jeans and leather jackets, and seemed to be arguing as they walked up to the house. He had to confess that she was her father's daughter: expensive tastes and a liking for the high life. He could see a great deal of himself in her, and in her boyfriend. They were well matched in many ways, not always positively. But, ironically, it had been Frederick who'd introduced them, so he'd only himself to blame.

Not long after, an older but equally glamorous couple arrived: Alexandra Davis and her current partner, James Forsyth. They roared up to the house in an open-topped sports car. Alex was wearing dark glasses and a headscarf; she looked like Audrey Hepburn. James was tanned, and sported a trim moustache.

Frederick had had a long and passionate affair with Alex. This was the affair that finally destroyed his marriage. But then Alex'd gone off with James, his former business partner. Frederick frowned at the memory. Most unsatisfactory – especially as, by then, he and James had already parted acrimoniously. Their venture, a dealership in luxury vintage cars, had gone bankrupt and James blamed Frederick for this failure. James now ran another, more successful business dealing in sports cars, but the wretched man was still a thorn in Frederick's flesh. Alex, though: so many wonderful memories! He would never meet another woman like her. Maybe someday they could . . .

Finally, a BMW moved slowly up the drive and crunched to a halt on the gravel. Frederick's former wife, Antonia, daughter of the Earl of Wensley, got out of one side and her new husband, Douglas Ramsay, the other. Frederick looked at Antonia carefully; she was what he called a 'handsome' woman, immaculately dressed and made-up but lacking that special sense of style and excitement that he'd found so irresistible in Alex. Douglas was a fat, balding businessman who sold furniture. Very successful by all accounts, and they lived in a massive converted farmhouse in Wensleydale, but just about as boring as Frederick's brother.

Douglas and Antonia completed the arrivals, which left Frederick's son, Alistair, and his wife, Katherine, as the final invited guests. They did not need to travel as they lived on the estate with their two little daughters, Caroline and Emily, in a comfortable, attractive house that had in more prosperous times accommodated the head gardener. The house was actually built into one of the walls of the old kitchen garden, and had had a large extension with a conservatory built on to the back. Alistair was more like his mother and indeed his Uncle Dominic: steady and sensible with a strong sense of the traditions of the house and family. Frederick suspected he would be a very worthy successor to himself; indeed, far better in terms of conserving the estate and spending money wisely. At last there would be a Lord Redmire who was neither eccentric nor a spendthrift. But how dull!

Frederick had sent a message to his people on the door that he was not available to speak to any of the arrivals. There were too many distracting and conflicting agendas among them, when he needed to concentrate on the main event of the day. He had instructed that all the family and special guests should be shown to their rooms with an assurance that he would see them for an early dinner at 6.30 p.m. He had no intention of revealing anything then either; that could all wait until tomorrow. He did, however, decide to see one person: his mother.

The dowager Lady Redmire, now well into her eighties, but very alert and active, lived in a self-contained flat on the ground floor of the house. She had a small sitting room with French windows that opened on to a small formal garden not open to the public. Her adjacent bedroom afforded views of the same garden, which she liked to maintain herself with help from the Hall's gardening team.

Frederick found her on the small patio outside the French windows, sitting in a deeply cushioned cane chair and drinking tea. He sat in an identical chair opposite.

'How are you, Mummy?' There was not a close relationship between them. Frederick had spent his childhood away at various boarding schools and he knew that she disapproved of his behaviour since he'd reached adulthood.

She gave him a sulky glance. 'As well as can be expected. I take it you're still going ahead with this wretched thing?'

Frederick responded with a smile. He'd pondered long and hard about whether to tell his mother about his reconstruction of his father's trick. He had known she wouldn't approve. For much of her long-suffering adult life, she'd had to cope with her husband's whims and obsessions, often being whisked around the world when she would have much preferred a quiet life at the Hall developing the gardens. She hadn't been the slightest bit interested in her husband's stunts, and her son's recreation of one of them merely reminded her of exasperating times in the past. But not to have told her would have invited trouble. She was bound to have become aware that something was happening, with all the activity and big television vans arriving. Then she would have been angry with him for concealing things. She retained a kind of proprietorial attitude towards the Hall and the estate; although her son was now in charge of it all, she still regarded it as fundamentally her residence and didn't like anything happening without her knowledge.

'Yes, Mummy, but don't worry about it; you don't have to be there. You'll see everyone at dinner and then you can come back here.' It felt like reassuring a child.

'But I don't like to think of all of these people swarming around the place, prying and interfering – especially television people. Why do they have to come? They're bad news, you mark my words.'

'They're the main reason I'm doing this, Mummy. People will flock here afterwards to see where this amazing trick took place. You'll see.'

'Humph! More people trampling over the grounds.'

'But, Mummy, it's the only way we can generate the revenue we need.'

She gave him a filthy look and didn't reply. He knew she was aware of his extravagances, and strongly disapproved of his gambling. He decided it was time to go.

'Well, Mummy, I'll have to be off; it's going to be a very busy evening.' She gave him another nasty glance. 'I'll see you later. You are coming over for dinner, aren't you?'

'No,' she replied. 'I couldn't bear to sit round the table with all those people, most of whom hate each other. I shall have a tray sent over. Tell Poppy to look in and see her grandmother but without that dreadful boyfriend. And Antonia: I should like to see her. They should come over together.' She looked at her son with contempt. 'Antonia was far too good for you, you know. What on earth possessed you to go off with that preposterous little tart Alex, I'll—'

'Mummy.' Frederick interrupted his mother calmly but firmly. 'Let's not go through all that again, shall we? There's no real point.'

Lady Redmire turned her face away from him. Frederick sighed, got up and left.

The day of his boss's grand illusion was proving very difficult for Richard Wilkins, Redmire's estate manager. He was a large, prematurely balding man with a perpetually harassed look. His suits tended to be a size too small and tight, and consequently he sweated a lot and often went red in the face. He'd been delighted, five years ago, to secure the job at such a prestigious place as Redmire Hall, but had soon discovered that it was very demanding. His previous position had been at a National Trust property, where the job description had been very clearly delineated. At Redmire, however, he found that he was expected to take charge of a whole range of things that had never even been mentioned at his interview. He was responsible for the house and the estate, with teams of people under his authority, some of whom had been at Redmire for years. They were not always very effective, but had been kept on as old retainers. The only area not under Wilkins's control was the gardens, which were managed independently by the head gardener and his team. Mr Carstairs – as Wilkins thought of Lord Redmire – was a demanding employer but also disengaged from the day-to-day business. He wanted the Hall, the estate and its farms to turn over a profit, but he didn't appear to have the slightest interest in how. Wilkins actually despised the man. He was the worst kind of aristocrat, with his profligate spending and his arrogant, lazy sense of entitlement.

Wilkins was at his desk in the estate office. This was in the former stables, which had been converted into offices, a gift shop and a café. He sat back in his chair and closed his eyes for a moment, reflecting on his situation. The stress of the job was affecting him: he was sleeping badly and also putting on weight, as he snacked too much on chocolate bars to try to keep his energy levels up during the day and had no time for exercise. And then there was this ludicrous stunt that Redmire was performing on live television. Guess who he'd put in charge of organising things? This had involved considerable extra work in coordinating with the television company, but there was little sign of appreciation from his employer.

Wilkins looked at his watch: four o'clock. He would have loved to lie down and have a nap but just at that moment the phone rang from reception at the Hall. He was needed. Wearily he prised himself out of the chair. He had a lot to do.

Meanwhile Frederick's family and friends had been making themselves at home in their rooms and speculating about what was about to happen.

Dominic Carstairs lay on the bed while Mary unpacked her clothes.

'I still don't understand what Freddy thinks he's up to,' he said moodily. 'How can he possibly have found out how my father did that trick? Who on earth's told him and why has he invited all of us?'

'Who knows how he's found out?' replied Mary, hanging up various outfits and still contemplating which one to wear for the evening. 'But you know how Freddy likes the limelight. He wants us all there to admire his achievement. There we are, his family and friends, supporting him live on television. And he knows we can't resist coming here to Redmire and staying in this marvellous old place.'

Dominic grunted. 'You might feel like that about Redmire, but it's not the same for me. The younger son always gets kicked out of the family home; it leaves you with a bad feeling, especially when a man like Freddy has it all given to him on a plate. Do you know, I don't think he's ever done a proper day's work in his life except at the bloody gaming table. I don't like to contemplate how much money he's gone through over the years.'

Mary was adjusting her hair and make-up at the antique walnut dressing table.

'No point being bitter, darling; you've not had a bad deal in life, after all. You've done well up to now. He's just a different kind of character. It takes all sorts to make a world.'

Dominic looked at his wife. She always seemed to find excuses for Freddy. He suspected that she was quite attracted to him – and that the feeling was mutual. This had hardly endeared his brother any further to him but unfortunately there were reasons why he couldn't afford to antagonise Frederick at the moment, and why he'd agreed to come to take part in this ridiculous business: he was hoping for at least a loan from Freddy.

He stretched his legs and got up from the bed. 'Well, he's up to something, if you ask me. Anyway, I'm off for a walk round the gardens, kill a bit of time before dinner.'

When Dominic left, Mary waited a moment and then picked up her phone. She tapped out a text and sent it, then put on a low-cut strappy top, a tight skirt and a fitted jacket that clung to her shapely figure. She opened the door, glanced up and down the corridor to check there was no one about and then left the room.

Poppy rolled off Tristram and lay beside him in the bed. She caressed his sweat-soaked chest while she gained control of her breathing.

'I love these old rooms and these big beds; there's something luxurious and sexy about them.'

Tristram laughed. 'You find everywhere sexy. That's one of the things I like about you.'

She picked up a pillow and hit him with it. 'I do not.' She laughed. 'You make me sound like some nympho tart.'

'Sounds good to me!'

She hit him with the pillow again and they had a play-wrestle and pillow fight on the bed. 'Anyway, it's time I made a move if I'm going to corner Dad.'

She got into her underwear, and then pulled on her expensive jeans and top.

'How are you going to do that? He's told everyone he's not available – getting ready for this trick or whatever it is.'

'Don't worry, I'll find a way. I know he can't refuse me; he's like all dads with their little girls.' She looked at her boyfriend's handsome body, naked on the bed. She was completely infatuated with him, but was not blind to his faults. Tristram was a gambler, like her father. In fact it was when she'd visited one of his clubs that Frederick had introduced them. Tristram was a successful male model and made a lot of money. Unfortunately, he also had a habit of losing large sums at the gaming table – and at the moment he had some debts outstanding to people well known to Redmire and his circle. Poppy believed she could persuade her father either to speak to Tristram's creditors and get them to reschedule the payments, or even to pay off some of the debt himself. Lord Redmire had already refused this once.

Tristram was sceptical. 'I really don't think you've any chance on this one.'

'Why?'

'I've told you: it's a matter of honour in gaming circles. You have to pay your own debts, otherwise you get blackballed and you won't get into any gaming club ever again.'

'Well, that wouldn't matter anyway, would it? Because you've promised me that after this you're giving it up: no more card-playing for money.' He looked down sheepishly. 'I mean it, Tristram. I don't care how good you are in bed. I'm going to get you out of this mess, but if you let me down again it's all over. I'm not staying with a character like my father who's gambled away half of his estate.'

'That's why he won't listen to you: he's had gambling debts himself and had to honour them, so why should he be sympathetic to me?'

'You leave it to me to speak to him.'

Tristram shrugged his shoulders. Poppy left the room without another word.

Alex Davis lay on the bed smoking, having cast off her expensive shoes. James Forsyth sat in an armchair by the window looking uneasy. He was also smoking. The window was open. They had been silent since their arrival.

'God knows why we've come here,' James eventually blurted out.

'Freddy puts on a good dinner and plenty of top-class wine. What more do you want?' replied Alex languidly.

'But why did he invite us, for God's sake? His former business partner and his former mistress? It's not as if we all parted amicably; he knows I blame him for our business going under. He never did a stroke of work, and look at me now: I'm succeeding without him. Shows who the weak link was. Anyway, I'm still going to make him pay.'

'Relax, it's all in the past. Maybe he's forgiven you. And what do you mean, "make him pay"?'

James laughed scornfully. 'Never mind. And I doubt he's forgiven me – not that he has anything to forgive me for; more the other way round.' He looked over at her. 'I think it's you he wants to see. I think he'd have you back in a jiffy, the old goat.'

This time Alex laughed. 'Now, now. No jealousy or bitterness. We can't have you two fighting over me; that would spoil the trick. Whatever it is.'

'Well, who knows. It's all a bit weird, if you ask me. But I mean it: if he tries anything on with you, he'll have me to reckon with.'

She was going to laugh again, but then she saw the look on his face. 'Good Lord, you're serious, aren't you?'

'Yes, I am.'

'Don't be ridiculous. Anyway, I'm going down to get a drink.'

'Well, I'm not coming; I don't want to run into him. I'm going for a walk round the gardens.'

'Suit yourself, but remember we're having dinner early, at half six, so don't get lost in the herbaceous borders.'

She went out, leaving James staring moodily at his phone.

As he was doing so, the phone pinged and the newly arrived text brought a smile to his face.

Antonia Ramsay stood at the window of her bedroom, which offered a view of the long borders down to the river. Douglas was lying on the bed, taking a nap. Her feelings about being here were very conflicted. She missed being the mistress of such a grand and beautiful property as this, but being here at Redmire again brought back some very painful memories of her husband's infidelities. Of course no one had any sympathy for you when you lived at a place like Redmire, but despite the material luxury of her life there she'd always felt miserable. Not only had she had to deal with the personal sense of betrayal, but she'd also had to hide her feelings from Alistair and Poppy, who witnessed the arguments and their father's long absences. Luckily she'd had an ally in Lady Redmire, who to this day always took Antonia's side against her son, and who was very fond of the children. Antonia knew the solidarity came from shared experience. Not of infidelity in the case of Vivian Carstairs, but of unreliability and being left with the offspring and domestic matters. It hurt, even if there were servants and nannies around to lighten the physical load.

Douglas was snoring – then suddenly woke up with a jerk, sat up and looked at his watch. 'Well, dear, we'd better start getting ready soon.' He yawned.

'Plenty of time,' replied his wife, with her gaze fixed on the long banks of flowers.

'I suppose so.' He looked towards her, uncertainly. 'You are sure you wanted to come this evening?'

She turned to face him. 'Of course. I wouldn't miss an opportunity like this to see Poppy and Alistair and the grandchildren all together.'

'Well, I know, but . . . well, here, in this house where he used to make your life a misery? That can't be easy. I can't ever forgive him for that, you know.'

She smiled at him. Of course he had no idea what it had really been like, but he cared about her and he was so dependable and reliable: just the opposite of Freddy. 'I know, darling; that's very sweet of you. But don't worry: I can cope.'

'Very well. As long as you're happy.' He got up and went into the bathroom.

She returned her gaze to the herbaceous borders. Her expression was sombre; she couldn't forgive her ex-husband, either. Douglas returned and she remained lost in thought.

'I think I'll just go for a short walk around,' she said after a while. 'I'd like to see one or two of the estate workers if I can, say hello. I know some of them miss me. Douglas?' She looked over, but her husband had fallen asleep again and begun snoring loudly.

In the gardener's house, Alistair Carstairs and his wife were having a glass of red wine as they sat in armchairs by the Aga stove before getting ready for the family dinner. The children were playing upstairs. Alistair was tall and thin with a perpetually worried air.

'I'm dreading this,' he sighed. 'The air is poisonous whenever the family gets together.'

'You'll survive,' replied Katherine as she picked dog hairs off her expensive gilet. 'You need to stick in there and fight for our interests and those of the children.'

'It's not just about us, or the children; it's the future of Redmire itself and the family inheritance down all the generations to come.' He twirled his wine glass nervously, an earnest look on his face.

'Surely you don't think he'll completely ruin the estate?'

'Why not? He won't show me the books, just tells me not to worry. But I know he's spent vast amounts over the years, one way or another. And what has he ever done to earn anything? One failed business venture, which actually *lost* money! Plus my sister's getting cash out of him all the time. How do you think they manage to live in Chelsea? I know lover-boy earns a fair amount, but not that much. And he gets through plenty with his gambling too.'

'Do you think that's why he's putting on this television-show thing?'

'Of course; it's an acknowledgement that things are bad.'

Katherine shook her head, drank her wine and then got up as the children came into the room. Alistair gazed at the floor, still fiddling with his glass, then sneaked a glance at his wife. There were other matters that were worrying him, but he decided not to tell her about them yet.

When Frederick had returned to the house after seeing his mother, he hadn't gone back to his office but to the secluded, long-neglected lobby that contained the door leading to the locked room. Preparations for the event had begun earlier in the week: the area had been generally spruced up and comfortable chairs arranged in rows facing the famous door. At the moment all the doors leading to this area were locked. A final rehearsal was taking place. The trick could not be performed alone, but it was vital that no one knew who his assistants were.

After the rehearsal, Redmire pronounced himself satisfied. His assistants left, taking care not to be seen and returning discreetly to their places among the many groups of people now assembled at the Hall. Redmire in turn left the house: he had an appointment to keep.

~

DS Stephanie Johnson sat in the passenger seat in her boss's shabby but comfortable old Saab, enjoying the drive through the countryside between Harrogate and Ripon. At the wheel, DCI Oldroyd was humming melodies from Strauss waltzes and admiring the mature horse-chestnut trees that lined the road. His side window was down, letting in cool air on the warm late afternoon. It was the most relaxed Steph had seen him for a long while.

'It's nice to see you in such a good mood, sir.'

'Well, why wouldn't I be?' replied Oldroyd genially, while casually easing the car round a bend. 'Here I am in the glorious Yorkshire countryside on my way to a beautiful stately home with marvellous gardens to see some kind of trick performed and no doubt also eat some good food. What's not to like?'

Steph smiled. She'd known her boss a long time, having worked with him since she joined the police force virtually straight from school.

He was known for his informality and jokiness, and their relationship was often like father and daughter. They both had family problems, which served as a kind of bond between them: Steph had grown up with a violent father who'd left the family and Oldroyd was estranged from his wife, whom he still loved. All this was rarely spoken about but was understood, and it never interfered with their professional work. Steph's partner, Andy Carter, was another DS at West Riding Police, Harrogate Division, and the three of them formed a very effective team.

'I wonder how Andy's getting on,' said Oldroyd.

Andy had taken leave to visit his family in the capital. He'd been brought up there, although he now regarded himself as an honorary Yorkshireman.

'He called last night. He took his little nephew swimming in the Serpentine; said it was so crowded you could hardly see any water.'

Oldroyd grimaced. 'I don't envy him; I can't stand big cities in weather like this.'

'No,' agreed Steph as she looked out over the fields and hedgerows, across the Vale of York to the hillsides of the distant North York Moors, where she could just pick out the chalky smudge of the White Horse of Kilburn on the hillside. She turned to her boss. 'Sir, I'm very curious about this thing we're going to. Can you tell me any more about it?'

Oldroyd had called her into his office late in the afternoon and said enigmatically that they were going out to Redmire Hall near Ripon later on to see a magic trick. It didn't sound like police work, but as she was on duty that evening she couldn't say no – and it promised to be more interesting than routine duties at police HQ. It was typical of Oldroyd to leave her guessing. He'd told her to go home and put on some smart clothes, so she was wearing a long dress and high heels. Oldroyd had turned up in his tuxedo.

'I knew you wouldn't be able to contain your curiosity,' he said, laughing. 'I expected you to break before we got to Killinghall; well done for lasting until here. Well, I got a call from Frederick Carstairs,

Lord Redmire – sort of a local aristocrat – asking if someone from the force could come out and witness an illusion he's going to perform at Redmire Hall. He said it would add authenticity to the event in case anyone thought it was a put-up job. You know, people would believe the police and all that.'

'I see.'

'At first I thought it was an odd request – and a bit arrogant, you know, thinking we had time to come and help him with a bit of entertainment.'

'It is, really, isn't it? Does he think we've nothing better to do?'

'Quite. But I like a bit of magic myself, and so I began to think, why not? No doubt there'll be some good hospitality. And I'll take Steph with me, I thought, as it will distract her from the loneliness she's no doubt feeling, with Andy in London.'

'Well, thank you, sir,' laughed Steph. 'What kind of an illusion is it, anyway?'

'Ah! Now, that's where it gets interesting, at least for me. You see, he mentioned it was something to do with a locked room and of course I immediately remembered the story of his father's famous trick in 1980.'

Oldroyd briefly outlined the legend of Vivian Carstairs's locked-room illusion. 'It was never explained, although some people have speculated about how it might have been done. If Frederick Carstairs is going to perform that illusion again after all these years, it will be quite sensational.'

'Right,' said Steph, sounding a little sceptical. She'd never been drawn to magic shows on television: magicians producing rabbits out of hats or making birds in cages disappear. Nor did she approve of female assistants in skimpy outfits.

'But if that's not your thing, I'm sure that the people there will be very interesting. There'll be plenty of opportunity to see how the other half lives. By the way, don't say anything to DCS Walker. I'm sure he'd agree with our initial reactions and not consider this outing as a good use of our time.'

'It could get back to him, sir.'

'I don't think so – and we certainly don't want it to. We get on fine but he's not a man given to frivolity. It's bad enough if I want to get away to a concert sometimes. Well, here we are.'

A brown tourist sign saying 'Redmire Hall' pointed to a country lane. Oldroyd swung the car down. After a few hundred yards' driving between high hedges full of honeysuckle and wild roses, they came to the formal entrance through ornamental gates. Then they proceeded down a long drive next to fields grazed by black-faced sheep. In the distance there was the spire of a church surrounded by magnificent copper beech trees. The drive curved and then they could see the house: mellow Regency-style stone and brick with ancient Cedars of Lebanon on the gravel area in the foreground. Above the house was blue sky with fleecy white clouds. It was all sublimely serene and beautiful.

Oldroyd smiled and shook his head. You had to hand it to the aristocrats of old: they knew how to live and insisted on the highest aesthetic values. Some of their fortunes may have depended on the slave trade, but at least they commissioned the finest architects and landscape gardeners to create estates of outstanding quality still enjoyed and admired today.

As they approached the car park, Oldroyd caught sight of the lorries and vans emblazoned with 'Ridings Television' in large letters on the sides.

'Oh bugger!' he swore loudly. 'That blasted Redmire said nothing about television. I was hoping to keep our presence here discreet; no hope of that if we're live on bloody TV.'

This seemed to actually make it more exciting to Steph, who had always fancied being on telly. 'I'm sure it'll be fine, sir, but I suppose you could just back out; tell him you weren't prepared for this.'

'Yes,' replied Oldroyd glumly, 'but I was looking forward to it, and such a lovely evening. Damn!' He slammed the steering wheel. 'We'll stay and risk it and just try to keep out of the limelight. Are you OK with that? I'll take responsibility if Tom Walker kicks off about it.'

'Fine, sir. I'm getting quite intrigued myself now.'

Oldroyd parked the car. 'OK,' he said with a gleam in his eye. 'Let's go and see what's happening.'

Frederick was slightly behind schedule, and found he had to hurry a little in his final preparations. However, he appeared his handsome, suave and confident self at the family dinner, dressed in dinner jacket and bow tie.

Despite the fact that many of the assembled group had not seen each other for a while, there didn't appear to be much in the way of friendly catch-up. The atmosphere in the elaborate red dining room was tense, and conversations were strained. Each of the guests had a different agenda with Frederick, who enjoyed playing them off against each other. He savoured the unspoken hostilities between them.

Usually the partners and non-family members tended to remain judiciously quiet during these family meals, but today it was Alex who eventually broke the awkward silence.

'It's a wonder to me that you manage to keep this place going, Freddy,' she remarked as she sipped delicately at a spoonful of lobster bisque. 'Of course, everything's just as splendid as ever.'

'Don't worry your pretty head about it, my dear,' replied Redmire, and James Forsyth glowered into his soup bowl. 'I have plans in hand to make the finances secure.'

Both Dominic and Alistair looked up sceptically.

'Such as?' asked Dominic.

'All in good time, little brother. All shall be revealed. But part of the plan is tonight's entertainment. The publicity is going to be huge.'

Dominic gripped his soup spoon a little tighter.

'In that case, I hope it goes well,' said Alistair. 'I'm not sure I agree with the idea that there's no such thing as bad publicity. We don't want the Hall to become a laughing stock.' Like his uncle and grandmother, Alistair thought the idea of the trick was ridiculous.

'Does it matter? Wouldn't the punters still come if everything went wrong?' asked Poppy. 'They'd still want to see the place they'd seen on television. I think Dad's brave to do a thing like this.' She was clearly trying to stay in favour. Her father knew what she was up to and smiled at her efforts.

Alistair's sour expression showed that he was also aware of his sister's machinations; he knew from experience how she could wheedle money out of their father.

'Don't you think the whole thing is going to downgrade the place?' he said. 'I'd rather people come here to see the gardens, the architecture and the artwork rather than to gawp at some cheap trick or other.'

'Alistair, you're such a snob,' said Poppy. 'Why does it matter why people come here if they're paying good money?'

Katherine Carstairs, who had so far maintained a judicious silence, gently kicked her husband on the leg beneath the table as a sign that he should shut up and not provoke any more arguments.

'Poppy's right.' Frederick had finished his soup and, after a quick check, he nodded to the staff to remove the plates. 'We're not the National Trust. We need to make money.'

Yes, to finance your gambling, thought Dominic.

'People want more than herbaceous borders, pieces of mouldy old sculpture and a few grand paintings these days. We need to attract more families.'

'In that case, why not just turn the place into another Alton Towers? Grub up the gardens and bring in the roller coasters?'

The suggestion of a wry smile on Redmire's face, unseen by his son, suggested that Alistair's angry comments were nearer to the truth than he imagined.

Antonia sipped her wine, an excellent Bordeaux. 'I'm sure your father would never go that far, Alistair,' she said. 'He wouldn't want to ruin Redmire; it's his children's inheritance.' She looked pointedly at her former husband, whose blank expression conveyed nothing.

'Huh!' snorted Poppy in disgust. 'How do you work that out, Mummy? We all know it goes to Alistair. I get nothing.' Non-family members looked down at the table in embarrassment, as it seemed that another family dispute was about to explode.

The Carstairs family had always had an aristocratic indifference to whoever might overhear them bickering, treating people outside the family like servants whose presence could be ignored.

Dominic's wan smile expressed some sympathy with Poppy.

'Poppy, I'm sure that's unfair,' said Mary. 'Your father has made very good provision for you, haven't you, Freddy?'

Frederick nodded to a waiter, who topped up his glass.

'Let's move on from this, shall we?' he said in his languid style, refusing to be drawn. 'It's not the time – and anyway, it makes me feel uncomfortable. You're talking as if I'm about to depart, but I can assure you I'll be around to torment you all for a while yet.'

There was polite laughter from Tristram and Douglas, but everyone else remained silent.

While Lord Redmire and his family dined in the luxurious red room, the rest of the guests were enjoying a rather sumptuous buffet in the large entrance hall. These visitors comprised various representatives from local businesses and tourism, politics and the media, along with DCI Oldroyd and DS Johnson.

'It's at times like this that I'm always so thankful we dress in plain clothes for detective work,' Oldroyd whispered to Steph as he sipped a glass of champagne and tucked into a large plate of canapés. 'Can you imagine how we'd be the centre of attention in uniforms?'

'Yes, sir,' replied Steph. 'But I'm surprised there aren't people you're familiar with here, given that you're well-known in this area.'

The hubbub of numerous conversations, along with the tinkle of plates and cutlery, echoed up to the high ceiling.

'Well, so far, so good. I've recognised one or two and I'm keeping away from them. That bald chap over there with the big belly, he's a shocking bore from the Chamber of Commerce in Harrogate. Tom Walker introduced me to him; he's one of his golfing chums. Mind you, I'm not surprised he's fat if he regularly comes to eating dos like this.' His eyes roved over the sumptuous pâtés, giant roast ham and whole poached salmon.

'True,' replied Steph as she nibbled bits from a much smaller plateful. She raised her eyebrows at Oldroyd. 'But go easy yourself, sir. You know you're always complaining about putting on weight.'

Oldroyd sighed. 'Yes, you're right, blast you. But at least I can manage a few glasses of this.' He twirled his champagne flute and looked at her mischievously.

Steph suddenly realised what he meant. She pretended to be outraged and put her hand on her hip. 'Oh, so that's why you've brought me along, sir? To drive you back after you've quaffed the champers! And all that about me being lonely with Andy away!'

'No, no,' protested Oldroyd, grinning far too widely. 'I assure you that was not the main reason. But I didn't think you'd mind,' he added archly.

'That's OK, sir. I'm not that fond of the stuff myself. But I'd go easy on that, too. It would look bad if I had to help my boss stagger to his car, drunk.'

'Worry not. I want to be alert to watch this trick, not slumped and dozing in a corner.'

Luckily for Oldroyd's waist, if not for his appetite, there was hardly time for dessert before the guests were asked to move to the part of the house where the locked room was located. Oldroyd's gaze lingered longingly on the strawberries, chocolate gateaux and millefeuilles before he joined Steph.

'Are you ready?' he whispered.

'Yes, sir; I'm sensing the atmosphere.'

The two detectives followed the rest of the well-dressed and excited guests down a corridor lined with huge Victorian paintings in massive gilt frames.

'I have to say, I'm feeling a bit underdressed, sir,' said Steph as she watched women with glittering dresses and fur stoles parade ahead of her.

'Not you,' replied Oldroyd. 'And anyway, as my mother used to say on occasions like this: "Nobody's looking at you."'

Just before they turned into the lobby, they passed a room that was filling up with yet more people sitting in front of a large screen. The evening's events were going to be relayed to this room. Oldroyd and Steph were ushered on into the lobby itself, where the bulky television cameras were in evidence plus snakes of thick cable around the room and powerful lights. Lord Redmire was shaking hands and welcoming everybody personally.

'Ah, Chief Inspector, very nice to see you. And this must be your detective sergeant. It's a great pleasure.' His handsome but rather debauched-looking face leered at Steph as he shook her hand. Steph cringed. 'Please come right down to the front; I have a special role for you tonight.' He led them to seats at the end of the front row and then returned to greeting people.

'Well, I don't like him, sir,' whispered Steph. 'He's one of those men who undresses you with their eyes and makes you feel uneasy.'

'Yes, I noticed. I've met him a few times at bigwig functions I've been to with Tom Walker. He's not a very savoury character – always had a reputation as a womaniser.' Oldroyd looked around, suddenly feeling uncomfortable himself. 'I don't like this; I didn't realise he wanted us to play a role in whatever's going to happen. He's a devious bugger. The mention of magic intrigued me and put me off my guard.'

'I suppose he'll get us up to check some equipment or other and say there's nothing fishy about it.'

'That's what I was thinking. Bugger!' he repeated.

'Come on, sir,' teased Steph. 'You were all enthusiastic a few minutes ago. Never mind. I think it's all very exciting.' She settled into her seat and looked at the door facing them. 'Is that *the* door?' she asked.

'Presumably,' replied Oldroyd, before adopting an exaggeratedly reverential tone. 'The Door to the Locked Room.'

At that moment, Lord Redmire came to stand in front of the door with a television presenter, who welcomed everyone with the usual jocular patter and outlined what was going to happen when the live broadcast began. There was a flurry of last-minute activity, with sound people moving their boom mics around and double-checking the positions of their cameras. Producers with clipboards called out and cameramen replied. At last things settled down and a voice said: 'Live in ten, nine, eight . . .'

Red lights went on over cameras, and the presenter smiled at the one in front of him.

'Good evening and welcome to a special edition of *Yorkshire Life*. We are coming to you live from Redmire Hall near Ripon, where tonight we are going to see something very special. Something that hasn't been seen for nearly forty years. I have here with me the owner of Redmire Hall, and the performer of tonight's magic trick, the Honourable Frederick Carstairs, Lord Redmire.'

During the brief applause, the presenter turned to Redmire, who looked confident and debonair in front of the camera. 'Well, I thought it was long overdue,' he quipped, to mild laughter from the audience. 'The truth is, I thought the secret of this trick had gone to the grave with my father. We didn't even have the key to that door. But recently certain . . . *information*, let's say . . . has come to light and I'm now in a position to repeat his grand illusion.'

'This trick was invented by your father?'

'Indeed, in the late seventies, with help from an Italian illusionist called Count Mazarini, one of the greatest illusionists of all time. A team of people came over from Italy to construct it.'

'I don't suppose you can tell us how you rediscovered these secrets?'

'No,' Redmire smiled. 'That would be telling, and a magician never explains his tricks.'

'Oh Lord! He's a magician now, is he? He gets more like our father every time I see him,' muttered Dominic Carstairs. Mary jabbed him gently with her elbow.

'Well, I hope he brings a bit more magic to this than he did to our business,' said James Forsyth softly.

'Quiet, darling,' hushed Alex.

'So,' continued the presenter, 'the door Lord Redmire mentioned is this one behind me.'

The camera panned to the door.

'Shortly we are going to open it and this will reveal a small room. Lord Redmire will enter this room, which will be examined for ways of escape. The door will be locked and . . . But I'm rushing on too quickly. Let's see inside.'

Dramatic music was heard from speakers at either side of the door as it opened. Dominic and James groaned. Oldroyd, on the front row, was torn between fascination and apprehension about what was to come next. The camera moved into the room.

'As you can see,' said the presenter, leading the camera into the room, 'it seems an ordinary sort of space, like a study: chair, small desk, window, bookshelf, rug.' He turned to Redmire again. 'And you're going to escape from here, Lord Redmire?'

'Indeed, but before we begin: I have invited Detective Chief Inspector Jim Oldroyd, from West Riding Police in Harrogate, and Detective Sergeant Stephanie Johnson to carry out a full examination of the room. This is to demonstrate that there are no exits from the room. This examination will be undertaken by unimpeachable people who cannot be accused of being in collusion with me.'

'Damn!' whispered Oldroyd to Steph. 'I just hope Tom Walker's not sitting at home in his slippers, watching telly. He'll choke on his whisky!'

'I shall be locked into the room,' announced Redmire, 'and you will pull this curtain across briefly and then back again. When the door is opened, I shall have disappeared.'

'Well, it sounds impossible to me, but can I now ask DCI Oldroyd and his assistant to come forward.'

More dramatic music, and Oldroyd got up reluctantly with Steph at his side, feeling a little more enthusiastic than her boss.

'So, Chief Inspector, I bet many of the criminals you catch would welcome a way of escaping from you like this.'

Oldroyd contorted his face into a fixed smile. 'I'm sure they would,' he replied through clenched teeth.

'So, if there's any way out of that room you'll find it?'

'Yes, I'm sure we will.'

'OK, off you go, then; the camera will follow you round.'

There followed several excruciating minutes for Oldroyd while he and Steph examined everything, including the small cavity under the floor, just as Vivian Carstairs's friends had done all those years before.

The presenter commented on every detail in an annoying manner that drove Oldroyd wild, but there was nothing he could do.

Steph was hard-pressed to avoid giggling during the filming.

Eventually they pronounced that there was no exit from the room other than by the door, which itself was a normal door with a simple mortice lock and two bolts. Steph returned to her seat, but the presenter detained Oldroyd.

'Very well, then. It is time for Lord Redmire to enter the room!' the presenter announced dramatically. 'And then the chief inspector will lock him in.' Oldroyd shot Steph a despairing glance and she looked down, trying not to laugh.

Redmire stepped up, handed a rather rusty-looking key to Oldroyd, entered the room and sat at the desk. A drum roll began.

'Ladies and gentlemen, the chief inspector will now close the door and lock it.' Oldroyd duly did as he was told. 'Can you hear me, Lord Redmire? Are you still there?'

'Yes, I'm here,' came the slightly quiet but clear reply.

'So now I will draw this curtain for only fifteen seconds.'

As he did this, dramatic music began once again. At the end of the fifteen seconds, the music stopped and the presenter drew back the curtain. There was silence. Every member of the audience in both rooms was enthralled. Oldroyd had forgotten his embarrassment as he unlocked the door and opened it. It was empty. This produced a chorus of 'ooh's from the audience, and even Oldroyd appeared impressed. He had certainly seen no way out. The small cavity was inspected but found to be empty, and the camera moved inside to confirm the fact that Redmire was not there.

'Well, ladies and gentlemen, as you can see, Lord Redmire has completely disappeared from a locked room. But that's not the end: he will now return. So I ask the chief inspector to close and lock the door again.' There was a repeat of the locking, curtain-drawing and music.

'And now, ladies and gentlemen, the chief inspector will once again open the door to this strange room and reveal . . . well, let's see!'

When the door was opened, Redmire was again sitting at the desk. Applause and shouts of 'Bravo!' came from the audience, but Oldroyd had a strange feeling: something wasn't right.

'And there he is, ladies and gentlemen! What an amazing trick! Lord Redmire, can you—?'

The presenter's patter stopped abruptly. Redmire had neither said anything nor moved until that moment. Then his body toppled sidewise out of the chair and the knife sticking out of his back became visible. Blood splattered on to the floor.

'Oh, bloody hell!' muttered Oldroyd to himself, before pandemonium broke out.

Two

On the Redmire Hall estate was a neat terrace of workers' cottages. In one of these, a retired estate worker was watching the transmission from the Hall, and was horrified when the body came into view. He was wondering what on earth was happening when he heard a knock at the door.

He opened it and looked out. The light was starting to fail, and the sun had set behind the big sycamore trees across the yard. A large moth fluttered soundlessly past his head, attracted by the light coming from the house. He saw a figure standing to one side of the door and recognised the visitor straight away.

'Oh, it's you. Come in.' He turned back down the short passageway towards the living room. 'This was—' He never finished the sentence because a garrotte had been looped around his neck. His assailant's grip tightened and, after a short struggle, the victim sank to the floor.

Back in the Hall, screams erupted all over the lobby and could be heard from the adjoining room, where people were watching the gruesome scene on the large screen; chairs tipped over as people sprang to their feet.

'Daddy!' shrieked Poppy. 'Oh my God!' She tried to run towards her father's prostrate body.

'Leave it to the police, darling,' said Tristram, holding her back.

'Freddy!' wailed Alex, and promptly fainted into the arms of James Forsyth.

'What the hell's going on?' shouted Dominic.

On television screens across the county, the camera wobbled, the picture cut out and the viewers were returned to the studio at West Riding Television Centre.

It fell to Oldroyd to try to establish some order. Setting aside the terrible personal implications of being involved in this horror live on television, and probably being watched by half of the West Riding Police Force and his superiors, he sprang into action.

'Stay back, everyone, and try to keep calm.' He stood in front of the door while Steph went into the room to check that Redmire was as dead as he appeared to be. Thank God she was here with him! Not that they looked the part of police detectives, in their smart clothes. 'This is an incident scene. No one must enter that room or touch anything. I am going to contact police headquarters and the ambulance service now. Please: everyone in this room remain here, as we shall need to take statements. I repeat: sit down and try to remain calm.'

'He's dead all right, sir. I think the knife has gone right into his heart.' Steph was reassuringly practical and composed. 'Shall I guard the door?'

'Yes, good idea. Some of the family will want to get in, no doubt, but don't let anyone through.'

Oldroyd called HQ in Harrogate, followed by the ambulance service. Then he surveyed the wreckage in the lobby. There were overturned chairs. Some people were cowering and sobbing in corners, while others sat white-faced and rigid.

The family had remained at the front, closest to the door, and Oldroyd tried to assess who might be in a fit state to take some control. Dominic Carstairs was still angry and ranting on about his brother's stupidity while Mary tried to quieten him. Poppy was still weeping hysterically while Tristram tried to console her; likewise James Forsyth was attending to Alex, who had regained consciousness. Alistair Carstairs was sitting with his head in his hands and Katherine's arm over his shoulder. Oldroyd decided that Antonia and Douglas Ramsay were the best bet and went over to them. They looked stunned but reasonably calm.

'Who's best placed to help me get control of things?'

Antonia struggled to reply. 'I think Richard Wilkins, the estate manager; he knows . . . Oh – that's him now over there.'

Oldroyd looked over towards the door and saw a portly man enter the room wearing a worried and puzzled expression. He walked briskly over to Oldroyd.

'Chief Inspector, isn't it?' Oldroyd nodded. 'I'm Richard Wilkins, the estate manager. What's going on? They said there's been an accident of some kind.'

'Worse than that, I'm afraid. Lord Redmire's been murdered.'

'What? No! Impossible. How? He was doing that trick, wasn't he?' Wilkins added lamely.

'He was, and I'm afraid that's how the killer got to him. He disappeared from the room all right, but when he reappeared he was dead – stabbed in the back. No sign of the killer.'

'But that's . . .' Wilkins seemed unable to comprehend what had happened.

'I've contacted police headquarters and the ambulance service; they'll be here soon. I have to stay here until they arrive so I wonder if you could make an announcement in the other room and . . .'

'What's happening?' A female member of the Hall staff rushed into the lobby and over to them. 'It's chaos in the other room. People are hysterical. What happened to Lord Redmire? I saw him fall and . . . Oh my God!' She looked towards the open door of the locked room and saw the body on the floor.

'He's dead . . . murdered,' said Wilkins. 'We've got to help the chief inspector here. We can't expect the family to do anything.'

'OK,' said Oldroyd to Wilkins. 'Go into the room where people were watching this being relayed and announce that everyone must stay where they are for the moment. And can you,' he said to the woman with Wilkins, 'go and get help from other staff to bring water and glasses for everyone.'

When they'd left, Oldroyd addressed the people in the lobby. 'Just try to stay calm, please. We just need to remain here until help arrives.'

'How can we do that when there's a murderer on the loose?' said an angry Dominic Carstairs.

'On that point, it's safer if we all stay together here. This murder has obviously been planned, so I don't think we've got some crazed killer on the rampage.'

'But that's ridiculous, I'm not . . .' Carstairs made as if to leave the room.

'Sir, please sit down and try to be patient. This is a murder enquiry and procedures must be followed.'

No one argued with Oldroyd when he spoke in this authoritative way. Carstairs did as he was told and the room went quiet apart from whispered conversations and muffled sobs from the still-distraught Poppy. The television crew had flopped on to the ground, with their backs against the wall. The presenter had his head in his hands. Oldroyd sat down on a chair.

'I've got to stop this; it's becoming a habit,' he remarked to Steph with grim humour, remembering the business at the Red Chapel in Halifax, where he'd witnessed a sniper kill a man in front of an audience of music lovers.

'Well, sir, I'm certainly glad I came now,' Steph returned in kind. 'It's proving very exciting – though not exactly in the way I'd expected.'

'I always say there's never a dull moment when you're working with me. I'm sure this is going to be fascinating, but the repercussions could be terrible.' He shook his head and thought about DCS Tom Walker and the odious Chief Constable of West Riding Police, Matthew Watkins. Live on television without permission and then this happens. It was just the kind of publicity they hated; no doubt he was going to be carpeted at some point.

To the detectives' relief, it wasn't long before they heard the sound of sirens, and pulsing blue lights eerily lit the now darkening sky outside. As the ambulance crew arrived in the lobby, Oldroyd was relieved to see the tall figure of Tim Groves, the forensic pathologist he'd worked with for many years, striding in unhurriedly and carrying his bag. He was always a very sane and sensible presence.

Tim smiled in greeting at Oldroyd. 'Jim, what on earth have you got yourself into this time? My wife was watching it; I was in the study upstairs. She called up saying I could expect a call from DCI Oldroyd as there'd just been a murder at Redmire Hall and you were there. I didn't believe her at first, but sure enough, here we are!'

'It's a huge embarrassment, Tim. It's not your wife watching that concerns me; it's who else has seen it – probably Tom Walker, Watkins and God knows who else. It's my fault: I'm a sucker for a bit of magic. Redmire – that's the victim – invited me to come and watch his re-enactment of his father's famous trick. He didn't say anything about the television being here.'

Groves laughed. 'Well, never mind, you're actually being super-efficient. Witnessing the murder means you're on the spot ready to go with the investigation . . . again! They should be pleased.'

'Well, I hope they see it that way,' said Oldroyd ruefully. 'Anyway, there he is.' He pointed to the body. 'I don't think it's going to be a hard one for you; the knife's still in his back, and we all saw him alive less than an hour ago.'

'OK. I'll have a quick look and then we'll get him back to the lab. I take it no one's touched anything?'

'No one's been in there except my DS, Stephanie Johnson. She went to check that he was dead. She had the privilege of accompanying me this evening,' he said ironically.

'Righto. Good for her.'

More officers were arriving now from Harrogate HQ, much to Oldroyd's relief. Quickly and very professionally the yellow-and-black tape went around the locked room, which had never, reflected Oldroyd grimly, held a more shocking secret than it did now. Detective constables began the task of taking statements.

Tim Groves finished his first rudimentary examination of the body. 'You're probably right, Jim,' he said, pulling off his rubber gloves. 'Can't see any complications at first sight; not been dead long; deep knife wound to the back, probably penetrated the heart. Anyway, I'll send you a report as soon as I can. We've got the murder weapon, but we'll be lucky if we get any prints. By the way: what was he doing in there? What was supposed to be happening?'

'He went into the room, which was then locked. When we reopened it, he'd disappeared. When we repeated the process of closing and locking the door, he reappeared, but in the state you see now.'

'Yes – not part of the act, you might say. So you've not only got to find out who killed him, but how they did it?'

'Correct.'

'And obviously someone else must have known how the trick worked and used it for their own purposes.'

'So it would appear.'

'Well, best of luck. You don't get the easy cases, do you?' observed Groves. He and Oldroyd had worked together a number of times on equally baffling murders.

'No, but it keeps the little grey cells going, as my fictional hero would have said.'

Groves departed with the body and Oldroyd and Steph went back into the main house to find somewhere they could set up an HQ. There was going to be a large amount of questioning of suspects about their movements and possible motives.

Richard Wilkins reappeared. 'I stayed in the relay room until your people arrived, and I think they have everything under control now, Chief Inspector. Can I be of any further assistance?'

Oldroyd explained that they were looking for somewhere to establish an incident room as a base for the investigation.

'Well,' said Wilkins, 'I think the office behind reception will be best. It's got computers and desks and stuff and it's linked to a small sitting room. I'll move the people who work in there into the general office temporarily.'

'Right, let's take a look, then.'

Wilkins led them to the room in question and Oldroyd pronounced himself satisfied. The sitting room would be good for interviews. There was the added benefit of having a good view of the entrance and part of the grand borders.

'This will be fine. Now, can you ask all the members of the family and the senior staff to gather in here briefly? There won't be chairs for everyone but I just need a quick word with them.'

'Certainly.' Wilkins went off to gather everyone. Oldroyd sank into a sofa.

'Well, Steph? Any initial thoughts?'

Oldroyd had a collaborative approach. He liked to know what his detectives were thinking. Steph seemed to like that.

'At the moment, sir, we assume that it's one of the family or someone who works here, because the killer must know the house well and a disgruntled family member or employee is likely to have a motive.'

'Yes, which is why I've asked to speak to them. We'll keep them here for questioning over the next few days. The rest of the audience, caterers, TV crew and so on, we'll allow to go for the time being. If any evidence crops up implicating any of them – which is unlikely – we'll track them down. I disagree with only one thing you said, which was that it's *a* person, singular: almost certainly there would have been more than one person involved. However that trick works, it's fiendishly clever and complicated and I just can't see only one person and Frederick Carstairs involved in this. Many of the great illusions had teams of people operating them.'

'I wonder if he's despised by the whole family. Apart from his daughter, they didn't seem that upset, did they?'

'No, although that could be shock. If any member of the family *is* responsible, of course, that person must have had at least one accomplice, as all the family were with us watching Redmire perform the trick.'

At that moment, the family started to file into the room, mostly looking stunned and subdued. Some sat on the available chairs and others stood around. When all were assembled, Steph shut the door and Oldroyd got up. Before he could say anything, Dominic Carstairs intervened.

'Chief Inspector, what is the point of this? We've all had a terrible shock. We need to be left in private to . . . to gather ourselves.'

'I won't keep you long, but I just need to explain one or two things. First of all, I want to express my condolences to you all concerning what has happened; I understand how awful it is for you.'

There was no response to this.

'Second, it will, unfortunately, be necessary for you all to stay here at the Hall for some time while we undertake some further investigations and questioning.'

There were murmurs of surprise and resentment.

'Is that necessary? We all need to return home after this horror, surely?' said Dominic.

It was Alistair who first realised the implication of what Oldroyd was saying. 'Chief Inspector, you surely don't suspect one of us, my father's friends and family, do you? I mean, we were all there watching the act.'

'I realise this adds to the unpleasantness,' replied Oldroyd kindly. 'But I'm sure you don't need me to tell you that the immediate suspects in cases like this are always people known to the victim. I don't think any of us really thinks that a crazed lunatic found their way into the house, knew what was happening with the trick, got into that room somehow and killed Lord Redmire for no particular reason. This murder was most likely the work of more than one person, so even if none of you could have actually wielded the knife, that doesn't mean you weren't involved.'

'But . . .' Alistair looked round at the others, but they looked away uncomfortably. It was clear that some of them would have liked to protest, but that they found Oldroyd's logic grimly inescapable.

'That's ridiculous,' muttered Douglas Ramsay, but without any conviction.

'That makes everything worse,' said Poppy. 'So not only is he dead, but you think one of us killed him!' She burst into tears again.

Antonia went over to her daughter and put an arm across her shoulder. 'Of course we'll all cooperate with you, Chief Inspector. Just tell us what you want us to do,' she said to Oldroyd, which seemed to prevent any further rumblings from the others.

Thank goodness for those sane sentiments, thought Oldroyd. It was always much easier if people cooperated from the outset in these circumstances.

'Thank you. It's really very simple: just remain here, in the rooms you were allocated, and we'll start the formal statement-taking and questioning tomorrow. You are now free to go to your rooms.'

They all started to file out – looking, if anything, worse than they had when they'd walked in.

Alistair Carstairs was last and at the door he turned to Oldroyd. 'Chief Inspector, can I have a word, please?'

'Yes.'

'Could I ask you not to say anything to my grandmother until I've told her what has happened? It will be a great shock to her and it ought to come from me or Uncle Dominic.'

'Of course. I didn't realise she was here.'

Alistair explained about her living arrangements, then glanced down the corridor as if nervous about something and continued in a half-whisper. 'I have to say, Chief Inspector, I don't trust that James Forsyth; he and my father had a business venture together that went wrong and I know Forsyth blamed my father. And, of course, he's with Alex; she had a long affair with my father and, well, who knows how Forsyth feels about that, especially when it was always plain to see that the spark between her and my father was still very much alive.'

'I see. Well, I'll be talking more with you all tomorrow, so let's leave it until then.'

Alistair looked a little crestfallen, but left without a word.

Oldroyd sat down with a sigh. He felt exhausted.

'What do you make of that, sir?' said Steph. 'Trying to deflect attention from himself?'

'Maybe. We haven't even begun to sort out all the relationships between these people yet – all their little rivalries, grudges and jealousies. Those exist in all families, of course, but in my experience they're always worse among the rich, where there's money and property to inherit.'

'Yes – do you remember that case on the other side of Ripon? Hunstone Hall, wasn't it?'

'I do. One of the younger members of the family, spoke like a young toff; he was steadily working his way through his more senior relatives so that he could inherit the estate, like Richard the Third in Shakespeare's play murdering his way to the crown. He was quite clever about it, but the nearer he got to his prize, the more suspicious the deaths became, until eventually he overreached himself and we caught him trying to poison one of his elderly aunts. Poor thing.'

'Do you think any other family members are at risk here?'

'Possibly. When we see the will and who benefits, that could be enlightening; he may have been threatening to change it. Anyway, let's finish up here for the night and get home. We need some rest, and maybe we're missing something tonight that we'll see with fresh eyes tomorrow.'

By the time Oldroyd arrived back at his flat overlooking the Stray in Harrogate, it was late in the evening and the last of the bars were clos-ing. A few late revellers were wandering the streets.

He opened the door and switched on the hall light. There was everything exactly as he'd left it. Not surprising, as he lived alone, hav-ing separated from his wife, but he didn't think he'd ever get used to the sharp stab of loneliness that hit him every time he came home and was reminded of his isolation.

At this time of year it was particularly hard. The days of family holidays were over, at least for him. His son, Robert, Robert's partner, Andrea, and their small daughter, Rosie, were currently camping in France. Oldroyd suffered a keen pang of regret when he thought of them and how little he saw of them these days. His estranged wife, Julia, was in a villa in Spain with some friends, and his daughter, Louise, was in Morocco, although he was due to pick her up at Leeds Bradford airport tomorrow. Even his sister, Alison, a vicar in a nearby village, was currently away at a retreat on a remote Scottish island.

He went to the kitchen to pour himself a glass of wine and saw the postcard his wife had sent him stuck with a magnet to the fridge. He picked it up and read again:

> You'd love it here: we're up in the Sierra Nevada near a mountain village. Lovely square with cafés and plenty of medieval architecture, great restaurants and great wine! Make sure you get away for some kind of break this summer.
> Julia
> P. S. Don't forget to pick Louise up from the airport!

As usual he found it difficult to interpret his wife's behaviour. Sending a postcard was a quaint thing to do in these digital days, and how many estranged wives sent postcards to their husbands, even if the message contained no terms of endearment? She seemed to be concerned about him but somehow at a distance. He put the postcard back and shook his head. He'd just poured out his wine when his phone rang.

It was Alison. 'Jim! I've heard the news and been trying to ring you at the flat. Whatever have you been up to now?'

'I'm fine – just got in. Tired, of course. How come you know about it? I thought you weren't allowed access to the news or even to talk to each other on these retreat things.'

'Not at all; we enjoy the discipline of quiet and meditation for part of the day, but we also keep in touch with the outside world and talk about what's going on. People think these things are otherworldly, but they're quite the reverse. We are helping each other to perceive more of the underlying truths beneath world events.'

Oldroyd smiled; he was used to little lectures from his sister on moral and spiritual matters and they were never dull.

'Dear me, I'm going on a bit,' she laughed. 'So much for mellowing in old age!'

'You'll never mellow,' laughed Oldroyd. 'I hope. Anyway, what are they saying on the telly? I've not seen any news. It's been a long evening.'

'I'm sure it has. Well, all I know is that this Lord Redmire was murdered during a live-broadcast performance of some kind of trick that his father invented. And you were there! There was a clip from the programme and you were examining this secret room or whatever it is. Now the family are all being kept at the Hall. That's it, really. Endless reruns of the same sequences: history of the family, lots of speculation, but no more facts.'

'That's because there aren't any; we've no idea yet what actually happened, never mind who was responsible. Of course, the family are the main suspects – that's why I'm keeping them there.'

'You still haven't told me why *you* were there.'

'Redmire persuaded me to go along. I've always loved magic tricks; he didn't say anything about the whole thing being televised. I'm going to have some explaining to do tomorrow at HQ.'

'Well, I'm sure you'll talk your way out of it, as usual. I suppose you're right about the family being under suspicion, but it's a strange affair, isn't it? The killer had to know how the trick worked, and you'd think, if that information was passed down, that Lord Redmire as the eldest son would be the one to know – but apparently he didn't until recently, when he claims to have discovered things. So who told him and how did they know? Anyway, I won't keep you; I'm sure you're ready for bed. Take it easy and don't go into any more secret rooms.' She laughed again.

'I won't,' replied Oldroyd, and ended the call. He always regarded Alison as a Mycroft to his Sherlock. What she said about his cases was always worth listening to. In this instance she'd managed to sum up the situation in a few words.

∾

When she got back to their waterfront apartment in the centre of Leeds, Steph rang Andy, who was staying with his mother in Croydon.

'How's it going?'

'Fine, except it's too bloody hot and the air's disgusting; it stinks of car fumes all over the place. I can't understand why I never noticed it when I lived here! I suppose you just get used to these things.'

'Yes. Is everyone OK, then?'

'Yeah. Mum's good. I don't think she'll ever get used to living by herself. Clare and the kids aren't far away, though; she sees a lot of them.'

'Good. What's their new house like?'

'OK but small. Ridiculous rent; typical for down here – I don't know how she and Sam survive. Anyway, what the hell have you and the boss been up to? I can't go away for two minutes without something ridiculous happening.'

Steph laughed. 'You must have seen it on the news, or didn't it get down there?'

'Just briefly. Some toff got bumped off doing a magic trick and you and the chief inspector were there? Sounds weird to me, but typical of the boss, I suppose. How come you two were involved anyway?'

'He was invited by Lord Redmire, the man who was murdered. Apparently he likes magic, but he didn't expect it to be on the telly. He might get into trouble now.'

'Bloody hell! Don't worry: he'll talk his way out of it. So I suppose you're going to be camped out at that big posh house for a while, interviewing rich people with titles? "This is very inconvenient; I'm having lunch with the Queen and I need to get my Bentley valeted . . ." That sort of stuff. I don't envy you.'

'I'm looking forward to it. It's going to take some sorting out. We don't even know how the murderer managed to commit the crime. It's all bound up with that magic trick, never mind who did it, and there must have been more than one person involved.'

'Things are never straightforward with him, are they?'

'No, but that's what makes it interesting.'

'I suppose you're right. OK, enjoy! I'm out with Jason at the moment, just taking your call outside the bar. Nice to get a bit of air; it's stifling in there.'

Jason Harris was an old friend of Andy's. He worked in the City and had a reputation for fast living.

'Not too wild, I hope! You know what he's like.'

'Oh no, he's changed a lot. Got a girlfriend now – living together and talking about having kids.'

'Jason! He'd never come home!'

Andy laughed. 'Well, we'll see. Should be a fairly sober affair tonight.'

'I think "sober" will be stretching it a bit.'

'Maybe! Anyway, bye for now – love you.'

'Love you too.'

The next morning, as Oldroyd predicted, he was called in to see DCS Tom Walker. Walker valued Oldroyd's skill and experience and was quite willing to protect him against higher authorities – especially the despised Chief Constable Matthew Watkins. They also shared a strong Yorkshire identity. Nevertheless, Oldroyd was expecting trouble after his unapproved appearance on television, but as he sat down he was surprised to see that Walker was smiling. He looked at Oldroyd with an inane grin on his face and nodded. He seemed to be struggling to speak.

'Sit down, Jim. I . . .' He couldn't continue, and suddenly burst out laughing.

Oldroyd sat speechless with astonishment as the laughter continued.

'Oh dear!' Walker took out a big handkerchief from his pocket and wiped his eyes. 'Sorry, Jim; it's just that I was watching it last night – me and the wife – and I saw you pop up unexpectedly on camera and then examining that room. My wife said, "Isn't that Jim Oldroyd?" and I said: "Yes, it is." I was flabbergasted to begin with. I thought, what the bloody hell's he up to? And then the door was opened and the chap was dead and . . . and, well, the look on your face when you saw the body . . . I've never seen anything so bloody funny in my life!'

With that he collapsed into further paroxysms of laughter. Oldroyd was relieved that he was clearly not going to get a dressing-down, but had to admit he found the super's sense of humour rather inappropriate, however hapless he'd looked at that awful moment. It was a while before Walker could settle himself down again.

'I'm sorry, Jim; I shouldn't be laughing when someone's been killed, but honestly, if you could have seen yourself . . . Anyway, I've had Watkins on the phone asking what the hell's going on. He wanted me to discipline you, but I said why? It's worked out well, you being there: you were a witness, and Stephanie. It means you're well placed to move the investigation on quickly. I told him you'd had a tip that something might happen so you accepted Redmire's invitation. He swallowed the whole bloody lot, the fool! So you're in the clear; just make a good job of it.'

Oldroyd saw the relish with which Walker had put one over on Watkins; it was clear that providing this opportunity, as well as some comic entertainment, had put him in his boss's good books. Walker didn't even ask him for the truth about why he and Steph had been there.

'Anyway, Jim, I presume you're off back there today, taking charge. Afraid I can't spare you any detectives: we've got a lot on at the moment. You can take Stephanie, of course, as your sergeant. I've been on to the Ripon station and they'll provide some help. I've also made it clear that you're leading things.'

'Thanks, Tom. Steph and I will manage as long as we can take some DCs from Ripon. There's going to be a lot of legwork; lots of people to question, you know.'

Walker agreed and Oldroyd went back to the office. Steph was ready to leave for Redmire Hall, rightly assuming that she would be Oldroyd's second-in-command on this investigation. Oldroyd explained to her about Walker's unexpected reaction to the events of the previous evening. Steph laughed at this.

'Well, sir, at least it's better than the bollocking you were expecting.'

'I suppose so,' agreed Oldroyd, 'but it was a bit annoying that he found me such a ridiculous figure when that body appeared. I wonder how many more people in the TV audience thought the same.'

'It's not like you to worry about what people think about you, sir.'

'No, I suppose not. Anyway, let's get off.'

They left the building, with Steph still laughing to herself about her boss's wounded dignity.

The atmosphere in the breakfast room at Redmire Hall was extremely grim. The family members slowly appeared, except Alex Davis and Poppy, who were still in their beds, completely distraught, and had declared themselves unable to eat anything.

Antonia ignored the tureens of food on the long sideboard, poured herself a strong black coffee and sat silently at the table, lost in thought.

James Forsyth sat opposite her with another black coffee. He fidgeted, desperate to have a smoke. After a minute or so he got up from his place, mumbled 'Excuse me' to Antonia and walked through some French windows on to a terrace, where he was able to light up. Tristram came in, looking very nervous, and sat at a corner of the large table, quietly eating some toast. Only Dominic Carstairs and Douglas Ramsay began piling their plates with the eggs, bacon, sausage and other breakfast items. They took their seats in the centre of the table.

Dominic looked around. 'Well, it's bloody depressing in here,' he declared.

Antonia looked up sharply. 'What on earth do you expect, Dominic? Have you forgotten what happened last night?'

'Of course not, but it won't do us any good moping around.' He sliced off a piece of the thick sausage on his plate, dipped it in egg yolk and thrust it into his mouth. 'The police are on the rampage and we've got to have our wits about us. I don't like the look of that chief inspector.' He waved his knife in the air. 'I think he's probably a socialist and he'll be delighted if he can pin the murder on one of us and get one over on the rich set.'

'Don't be ridiculous, darling.' Mary Carstairs had entered the room and was standing behind her husband, pouring some tea. 'You're talking as if poor Freddy's murder might be the start of a Bolshevik revolution.' She sat down next to Antonia. 'The police are only doing their job. I thought they were very nice, that detective and his glamorous assistant. Very polite and understanding.'

Dominic glared at his plate, rolled a rasher of bacon around his fork and stuffed it whole into his mouth.

'You're always so gullible; don't let them take you in. They're still the police, however nice they seem.'

'Well, *I've* nothing to hide, so it doesn't concern me.'

Dominic bridled at this. 'What on earth are you implying? You don't . . .'

Douglas Ramsay, who was tucking in to kippers and scrambled eggs, laughed. 'She's pulling your leg, Dominic. Calm down, for goodness' sake.'

Dominic scowled and, without another word, continued to eat aggressively.

'Do you really think the police believe it's one of us?' They all turned to Tristram, who'd spoken for the first time since he entered the room.

'Well,' said Douglas, 'as the inspector told us last night, it's the logical place for them to start their enquiries. Whether we like it or not, we have to accept that, at least for now, we are the main suspects.'

Tristram shook his head, and Dominic muttered something into his plate.

Mary turned to Antonia. 'How are you feeling, darling? It's much worse for you than for some of us; I mean, you were married to him for all those years.'

Antonia gave her a weak smile. 'Yes, it was all so sudden and shocking. Freddy and I had our disagreements, but I wouldn't wish that on anybody.'

'Of course not, darling; it was absolutely hideous, seeing him fall over with that knife in his back. I don't think—'

'Good God, I don't believe it!' James Forsyth suddenly came rushing back into the room.

'What's going on?' asked Douglas.

'One of the police officers came over, gave me a message – said could I tell the rest of you . . .' He stopped, as though he couldn't bring himself to finish the sentence.

'Well?'

'There's been another murder.'

Antonia let out a little cry.

'What the—!' Dominic threw down his knife and fork with a clatter.

Forsyth continued. 'A man who worked on the estate – a mechanic, retired, name of Robinson. Found him this morning in his cottage, strangled.'

Horrified glances were exchanged, but no one seemed capable of any further comment.

While Oldroyd and Steph were on their way, HQ radioed the news that another body had been found at Redmire Hall. Steph took the call.

'An old chap in one of the estate cottages?' said Oldroyd after she reported it all to him.

'Yes, sir. Looks like he was strangled; there are marks round his neck. Forensics are on their way.'

'Right. Well, it can't be a coincidence.'

'You think it's connected?'

'Surely. I mean, is it plausible that some random robber or madman breaks into a cottage and kills someone on the same night that the owner is also murdered?'

'It's possible.'

'Yes, but my instinct tells me that it's not the case. I think that person was probably killed because he knew something, and it will be very informative to find out what.'

Oldroyd turned off the main road and on to the approach to the Hall. It was still beautiful but had lost the glamour lent by last night's excited anticipation before the horror of the unfolding events. The sky was glaringly bright but overcast. As they reached the house, they could see yellow-and-black tape across the door of one of a row of pretty red-brick terraced cottages.

'We'd better go in there first,' said Oldroyd as he drew the car to a halt.

Police officers from the Ripon station were on guard and a young detective constable from Ripon met them at the door. He was energetic-looking and had a brisk, efficient manner.

'Good morning, sir; DC Jeffries. The deceased's name was Harold Robinson, known as Harry. He was seventy years old; wife died a few years ago. A retired mechanic – worked on the estate here for forty years maintaining the family's cars and other odd repairing jobs. Found this morning by the chap who lives next door, John Cooke, concerned he hadn't seen the deceased out and about early on, which apparently was his habit.'

'Any sign of a break-in? Anything taken?'

'Nothing obviously stolen, sir. Television set, et cetera, all in place and no signs of forced entrance. The front door was unlocked, suggesting the victim may have known the attacker and let him or her inside; then this assailant simply closed the door behind them when they left.'

'Indeed. Thank you. Let's take a look inside, then.'

Oldroyd and Steph went through a narrow entrance hall and into a small sitting room decorated in a rather old-fashioned manner, with a chintzy sofa and heavy curtains, but everything seemed of good quality. On the floor was sprawled the body of the victim, face down on an expensive-looking Persian carpet. Oldroyd examined the room.

'Well, I can't think the motive was robbery. There are some quite expensive things here – pottery, ornaments, silver candlesticks – all of which would be worth a bit and easy to carry away.'

'Unless there was one particular item they wanted and they just took that,' suggested Steph.

'Of course, but given that this chap was an estate mechanic all his career and wouldn't have earned a great deal, he seems to have acquired some valuable stuff – unless he had some other means of income.'

'Sounds like a job for me, sir; I'll investigate it,' said Steph.

'Good,' replied Oldroyd. 'See if there's any kind of inventory anywhere that might include something that's now missing, and look into his accounts. Ah, here's Tim.'

Tim Groves appeared, his lanky frame ducking through the low doorways of the cottage. 'Good morning,' he announced breezily. 'So I take it last night's operation was part of something more complex than you thought, or do you think these murders are not linked?'

'On the contrary, Tim: I'm pretty sure they were. No sign of robbery here, nobody forced their way in. I think he knew something.'

'Killer lost no time in shutting him up, then. It's the old "S" murder in your taxonomy. Right, let's have a look.'

'S' stood for 'Silencer', referring to someone being murdered because they knew too much. Oldroyd had a habit of inventing these acronyms for deaths, maybe as a way of bringing humour to a subject he found difficult to contemplate despite his regular contact with its brutal reality. There was MTAP, 'Malignancy of Time and Place', which mainly applied to the unfortunate victims of serial killers who'd just happened to be in the wrong place at the wrong time. BM stood for 'Blackmail', KFTM for 'Killed for Their Money', LJ for 'Lust and Jealousy', and so on.

Oldroyd's current favourite was NBI: 'No Bloody Idea', applied when there was no obvious suspect and the investigation was slow. At least these acronyms were more creative and humorous than the dreary stuff produced by management.

'And what do you think he knew?' asked Groves as he deftly carried out his examination, peering closely at the red marks on the body, which Steph had already noticed.

'Well, given that he was a mechanic, I'd say he may well have known something about how Carstairs's trick worked. There's a way in and out of that locked room, and it's concealed in an extremely clever way. Sometimes illusions like that are breathtakingly simple, but often the mechanisms behind them are very complicated. Given the victim's age, he was probably involved when the old Lord Redmire had that room installed. The story is that an illusionist came from Italy to set it up, but someone based here on the estate with technical knowledge would have had to know how it worked in case anything went wrong or needed repairing. I'll bet it was this man and that he knew the secret of the trick.'

'I didn't know until last night you were a magic-and-illusion buff,' observed Groves with a smile.

'Yes! I think it's because magic tricks are puzzles, a bit like crimes, and I like to try to work out how they're done.'

'Same for me sometimes,' replied Groves. 'But not this time, I think. Fairly straightforward: throttled by some kind of thick cord; probably a man – quite a bit of force, judging by the depth of these marks.'

'It might be important to know what kind of cord, Tim. Any chance of finding out?'

'Well, I'll have a closer look back at the lab, see if I can find any fibres. I've still got to examine the knife that killed His Lordship, by the way – see if there's anything interesting about it.'

'Good. Well, let me know as soon as you can. We'll have to start questioning them all today up at the Hall.'

'Good Lord!' chuckled Groves. 'It's a real old Agatha Christie "murder at the big house" job, isn't it? Maybe it was the butler! People are often not who they appear to be in her stories, are they? Maybe someone's a Russian agent or has a secret past.'

'You can laugh, but Agatha had a fine brain. I've learned a lot about how to think about difficult cases by reading her novels,' replied Oldroyd, and then suddenly went thoughtful.

'*Mais oui*, Hercule. I'll be in touch.' Tim Groves went off laughing to himself as his assistants prepared to move the body.

'Sir?' asked Steph, who'd been listening to the conversation. 'Do you think Robinson could have carried out the murder himself if he knew how the trick worked?'

'Quite possibly, but it's more likely that he provided the technical know-how. But I think there were more ruthless people than him involved, and now they've got rid of him because he knew too much; I think they were probably the ones who actually killed Redmire. But it's all supposition until we get some actual evidence. Ah, Jeffries!'

The keen young DC was still there, waiting for his next job.

'I want you to prepare a portfolio for tomorrow, containing as much information as you can about Redmire's family and friends and also a list of all the people who work here. You can get the latter from that estate manager, Wilkins, and I want all his background information on the employees too.'

Jeffries's eyes brightened. 'Yes, sir.'

'And tell your superior at Ripon . . . Inspector Parsons, isn't it?'

'Yes, sir.'

'I'm going to need you to work with me until this case is finished. If he doesn't like the idea I'll have a word with him.'

A broad smile filled Jeffries's face. 'Yes, sir!' He practically ran off to complete his task.

Oldroyd turned to Steph. 'Well, he'll be very useful, I think.'

'I think he'll want your autograph at the end of the case,' laughed Steph.

Oldroyd laughed too. 'Come on. We'd better get cracking up at the house.'

Oldroyd and Steph left the cottage, which was still being guarded by uniformed officers. Everything was strangely quiet as they strolled along the gravel paths towards the Hall. Instead of the usual steady stream of visitors exploring the grounds, everywhere was deserted.

Oldroyd reflected on what Tim Groves had said. Some people among that group of friends, family and estate workers were playing roles, nurturing deceits, their own personal illusions as deadly in their way as the locked room that had proved a deathtrap for Lord Redmire. It was his and Steph's job to unmask whoever it was and to solve the mystery of the trick.

He frowned. This was starting to seem a tall order.

'Harry Robinson – I remember him,' said Antonia. 'He was a mechanic. He serviced the cars and things like that; he did all sorts of odd jobs.

He was a really nice man, very loyal. He retired just before I left. What on earth's going on?'

Most of the family were still in the breakfast room, trying to absorb the shocking news of the second murder.

'It seems a coincidence,' said Douglas. 'But I would imagine the police will think the two murders are linked.'

'The whole estate's under attack,' said Dominic. 'Who knows what's behind it? Freddy may well have borrowed money from some gangster types in London and when he couldn't pay back they decided to come here to take revenge and whatever loot they could put their hands on.'

'That's a bit wild, old boy,' said Douglas. 'I mean, I can't imagine why such people would attack a retired estate worker.'

'Those types always go for the most vulnerable, mark my words.'

'Anyway, the plot thickens,' observed James Forsyth. 'I'm glad *I* don't have to get to the bottom of it.'

'First Freddy and now this,' said Mary Carstairs. 'It's a nightmare.'

'It is,' said Douglas. 'And it's one we're going to be trapped in for some time.'

'So before we start, let's recap some of the basics.'

Oldroyd and Steph were in their makeshift but rather comfortable 'office', reclining in the easy chairs in the little sitting-room section. Coffee and biscuits had been provided.

'First, we believe these murders are linked, but we don't yet have the proof. Second, they are likely to be the work of a number of people, because of the complexity of what's involved with that trick. Robinson probably had some technical knowledge and has been silenced.'

'So, sir, you're thinking of probably about three or four people?' said Steph as she sipped her coffee. She needed the caffeine: last night had been very long and traumatic, and she felt tired.

'Yes. Any more than four is rare and leads to complications, in my experience; someone usually rats on the others for a reward or to try to get themselves out of trouble. Then there's the question of motive. We're starting with the family, which is always the most likely place to find someone with a motive for murder.'

'As they were all there in that room with us watching the trick, they were clearly not directly carrying out at least the first murder.'

'Yes – and they've thus provided themselves with a wonderful alibi. However, rich people never do their own dirty work, even if they've planned it – they get others to do it for them.'

'Do you think the murders were carried out by a professional hit-man?' Steph refilled her cup; she was feeling better already.

'No, not in this case. The killers all had to know about the trick and there must have been meticulous planning; you couldn't just bring in outsiders to do it. It also involved gaining the confidence of the victim.'

'Yes: Lord Redmire knew his killers; they were the people who shared the secret of the locked room with him and operated it last night.'

'Exactly. In fact, you could say that he planned and cooperated in his own murder.' Oldroyd shuddered; it was not an agreeable thought. Death was never pleasant, but the idea of unwittingly planning your own violent demise was positively macabre.

'How do you think it was planned, then, sir?'

'Clearly Redmire knew nothing of the trick until recently, or he would have used it before. Maybe he was gullible because he could see the financial rewards of the live TV performance and the consequent visitor potential. What I think could have happened is that these people, whoever they are, approached him saying they'd discovered how this thing works. They agreed to stay quiet and help him, maybe for a reward. They stayed quiet all right: they weren't going to reveal the murder method!'

'Wow!' exclaimed Steph softly. 'And then they got rid of one of the group. Why Harold Robinson, sir?'

Oldroyd shrugged. 'We don't know yet. Maybe he was threatening them somehow or they couldn't trust him for some reason. The fewer people in the know, the better. And that's assuming we're right that the murders are linked.' They'd both finished their coffee and Oldroyd stretched in his chair. 'Well, better get started. I expect it's going to be long and complicated. I want you to tell me what you instinctively feel about them all. I know we have to have evidence but an experienced detective develops a feeling – almost a smell – for falsity, guilt and lies, and it's often a good place to start. You often find then that the evidence follows to support your hunches.'

'As long as you don't try to fit the evidence to your hunches,' replied Steph with a mischievous smile.

'Absolutely; we're not into that. That's when the police start to make fools of themselves and get people wrongly convicted. Let's start with his ex-mistress and her boyfriend.'

Richard Wilkins was out on what he called his 'rounds'. He was tired after a poor night's sleep, but part of his normal routine was to spend some time walking around the estate checking that everything was going smoothly. The Hall had been closed to visitors for an indefinite period. He hoped the police would not take too long in their investigations because the estate badly needed the revenue.

He passed the estate entrance and the Redmire Hall gift shop, both in darkness, and the forlorn, empty café with its terrace overlooking the walled kitchen garden. He looked up at the now brightening sky in exasperation: that terrace and the garden should be full of people on a day like this, bringing the money rolling in. He continued through an opening in the ancient brick wall overhung with a beautiful climbing rose and reached the main herbaceous borders.

The gardens were constructed as a series of 'rooms', divided by hedges and linked by paths. Redmire's grandfather, a keen gardener, had taken inspiration from Lawrence Johnston's famous gardens at Hidcote Manor in Gloucestershire. The expansive double borders running from the house down to the river created the largest 'room' and one of the showpieces of the house.

Wilkins found the gardening team at work here, no doubt taking advantage of the absence of visitors to get ahead with their tasks. Wheelbarrows and buckets lined the edge of the central lawn and the gardeners were weeding between the huge, colourful clumps of delphiniums, rudbeckia and phlox. The head gardener, David Morton, was directing his team. Morton had worked at the estate since he left school in the late 1960s. He was past retirement age, but was deeply devoted to the gardens at Redmire and refused to step down. As he was so skilful, and because under his leadership the gardens had won several awards, there was no immediate pressure on him to go. Wilkins went over to have a word.

'Morning, David. Taking the chance to get on with things without having to work round the public, I see.'

Morton stood up and leaned against his border fork. He was strongly built, with a greying beard.

'Morning, Richard. Yes, the show has to go on, doesn't it? The weeds don't stop growing because His Lordship's dead.' He shook his head as if he could still barely believe that fact.

'No, and I'm sure he'd have wanted you to carry on keeping things as good as they are.'

'Yes.'

'Have the police been to talk to you yet?'

'No. I'm expecting them at some point.'

'Yes. They'll want to talk to everyone who works here and had anything to do with the people who were murdered; anyone who they think may have had a motive for killing them.'

'To be honest, we know His Lordship was a bit of a rogue – I can imagine there were lots of people who might be glad to see the back of him. But Harry? I've known him for years. Nice chap, harmless; no enemies that I can think of. Who'd want to kill a man like that?'

'Well, someone did. Anyway, I'll be off and leave you to get on. I sometimes think you lot would have an easier job if there weren't any visitors; they get in your way, don't they?'

Morton laughed. 'Yes, the public can be a nuisance, stumbling into plants and breaking them, leaving litter, trampling on the grass instead of staying on the paths. Still, I don't suppose we could do without them. See you later.' He returned to his border and Wilkins headed back to the estate office.

As he passed across the front of the house, Andrea Jenkinson came out to greet him. 'Richard, how are you?' She looked concerned.

'OK, I think – bearing up, as they say. What about you?'

'The same. I've been ringing round cancelling things and there've been a lot of calls giving condolences. It's all really weird.'

'I know.'

'It's worse for you, though; it's a hell of a responsibility to organise things for the police and the family and then keep everything going when we – *you* – reopen.'

Wilkins shrugged. 'All part of the job, I suppose.'

'Maybe, but don't overdo it. Don't make yourself ill for them.' She nodded back towards the house. 'They're not worth it.'

'I know.'

'Anyway, better get back; no doubt the phone will be going. Bye for now.'

'Bye.'

Wilkins continued on to the visitors' entrance, where everything was quiet. The house was not as popular with visitors as the gardens and play areas. Entry cost extra, which deterred families, and there was not a great deal inside for children anyway. Nevertheless, the interior had some magnificent decorative plasterwork, paintings, furniture and collections of china. Most people who made it into the house were not disappointed.

Celia Anscomb was in charge of the interior. She organised the voluntary guides and supervised conservation work, which was ongoing and expensive. Wilkins popped into her small office next to the entrance. She was in there alone.

'Good morning, Celia, how are you?' Celia had very short hair and she wore large glasses and a long skirt. She looked very worried.

'Hello, Richard. What on earth's going on? I can't believe it. Two murders here last night, in a quiet stately home in the country? Is the world going mad?'

Wilkins blew out his cheeks and shook his head. 'I know, it's unbelievable.'

'Do the police know who did it? Harry was a nice man; I can't think who would have wanted to kill him. I can imagine that Lord Redmire might have had some enemies, though.'

'Yes, but the answer to your question, I think, is that the police not only don't know who killed either man; they also don't even know *how* Lord Redmire was murdered.'

'So we'll have to stay shut for the time being?'

'I think so.'

'I thought as much, but I wanted to talk to you about that, Richard. We can't really afford to lose the revenue, otherwise the conservation programme is going to grind to a halt.'

'Yes, I understand.'

'I spoke to Lord Redmire only the other day and told him that we're underfunded here in the house, but he never seemed to see it as important. Quite the reverse. He's been poking around recently looking at stuff and asking me to get valuations on things. Even the Gainsborough.'

A huge portrait of an eighteenth-century Lord Redmire and his family that hung at the top of the stairs was the centrepiece of the Redmire art collection. It had been commissioned by that lord and been on the same wall in the house ever since its completion.

'It obviously made me wonder if he was thinking of selling things to make ends meet. We all know – because enough rumours have been going round – that he was always short of cash because of his gambling. That was bad enough. But now, the longer we're closed, the worse it will get. That plaster in the green bedroom will literally start falling off the ceiling if we don't start work on it soon.'

'I know, I know,' agreed Wilkins. 'Look, between you and me, Lord Redmire did have some plans to generate revenue but I don't know any details. It might have involved selling some valuable objects in the house – I don't know. He never discussed the details with me. It's probably the wrong thing to say, but, for everyone who's worked hard to keep the house and the rest of the estate in the condition it's in and wants to see it all remain intact, it'll be much better when Mr Alistair takes over. I've just been talking to David Morton and I'll bet he feels the same.'

Celia raised her eyebrows. 'Well, I suppose you're right, Richard; I hadn't thought of it like that. Mr Alistair certainly gives the impression of being really attached to the place. So maybe every cloud has a silver lining, eh?'

'You could put it like that. Let's not pretend that his father was the greatest person to work for, though I know you shouldn't speak ill of the dead.'

'No, I agree.' As Wilkins turned to the door, Celia said, 'Just before you go, Richard, could you have a word with the police? Just to ask them when we can reopen? Explain the financial difficulties.'

'I'll do my best but I don't think it'll cut much ice. They've got a murder enquiry on and that will be their priority, not the viability of this place. Anyway, bye.'

'Bye.'

He trudged back to his own office, feeling weary and hoping for a break, but when he arrived he found the ever-keen DC Jeffries waiting for him with a long list of demands for information.

Three

'So, I understand that you and the deceased Lord Redmire had a relationship over a number of years?' Oldroyd and Steph were interviewing Alex Davis, who had been persuaded downstairs and now looked uncharacteristically tense and uncomfortable in the makeshift incident room. She was wearing dark glasses and a cashmere cardigan even though it was a warm day.

'Yes, Chief Inspector,' she replied wearily. 'It was well known; we didn't try to conceal it. Freddy and I were very close for a long time.'

'And what brought the relationship to an end?'

She gave Oldroyd a filthy look, but knew she had to reply. 'Oh, this and that. Time passes, things change. Freddy's not renowned for his fidelity; he began to stray.'

'How did you feel about that?'

'By that time it was obvious that he was ready to move on; I'd started to stray, too, with James, who became my partner.'

'And had been Lord Redmire's business partner?'

'Yes.'

'That sounds extremely messy. I assume Lord Redmire wasn't too pleased about it?'

'No. But he could hardly complain, could he?'

Steph watched Alex Davis closely. She felt ambivalent about this woman: she was part of that arrogant rich elite who'd been 'born with a silver spoon in their mouths', as her mum would have said, but she admired the way she had not allowed powerful men to trample all over her and in fact had given as good as she'd got.

'Nevertheless he must have felt it more keenly, as you went off with his friend,' continued Oldroyd.

Alex sighed. 'I'm not sure that James was really Freddy's friend. I don't think Freddy had any proper friends.'

'Well, whatever their relationship was, I take it this must have soured it.'

'Yes.'

'And was that when their business venture came to an end?'

'It was certainly a factor, but it was more complicated than that. You'll have to ask James.'

'Did you know anything about what was planned here last night? Did Lord Redmire tell you anything about this locked-room trick?'

'No, nothing. James and I got the invitation and I wanted to come, because I thought it would be fun. We don't get many invitations to stately homes like this.'

'And what did you do when you arrived?'

'James and I were shown to our room. Later I came down to get a drink in the drawing room. James went for a walk in the gardens, then we all met for dinner and after that, you know.'

'Have you ever met Harold Robinson?'

'No.'

Oldroyd paused and looked at her. 'It must have felt awkward, coming here; you knew Lord Redmire's ex-wife and his family would be around. Are you sure it wasn't because you wanted to see him again? How did you feel about him? Were you still angry?'

Her answer was unexpectedly frank. 'Yes, I was angry with him – I still am. Freddy and I had the kind of feelings for each other that never entirely die, although I'm happy with James and would never have gone back to Freddy.'

'Were you still in love with him?'

She took off her glasses and looked straight at Oldroyd. 'I always will be, Chief Inspector. That's why I left him: because he had the power to hurt me and he did – too many times. But I didn't kill him.'

Despite the fact that he seemed the epitome of cool, in a cream linen jacket, blue jeans and brown brogues, Oldroyd and Steph could sense the tension in James Forsyth, who lounged in his chair in a rather exaggerated fashion.

'You knew Lord Redmire for many years, I believe.'

'I did.'

'How would you describe your relationship with him?'

Forsyth thought for a moment. 'Freddy and I got on very well when we first got to know each other through the Vintage Sports Car Club. We were young in those days and we both liked driving fast cars, going for a drink afterwards – you know the sort of thing.' He smiled.

Steph knew that there were few things Oldroyd despised more than wealthy young men, probably alcohol-fuelled, tearing around the rural roads putting people's lives in danger.

Oldroyd said nothing, but did not smile in return. 'Did this fast life include pursuing women?'

'I can't deny we did a fair amount of that too, Chief Inspector. They were very exciting times. There's nothing a woman likes more, in my experience, than being driven at speed through the countryside in an open-topped sports car.'

Steph shook her head and bit her tongue. 'I think you were probably doing more than driving them around in sports cars.'

'Yes, we were.' Forsyth's smirk sickened Steph. It reminded her of men she encountered in bars who came up behind you and started massaging your shoulders.

'Am I right in thinking that Lord Redmire was still messing about with women after his marriage?'

'He was, though I have to say not with my approval. I was very sorry for Antonia.'

I don't believe you, thought Steph. You're enjoying this. You haven't even asked why we're asking you about your private life.

'I'm just trying to establish the origins and background of your relationship. Can you give me some idea of the time frame in relation to when you went into business with Lord Redmire and when Alex Davis came on the scene?'

'Freddy and I had known each other for about ten years when he suggested the idea that we should start up a company selling vintage cars. I should have known better; going into business with Freddy was always going to be a mistake. He only suggested it because his funds were low; his lifestyle and his gambling consumed vast amounts of cash. I should have realised that he had no idea about running a business – or work of any kind, for that matter. He'd lived like a playboy all his life.'

'What about you?'

'My father ran a business: high-class furniture – very successful. So I had much more business knowledge than Freddy.'

'And Alex Davis?'

'She appeared at about the same time, when we'd just started. She came to look round the showroom with her then boyfriend, some freak from the racing-car world who went round saying how underpowered the cars were compared to the ones he drove. I could see from Freddy's expression that he was instantly smitten with Alex. From then on, he spent even less time at work and more time chasing her until he was successful. He paraded her round quite openly; I think that was the last straw for Antonia and she left him. Poppy had moved in with Tristram by then.'

'So I take it the business didn't prosper?'

'How could it? It was a one-man show. It was too much for me.'

'What happened between you and Alex Davis?'

'Freddy was still womanising. I was sick of it by then, and sick of him too. I mean, it's one thing sowing your wild oats, but another when you've destroyed your marriage and you're now cheating on a woman like Alex. He was cheating on me too: he was leaving me to run the business alone and I couldn't do it. Alex started to come round to the showroom to talk to me about Freddy; we were both very upset about it all. Then one day she came to my apartment and it all went on from there.'

'Were you aware that she retained some affection for Lord Redmire?'

Forsyth looked up, surprised. 'Did she tell you that? Yes, I know she still had a soft spot for Freddy – so did I. He was that kind of character: very charming, great fun . . . but totally unreliable. It's all very sad.'

'What happened when the business crashed?'

'We had a big row about it. Alex supported me and Freddy realised what was happening between us. It all turned nasty and we lost a lot of money. I started again with a different business partner and we're doing fairly well in a tough market; we're in the sports-car trade.'

'How would you describe your relationship with Lord Redmire recently?'

'I've had nothing to do with him since then.'

'Why did you think he invited you to this event? Did you know anything about this trick?'

'No, I didn't; the whole thing was a surprise – a ghastly one, as it's turned out. I didn't really want to come, to be honest, but Alex talked me into it. She likes coming to glamorous places like this. I'm not sure why he invited us and I wonder if, in Freddy's mind, he was in some way trying to win Alex back, you know, by impressing her. I certainly wasn't expecting him to compensate me for any of the money I lost.'

'According to Alex Davis, you arrived here yesterday, went to your room and then she went to get a drink while you walked around the gardens before dinner.'

'Correct.'

'Had you ever met Harold Robinson?'

'No.'

Oldroyd took a drink of water and looked searchingly at Forsyth. 'OK. I want to ask you again about Lord Redmire. How did you really feel about him after everything that had happened?'

Forsyth fidgeted and then seemed to choose his words carefully. 'I'm being absolutely honest with you. I'm still angry with Freddy for letting me down over the business and losing my money. I normally kept Alex well away from him. I thought that was the best way.' He looked directly at Oldroyd. 'I know what you're thinking, Chief Inspector. I had a motive to kill Freddy: anger over the business, money and jealousy about Alex. But I didn't do it.'

Accompanied by Tristram, Poppy finally made an appearance downstairs, joining the rest of the family in the main drawing room, where they were gathering to await their calls through for interview. She flopped on to a sofa next to her mother. Antonia put her arm around her. Tristram stood behind the sofa looking uneasy, while Douglas – apparently quite calm – sat in an armchair digesting his breakfast. Dominic Carstairs paced up and down the room with his hands in his pockets muttering to himself. Mary was pouring herself a gin at the drinks tray on the sideboard.

'It's a bit early for that, isn't it?' Dominic called out irascibly to his wife.

'Surely not in the circumstances,' replied Mary, unruffled.

Dominic shook his head and flung out his arms in contempt. 'Here we all are. It's like waiting for a bloody job interview. That damned detective again – how dare he treat us like this!'

'Sit down and relax, old boy; you're making us all nervous,' observed Douglas.

'Bah!' exclaimed Dominic, and went outside through the French windows.

'Are Alex and James with the police?' asked Poppy.

'Yes,' replied Antonia. 'They went to be interviewed together, but I think the police will speak to them separately.'

'Oh God!' cried Poppy, and put her head on her mother's shoulder.

'Nothing to worry about, darling; just answer their questions clearly and you'll be fine,' said Antonia.

'But it's so awful after what happened to Daddy and . . .' Poppy started to weep again. Tristram stroked her hair.

'I'll go with you and I'll be outside waiting for my turn,' he said.

'Will we be able to go afterwards? I don't want to stay here any longer.'

'I'm not sure about that, darling,' said Mary. 'The police aren't concerned about our convenience. They just want answers. It's early days yet, so I think we'll have to stick around a bit longer until they've got everything they can out of us. Anyway, I think it's right that we do, really; we've got to help Alistair and Katherine with the funeral arrangements, handling the press and things like that. We can't all just disappear and leave them to it, even if the police would let us.'

'I agree,' said Antonia. 'We should all stay together and work through it all.'

As if to emphasise the point, a duty constable called for the Ramsays to go to the interview room.

Oldroyd was impressed with Antonia Ramsay, who looked dignified and stoical despite suffering the shock of seeing her former husband murdered. She sat erect in the chair.

'I already know quite a bit about your relationship with your former husband, but I have to ask you nevertheless.'

'There's not much to say.' Her tone was flat, resigned. 'Freddy started seeing other women not long after we were married. He never made much of an attempt to conceal it and word always got back to me, even though he conducted most of his affairs in London. He owns a flat in Kensington. Eventually I'd had enough. I waited until the children had left home and then divorced him. I'd already met Douglas, but we didn't start our relationship properly until I'd left Freddy. Some of us have standards of behaviour that we try to maintain,' she concluded. She sounded rather bitter and self-righteous, thought Oldroyd, but he could hardly blame her. This was a woman who'd suffered serial humiliations over many years.

'Are you happy now with your new husband and financially secure?'

'Yes. Douglas is the exact opposite of Freddy: steady and reliable. He's exactly what I needed.'

'OK. Good. Can I ask you about your children, Poppy and Alistair? How were they affected by their father's behaviour and the divorce?'

'I tried to protect them as far as possible; I was helped by the fact that Freddy was away in London for long periods so we weren't having rows all the time.'

'And now?'

She frowned. 'Alistair's very sympathetic; he's got a family of his own, and I think he understands what it must mean to have an unreliable partner. But Poppy's immature, and takes after her father too much for my liking. She could get money out of Freddy whenever he had any, and I now know she hands some of that over to her boyfriend. Which baffles me, as he's a gambler like her father, and she's seen how he frittered the family inheritance away.'

'I see.' Oldroyd thought about his own daughter, Louise, who still relied on the Bank of Dad at times; at least she didn't gamble. 'Did Lord Redmire, his father or anyone else ever tell you anything about the locked room and how it worked?'

'Never. I remember Vivian would never say anything at all except that he considered it one of his greatest achievements. I liked Vivian. He was an amiable old eccentric – hopeless with money, like his son, but not a womaniser or a gambler. My feeling is he wouldn't have trusted Freddy with the secret. He knew his son's weaknesses and that he'd just exploit the trick for gain, which was exactly what he was trying to do, wasn't it?'

'Yes. How do you think Freddy got to know about it, then?'

'I've absolutely no idea. The whole thing was completely forgotten about; nobody went near that room when I lived here. It's a mystery to me how the secret has suddenly resurfaced.'

'I assume you knew Harold Robinson?'

'Of course. Lovely man, very reliable. He was devoted to Redmire. I can't see who would want to kill him.'

'Right. And can I ask you about your movements when you arrived yesterday?'

'Douglas and I went to our room. He had a nap while I went for a walk. I met one or two estate workers I hadn't seen for a while and had a chat with them. Then I went back and we had dinner.'

'Well, Mrs Ramsay,' said Oldroyd, bringing the interview to an end. 'I know I don't need to tell you that your treatment by Lord Redmire constitutes a motive for murder.'

Antonia smiled and looked unconcerned. 'Yes, I appreciate that, but I'm sure you're expecting me to deny it – and I do.'

'Quite. But as the person who knew him and all his affairs – business and otherwise – so well and for so long, do you think he had any special enemies who might be responsible?'

She laughed scornfully. 'Well, take your pick, Chief Inspector; I'm sure you're already compiling your own list of people with a motive. Freddy made enemies, he had debts – people stood to gain from his death.' She paused and looked very seriously at Oldroyd. 'But I don't know anyone who would be capable of organising and carrying out a murder like that. It was clever and it was brutal.'

Douglas Ramsay was amiable and cooperative compared to previous interviewees.

'Terrible business, Chief Inspector. Of course I didn't like the man, can't pretend otherwise. I could never forgive him for the way he treated Antonia. That man was, well, I know it's old-fashioned, but he was a cad.'

Steph smiled at the antiquated term.

'You must have found it difficult to come here, then,' said Oldroyd.

'Yes. I only came because Antonia wanted to; she likes to take every opportunity she can to see Poppy and Alistair and also, although she'd never admit it, she enjoys coming back here, you know. It can't have been easy to give up being mistress of this wonderful place, and I understand she got on so well with everyone on the estate.'

'I take it you'd never met Harold Robinson?'

'No, though I've heard Antonia mention him.'

'And can you confirm that when you arrived yesterday, you stayed in your room having a nap until it was time for dinner while your wife went out for a walk?'

'That's right.'

'I must say, you have a very generous attitude, Mr Ramsay. You can't have felt very comfortable coming to this house, but you did it for your wife. How do you find the family?'

'To be honest, not always easy. Alistair's fine, nice young family, but I don't warm to Poppy: spoiled young woman, boyfriend's a bit of a waster. Please don't say I said so to Antonia. Dominic's a grumpy sort of character, seems to resent his brother getting the estate. Can't say I blame him, but it's made him very bitter.'

'You said you didn't like Lord Redmire. Did you dislike him enough to want him dead?'

Ramsay laughed a little nervously. 'No, of course not, Chief Inspector. Antonia suffered at his hands for many years, but Freddy had very little to do with us. We're happy together and Antonia has a new life. There's no reason why I should do anything to spoil that.'

'I take it you think there were plenty of people who might have wanted him dead.'

'I suppose so, but I don't know. The way Freddy was killed, and now this other man . . . It's all so shocking.'

Andrea Jenkinson was alone in the small office that had previously belonged to herself and Lord Redmire. She looked down the long borders, as Lord Redmire had done not long before his violent departure. She could see David Morton and his team at work and he waved to her. It was very quiet in the office but there was little work to do in the circumstances. She knew she had to talk to Alistair Carstairs, the new Lord Redmire, about her role and what the future held, but she'd already decided to leave Redmire Hall and make a new start. She'd only been here two years, but it hadn't been easy working with the late Lord Redmire. He'd been lazy and demanding, making last-minute requests for her to change things or deciding not to do what she'd spent a lot of time arranging. He was often late, and would blame her unfairly when things went wrong. And then there'd been the unwanted attentions. She had known about his reputation when she'd gone for the job, but it had still seemed a good opportunity, working for a lord. Luckily, he'd never tried anything on directly, although the way he looked at her had often made her feel uncomfortable. The fact that he was old enough to be her father hadn't seemed to concern him. Of course, that was never a problem for philanderers like him, as she was aware.

When she'd shown no interest in him, he had for a while made things even harder for her, until he'd started to appreciate her work: how efficient she was and how she was able to extricate him from difficulties. Nevertheless, now seemed to be the time to go, as there were other complications in her life at Redmire.

Her thoughts were interrupted by a knock on the door. She knew who it would be.

'Well, talk of the devil. Come in, there's no one here.'

Richard Wilkins came in, looking around tentatively. When he saw the office was indeed empty, he strode over to Andrea and kissed her. He sat in a chair next to hers.

'Who were you talking to about me, anyway?' asked Wilkins as he gazed at her very fondly.

'No one, but I was thinking about you.'

'Good, I'm glad to hear it.'

She looked away from his gaze. 'I've also been . . . been thinking about what's going to happen now, you know, with my job and everything.'

'Aren't we all? Everything's very uncertain.'

'Yes, but most people will stay on, surely? The estate will still need them when the new regime takes over.'

'Well, that goes for you too.'

'Yes, Richard, I know, but I don't think I . . . want it.'

'What do you mean?'

'I'm going to leave Redmire, even if they say I can continue.'

'What?'

'Yes. I've had enough of it here.'

Wilkins grabbed her hand. 'You don't mean that; I thought you liked it here, and what about, you know, us? It's going to be a lot more difficult if . . .'

'It's over, Richard.' She pushed his hand away, and faced him. 'I've been meaning to tell you for some time, but it's been difficult.'

She'd raised her voice a little and Wilkins looked round as if people might be listening. He looked at her desperately.

'You're not serious. It's the shock of what happened that's upset you.'

'I am serious. I don't want to carry on having an affair like this, here at work, and then you drive home to your wife and family every night.'

'But it's wonderful, what we have together.'

'It's wonderful for you, but there's no future in it for me. You've made it clear that you'll never leave Laura.'

'It's not her, it's the kids. It's not fair to leave them without a father.'

'Fine, and you just expect me to go on being your bit on the side at work?'

'But we've talked about this so many times; I thought you were happy that at least we could be together here?' He tried to put his arm around her but she resisted.

'I was.' She sighed, and looked down, as if contemplating the past. 'But, well, maybe you're right: what's happened has affected me. In fact it's shocked me into realising certain things and asking myself big questions, like: where is my life going? What I've decided is that I've no future here.'

'But where will you go? And . . . and I don't want to lose you. I . . .'

She raised her head again and her eyes blazed with anger. 'It's all right saying that, but if I meant so much to you I wouldn't always have come second.'

'You don't always come second, I—'

'Stop it, Richard – I don't want to hear any more. I want you to go. All our meetings from now on will be strictly to do with estate business while I'm serving my notice. I intend to hand in my resignation soon. In fact, I'm telling you now, as the most senior figure in the management structure until Alistair Carstairs has confirmed that he's taking over the running of the estate. Just don't say anything yet.'

He looked at her pleadingly, but she merely shook her head. He got up and left the office without another word. When the door was shut, she breathed out a sigh of relief. She felt much better now that that was done.

Dominic Carstairs sat bolt upright in the chair with his arms folded and glared at Oldroyd.

'I want to make it clear that I think these, these . . . proceedings are an outrage,' he spluttered.

Outrageous because he thinks a member of the land-owning classes like him is above the law, thought Oldroyd. This interview was not going to be easy, but somehow he had to remain objective.

'I'm sorry you feel that way, sir,' he replied in a sternly formal manner, 'but this is a murder enquiry and we need to ask you some questions. I'm sure you will cooperate.'

He glowered at Carstairs in such a ferocious manner that the man visibly wilted and Steph had to look away as she smiled.

'Did you know anything about this illusion of the locked room? Did your brother or your father ever say anything about it?'

'No – probably because they knew I wouldn't be the slightest bit interested in it. I'm a practical man; I've no time for magic, illusions and other such piffle. If the gullible public want to pay to see someone apparently disappear when of course they haven't, that's entirely up to them. The trick seems to lie in getting people's money out of them for nothing.'

'Well, as a businessman, wouldn't you be interested in it from that angle? Obviously your brother was: he clearly thought it would be an excellent money-spinner.'

Carstairs grunted with contempt. 'Some of us, Chief Inspector, have more self-respect than to make fools of ourselves trying to con people by getting locked up in some so-called "magic room", or whatever it's supposed to be. Typical of Freddy, of course. A scheme to make money that didn't involve any work.'

'You don't appear to have a very high opinion of your brother.'

'He is – was – an idler and a spendthrift; people like him give our class a bad name. What's more, he was a serial philanderer and he caused Antonia a lot of distress; never deserved to have her in the first place.'

'I wonder if there's any long-standing bitterness here? Do you resent the fact that your older brother inherited the estate and the title?'

'Yes, I bloody well do, as a matter of fact. It was completely undeserved and it left me having to struggle to earn a living. At least it'll now pass to my nephew, who's a sound sort of chap. He won't gamble it away. It would be nice, though, if I could have relied on that kind of inheritance to pass on to my children. They have to work for a living, like me. Still, I suppose it doesn't do them any harm.'

Oldroyd felt no sympathy. Carstairs didn't exactly look poor, yet here he was bleating on because he'd not got the lion's share of the family fortune when clearly he'd had so many other advantages all his life.

'Did you know Harold Robinson?'

'Yes, vaguely. He's been here a long time. He was the estate mechanic when I was a teenager here, but I never had much to do with him.'

'Did he have any enemies?'

'I wouldn't know.'

'When you arrived yesterday, what did you do?'

'After we settled in, I went for a walk and Mary stayed in the room until we all met for dinner.'

After these routine questions, Oldroyd decided to go in for the kill. 'Did you dislike your brother and his good fortune enough to want to murder him?'

Carstairs laughed derisively. 'Much good that would have done me: the estate would still have gone to Alistair. Hardly worth the effort.'

'Maybe not in financial terms, but if you hated him badly enough there would have been the satisfaction of destroying him.'

'So I'm not only jealous but a sadist too, who takes pleasure in murdering his own brother.'

'So did you?' persisted Oldroyd, pressing for a clear denial.

'No, I did not!'

Mary Carstairs seemed the most composed of the interviewees so far. She relaxed in the chair and smiled at Oldroyd and Steph.

'Nasty job you've got, I must say,' she remarked. 'I don't envy you trying to find out who's committed these murders.'

'Why's that?' asked Oldroyd.

'Well, they were obviously well planned, weren't they? A very efficient job.'

'I agree and I'm sure you want to help us in this difficult task.'

'Of course. Fire away, Chief Inspector.'

'First, according to your husband, after you arrived you stayed in your room on the afternoon before the murder.'

'Yes.' Oldroyd picked up on a moment's hesitation.

'Did you know Harold Robinson?'

'No.'

'How would you describe your relationship with Lord Redmire?'

She smiled again. 'Freddy and I got on well. He was always very charming, a good laugh, and knew how to enjoy himself.'

'Did he ever tell you anything about the locked room?'

'No.'

Oldroyd looked at her closely. 'You don't seem very upset, despite the fact that you've lost someone you were close to.'

'I wouldn't say we were that close, Chief Inspector; I didn't see Freddy that often.' She sighed and her tone became more sombre. 'Anyway, what's the use in moping about? That never brought anyone back. But yes, I will miss him. I don't think I speak for everyone, though.'

'And why's that?'

'Well, there were too many . . . Oh, Lord! I was about to say "too many knives out for him", but that's hardly appropriate, is it! Too many people had issues with him. I'm sure you don't need me to tell you: James and Alex and all that love-triangle stuff. The car business with James. The long-suffering Antonia . . . Poppy forever after his money and so on . . . to say nothing of my bitter husband. Mind you, don't get me wrong: I'm not saying I think any of them would have bumped him off, nor that other poor chap.'

'Should we add you to that list?'

She laughed out loud. 'Me? Why ever would I want to kill poor Freddy? I was his only real ally in the family.'

David Morton, deadheading roses in one of the rose gardens, saw Richard Wilkins storm out of the house with a face like thunder and march back through the gardens to his office. This time he did not come over for a chat, and the gardener wondered what had happened. Maybe the stress of being in charge in these unusual circumstances was proving too great. He felt glad that he was well out of the trouble. All he had to do was organise his team and maintain the gardens. It was a specialist area and no one interfered much with him, especially as he clearly did an excellent job.

Suddenly a voice called out. It was Lady Antonia. He still called her that, even though she wasn't the mistress of Redmire anymore. She was coming from the direction of the house and wearing an elegant pale-green trouser suit.

'David, how nice to see you again. Please carry on.'

'And you too, Your Ladyship.'

Morton didn't exactly touch his forelock, but came very close. He carried on carefully applying his secateurs throughout the conversation.

'I see the Jacques Cartier have bloomed well this year,' she said, looking at the pink rosettes of the old rose and smelling its fragrance.

'Yes, I think we'll get a second flush in September if we're lucky.'

'Wonderful! I have some of these in my rose garden, but they never flower as well as these. The gardens here are special, and it's mostly down to you, David.'

'Well, thank you, but I don't think it's just me: there's something in the soil and the air here. It's a very special place.'

'I agree, but I also think you're being over-modest; the work you've put in over the years . . .' Her tone changed. 'By the way, I'm sure you're shocked by what's happened, like everyone else, but I know my son will want you to stay on when he inherits, so don't worry.'

'Yes, I've no worries there, Your Ladyship – I get on well with Mr Alistair. He's going to make a good master of Redmire; he really cares about it.'

'Quite,' replied Antonia, but she hadn't missed the subtle sentiment, probably shared by most of the estate staff, that her ex-husband had not really cared for Redmire.

After Antonia had walked on, another person approached Morton. Ian Barden had the unusual job of maintaining and driving the miniature railway engines, which he did with skill and care. He was also an obsessive character, lacking in social skills and apt to talk at people for lengthy periods about obscure details of model engines or some odd fanatical, paranoid notion he'd got into his head, such as his fear that radiation from electrical appliances was going to kill everyone.

The shed where the engines were housed was near the rose garden. As Redmire Hall was closed, Ian had time on his hands and had spent the morning overhauling the reserve engine, a scale model of the *Duchess of Hamilton*, the famous Princess Coronation Class steam locomotive, complete with streamlined casing. Barden was a thin man with staring eyes. He was dressed in blue overalls and his hands were oily. He was wiping them on a rag as he came over.

'Morning, David.'

'Morning, Ian. How's the *Duchess*?'

'Fine. I've been stripping her pistons and greasing round.' Unusually, he went no further on this topic. 'It's a right bloody carry-on, isn't it, these murders?'

'Aye, it is,' replied Morton as he continued with his deadheading. He didn't particularly want to hear Ian's thoughts on the matter.

'It's bad enough that t'gaffer's been done in, but Harry, he were one of us, like, and a good mate o' mine too.'

'He was.'

'Word's going round that Harry knew something, you know, about Lord Redmire's murder. What do you think?'

Morton stopped and turned. 'Harry? Maybe, but he would never have hurt anybody.'

'No, I reckon not, but all the same there must have been a reason he were done in an' all. It's very fishy, if you ask me, and it's not nice thinking there's a killer around, is it? I mean, who's next?'

'Ah, I wouldn't worry about that. Unless you know something . . .' Morton laughed.

'Well, there's a point, but I'll say no more for the moment,' Barden whispered conspiratorially. 'Anyway, better get on. See you later.'

Morton watched him go, and shook his head.

Barden walked back to the little engine shed. He'd meant it when he said that Robinson had been a good friend of his, and he wanted to know who'd killed him. In fact, he intended to conduct an investigation of his own and already had some ideas. This had to be stopped before anyone else was killed. Where would it end? Maybe the whole of Redmire Hall would be wiped out by some terrible serial killer, like the ones he'd seen on television. Admittedly they were usually in the direst neighbourhoods of big American cities and not in small Yorkshire villages, but who knew? He was going to leave nothing to chance.

Poppy was shaking as she entered the room and sat down.

'I know this is going to be difficult for you,' began Oldroyd. 'You were obviously close to your father. We just need to ask you some questions and some might be a bit upsetting – OK?'

She nodded.

'Can you tell me what you did yesterday when you arrived?'

She looked as if it was a difficult question.

'Tris and I spent some time in our room, and then I went out for a while, just for a walk, then we had dinner and then . . .'

'OK. Can you think of anyone who would want to harm your father?'

She shook her head. 'I know not everybody liked him, but I don't know anyone who would have harmed him.'

'Did you always get on well with him yourself?'

'Yes.'

'How did you feel about him being unfaithful to your mother?'

'He behaved badly, I'm not saying he didn't, and Mum suffered because of him, but that wasn't everything about him. He was my father and I know he cared for me. We had lots of fun together when Alistair and I were little and he helped me a lot and now . . .'

She broke down in tears, and Steph handed her a tissue.

'Thank you,' Poppy murmured.

'When you say he helped you, do you mean financially?'

She hesitated. 'Yes. Daddy was very generous, because he always believed in me. He understood that the academic route wasn't for me and I had to . . . sort of . . . try different things.'

In other words, you dropped out of school and Daddy financed his little girl in every scheme you've come up with since, thought a cynical Steph. She recognised some envy in herself, as her own drunken and violent father had abandoned his family when she was a young girl and her mother had always struggled with lack of money after that.

'I see,' continued Oldroyd. 'Did his generosity continue or did he refuse you money in recent times?'

Poppy looked startled. 'How did you know?'

'I don't know anything. I'm just asking.'

She looked a little sheepish. 'Well, he did turn me down not long ago, but it wasn't really for me; it was for my boyfriend, Tristram. You see, he's got into debt – he gambles. Daddy said he would have to pay his gambling debts himself. It was a matter of honour or something.'

'Was he angry?'

'Not with me; I think he disapproves of Tristram's gambling but he likes Tristram otherwise. He introduced us in London.'

I'll bet he regretted that, thought Oldroyd. 'Did your father ever talk about this locked-room trick to you?'

'No, never. To be honest, I haven't taken much interest in the Hall since I left for London as a teenager. That's all Alistair's thing. He's always lived here, and now he's going to inherit it.'

'And what about you? Do you think Alistair will be as generous as your father if you run into . . . difficulties?'

'Probably not; he'll have the estate and his family to consider. But Tristram and I will be OK if he can stop his gambling. Tristram earns a good whack from his modelling and my photography business is . . . developing.'

Oldroyd looked at her, realising she was too young to appreciate the pun she'd just unwittingly made.

'Did you know Harold Robinson?'

'Not really. I know he worked for Daddy.'

'So you have no idea who'd want to kill him?'

'No.' She looked upset again. 'I grew up here and I was happy. Now it's a place where people get murdered. I don't understand it.'

Tristram Benington looked cool as he sat with the poise and composure of the professional model.

'You arrived here yesterday, went to your room, stayed there until dinner, and Poppy went for a walk by herself.'

'You've got it.'

'We understand that Lord Redmire introduced you to his daughter, Poppy, and that was the start of your relationship with her?'

'Yes, he did, but it was just a casual thing. We were coming out of the Red Hot Poker in Soho – that's a gambling club – and Poppy was there; she'd come to meet her father, so he just introduced us.'

'Did you know Lord Redmire well?'

'No, only through the club. You get to know all the regulars, all ages and professions, and you talk about your strategies and your winnings and losings and so on – mostly losings.' He sounded very jaded with the whole business, thought Oldroyd.

'Do you think he regretted introducing you?'

Tristram shrugged. 'Maybe. He probably didn't want his daughter to be in a relationship with a gambler like himself.'

'Was he hostile to you in any way, or threatening?'

'No. He knew I earned plenty of money and I treated Poppy well; it would have been hypocritical of him to come down heavily on my gambling, wouldn't it, given his record?'

'Miss Carstairs said that he refused to pay off any of your gambling debts.'

'That's true. I never asked him to do it, though; it was Poppy who thought she could get round him. I would never ask a favour like that.'

'Why?'

'I tried to explain to Poppy: it's an honour thing; you have to pay your own debts when you're gambling with people. It's frowned on if it gets around that other people are having to give you money.'

'Why does it make any difference?'

'You just get a bad reputation. If you're borrowing to pay, you're just transferring your debt. Then people won't play with you, won't risk it in case you can't pay if you lose. Then, if it continues, you'll be thrown out of the club.'

'I see.'

'It would also have reflected badly on Lord Redmire – he would have been breaking the code too.'

Oldroyd tried to imagine this high-risk world of gamblers: tuxedos, playing cards, tumblers of whisky and money, money, money.

'Did Lord Redmire make any enemies through his gambling?'

'Not to my knowledge, but I only knew him through the Red Hot Poker; he was a member of other clubs too.'

'So you didn't know anyone who would have wished him harm?'

'No, and to be honest I liked him. I know he felt protective about Poppy, but I think he liked me too. We both enjoyed having a good time, you know. I was hoping that Poppy and I would get married soon and he would have been at the wedding. Now he won't be.'

Oldroyd found it difficult to gauge exactly what Benington felt about this prospect.

'OK, then, what did you think of all that?'

Oldroyd and Steph were having a working lunch, eating some very good-quality sandwiches with salad and fruit organised by Richard Wilkins. There was also a large cafetière of coffee.

They were just beginning to analyse their questioning of the family and guests.

'I can't say anyone in particular stood out as more suspicious than the others, sir,' Steph said through mouthfuls of a smoked salmon sand-wich. 'But they all had some form of motive.'

'Yes. What about a crime of passion? Could James Forsyth have plotted to kill Lord Redmire through jealousy?'

'Or because of the business failure – two possible motives there.'

'We'll need to check the details of what happened with that busi-ness, although it doesn't look as if Forsyth was actually ruined; he seems to be doing fine now.' Oldroyd popped the last piece of an excellent mature Cheddar sandwich into his mouth.

'On the passion side of things,' continued Steph, 'Alex Davis was pretty candid about her feelings. I wonder if Redmire's affairs left her with a deep sense of hurt, and so she planned to get her revenge?'

'Rather unwise to be so frank with us, then. But of course that could have been a double bluff.' Oldroyd eyed the sandwiches greedily. He'd already eaten three and knew he should stop, but they were so good he decided to have another: this time bacon and avocado. 'I'd like to know a little more about her background. Did she ever have a job or has she always been a wealthy socialite?'

Steph poured out coffee. 'As far as the Ramsays are concerned, I find it difficult to think that the husband could be the killer. He seemed an amiable sort of bloke who didn't want to rake up the past. Redmire's ex-wife, though . . . Now there's a woman who suffered and could have been nursing a grievance. Also, living here for so many years makes it more likely that she may have been the person who somehow discovered things about the trick.'

'Yes,' replied Oldroyd, sipping his coffee. 'I thought she may have some hidden depths below that controlled exterior. She was the opposite of Dominic Carstairs, who was all irascibility and bluster, full of resentment and anger. He seemed intent on making himself a suspect, but apart from revenge on his brother for being older than him and inheriting the title and the estate, he didn't stand to gain anything, so I don't see him as a strong suspect. His wife, though, was curiously calm about it all, didn't seem shocked or particularly upset, which makes me suspicious.'

'But what would her motive have been, sir?'

'I've no idea at the moment, but it occurs to me that maybe she could have been another of Lord Redmire's conquests who was then abandoned; so we'd be back to the fury of the woman scorned.'

'Poppy's a spoiled rich kid,' observed Steph, 'and I think she laid on her grief for her father a bit. She'll miss him all right but mainly because there'll be no more handouts. I can't really see her planning to murder him, though; first, because I don't think she'd be capable of it, and second, it would have been against her interests.'

'Same goes for the boyfriend, really. They both needed Redmire alive to preserve their source of income – unless they were so desperate for money that they wanted to get their hands on Poppy's inheritance, but that may not have been worth that much. So . . .' He slapped his hands on his legs and summed up: 'I agree that that didn't yield very much. They were all in the lobby at the time of the murder; no one saw anything suspicious; all deny any knowledge of the trick; and they all claim to know no one who would have wanted to kill him.'

'Are you going to let them all leave now, sir?'

Oldroyd pulled a face. 'No, I don't like them – all rich and privileged – so they can stew for a bit longer.'

Steph laughed as she crunched into an apple while Oldroyd unpeeled a banana.

'Sir, that's not a very professional reason to keep them here!' she said between mouthfuls.

Oldroyd ate his banana and smiled. 'You know I'm only joking. I'm not ready to release them yet. We've got more people to interview: the resident family and the employees. We'll wait at least until we've been through them; they might have some interesting information on the people we've already seen. Let's start off with the rest of the family. We'll have to spread ourselves out a bit or it's going to take forever. You take the dowager, and I'll go after the new Lord Redmire and his family. I find it hard to believe that the dowager could have conspired to kill her own son, but who knows? These minor aristocratic families can be very strange. At least you might get some useful history. Remember, she was there for the original performance of the trick. See what she remembers about it.'

'Sit down, my dear.' The dowager Lady Redmire gestured with a wizened hand towards an ornate old-fashioned sofa next to her high armchair. She was wearing a flowery print dress and a woollen cardigan. She looked calm and unruffled.

'I'm sorry about your loss,' began Steph. 'Is it OK if I ask you some questions?'

'By all means,' replied the old lady with surprising equanimity. She paused and looked into the distance. 'All I can say is that, in a way, I'm not surprised; he always seemed to have something like this coming to him.'

'Why was that?'

'He was reckless with money, and with people's feelings. His father wasn't good with money either, but Vivian was a kind man and he didn't get involved with other women. Men like my son, I expect, make a lot of enemies.'

'Do you know of anyone in particular who would've wanted to harm him?'

'No. I had no idea who he saw or what he did; he never told me anything about his life. I know he lost money gambling – he didn't get that habit from his father either. And he had lots of affairs. I don't know how Antonia put up with him for as long as she did.'

'Antonia must have been very bitter about the way she was treated.'

Lady Redmire looked at Steph archly. 'Yes, and I know what you're getting at, but no, Antonia would never have done anything violent. She's far too dignified. She did the right thing and just left him, divorced him, and now I think she's happy with Douglas; she deserves it. She still comes to see me regularly – lovely woman. I think of her as the daughter I never had and I told Freddy only yesterday that she was always too good for him.'

'When did you last see Lord Redmire?'

'He came over at about five o'clock. We argued as usual.'

'What about?'

Lady Redmire frowned and shook her head. 'I didn't approve of his ridiculous idea, this reviving a trick of his father's. It was bad enough the first time round. I never knew what Vivian was going to do next, although I always knew it would cost money. Freddy got the television people involved. He tried to keep that from me for a while but he didn't dare not tell me in the end. What a carry-on! One of the best things about Redmire is the peace and quiet. I couldn't believe he wanted to carry out such a stunt and have the place swarming with people. At least Vivian only performed his tricks for his friends; it was an expensive way of showing off, I suppose.'

'Did your husband ever tell you anything about this locked-room trick – about how it worked and so on?'

'Goodness me, no! He never told me anything about any of his ridiculous obsessions.' She laughed. 'It was all fun for him – and harmless, I suppose, if it all hadn't cost so much. The problem with them both was they were brought up with money, never had to work for it, so they were completely careless about it.'

'He had people to help him, you know, to sort of install the thing?'

'Yes, he did. I remember that he placed that part of the house out of bounds to everyone – myself included – for months, and I remember people arriving with things in vans, but I don't know who they were. Some of them came from Italy, I think, but he put them all up at the inn in the village so they couldn't mix with anybody at the house and I imagine they were all sworn to secrecy. The only person who I think might have had something to do with it was poor Harry Robinson; he was a kind of mechanic and I think he was in on it.'

'He almost certainly was and that's probably why he's been killed: so he couldn't talk to us.'

'Was he part of this terrible plan, then? I can't believe that. The family always treated him well and he was devoted to Redmire Hall – spent his whole working life here, I think. I can't think why he would have had any kind of grudge against Freddy.'

'We don't know the extent of his involvement, but it was probably his knowledge of the mechanics of the trick that was used to set it up again.'

'I see. Then he was disposed of. How dreadful.'

Dreadful it certainly was, but again she seemed very sanguine about it all. She's a tough old bird, thought Steph.

'What do you remember about that night when your husband performed the trick for the first time?'

'Well, it's a long time ago, but I remember Vivian put a lot of effort into planning it all. He was single-minded to the point of obsession when he really got his teeth into something. He organised a dinner – at great expense, of course – and he hired some kind of actress to be his "beautiful assistant", as they say. He dressed her up in a sparkly costume and got her to speak in a foreign accent. It was all a bit clichéd, but Vivian could always laugh at himself.

'I'm afraid to say that on the night itself, I wasn't really concentrating; my sister had come to stay and she had quite young children, two girls. They wanted to stay up to see what was happening but of course it didn't really work out. They soon got bored, didn't really understand what was going on. Rose and I had to watch them all the time, but they were quite good. They sat at the side, playing. Marbles, I think it was. I remember that Olivia, she must have been about eight, went over to look into that room before Rose called her back. Anyway, I just let Vivian get on with it. Everybody was terribly impressed. Vivian was elated, said it had been a triumph. The problem afterwards was that he refused to repeat the trick for fear that it wouldn't make as much of an impression the second time, or that someone might work out how he'd done it. That sort of left him with nothing more he could do with it, so he turned his attention to something else and the room was just left. Locked up and strictly out of bounds to everyone. I thought it was a lot of money to pay for one performance for his friends, but he always said it was his greatest achievement.'

'As far as you know, is there any record of who was here that night and saw the trick performed?'

'Oh, I shouldn't think so. Viv never bothered with anything like that. Most of the people I can remember being there are dead now.'

'What about your sister and your nieces?'

'I'm afraid Rose is no longer with us. Died in her fifties – cancer. Charlotte's in America; she was only five at the time. Olivia . . . now, Olivia: she comes to see me now and again. I don't have an address for her but her surname's Pendleton. She's in London somewhere; she's a fashion designer.'

'Do you know who she works for?'

'No, I think she's freelance, not famous. I always get the impression she struggles. Let me see, she'll be in her mid-forties now. Can you believe it!'

Steph decided to move on. 'So you didn't really approve of the way your son ran things here?'

'No. The fact is, he was forced into things because he was short of cash, and he was short of cash because he gambled. Dominic would have made a much better job of things – boring but practical – and I have high hopes for Alistair, who's a very sensible young man. I think he'll get the estate back in order.'

'When you say your son was "forced into things", what do you mean?'

For the first time, the dowager Lady Redmire seemed to weigh her answer carefully. 'I think he had some plans for the estate, but I don't know any details. We women never get consulted in these old aristocratic families. Women are just there to provide an heir, and ideally a male heir. He probably wouldn't have dared to tell me about them because he knew I would have disapproved. I don't think Freddy really cared about Redmire at all; it was just somewhere to make money for him.'

'So what do you suspect he was planning to do?'

'I can't imagine and I don't like to think about it; but at least now it'll never happen.' She smiled at Steph, seeming almost relieved that her son was dead and that his awful plans, whatever they were, could never come to fruition. Steph found it rather chilling.

Alistair and Katherine Carstairs sat together on a sofa in their modest living room in the former head gardener's house, looking very sombre as Oldroyd appraised them with his shrewd grey eyes. Was it genuine grief that made them look so serious, or was it their impending responsibilities as the new master and mistress of Redmire?

'I want to say at the outset, Chief Inspector,' said Alistair, rather formally, 'that if there's anything we can do, don't hesitate to ask.' His wife nodded. 'What's happened is absolutely dreadful: my father and poor old Harry Robinson both murdered in one evening.' He shook his head. 'I can't make any sense of it.'

Very helpful, thought Oldroyd, but they seemed to assume they were completely above suspicion themselves, whereas in fact they had one of the strongest motives.

'Did your father have any enemies – people who might want him dead?'

The couple exchanged glances. Alistair replied for them both. 'I'm sure you've already found out from the others that my father was the kind of person who often left trouble in his wake. His financial dealings and his . . . his personal life . . .' Oldroyd saw him struggle for a polite term to describe his father's philandering. '. . . were such that I would be lying if I said there was nobody with a grudge against him, but killing is another matter.'

'I agree, Chief Inspector,' said Katherine. 'I don't believe my father-in-law had done anything bad enough to justify anyone wishing to murder him.'

'That's in your opinion,' replied Oldroyd, who looked deceptively relaxed in an armchair with his arms resting on each side, though his keen eyes were as alert as ever, 'but other people might see it differently, especially where money and, shall we say, passions are involved.'

'I suppose so.'

'We've started to build a picture of your father's relationships: the failed business, the gambling, the affairs, the divorce from your mother. What I wanted to ask you was how far you were involved in running things here. Did Lord Redmire consult with you as his heir?'

Alistair shook his head. 'He didn't, I'm afraid. My father considered it his responsibility to run affairs here and he never discussed things to do with the estate with anyone, as far as I know, except the estate manager – who, of course, is a professional and not part of the family – and even then the consultation was limited. If you tried to ask him about it he could get very tetchy.'

'Do you think that was because he had things to conceal?'

'What kind of things?'

'I'm thinking mainly of the overall state of the finances here. There seems to be a feeling that things were not in good shape, due to your father's gambling and so on.'

Alistair frowned. 'I assume Uncle Dominic's been saying things to you. I get on all right with him, Chief Inspector, but he's made no secret of the fact that he's bitter about my father inheriting the estate and that he considered him both a waster and a useless businessman.'

'Did you agree with his views?'

Alistair appeared to hesitate.

'My husband doesn't want to be disloyal to his father, Chief Inspector.' Katherine looked across sympathetically at her husband. 'But we knew what he was like with money and it was a constant worry for us: what might be happening to the estate and what exactly would we inherit.'

'Did you assume that things were gradually deteriorating?'

'I suppose so, yes,' replied Alistair, hesitantly, glancing back at his wife. He seemed to be calculating how much to say. 'I was aware that he had plans of some kind, and so was my grandmother. He let one or two things drop occasionally; never gave any details, though.'

'What kind of things?'

'Oh, if we were talking about Redmire, he'd say that things never stayed the same in life, that everything had to change eventually. Just hints, really.'

'Do you think he discussed these plans with other people?'

'As far as I know, not with anyone except the firm of property developers he dealt with.'

'It sounds as if he knew his proposals wouldn't be popular.'

'Maybe, or maybe he just wanted to do things in his own way without interference; he was very stubborn like that.'

Oldroyd casually tapped the tips of his fingers together as his elbows rested on the chair arms. 'Had your father behaved strangely in any way recently? Had you noticed anything unusual around the estate?'

The Carstairs exchanged glances again. 'Well, that's a bit difficult to say, Chief Inspector, with all the preparations going on for the event; things weren't exactly normal. My father seemed in good spirits. I think he really believed that this trick and the spin-off, as it were, would generate money.'

'So he didn't seem worried at all, as if he was afraid someone might attack him?'

'No. I'm sure he wasn't expecting anything of the kind.'

'There was something odd that happened, but it's a little while ago now, Chief Inspector,' said Katherine. 'I told Alistair about it at the time.'

'Yes?'

'One night – it was several months ago – I couldn't sleep so I got up and went downstairs. It was about two o'clock in the morning. From our kitchen we can see over to the estate office, where Richard Wilkins and his staff work. I noticed there was a light in one of the rooms. It looked like a torch moving around, and I could see the shadow of some-one. It was all a bit spooky. I immediately thought about burglars, and I watched for a while. And then the light went off. No one came out of the outside door that I could see, but there is another one at the back, which was out of sight. I called the police and went over with them, but by that time there was no one in the building. The door was locked. We found a broken window at the back, which was open, so that was how they must have got in, and the room I'd seen the light in was Richard's office. Anyway, I went over first thing in the morning and told Richard when he arrived.'

'Very interesting,' declared Oldroyd, who was listening intently. 'So what was the outcome?'

'Nothing, really. The police never found a suspect. There were no unexpected fingerprints on any item, and it was strange that nothing appeared to have been stolen. The room was in order. If it hadn't been for the broken window, I might have thought I'd imagined it.'

Oldroyd shut his eyes and paused to think. 'Thank you very much for that. Well, that's all for now.' He looked at them both. 'I suppose you're going to find out soon enough about the estate finances. How do you feel about your inheritance? Becoming the new Lord and Lady Redmire?'

The couple exchanged glances yet again. Neither seemed to want to speak without the other's permission.

'To be honest, Chief Inspector, we haven't had time to think about it,' said Katherine.

'We have other things to think about now: funerals, and who on earth has done these terrible things,' added Alistair.

'Yes,' said Oldroyd.

The interview ended where it had begun.

Four

Oldroyd stood by the arrivals gate at Leeds Bradford airport, waiting for Louise to come through.

It was early evening and the weather had abruptly changed, as it was apt to do in the Yorkshire summer. It was cloudy and there was a chilly breeze from the north-east. Oldroyd had felt a few spots of rain as he'd walked up the tarmac path from the short-stay car park. However, he was glad to be here.

Louise, who still lived a semi-nomadic life during the university holidays, moving between his flat, her mother's home and the student-style houses of various old school friends in Leeds, was coming to stay with him for a while. She had thought that avoiding the temptations of Leeds nightlife after her Morocco trip might encourage her to get on with her vacation reading. In October she was returning to Oxford for her final year. Oldroyd enjoyed it when she stayed at his apartment and he didn't mind his daughter's untidiness. It was a break from his unwanted solitude and he'd always got on well with her. She was a lively, feisty character committed to all kinds of progressive causes and political activism. They shared many views, but Oldroyd liked to tease her by playing devil's advocate or playfully pointing out discrepancies between her views and her lifestyle.

He saw her coming down the corridor to the arrivals area and waved. She waved back. She looked tanned and had her hair tied back; she was wearing a T-shirt and grubby-looking shorts. He gave her a hug.

'Hi, Dad, thanks for coming. God, it's absolutely freezing here! When the plane came down through the murk it was like landing on a different planet!'

'Welcome to Yorkshire!' laughed Oldroyd. 'You'll have to get your jeans on and a jumper.' They walked back down the path to the car.

'You're not kidding. I wish I'd asked you to bring something for me to change into. Has it been like this all the time I've been away?'

'No – mixed, you know. We've had some really good days, pretty hot.'

'I'll bet; you mean you were able to go outside without a coat on.' She laughed.

They got into the car after Louise had put her small, well-worn case in the boot. Oldroyd drove out of the airport, turned right and headed towards Pool Bank. Rain started to spatter on the windscreen and he turned on the wipers.

'I've forgotten what rain is like,' sighed Louise. 'It was in the top thirties every day.'

'That would be a bit too much for me,' replied Oldroyd, 'especially when you're walking around a city. I'd have to be sat in the shade by a swimming pool.'

'Oh, we loved it.'

'Who did you go with?'

'Josh and Amelia – friends from uni. They've been seeing each other since the first year.'

She never said anything about any men in her life and he didn't like to ask. Maybe there were women in her life. He would be fine with that, and he was sure his wife, Julia, would be too. She'd long ago turned away from her conservative upbringing in the Home Counties.

'What do you fancy for tea?'

'Anything. I'm not bothered. They fed us on the plane, though it was pretty awful.' Louise was vegetarian and actually quite particular about what she ate.

'I could do my famous egg-fried rice.'

'Fantastic. Looking forward to it.'

Egg-fried rice was the only real vegetarian dish that Oldroyd could cook, so he tended to eat it quite a lot when Louise was staying.

'What've you been up to, then, Dad?'

'Oh, nothing much, just work. I'm involved in a very interesting case at the moment.'

He told her about the Redmire Hall Locked-Room Mystery, as he'd taken to calling it.

'Wow! That does sound interesting. I wouldn't fancy having to deal with all those rich people, though,' she said, echoing Andy Carter's opinion. 'I've had enough of those types at Oxford, with their sense of entitlement. I'm sick of their expensive clothes and their plummy voices.'

'No jealousy involved there, then?'

'Shut up, Dad!' she laughed. He liked that she could always take a joke against herself, and he admired her idealistic political views. However, he decided, this was not the right time to remind her that, in world terms, she was also part of the rich elite. 'Anyway, I got some great clothes cheap in the souk in Marrakesh – all handwoven and organic and still a lot cheaper than here.'

Despite the stated low cost, Oldroyd wondered what she was using for money, but decided not to broach this issue at the moment. He didn't want a potential conflict so soon after she'd got back. This is where he played a tactful game with his daughter, to subtly discover how much debt she might be in. He suspected Julia jumped in and made things worse, resulting in the big rows she sometimes mentioned.

'And not made under exploitative conditions?'

'No! Dad! Are you taking the piss? If you are, you won't get your present!'

'Ooh! A present! Well, I didn't even know I was getting one.'

'Behave yourself and we'll see.'

Back in Harrogate, Louise went into the spare room of Oldroyd's flat and called out, 'Dad, can you make some coffee while I unpack a bit?'

'OK.'

Oldroyd got to work and after a while she came out with all her dirty clothes and crammed them into the washing machine.

'Making yourself at home, I see,' quipped Oldroyd.

'Yes,' she replied, 'and thanks.' She took the coffee and went to the fridge to get some milk and noticed the postcard from Julia. 'I see Mum's sent you a card.' She sounded surprised.

'Yes.'

'Right. I was wondering how she's getting on. She's gone with Anne and some of her friends from work. Peter's gone too.'

'Peter? Who's Peter?' Oldroyd suddenly felt a little sick.

'Peter Jones; he works at the college – art teacher. He and Mum are . . . friendly . . . I think.' She chose her words carefully, as she saw the effect this news was having on him. She hadn't realised that he knew nothing about her mum's new relationship.

Oldroyd sat down. This was what he'd feared ever since his wife had asked him to leave. He hadn't wanted to go and had lived ever since in the hope that they could get back together. So far this hope had been sustained by the absence of any other men in her life. This news was a bitter blow and he felt angry.

'Why the hell did she send me a card, then? She's on holiday with her boyfriend and she sends a postcard to her husband?'

Louise sat down next to him. 'I didn't say he was her boyfriend – I don't know. You know Mum can be a bit secretive and, well, unpredictable; she doesn't tell me much. They've been seeing one another a bit, that's all, I think.'

Oldroyd put his hands to his face and sighed.

'Dad, I'm sorry. I thought you knew.'

'I didn't. Why didn't she just tell me?'

'I don't know, but Dad, you must have known this could happen sooner or later. You can't carry on as if Mum's just going to pick up the phone one day and plead with you to come back.'

He looked at her. How mature and sensible she was! It seemed that only five minutes ago they had been building houses and animals from Lego together, and now she was counselling him in matters that were deep and personal. Young people, especially women, handled these things far better than their parents: they were straight and open about relationships.

'You're right,' he said. 'That's exactly how I have been living and I've deliberately avoided getting into any relationships myself, to show that I'm . . . well, that I'm . . . still committed to her.'

'Well, you'll have to be a bit more realistic, Dad. It might never happen.'

'How do you know? Has she said anything?'

'No. I think she still cares about you; that's why she sent you the card. But she's probably not sure whether or not it would work out if you came back. I think her feelings are confused.'

It was a perceptive summary, but it felt strange to hear it all from his daughter.

'I would do things differently.'

'Would you, though? You're still as deeply involved in your work as ever and she knows that. You're often in the news, for one thing.'

'You sound like your Auntie Alison.'

'Well, that's a compliment; you should listen to her more often. Anyway, whatever, you're just going to have to accept what Mum does and see what happens. Look, I'll make tea – you have a rest. Have a drink or something.'

She got up, leaving Oldroyd to brood for a few minutes. Then he followed her advice and opened a bottle of red wine to prevent himself from sinking any deeper into self-pity.

'This is very good,' he said as they sat at the table together and he tried her egg-fried rice. It was much better than his effort.

'Thanks. Are you feeling better now?'

'Not really.'

She frowned at him. 'You're such a romantic, and it's very sweet, but there's no point deceiving yourself. It may be over for good with Mum.'

He winced. 'Do you talk to her about things like this?'

'No. I told you, she doesn't say much about personal stuff.'

He drank some more wine. 'Mum and I were together for so long. I suppose I still can't believe that I made such a mess of things that they can't be put right again.'

'Well, regretting the past isn't going to help, Dad. I think it's time you thought about what to do with the rest of your life, if you see what I mean.'

Oldroyd finished his glass of wine. He knew what she meant but he didn't know where to start.

The next day, back in his 'office' at Redmire Hall, Oldroyd made a big effort to concentrate on the task in hand, hoping that immersion in the work that had caused so much damage to his marriage might enable him to forget the pain in his private life. DC Jeffries had joined them, clutching a large portfolio.

'OK,' began Oldroyd, 'we've interviewed all the immediate family and friends who were here on the night; let's review what we've learned from that. How did you get on with the old dowager?'

Steph looked at her notes. 'She was very together; didn't seem upset about her son's death; seemed more relieved that her grandson was going to take over; thought her son had no feeling for Redmire; just saw it as a place to make money. She also seemed to think he had plans for the estate that she wouldn't like.'

'Any details?'

'No. She just didn't trust her son, said he had no real feeling for Redmire.'

'It'll be very interesting to find out if there were any such plans. They might have affected a lot of people.'

'It seems like he kept them secret, though, sir, so it's unlikely they could have provided a motive.'

'True, but some people must have known; we'll need to get on to that quickly.'

'I also asked her about her memories of the first time the trick was done. She said she and her sister were there but looking after her sister's kids, so she didn't see much of what was happening. The good news is that one of those kids, a little girl called Olivia, about eight years old, apparently looked into the locked room while the trick was under way. So she may have seen something. According to Lady Redmire, she's in London now. I'm sure we can easily track her down.'

'Good. She may be our only hope of understanding what could have happened. I can't imagine many of the adults who were there that day are still alive and, if they are, they probably don't remember much about it. A child is different: it would probably have made an impression on her, though I can't think she could have seen anything particularly significant. Anything else?'

'No. But there was something about her that I found a bit chilling. Despite her age, I don't think we can leave her out of things.'

Oldroyd raised his eyebrows. 'Even though it was her own son who was killed?'

'I know, but isn't it true that for some of these people the estate, the family tradition, you know, all that stuff, is what really matters? Maybe she thought her son's behaviour – wasting money, gambling and so on – threatened that and that his plans were going to change or damage things in some way.'

'So the only solution was to get rid of him?'

'I know it sounds a bit extreme, but I wouldn't rule it out. Obviously she couldn't have done it herself, but she could have encouraged others.'

'Right. Well, I didn't get much from the young Carstairs – now Lord and Lady Redmire, of course. They seem very straight, conscientious types. I had the same stuff about his father gambling and concern about what he might be planning for the estate. We really need to find out more about that.'

DC Jeffries, who'd been listening intently and was eager to contribute, couldn't restrain himself any longer. 'Sir, the estate manager would be a good place to start. When I was getting this information about the employees from him' – he indicated his portfolio – 'I asked him about all the information he had about the estate, as I knew you'd need that too. All the estate records are held in his office, but he was very cagey about access as there was confidential stuff in there.'

Oldroyd smiled at the DC's keenness to please. 'Well done, Jeffries. You're right: we'll get on to that as soon as we can. Can you organise the warrant if we need it?'

'Yes, sir.'

Oldroyd continued, 'There was something interesting I got from the Carstairs. Katherine Carstairs saw someone in the estate office during the night a while back and the police were called. Someone got in through a window but the strange thing was that there appeared to be nothing missing. There's another job for you, Jeffries: look up the report at Ripon station about that break-in and confirm the details.'

'Yes, sir.'

'It may come to nothing but we need to follow it up, especially as it seems there are important documents in there. So, you've clearly compiled the information I asked for. Has anything struck you as significant?'

Jeffries was a little nonplussed. As a lowly DC he probably wasn't used to being asked his opinions. Oldroyd could sense Steph smiling; she was familiar with Oldroyd's expectation that everyone working on a case with him should be thinking about it and having ideas.

'Well, sir,' Jeffries began, summoning up his courage, 'as far as the employees go, there is a staff of twenty, including workers in the estate office. Gardeners, kitchen staff, a waiter, cleaners, people who operate the shop, and an odd-job man who presumably replaced Harold Robinson when he retired. They've all been interviewed and their backgrounds checked. There's nothing to suggest a motive for the murders in any of them, but I think the three senior people . . .' He checked his notes. 'That's Richard Wilkins, the estate manager, Andrea Jenkinson, Lord Redmire's PA, and Celia Anscomb, who supervises the interior of the house – would be worth talking to, as they knew Lord Redmire and the workings of the estate better than anyone else, even the family.'

Oldroyd nodded encouragingly. 'Absolutely right, Jeffries. We'll need to follow them up closely.'

'I'm still gathering information about the family but there's probably not much you don't already know.'

'Go on.'

Jeffries looked again through the sheets in his portfolio. 'We did find out that Dominic Carstairs's company is in financial difficulty.'

'And why might that be important?'

'I wonder if he hoped his brother would help him out but Lord Redmire refused.'

'Very good – and it might partially explain his general hostility and grumpiness, although I think that's also his regular personality.'

'The next thing, I would suggest, is to investigate the gambling club in London where Redmire and Tristram Benington played.'

'And lost,' interjected Oldroyd.

'Yes, sir, and I wonder just how much Benington owed and how serious was his need for cash.'

'Well done again, Jeffries,' said Oldroyd. The young officer beamed. 'Right, we've got quite a lot to work with now – so you go ahead and contact the Red Hot Poker Club, and then see if you can track Olivia down.' Oldroyd turned to Steph. 'We need to talk to Andrea Jenkinson and Richard Wilkins and have a proper search through Redmire's office, but first it's high time we had another look at the crime scene. We still have to work out how the first murder was committed, never mind who did it.'

Oldroyd and Steph made their way through the deserted lobby area, which was still taped off with a PC on guard. The chairs were still in disarray, frozen as they had been in the moment of horror and panic when Redmire's body was ghoulishly revealed. The door to the room had been left open, and the key was still in the lock. Oldroyd and Steph entered gingerly. It was hard to resist the feeling that the room itself might be dangerous. Oldroyd examined the furnishings and the bookshelves slowly and with even more care than he had on the night of the murder.

'I think these are all the original furnishings from the late seventies, cleaned up for the new performance; they must have been a bit dusty after all that time. Look at those old volumes on the shelves.'

'Maybe that's something to do with the trick, sir – maybe nothing could be replaced because it plays a part somehow.'

Oldroyd frowned. 'You could be right. I wonder . . .' He started to move the furniture around as if he hoped to trigger an opening to a secret exit. He fiddled with the window fastening and then he pulled a book off the shelves.

'Ah! Now that's interesting: these books aren't real. Look.'

Steph examined the 'book', which was actually a very realistic but hollow cardboard replica.

'I suppose that would make sense, though, sir – I mean, it's all a façade really, isn't it, so why bother having real books?'

'True, but it also means these "books" can be easily removed. I wonder what's behind them?' He took them all off one shelf to reveal the wall behind, but there was nothing there. He repeated the process with all the shelves, but again found nothing. He turned his attention to the floor. 'We're going to have to get this floor minutely examined: every floorboard needs to be looked at in case there's a catch or something that might release some kind of trapdoor. If there is one it's fantastically well concealed,' he said, moving the rug to see if the floor was any different underneath. It wasn't.

Turning his attention to the walls, he prodded and probed but everywhere the plaster was smooth and gave no possible indication of a door or recess.

He sighed. 'What about the ceiling?'

Steph, who'd also been poking around without success, frowned. 'It doesn't look likely, sir. I'd swear this place has no way out except the door we came through.'

'That's what it's meant to look like. Remember, a specialist team came from Italy to construct this illusion, and it seems to have taken them some time. Finding the answer is not going to be easy.'

He climbed on to the chair, and pushed and tapped at the ceiling. Then he fiddled with the light fitting. Nothing.

'Let's have another look at that trapdoor,' he said.

He pulled the door up by the brass handle and got down to look into the cavity, just as Vivian Carstairs's friends had done many years before. It was just the same: wires and junction boxes, concrete floor and walls, no way out.

'Go outside and shut the door,' he said to Steph. 'Let's see if closing it causes anything to happen.'

Steph went out and closed the door behind her. Oldroyd sat in the chair like Redmire had previously, and felt a tingle of fear. It was claustrophobic and strange to be alone in the locked room itself. The last person who'd done so had not emerged alive. But nothing happened.

'Turn the key, Steph!' he called out. 'Maybe the lock activates something.'

Steph again obliged – again with no result.

'Open up. Nothing's happened.'

Steph re-entered the room to find Oldroyd still sitting in the chair, deep in thought.

'Well, it beats me,' he said. 'We'll have to contact the Italian police and see if we can find anyone connected to the Italian illusionist who invented this thing – Count Mazarini, I think he called himself. I don't know whether he was a real count or whether that was just a stage name. I doubt if he's still alive, but someone over there might know something. I'm going to research him myself when I get the chance. We also need to find out more about Harry Robinson; see if he ever spoke to anyone about this trick.'

'Do you think if we can find out how it was done, it will lead us to the killers, sir?'

Oldroyd looked round the room again with a mixture of frustration and admiration. 'Who knows? It's another double-puzzle case, isn't it? We don't know how or who, but you can bet that the identity of the killer is linked to the secret of the illusion.'

Suddenly he had an idea.

'Let's go and have a look at things from the outside. It might give us some ideas.'

They left the room and the lobby and crossed to the nearest external door, which opened at the end of the east wing of the house. It was then a short walk round to the rear. Oldroyd peered at the building. They were standing in a small courtyard with three sides. Part of the main house formed one side and a low wing ran parallel on the other. Between them, at right angles, ran another section of the house, which formed the third wall. On this section an extension had been built out with wide stone pillars at either end.

Oldroyd pointed to the extension. 'Right. Well, that must be the back of it. That's the window and that extension looks about the size of the room. I think . . .' He looked carefully and it seemed to fit but something didn't seem quite right. What? He shook his head and went to the window. Sure enough, he found himself looking into the locked room. He could see the desk, the books and the chair. He tried to look at the roof but couldn't get a clear view. 'We'll have to get people on to the top of that to confirm there are no trapdoors and suchlike, but there was no evidence of anything on the inside.'

Steph was looking hard at everything in an attempt to find something of significance, but without success.

'I can't work it out, sir,' she confessed. 'Maybe Lord Redmire's study will tell us more.'

Oldroyd frowned at the building, as if he felt he almost had the answer but it was eluding him. 'You're right. Let's go and have a look and hopefully speak to his secretary.'

At the Hall, people were dealing with the tension in different ways. Douglas Ramsay and James Forsyth were playing chess at a small table in a corner of the large living room. Poppy and Tristram had gone riding. Dominic Carstairs had stomped off angrily for a long walk around the estate.

Alex Davis and Mary Carstairs were walking down the long borders towards the river. The weather had settled again. A warm breeze blew huge white clouds across the blue sky and the flowers were in their high-summer splendour. Tall mauve delphiniums were mixed in with pink roses, purple echinacea, white phlox and blue campanulas. The scented air hummed with bees, and butterflies moved between the flowers.

Alex dragged nervously on a cigarette. 'Look at this place.' She waved with her free hand at the borders. 'Freddy had everything going for him. Why couldn't he keep away from the bloody gaming table?'

'I know, darling. He had all that charm and influence over other people, and absolutely no self-discipline.'

'None. I have to admit he treated James very badly, left him all the work to do; no wonder their business failed. There's the idle rich for you. Still, we've got room to talk.'

'Well, speak for yourself, darling,' laughed Mary. 'I wouldn't say we were filthy rich at the moment. That's why Dominic's always so grumpy: he can't upgrade his Merc. But, First World problems, as they say!' When she'd laughed again, Mary looked more seriously at Alex. 'Do you think James was still angry with Freddy? You know, enough to . . .'

A spasm of anxiety crossed Alex's face. 'No,' she said without conviction. 'They've never been reconciled, but James is not violent.' They'd reached the river and stopped walking. 'Actually, I was going to ask you the same. Dominic never seemed to get on with his brother, did he?'

'Oh, no,' replied Mary breezily. 'He could never accept Freddy inheriting the estate – thought it was terribly unfair, Freddy didn't deserve it and so on – but Dominic would never sully himself with any nasty murder schemes; he'd consider it ungentlemanly and beneath him. Do you fancy a row out on the water?'

Where the long borders reached the river there was a small landing stage and a rowing boat was moored at the water's edge.

'Yes. Why not?'

Mary held the boat while Alex climbed on board and then she pushed off and rowed upstream. She'd done quite a bit of rowing at her boarding school near the Thames. The boat moved through the calm water, past the drooping branches of the weeping willows. Mallard and red-beaked water hens swam near the bank, shepherding their offspring, which were paddling desperately to keep up with the adults.

Alex lay back in the boat and trailed her hand in the water.

Mary looked at her. 'How do you – did you – feel about Freddy?' she asked tentatively.

'How do you mean?' murmured Alex without opening her eyes.

Mary turned the boat around and let it slowly glide downstream. 'Did you still have . . . feelings for him?'

'Of course. I told the police. There was always a spark between me and Freddy.'

'And with me too,' said Mary quickly.

Alex sat up and opened her eyes. 'What? Oh my God, I didn't know that!'

'No one does, darling. I've never told anyone. But now he's gone I feel I've got to tell someone, and I thought you . . .' Tears were welling up in her eyes. Alex turned round and saw that the boat was drifting towards the weir, which was downstream from the gardens.

'Mary, row to the side and let's pull in.'

In a few moments, the boat was moored at the bank and the two women were sitting together under the shade of a tree.

'I thought you would understand,' Mary said.

'How long had you been seeing him?'

'For the last two years, but not often. Sometimes we met in London when I visited my sister, and we tried to arrange something when we came here. In fact . . .' She started to cry again. 'I must have been the last person to see him – you know, intimately. We met up in a room by the stables before we all had dinner on that last evening.'

'I see.'

'Do you hate me now?'

Alex smiled. 'Not at all. Freddy was a very alluring man. My time with him was over, though; there's no jealousy or anything. I'm glad you told me, if it's made you feel better.'

'It has. Dominic is, well . . . Oh my God, he's as boring as hell!' She laughed with relief. 'There, I've said it! But don't breathe a word to him about anything. It'll be more than my life's worth – because of the shame, you understand, not because he really cares for me, and especially as I did it with his despised brother.'

'Don't worry, I won't say anything. But how do you cope with being married to him? It must be ghastly.'

'Marriage of convenience, darling. He keeps me in reasonable style; at least, he has until now – as I said, things aren't so good. His recruitment consultancy is not doing well, actually. He's too old-fashioned, wants to operate through the old boys' network, doesn't like helping to promote women and people from ethnic minorities to good positions. I think he hoped that Freddy would help him out at some point. Too late now. I didn't tell the police – didn't want to give them a reason to suspect Dominic.'

Two white swans glided elegantly past, scarcely disturbing the smooth surface of the river, and cows were grazing in a field on the opposite bank.

'It's a funny old business and it all makes you think.' Mary turned to Alex again. 'Do you worry about James – you know, that he could be involved in all this?'

'No,' she replied, though a shadow passed fleetingly across her face. 'I don't think any of us is involved, and anyway, James didn't dislike Freddy enough to want to kill him.'

'I hope you're right, darling. The problem is, too many of us had some kind of motive to want to get rid of Freddy, despite how we might protest our innocence. There's one thing I didn't tell you: I got to know that Freddy was seeing someone else as well – a woman in London that he'd met through his gambling somehow. Not that I didn't expect it – I mean, it was par for the course with him – but if the police find out, that gives me a motive: the woman scorned.'

'Hell hath no fury . . .'

'Exactly, darling. And I'm afraid that goes for you too.'

Oldroyd and Steph found Andrea Jenkinson alone in Redmire's office.

'Come in,' she said, and gave a wan smile as she opened the door for them. 'I've been expecting you.'

There was an expensive-looking wooden desk facing the window, which Oldroyd took to be Lord Redmire's. Andrea's desk was smaller and placed near the door. The room was quite compact, so Oldroyd sat on Redmire's swivel desk chair and Steph squeezed into a chair by the side wall.

'Obviously we'd like to ask you a few questions, and then have a look at what he had in the office here.'

'Of course, but I doubt you'll find any important documents. Those are all kept in the safe in the estate office.'

'So we need to talk to Richard Wilkins about that?'

'Yes.'

Oldroyd looked at Andrea. She was conventionally dressed in a blouse and skirt. Her accent was from London.

'How long have you worked for Lord Redmire?'

She faced him confidently. 'Two years next month.'

'Where were you before that?'

'In London; I was PA to a chief executive of a finance company.'

Oldroyd raised his eyebrows. 'That must have been well paid. Better than this. Why did you leave?'

'I was fed up of London and the job in that awful world of money. Yes, I did earn more, but I was sharing a house miles out of the City, and commuting for hours every day. I fancied a change, and this came up, which was so different that I thought, why not?'

'And how have you found it? How was Lord Redmire to work for?'

'Fine. The work is less stressful and high-powered; sometimes I feel underused but it's been restful. I rent a lovely apartment in Ripon overlooking the River Skell.'

'Did Redmire ever try it on with you? He had a reputation as a womaniser, didn't he?' asked Steph.

'No. He was always professional – although you sensed he was sometimes looking at you in a certain way. But I can cope with that; I've had plenty of it from men in the City, believe me.'

'I do,' replied Steph. She still occasionally had to put a male police officer in his place, despite all the training given in sexual harassment and equal opportunities. 'How much did he involve you in the preparations for the night of the illusion?'

'My role was to organise the invitations and liaise with the media. Richard was responsible for the logistics.'

'He didn't tell you anything about the illusion itself?'

'No, that was all kept highly secret.'

'What were your movements on the evening of the murder?'

'It was a hard day working with Richard to finalise the arrangements. When everything was completed I went home. I didn't want to stay and see it; things like that don't interest me. Richard stayed on duty.'

'Had anything unusual happened recently: any telephone calls, letters? What kind of a mood was Lord Redmire in?'

'He was actually very upbeat. He seemed very confident that the locked-room business would be a success and he was looking forward to it. He loved being at the centre of things like that. I don't recall any calls or letters that affected him, but I know that members of his family had requested money from him.'

'Who?'

'His daughter, Poppy, and his brother, Dominic.'

'Did he discuss any of this with you?'

'No, but as a PA you inevitably see letters and emails, or you over-hear conversations, so you pick up a lot of sensitive information.'

'Were you aware of any enemies Lord Redmire might have had?'

There was a brief pause while she considered. 'It was common knowledge that he was a gambler and, as you said' – she nodded to Steph – 'a womaniser who'd cheated on his wife. I also knew about his failed business venture with James Forsyth. I'm sure you know about all this already, and I'm not saying I thought anyone in particular was capable of murdering him and the other poor man.'

Her answers were clear and efficient. Her expression conveyed nothing of her inner thoughts. She had the manner and demeanour of an efficient PA who maintained a detachment and objectivity in her professional life.

Steph got up to examine Redmire's desk and its drawers while Oldroyd continued his questioning.

'We've been told that Lord Redmire had plans for the future of the estate, plans that may have been controversial. What do you know about those?'

'Again, very little. He told me that there were some changes to the estate and the business coming up because there was a need to increase revenue, but he didn't tell me any details.'

'Did you interpret this as his need for money to finance his gambling?'

'Yes. As far as I know, there were no other pressing financial problems; the estate was doing well. But, again, Richard might know more.'

Steph had finished looking through Redmire's desk but had found nothing. 'How well did you know Harold Robinson?' she asked as she sat down again.

'Harry – we called him Harry. Not well personally. He retired before I came to work here. I used to see him walking round the grounds. He introduced himself to me; he was a charming old man. I can't imagine who would want to kill him. However, I got the impression that, like so many other people, he didn't like Lord Redmire.'

'Any idea why?'

'No. It was just that he made a few snide remarks about him, and he never came to the office.'

'I see. Well,' said Oldroyd, 'from what you've told us it seems that Mr Wilkins is the person we need to speak to next.'

He and Steph got up to go, but Andrea suddenly stopped them.

'Just before you leave, I did see something just as I was leaving that evening.'

Oldroyd sat down again. 'Go on,' he said.

'I went out of one of the back entrances towards the staff car park and I heard raised voices. It was Lord Redmire and Poppy. They were standing near the door, behind some bushes, but I could still see them. All I heard was Lord Redmire saying something like: "You're getting no more out of me." And then Poppy shouted, "You've never liked him, have you?" and she started to cry. I pretended I hadn't seen them and walked on to my car. I assume she'd been asking him for money for Tristram. It was common knowledge that he also had gambling debts.'

Oldroyd nodded. 'I think you're right,' he said. 'Well, thank you for your help. It's OK to carry on with your work here, though I suppose your main purpose has been suspended for the moment.'

'Yes, until I speak with Mr Alistair.'

'Of course.'

Oldroyd and Steph left, and Andrea returned to work. After a few minutes there was a knock on her door.

'Come in.'

Ian Barden opened the door and Andrea's heart sank. Ian was one of those well-meaning but tiresome people who were often hard to get rid of. He usually had some notion in his head that he was keen to explain in tremendous detail but that made no sense to anyone else. He was dressed, as ever, in his blue overalls. She didn't invite him to sit down, as he might get oil on the chair.

'Ian. What can I do for you?'

'Well, I'm going round talking to everyone about what's been goin' on.'

This didn't bode well; it sounded like he'd appointed himself to DCI Oldroyd's team.

'Yes, it's terrible, Ian, but don't you think it's all best left to the police?'

'Maybe, but they don't know this place as well as I do.' He leaned forward. 'And I've seen things.'

'What things?'

'I can't say yet.' It all sounded very mysterious.

'You should go to the police, then.'

'Yes, but will they move quickly enough? I mean, who's next on the list?'

'Probably no one. I expect they'll find it was someone with a grudge against Lord Redmire – and I think there were quite a few of them.'

'Let's hope you're right. Anyway I'd better be off,' he said, to Andrea's relief. 'Just take care of yourself.'

'I will, Ian.'

Oldroyd and Steph found Richard Wilkins alone in the estate office. His staff were still on stand-down.

'Please, take a seat,' he said. 'Are you getting everything you need? Is that room OK?'

'Yes, everything's fine,' replied Oldroyd. 'You look very tired. I expect it's been very stressful and demanding for you.'

Wilkins sighed. 'Yes, Chief Inspector. I've just been on the phone to Lord Redmire's solicitors. A representative's coming over tomorrow to read the will. Someone has to take charge of these things and no one in the family can do it. They're not used to organising anything practical – they don't know where the cutlery drawer is, so to speak. They leave it to their minions.'

'I see. You sound a bit resentful about that?'

Wilkins looked at the two detectives and frowned. He sat back in his chair. 'I'm going to be frank with you: I don't particularly like it here, and I didn't like Lord Redmire either.'

'Why was that?'

'My last job was with the National Trust. They were good to work for; it was a team effort, and everyone cared about what they were doing. Redmire was very demanding and really wasn't interested in the estate except in so far as it could make money. I really couldn't warm to him at all.'

'Were you aware that he had any enemies, other than yourself?'

Oldroyd smiled at his little joke, and Wilkins laughed. 'Well, I didn't dislike him enough to kill him, Chief Inspector, and I can't think of anyone who would, although there were lots of people he didn't get on with, even in his close family.'

'Who in particular?'

'I've overheard some angry phone calls between him and his brother. There was no love lost between them.'

'What were they arguing about?'

'I think Dominic Carstairs had a big chip on his shoulder about being the younger brother who had to earn his living. From what I could gather, his business has not been doing that well recently, and he was asking Lord Redmire for help.'

'It seems as if it was no big secret that quite a number of people were out to get money from him.'

'Yes, but the problem was he didn't have any to give.'

'He hoped the locked-room performance would be a money-spinner, then?'

'He did – that and his plans for the estate.'

Oldroyd sat up. 'Yes, I was just coming to those. Andrea Jenkinson seems to think you may know something about them.'

'Sorry to disappoint you. As I said, I was just a minion. He never consulted with me about important things like that.'

'Who did he speak to about it?'

'I assume it was some firm of property developers.'

'Do you know who?'

'No, but he kept documents in the safe here, sealed up.' He pointed to a heavy metal safe on the wall. 'I never saw the contents but one of them had something written on it like "Estate Development".'

'We need to see those.'

'Of course.'

Wilkins got up, took some keys from a drawer and walked over to the safe. He removed a pile of papers and began to sort through them. After a while he stopped, and looked puzzled.

'Well, that's very strange. They're not here.'

Oldroyd glanced at Steph. 'When did you last see them?'

'I don't remember – some time ago – but I've had no reason to get them out.'

'Who else has a key?'

'Only Lord Redmire. He must have taken them.'

'According to Katherine Carstairs, you had a break-in here a few months ago.'

'Yes, she reported seeing someone in this office during the night. It was investigated but nothing was missing.'

'Did you check the contents of the safe?'

Wilkins looked a little sheepish. 'Actually, no. I didn't think about it. It hadn't been tampered with and I thought, even if there had been someone in here, they would have been looking for something accessible: money or equipment.'

'Maybe, but it seems that if there was an intruder, those documents are what they were looking for, unless Lord Redmire had a reason for removing them. I assume these consultants, whoever they were, will have a copy.'

'Yes, I'm sure they will,' replied Wilkins. He sounded distracted, and his expression was suddenly anxious.

'Are you OK?' asked Steph.

'Yes, fine. I'm just shocked that those documents have gone. It just seems to be one thing after another at the moment.'

'Did you know Harry Robinson?' asked Oldroyd. Wilkins's face brightened.

'Yes, nice old chap. He retired just after I came to work here. I used to see him quite a bit, as he lived on the estate. He was often in the pub too. No one has any idea who would have wanted to kill him.'

'Which pub was that?'

'The Pear Tree. It's in the local village, Little Aldington. It's just a walk over the fields from here. I sometimes call in there after work. It's the Redmire Hall local, if you like. Harry must have been going in for years; there must be a lot of people in there who knew him.'

'Well, thank you for that, and we'll leave you to it.'

'Not at all.'

Ian Barden was working hard on his mission to warn everyone of the danger at Redmire Hall and, with the gardens and the railway shut, he had plenty of time to go round the estate speaking to people. When he left Andrea Jenkinson, he wandered over to the house to see if he could get a word with Celia Anscomb. The visitors' entrance was open, so he went in quietly. He spotted Celia looking at the visitors' book in the hall and came up noiselessly behind her.

'Anyone interesting been here lately?'

Celia gave a little scream and jumped round. Barden laughed a little too loudly.

'Ian! For goodness' sake, don't ever do that again.' Celia gripped the table to steady herself. 'Don't you know we're all as jumpy as anything after what's happened?'

'Oh, yes, and with good reason,' replied Barden, leaning forward in his serious manner. 'You shouldn't be here by yourself, you know. They could strike again even in broad daylight.'

'And who are "they", Ian?'

'I couldn't say at the moment, but I'm letting everyone know that I've seen things.' He nodded enigmatically.

Celia decided to humour him. 'Well, it's good to know that you're looking out for us, Ian. I'm sure everyone's told you that you must go to the police if you know something important.'

'Yes, maybe. All in good time.'

'So you've no customers today, then?'

'No, but it gives me a chance to do a bit of work on the *Duchess*.'

'The what . . . ? Oh, the engine! Yes, well, I'm sure she needs your attention, so you'd better be getting back to her.'

'Yes, you're right, but you just be on your guard.' He pointed at her, then turned round and left.

Celia sighed, shook her head and continued to peruse the visitors' book. It always fascinated her to see where visitors came from, especially those from distant places such as New Zealand and California.

'Good morning!'

For the second time she turned around startled.

Steph hadn't intended to startle Celia, but the woman certainly acted like Steph had appeared from nowhere.

'Oh! Hello. They said you'd want to talk to me; please, come in.'

Celia led Steph into her small office, and they both sat down. Steph looked around appreciatively at the stylish artwork on the walls and the orchids on the window ledge. 'This is a very nice office.'

'Thank you.'

'You're obviously a very arty person. Do you use those skills in your work here?'

'Oh, yes. I don't just organise cleaners and tour guides; I'm responsible for conservation too.'

'What does that involve?'

'I regularly inspect the internal fabric of the house and the paintings and furniture for signs of wear and decay, and then I organise a programme for the specialists to come in and do the work.'

'That sounds expensive.'

'Yes, it can be.'

'So, in light of the financial difficulties here at Redmire, have you found it difficult to have this work funded recently?'

'It hasn't been easy.'

'Has it caused conflict between yourself and Lord Redmire?'

'Not particularly, but I was worried about other things, which I might as well mention now as I know you'll find them out.'

'What were those?'

'He hinted that some of the paintings and furniture I look after might be put up for sale. He even asked for me to arrange a valuation on one painting, our most valuable. Obviously that was a shock. It would have degraded my position; I would have had fewer things to conserve and it would have broken up the great collection we have here.'

'So were you very angry with him?'

'His ideas hadn't come to anything and I was hoping that he'd change his mind.'

'How long have you worked here?'

'Five years. I used to work in London; I had a very lowly position at the V&A. This is much more responsibility. I have a lot of freedom.'

'How did you get on generally with Lord Redmire?'

'What do you mean?'

'I understand he could make women feel uncomfortable. He had a reputation for womanising, didn't he?'

Steph noted Celia's expensive clothes, slim figure and air of sophistication. She could imagine her being a target for Redmire's attentions.

'You had to be used to him and know what to expect. It was obvious that he was appraising you and he made comments. I spoke to Andrea Jenkinson about it. We agreed that if you were firm in not responding, he would give up.'

'As he was the boss, I suppose there was no one higher up to call him out to, was there?'

'No.'

Steph appreciated Celia's difficulty in coping with unwanted sexual attention from a superior. She'd never experienced anything from Oldroyd but she was wary of certain officers back at Harrogate HQ. She went in for the kill. 'So, did you dislike Lord Redmire enough to want to see him dead?'

Celia looked shocked. She was a less worldly character than the tougher Andrea Jenkinson, or at least that's how she appeared to Steph. 'No, of course not. Anyway, I don't know anything about magic tricks,' she added lamely.

'But you had a motive in protecting the collection?'

'Maybe. I can see why I'm on your list, but I didn't kill him.'

Steph was inclined to believe her, but just how miserable Lord Redmire had made Celia Anscomb's working life remained an intriguing and relevant question.

DC Jeffries was getting on everyone's nerves at Ripon Police Station. He paraded around jauntily, with a Cheshire-cat smile on his face, missing no opportunity to remind people that he was working for Chief Inspector Oldroyd.

He was pleased with himself for having compiled all the information DCI Oldroyd had asked for about employees at the estate. Now his task was to contact the Red Hot Poker Club in London to enquire about the gambling activities of Lord Redmire and Tristram Benington.

He called the number, spoke to a very snooty receptionist and was passed on to an even more ostentatious official who declared himself the manager.

'What can I do for you, Constable?' the manager drawled.

'We're investigating the death of Frederick Carstairs, Lord Redmire, who I understand was a member of your club.'

'Yes, well, obviously we've seen the news and we're extremely sorry about the death of Lord Redmire, but I'm afraid Red Hot Poker policy prohibits staff from entering into any discussions about club members.'

Jeffries took some satisfaction in asserting his authority while remaining as scrupulously polite as the man to whom he was speaking. 'Sir, I'm afraid I have to remind you that this is a murder enquiry and that your cooperation is required regardless of any club rules that may normally apply.'

He was proud of that and it proved effective.

'Very well,' said the manager reluctantly.

'So can you first of all confirm that Lord Redmire and Tristram Benington are members of the Red Hot Poker Club?'

'I can.'

'And were you aware that both of them had accrued debts?'

'I couldn't comment on that, Constable, for the simple reason that debts are private matters between club members, and the club has no knowledge of the details.'

'But surely, sir, the club must take an interest in such things? You must be reluctant to allow people, even if they are members, to take part in high-stakes games if you are aware that their finances are unsound. It could cause serious problems, couldn't it, if people are playing who are unable to honour losses?'

'Maybe . . .'

'So, do you have any information on this that might have a bearing on the case?'

There was a pause, and Jeffries could sense that the manager was trying to decide what to do.

'This is strictly confidential, Constable. If it ever emerged that someone in my position had discussed the private matters of club members with someone outside the club, it would cause a terrible crisis here. And, of course, my position would be in jeopardy.'

'OK, I understand.'

'Lord Redmire has been a member for many years and we were aware that he'd lost a great deal of money and had incurred debts, but how he was dealing with them was his own concern. As far as Mr Benington goes, we knew that he also was in debt and recently . . .' He paused again, clearly finding this extremely difficult. 'Mr Benington and Lord Redmire were overheard arguing about money. It appears that Lord Redmire was refusing to help Mr Benington pay off his debts. I have to say that it is part of the code of people who play at the table that any debts have to be honoured personally – so Lord Redmire was quite right to refuse assistance.'

Jeffries smiled as he considered how much discreet 'overhearing' went on in these institutions.

'I hasten to add, Constable, that I'm sure that this altercation had no bearing on the recent unpleasantness at Redmire Hall.'

Jeffries didn't comment on that final remark but thanked the man for his help and rang off, very pleased with how he'd handled the interview. He beamed to himself at the prospect of informing Oldroyd that Benington had asked Redmire for financial help and clearly been angrily rejected.

It was early evening, and Oldroyd had released Steph for the day. She set off for the drive back to Leeds, while Oldroyd decided to stay and pursue the lead Wilkins had given them. What better tip-off than one that involved going to a pub?

He decided to walk the short distance to Little Aldington from the estate, as it was a pleasant July evening. The path from the estate ran along the edge of a field of barley. Oldroyd thought that this was a route that would have been very familiar to Harry Robinson. Looking across the green, whiskery crop, Oldroyd could see the narrow spire of the local church protruding above a group of majestic copper beech trees. In the distance the squat shape of Ripon Cathedral was visible and, further away still, the fells of Wensleydale.

The footpath entered a lane enclosed by weathered stone walls, over which Oldroyd glimpsed a paddock with sheep grazing under large sycamore trees. He emerged from the lane on to a quiet road. There was a wide village green bordered by picturesque rosy-brick cottages with gardens full of roses, delphiniums, hollyhocks and carnations. An inn sign with a picture of a fruiting tree hung outside the pub, a black-and-white building that formed part of a long terrace of small cottages. A black sandwich-board sign on the footpath announced that food was being served and that there was a beer garden at the back.

Oldroyd entered to find what he'd hoped for: a number of people who looked like locals were gathered at the bar. Some of them were rather elderly. They must have known Harry Robinson, he thought. He walked up to the bar and gestured to the barman, who came over intending to serve him. Oldroyd held up his identification.

'Chief Inspector Oldroyd, West Riding Police. I'm investigating the murders at the Hall. I'm here to talk to anyone who knew Harry Robinson. I assume I'm right in thinking he was a regular here.'

This announcement silenced the conversation at the bar.

'I see,' said the barman, a portly middle-aged man. He turned to the group of men propping up the bar. 'Bill, Frank, you knew Harry a long time, didn't you?'

Two of the older men in the group, both wearing flat caps and holding pint glasses, turned to look at Oldroyd. 'Aye,' one of them said. 'We've known Harry for donkey's years. What the bloody hell's going on over there?'

'Let's sit down.' Oldroyd indicated a vacant table. 'I'll have a pint of bitter, by the way,' he said to the barman. He knew he shouldn't really drink on duty, but then, he worked so many hours that he lost track of when he was officially working and when he wasn't – so stuff it.

The two sat down, eyeing Oldroyd rather suspiciously. The barman brought Oldroyd's pint over to join the other two on beer mats.

'So you are . . . ?' began Oldroyd.

'I'm Bill Mason,' said the man who'd spoken at the bar, 'and this is Frank Bridges.'

'Good. So how well did you know Harry Robinson?'

'I went to the village school with him when we were kids,' said Bridges. 'We've lived round here all our lives. School's gone, though, now – shut years ago.'

'I was brought up in Ripon,' said Mason, 'but I've lived here more than forty years.'

'Did he have any enemies, as far as you know? Anyone who'd want to harm him?'

'Harry? Never in this world,' said Bridges. 'He was a nice chap – never wanted much in life. He was happy with his steady carry-on up at the Hall. Him and his wife had a nice little cottage there. No children. She died a few years ago.'

'What did he do up there?'

'Just a handyman, wasn't he, Frank? On the mechanical side. He used to say he'd done his apprenticeship in a garage in Ripon. He maintained their cars and did other odd jobs: electrics, plumbing, stuff like that.'

'Another drink?' asked Oldroyd, noticing that the men's glasses were empty.

'Aye, thanks.'

Oldroyd went to the bar and returned with two pints of bitter, which he set down on the table.

'Did Harry ever tell you anything about this locked-room business? We know he was involved in setting it up originally, back in the seventies.'

The two men looked at each other. Mason replied, 'It wasn't long after I came here. I remember there was a great palaver about it. It was in the local paper.'

'Harry was full of it,' said Bridges. 'I remember him saying it was very clever, but we couldn't get him to tell us anything – said he'd been sworn to secrecy and he'd been rewarded.'

'Rewarded how?'

'He never said.'

'So he never revealed anything about the trick?'

'No, however much we tried to get it out of him.'

'Did Harry say anything recently about the trick being revived?'

'No,' said Mason. 'He hadn't talked about it for years and we were as surprised as anyone else when it was suddenly announced that Lord Redmire was going to perform it again after all this time.'

'Is there anything else you can remember about Harry and the locked room? You see, we're pretty sure he was murdered because he knew how it worked.'

'Bloody hell,' said Mason. 'Well, no, I don't think so. He was in here the night before. He wouldn't say anything about it, but he did seem quiet, as if he had things on his mind. Wasn't he, Frank?'

'Aye. He didn't seem to be looking forward to it; I don't know why, because he always seemed proud of it before,' replied Bridges.

'Do you think he knew what was going to happen?' asked Oldroyd.

'What? You mean Lord Redmire getting stabbed? Harry?' Bridges shook his head.

'Can't see Harry involved in killing anybody – though I will say he didn't like Redmire,' said Mason. 'He often said stuff about him in here. Said he was a mean bugger, not a patch on his father to work for.'

'Aye, but that's different from saying he helped to bump him off.'

'Yes,' said Oldroyd, intervening before things got heated between the two men. 'Well, thank you very much for your help; it's been very useful. If you remember anything else please contact me.' He gave each of them a card.

The bar was starting to fill up with evening drinkers and diners. Oldroyd made to leave and was about to go out through the door when someone called to him. 'Can I have a word?'

Oldroyd turned to see a tall, thin figure wearing a hoodie. It was a young man with an untidy moustache and a swarthy complexion.

'Yes?'

'You're investigating those murders up at th'all, aren't you?'

'I am.'

'I saw something.'

'Right. Let's go in here.'

Oldroyd led the way into the small bar at the back and sat down. The young man joined him, looking uncomfortable, slouching back with his hands jammed into his pockets.

'Can I get you a drink?' asked Oldroyd.

'No. I've got to be off in a minute.'

'So what did you want to tell me?'

'Old Harry, he was a friend of mine. He was a nice old bloke; he knew me dad when he was around and he used to show us round th'estate, you know. I grew up in t'village. I used to go with him trapping rabbits and stuff.'

'OK.'

'I want you to catch the bastard who killed him.'

'Right, so what was it you saw?'

'So, on that night, I was in those woods behind th'all.'

Oldroyd refrained from asking what he was doing there, so as not to put him off. It was most probably a bit of poaching on estate land. Harry Robinson would have taught him about the best places.

'And I came across this car. It was hidden in t'trees; there's an old track that leads in from t'drive up to th'all. There was nobody in it and I thought nowt about it at the time. I saw all t'posh people going in and all them TV vans and it was a good time to . . . do what I was doing.'

Again Oldroyd maintained a judicious silence about what the man may have been doing. 'So you think this car was hidden for a reason?'

'Yeah. Well, someone bumped off His Lordship, didn't they? And Harry. They could have got in that car and driven off.'

'Yes, it's suspicious. So what make of car was it, and did you get the number?'

'No, I didn't get t'number, but it was a VW Polo: quite old, red. I know me cars.'

'Have you any idea how long it stayed there?'

'No, but I went back yesterday and it was gone. One other thing I saw was that there was more than one set of tyre tracks; another set that were old, so I thought maybe that hiding place had been used before.'

Oldroyd smiled. 'Well done – very observant. Have you ever thought of joining the police?'

'What, me? That's a joke.'

'Never mind. Thank you anyway. If you see anything else, give me a call.' He gave the man another of his cards. 'And your name is?'

'Scott Handley, but . . .'

'Don't worry: I'm not going to check your name against our records. It's not relevant.'

The young man looked relieved. 'I'm off, then,' he said abruptly, and walked out of the bar, leaving Oldroyd with plenty to think about.

Oldroyd decided to stay in the pub and try the food, opting for a steak-and-kidney pie with chips and peas. As he ate he considered the new information.

Despite the protestations of the man's friends, it seemed even more likely that Robinson had indeed been involved in setting up the murder of his employer. Why did he dislike him so much? It was clear that Redmire was not a pleasant character, but there must have been a deeper reason if Robinson was prepared to see him dead.

Oldroyd paid his bill and continued to ruminate as he left the pub. The light was fading as he retraced his steps across the field. It was a beautiful warm night and he stopped for a moment to gaze up at the stars. A tawny owl floated silently past between two large trees. A gentle breeze rustled the barley. Was this car Scott Handley had reported of any significance? They would have to check car ownership among the people at the Hall. It would—

Oldroyd had reached the edge of the field, where two hedges joined and there was a stile, when suddenly there was a crack and a bullet narrowly missed him, burying itself in a tree by the hedge. Stunned and alarmed, he leaped over the stile and hid behind the hedge, panting, with his heart racing. He tried to get a view of the field while calming himself.

Halfway across the empty stretch of grass was a large horse-chestnut tree and Oldroyd could see a figure peering round it in his direction and holding a rifle. Oldroyd moved away carefully, remaining out of sight behind the foliage until he was able to make a dash towards the shelter of a copse of trees by the house.

He waited to see if anyone would appear, but everything remained still and eerily silent. Eventually, he made a run for the house, and round the front of the building to where his car was parked, feeling that at any moment he might hear another crack and feel the impact of a bullet. Here there was a PC on duty, who was startled by Oldroyd's sudden appearance.

'Sir?'

'Someone's just taken a shot at me,' Oldroyd blurted out. 'In the field at the back.' He pointed back to where he'd run from. 'They may be following me. Let's get into the house, quick.'

Inside, the PC locked the door and radioed for help. More officers appeared and quite soon were joined by armed officers from Ripon. There were no more shots from anywhere and a search of the immediate vicinity revealed nothing.

Oldroyd took some time to recover. When it was deemed safe, he left his car at the Hall and was driven back to Harrogate in a police van, reflecting that whoever was behind these crimes was clearly more ruthless and determined than he'd realised.

Five

Oldroyd slept in a little the next morning. He'd opened a bottle of wine when he got back to Harrogate the previous night and listened to some late Mozart piano concertos on his headphones in order to calm down after his experience with the shooter.

It was a long time since he'd met personally with violence in his investigations, not since a seemingly mild-mannered man who'd in fact killed his own wife had suddenly produced a knife and lunged at Oldroyd when the latter had cornered and exposed him. Oldroyd had moved deftly to one side, grabbed the man's arm and forced it back. The elbow joint had cracked and the man had screamed as he dropped the knife. Oldroyd could look after himself if he had to, but people hiding and taking potshots at you was hard to defend against.

He slouched, yawning, into the kitchen to find a note from Louise and a little package.

Hi Dad

Got up before you, that's a first! Looks like you were
hitting the wine last night!

Gone to see Ben and Clare, may stay overnight. Hope
you like your pressie!

L xxxx

Oldroyd filled the kettle, put a couple of slices of bread in the
toaster and then sat down to open his present. Inside the wrapping
was a wooden doll of the Russian type, clearly meant to be Beethoven.
Inside Beethoven was Mozart, and inside Mozart was Schubert. They
were all quite small but very well made.

It was a lovely present, although again he found himself wondering what she'd used for money, as it didn't look cheap. He examined
the intricate detail of each figure and then, as happened so often with
Oldroyd, something clicked unexpectedly in his mind. He gazed into
the distance. No, it couldn't quite be that, but . . . maybe. For a while
he was lost in thought while the kettle boiled and the toast started to
smoke.

Steph Johnson got into the Harrogate station early as she wanted to
make progress on tracking down Olivia Pendleton, the dowager Lady
Redmire's niece, but she couldn't resist a quick call to Andy first. He was
a long time answering and sounded extremely woozy.

'So who's been out on the piss, then? I thought you were only having a sober do with Jason?'

'God, I wish it had been. I feel like shit.'

'Serves you right – no sympathy. You bought it, as my granddad
would have said.'

'Too right. God, I feel sick!'

Steph had to laugh.

'Well, great – I ring my boyfriend up and he threatens to vomit down the phone at me. Nice to speak to you, too!'

'Don't talk so loud – it hurts my head!'

'Oh dear me; the poor thing. Anyway, those of us who are working have jobs to do and as a punishment for enjoying yourself without me, you can help.'

'How?'

'I've got to track a woman down. Olivia Pendleton – she's a cousin of the murder victim, Lord Redmire, and she's a fashion designer in London.'

'I don't know anything about fashion designers.'

'No, but you've got mates at the Met who do. They can do a quicker search than I can, so give them a quick ring and get them to send me the information when they find it.'

'I'm supposed to be on holiday.'

'Yes, but I know you won't mind doing this little thing for me. That is, when you've sobered up. The boss'll be really pleased you helped, and you know how you like to impress him.'

'OK. What was the name again?'

Steph gave him the details. 'So, when are you coming home, then?' she asked.

'In a couple of days. I want a bit of time back in Leeds before I go back to work.'

'OK, well, get on with this job, then. I'd like to have something to show the boss later today.'

'Today! That's asking a bit.'

'Get away! Those old mates of yours will get it done for you in no time. So I'll leave you to it. Bye.' She grinned as she ended the call.

'Is he missing you, then?'

Steph looked over to the door and her grin died. Detective Inspector Derek Fenton was watching her with an unpleasant smile on his face.

He was a plump middle-aged man who wore clothes that were too tight. He often had sweat stains under his arms. Steph felt uncomfortable in his presence. He made personal remarks and sometimes stood a little too close to her, but had so far done nothing further.

'Maybe.'

'He ought to be, lucky man.'

'Would your wife like to hear you say that?'

The words were out of her mouth before she had time to think of the consequences.

Fenton walked into the office and shut the door behind him. 'I beg your pardon?'

'You heard me.'

'I did, Sergeant; and just because you're using DCI Oldroyd's office, don't think you can speak to me as if you're him.'

Steph went bright red with anger and frustration. 'I'm sorry, sir,' she mumbled, unable to look him in the face.

Fenton sat down in a chair next to her and lowered his voice. 'You're very pally with the chief inspector, aren't you? We know he took you out with him all dressed up to Redmire Hall, where he made a fool of himself. The dirty bugger – old enough to be your father. What do you do for him, then, in the back of that old Saab of his? Anything for a promotion, is it? Does Carter know about that?'

'There's nothing like that going on,' she said, and then added, 'sir.'

'I'll bet. Well, rumours travel quickly, don't they? And if you don't want them to, you'd better be a bit friendlier.'

He got up and walked out of the office.

Steph felt hot tears behind her eyes. She had a strong urge to shout 'Bastard!' after him, but was able to resist. She sat for a while, trying to control her breathing. It had all happened so quickly and had hit her unexpectedly. She went to get a glass of water and returned to the office. There was no sign of him.

She considered whether she should report what had happened but decided against it. It would be a serious allegation against her superior, and she had no evidence to support her. She was going to have to deal with it herself.

~

Another tense and dreary day of waiting had dawned at Redmire Hall. After breakfast, Poppy and Antonia walked over to see the dowager Lady Redmire, Poppy with some reluctance.

'I hope she doesn't go on about Tristram again, Mummy. Last time she never stopped making snide remarks about him: when was he going to get a proper job? Was I supporting him? He earns more than me, you know! The problem with Granny is she has no tact at all; she says the first thing that comes into her head and she doesn't mind her own business.'

'That's what old people can be like. My mother was the same. They've got past the age of caring what people think. People from your grandmother's generation often have fixed views about things to do with families and the roles of men and women, and they won't shift.'

They reached the garden entrance to the dowager's flat and found the old lady sitting in a cane chair on the patio. It was a warm morning, but she was wearing a cardigan as usual.

'Oh! It's you two,' she said. 'Well, thank you for coming over; it's nice to see you, especially as things have been so absolutely beastly.'

'How are you feeling?' asked Antonia.

The dowager Lady Redmire frowned and shrugged her bony shoulders. 'What can one say? I told that young woman detective: I always thought Freddy would end up like this.'

Poppy was shocked. 'What do you mean, Granny? Murdered!'

The dowager Lady Redmire turned a hard face to her granddaughter. 'Your father was a reckless and selfish man, Poppy. He had something bad coming to him. That's all I'll say.'

'Well, we all know about Freddy's bad points.' Antonia moved in to calm the conversation. 'But what happened was terrible and we're all shocked. We must just try to support one another.'

'Well, he didn't treat you very well.'

'No, that's true, but one has to try to forgive and move on.'

The dowager Lady Redmire gave her a look of admiration. 'You were always such a good woman, Antonia. You were far too good for Freddy. I told the police as much. I told Freddy, too, more than once.'

Gratifying as this was to hear, Antonia tried again to move things on. 'Anyway, Poppy wants to tell you about her photography.' Antonia gestured to Poppy behind the dowager Lady Redmire's back.

'Oh yes?'

'Yes, Granny. I'm freelance, but I get commissions from all kinds of people. I got one from an upmarket estate agent last month to take pictures of their properties in St John's Wood. That was really interesting.'

'Does it pay well?' said the dowager Lady Redmire abruptly. 'You'll need it to if you're still keeping that boyfriend.'

Antonia winced. Poppy looked angry and deflated.

'What's his name again?' continued the dowager Lady Redmire, seemingly oblivious of any offence she might have caused.

'Tristram,' sighed Poppy.

'Yes, well, I'd never trust a man who was a model. What is he a model of, anyway?'

'Clothes, Granny – expensive clothes. He earns more than me, as I keep telling you.'

'Just for wearing clothes? Well, it's not much of a job for a man, is it? And you can't be doing well with your photography if he earns more than you. Mark my words, no good will come of it. Now, your brother, Alistair—'

Antonia interrupted before the dowager Lady Redmire could get herself properly launched on another contentious subject. 'Have the others been over to see you?'

'Which others? I don't know who's here. Dominic popped his nose in for five minutes yesterday; brought Mary with him. He's still playing the disappointed man. I don't know how she puts up with him.'

'I don't suppose Alex or James have been over?'

The dowager Lady Redmire sniffed. 'That little minx wouldn't dare show her face here. She knows what I think of her. I'm surprised you're so generous towards her. You're so noble, Antonia. I always felt sorry for James, though. He was another of Freddy's victims. I tell you, is there any wonder somebody wanted him dead?'

'And how are you keeping?'

'Oh, very well. I can't complain. I'm perfectly content here. It's a wonderful place to end one's days.' She paused to reflect. 'One just wishes that one's family had turned out better. I blame Vivian, really. He wasn't a bad man but there was never any stability, and . . .'

'I think we'll have to be getting back, Ursula.' Antonia had given up the struggle.

'Getting back? But you haven't been here five minutes.'

'No, but we'll come back again soon. We need to prepare ourselves for the will. The solicitor's coming this afternoon. Are you coming over to the house to hear it?'

'No, I'm not. Alistair will inherit the estate and that's all that matters. Things should improve after that.' She looked away as if indicating the end of the conversation.

Not surprisingly, Poppy was in a silent, sullen mood when they returned to the main house, and Antonia was left to reflect yet again on the cruelties of aristocratic family life.

'So, someone took a potshot at you, sir?' asked Steph.

'I'm afraid they did – and of course it means that we really have to watch our step now. Whoever's behind this is ruthless and determined. No walking around quiet parts of the estate and its environs by ourselves, particularly at night.'

Oldroyd, Steph and Jeffries were sitting in their Redmire Hall office. Jeffries tried to maintain a sombre expression but was secretly thrilled and excited: this was real, dangerous police work.

'Unfortunately the trip to the Pear Tree, which was nearly the end of me, didn't yield a great deal.' Oldroyd told his two detectives about what the rough-looking man had told him in the pub. 'So we need to check car ownership here at the Hall and widen out to the neighbourhood if necessary.' He nodded to Jeffries, who immediately made a note of his next task. 'As far as this trick goes, I think we have to approach it differently.'

'How, sir?'

'I'm not sure, but as I've said to you many times, we always need to avoid getting into a rut and making assumptions. If things are not working out, we need to think "outside the box", as people like to say nowadays.' He smiled as he thought of what Tom Walker would make of that. 'Anyway, Jeffries, what have you got to report?'

Jeffries seized his moment enthusiastically, and told the two senior detectives what he'd discovered in his call to the Red Hot Poker Club, including the interesting fact that Redmire and Benington had argued about the latter's debts before the murder.

'Very good,' said Oldroyd. 'He didn't tell us about that, did he? Probably thought it would incriminate him and he's right. We'll have to get back to him.'

There was a knock on the door, and a PC entered the room. 'Excuse me, sir, just an update on the attack last night.'

'Yes?'

'We've continued the search in daylight, particularly in the field by that tree from where you said the assailant fired at you. No shell casings were found, but the good news is that the bullet has been found in the tree near to where you were standing. It's going to take some getting out, but then ballistics should be able to match it to rifles.'

'Excellent work, thank you,' said Oldroyd, and the PC left.

'Not sure how much help that will be, sir,' said Steph. 'There are always lots of guns around in a country place like this, and plenty of places to hide them. Farmers have them to shoot crows and rabbits and stuff. I'll bet there are shooting clubs in the area too.'

'True, but all information is useful. It may prove to be extra incriminating evidence at some point. If we can identify the murderer.'

'I got two DCs to complete the inventory of Harry Robinson's possessions and the estimate is that they were worth a great deal. I think I know now how he paid for the stuff.'

'Well done,' said Oldroyd.

'It was easy. I looked at his bank account and his monthly payments in were very substantial. For some reason, the Redmire estate was paying him an extremely generous pension.'

'Was it indeed? There must have been a good reason for that and I'll bet it was something to do with his knowledge of the trick.'

'I've managed to track down Olivia Pendleton,' said Steph. 'And I have to say it was with Andy's help. He used his contacts at the Met; they found her in no time. She runs a fashion house called Zorba. Their premises are in Islington. I've spoken to her, and by chance she's coming up to Yorkshire to see her aunt, who owns another big house near here: Belthorpe Manor.'

'Yes, I know it – bit of a rundown eccentric place on the other side of Ripon. We'll catch up with her there. Well done and pass on my thanks to Andy; that was beyond the call of duty, working on his holidays.' Oldroyd got up. 'OK. I want you two to track Benington down and see what he has to say for himself. After that you can follow up with

Miss Carstairs and see what she has to say about being seen arguing with her father. I'm going to have a search through Redmire's possessions in the house to see if there's anything interesting there. There's also the question of his will. The solicitor is coming this afternoon, apparently; the family must be in suspense. We'll get a copy at the same time so let's see if it contains anything interesting.'

The family were indeed in suspense about many things, the latest, since Richard Wilkins had informed them of the solicitor's visit, being the contents of the will. The stress of living on top of one another was getting unbearable, especially as many of them disliked each other. Now suspicions and jealousies were rife and in the tense atmosphere conversation was limited.

After breakfast, Tristram was sitting in a corner of the sitting room trying to keep out of the way of everyone and wondering how he'd got caught up in this awful family. He still thought Poppy was worth it, however; and shortly she might have the money to solve their financial problems.

James Forsyth came into the room. 'Morning, Tris,' he said jovially. He sat down near him, leaned over conspiratorially and said in a hushed voice, 'It's bloody terrible, isn't it? If looks could kill, as they say. I'm glad I shan't be there when the damned will is read; it could be a bloodbath!'

'I know.'

'I'll tell you what, do you fancy going out for a spot of shooting? Alex has a headache so she's lying down. It'll get us out of the house. It's not the game season, but we could see if we can bag a few rabbits and reduce the crow population.'

'Good idea,' replied Tristram. 'Poppy's gone to see her grandmother. Do you know where the guns are kept?'

'No problem. I've been out many times with Freddy. There's a gun-room near the stable block. We'll get one of the estate workers to sort us out.'

Half an hour later the two men were striding over the fields in the direction of a copse. They were wearing boots and brandishing two .22-calibre rifles, all supplied by Lord Redmire's gunroom. One of his many expensive pursuits had been organising shooting parties and providing clothing and equipment for the guests.

Forsyth turned to his companion. 'I suppose you and Poppy stand to gain now Freddy's gone.'

Benington looked at him sharply.

'No, don't get me wrong,' Forsyth said. 'I don't mean you did anything to bring it about. I just mean it will be a help, because I hear you're . . . struggling a bit. Look, there's a rabbit!'

A rabbit was standing still at the edge of the field. Forsyth raised his rifle, shot but missed. The rabbit bounced away at great speed, showing them its little white bottom.

'Damn!'

'I'm not sure how you got to know that.'

'It's that poker club, I'm afraid. I go there myself a bit sometimes, but I made sure Freddy was never there. Surprised I've never seen you. It's a gossip factory, that place – no secrets. The word was going round that Freddy had refused you money.'

'I should never have approached him there, in public.'

'No, someone will have been listening in all right. But I think it was a good thing he refused; he was not a man you wanted to have any financial dealings with, believe me. I learned that from bitter experience.'

'Did he leave you badly in the lurch?'

'Yes. Supposed to be a partnership; he never did a stroke of work and then pulled out, leaving me to pick up the pieces.'

They had reached the copse, a small group of mainly sycamores on a small round hill at the edge of the field. Forsyth looked up into the branches.

'Well, that's a stroke of luck,' he said. 'Look up there: a nice pair of black crows to have a shot at. Fancy a go?'

With some reluctance, Benington raised his rifle. He was not very experienced in handling guns, though he had done some shooting at his private school in Berkshire. He took aim and fired. One of the crows flapped off croaking, but the other fell off the branch in a flurry of feathers, thudded to the ground and lay lifeless.

'Bravo!' exclaimed Forsyth. They went over to examine the dead bird. 'Look at that beak: fearsome thing, isn't it? No wonder they can peck a lamb's eyes out . . . No,' he continued, 'you're better off getting the money from Freddy this way.' He gave Benington a sardonic smile.

'I very much agree,' replied Benington, and returned the smile.

Forsyth saw some figures approaching from the direction of the house. 'Hmm, better put our guns away; here come the police again. Mind you, it's that female detective sergeant – she can interrogate me any time she likes.' They both sniggered.

Forsyth had seen Steph and Jeffries walking across the fields towards them.

Steph had been informed that the two men had gone out shooting and she approached them with some caution, considering what had happened the previous night. She kept her eye on the guns, as did Jeffries, standing at her side.

'Mr Benington. I'm afraid I need to ask you some more questions.'

'I'll walk on into the wood, Tris. You can catch me up.'

'OK.' Forsyth gave Steph a lingering look and walked off, following a path between the trees.

Benington's gaze then settled on Steph. She came straight to the point with a steely glare. She was in no mood for any more harassment after what had happened earlier back at the station. 'We've been informed that you were involved in an argument with Lord Redmire at the Red Hot Poker Club not long before he was murdered. Is that true?'

Benington laughed. 'My God, James is right about that place. I assume you've been talking to someone there?'

'We have and they state that you had a heated argument about money.'

'All right, it's true. So what?'

'Can you tell me more about what was said?'

Benington shrugged his shoulders. The rifle he was carrying was slightly raised.

Steph stepped back. 'Be careful with that rifle, sir. I think it would be better if you laid it on the ground.'

'OK. You seem very jumpy.' He put the rifle down on the grass.

'Someone took a shot at Chief Inspector Oldroyd last night so we're not taking any chances.'

'I see,' said Benington. 'Well, the truth is, to put it simply, I've run up some gambling debts at the club and I was asking Lord Redmire if he could help me out. He refused and was angry that I'd asked him.'

'Why?'

'Because it's a matter of principle at a club like that: you honour your own debts. He was right. I should never have asked him.'

'Did Miss Carstairs have anything to do with it?'

'No. I haven't told her that I asked her father for help. Poppy doesn't understand how the club works. She's been trying to get me to ask Lord Redmire for help, not knowing I'd already done so. And the fact is I shouldn't have asked him; like I said, there's a code of honour about these things.'

'She was also seen arguing with her father on the evening he was killed.'

'By whom?'

'A witness, sir; I can't divulge names.'

'She cornered him before dinner that night, but she got the same response as me. I don't think she'd given up on the idea, though; she can be very stubborn when she decides she wants something.'

'So, sir, why did you conceal your argument from us when we interviewed you?'

Benington shrugged again and Steph bristled. She found his nonchalance in these circumstances arrogant. 'Obviously it doesn't look good for me that I'd argued with him not long before he was killed. I thought it better not to mention it.'

'That was a mistake, sir. Being open always means we're less suspicious.'

He gave her a sneering little smile. He wasn't going to accept a lecture from her.

'So your anger at Lord Redmire's refusal didn't lead you to plan his murder?' Steph asked.

Benington laughed contemptuously. 'No.'

'Even though his death might well solve your financial problems?'

'Certainly not.'

Steph gave him a hard stare. 'OK, sir, that's all for now. Off you go to bag a few more crows.'

She turned quickly and walked back across the field, followed by Jeffries, who was chuckling with admiration at the way she'd handled the two men.

Before going to search through Redmire's papers and possessions, Oldroyd decided to go for a walk around the gardens. He felt he needed to relax after the double traumas of being shot at and discovering his wife had a new man. Under this stress there was a chance that he could lose focus on the case.

He walked up and down the main borders, admiring the colourful perennials, and then wandered into some of the side areas. He walked through a white garden, a fuchsia garden and an elaborate rockery and eventually found himself on the edge of the garden area in a peaceful walled section known as the 'tropical garden', presumably because delicate specimens were grown against the rosy-brick walls, which retained heat and provided shelter against cold winter winds. He was admiring the pale-blue flowers of an abutilon when he heard a voice behind him.

'Morning.'

Oldroyd turned to see a stocky, bearded figure in a flat cap, brandishing a pair of secateurs in his left hand, and he stuck out his right.

'David Morton, head gardener. I think you're in charge of the investigation, aren't you?'

'Yes. Chief Inspector Oldroyd.'

They shook hands. Oldroyd noticed that Morton's were red and toughened by outdoor work.

'I was just wondering who was walking around here,' Morton said. 'We're still closed to the public, but I recognised you, even though neither you nor any of your officers have been to talk to us gardeners. We're feeling left out.' His weather-beaten face crinkled into a smile.

'We were going to get round to you at some point. We're concentrating on the family and close friends of the deceased at the moment. I don't suppose any of you witnessed the first murder?'

'Oh, no, we weren't invited to that. Far too posh a do for the likes of us. We might bring in mud on our shoes! Anyway, gardeners are too nice to get involved in nasty stuff like murder. We nurture and feed living things; we don't kill them.'

'Well, you've certainly done a good job here.' Oldroyd looked at Morton, and considered how it must feel to work for so long as the steward of such a wonderful garden. 'I suppose you must become very fond of this garden and the plants, when you've looked after them for so long.'

'Oh, yes,' replied Morton enthusiastically. 'They become like your family, especially if you're like me, with no family of your own. I've always been wedded to the job, so to speak. That abutilon you were looking at' – he pointed at the slender branches of the flowering shrub – 'is tender, very difficult to grow so far north. I planted it there years ago when it was very small. I've watched it grow and looked after it, protected it from the winter winds and pruned it properly every year, fed it in the spring, and look at it now.' He gazed admiringly at the perfect blooms.

Oldroyd's interest was roused. 'As we've met now, I might as well ask you a few questions.'

'OK, follow me – let's go and sit down.'

Morton led the way out of the tropical garden, round to the other side of the high wall and into a long, low brick extension, which turned out to be a clean, well-equipped former potting shed now partially converted into an office. Oldroyd and Morton sat on two rather battered wooden chairs at the far end of the shed, where the gardener had an untidy desk, strewn with brown, earth-stained papers and seed catalogues.

There were a number of dusty cardboard certificates in gold and silver displayed on the wall, a record of success at various local horticultural shows. A long potting bench extended down the shed on the window side and above this on various racks were small gardening tools: trowels, forks, dibbers, secateurs, heavy-duty scissors and some knives. It was definitely a gardener's lair.

Morton offered tea but Oldroyd declined when he saw the pile of dirty crockery and the grubby kettle by an ancient sink in a corner of the room.

'So,' began Oldroyd, 'how did you get on with Lord Redmire?'

Morton shrugged. 'As well as I did with his father and probably would have with any of these wealthy estate owners.'

'Why do you say that?'

'They mostly don't really appreciate their gardens. They expect them to be there, because it's what you have if you're part of the landed gentry. They also like them to make money when they're open to the public, but they don't understand them and their beauty and what's involved in maintaining them.

'Now, old Mr Charles Carstairs – he was Lord Redmire in my father's time – he was different. He designed the gardens; he was an expert. He knew what he was doing and where to get some rare plants. Wealthy chaps were still making long trips abroad to far-off places and bringing specimens back. We've still got some of them here, like that big magnolia against the wall near the abutilon. It's been here eighty years; my father helped to plant it when he was a young lad.'

'So he worked here as well?'

'Oh, yes. He was the head gardener before me, and my grandfather worked here as well.'

'So you must've been brought up here and you've lived here all your life?'

'Aye. In the old days we used to live in that house where Mr Alistair lives now. I had to move out when he got married, but I didn't mind. I've always liked Mr Alistair.'

'So where do you live now?'

'One of the cottages near to poor Harry.' He frowned. 'I've known Harry a long time; I hope you find t'bugger who killed him.' Morton's anger seemed to make his speech broader.

'I'm sure we will. By the way, can you tell me where you were on the night of the murders?'

'I was at home for a bit, got away from the noise and crowd. Those television people were a pain in the arse, laying their cables over the lawns and churning things up. Later on I went for a drink at the Pear

Tree. The news came through while I was there, and we were all talking about it. They don't have a television in the bar or I suppose it would have been on, but someone came in and told us what had happened.'

'You didn't fancy staying in and watching it yourself, then?'

Morton shook his head. 'Naw; I don't like all that magic stuff, and I didn't want to see Lord Redmire make a fool of himself. I mean, he was no magician, was he? Couldn't see how he was going to pull it off, but apparently he did – until it all went wrong. Sorry, I'm forgetting, you were there and saw it all.'

'I did,' replied Oldroyd, avoiding any further detail. 'You don't know how he found out how to perform this trick?'

Morton shrugged. 'No idea. It's been a secret for years; I was here when Mr Vivian did it first, though we weren't invited then either. It was common knowledge that Harry knew something, but he was sworn to secrecy. I expect he must have told someone – I don't know who or why – and that was why he was killed. Am I right?'

'It appears that way.'

'He should have kept his mouth shut, poor bugger.'

'Do you know of anyone who might have been trying to find things out?'

'No. As I said, it's been a secret for ages and people had just about forgotten about it. No one round here expected it to be done again.'

Oldroyd had to agree with that. It was strange how the whole thing had been resurrected and then used for murder. He sensed that something very dark was at work.

Shortly after lunch, a BMW drove slowly up the drive and parked near the entrance, before a fat, balding man in spectacles got out and heaved himself up the steps to the house carrying a briefcase. This was Irvine

Sidgwick, Lord Redmire's solicitor. He was part of a family business in Ripon that had been solicitors to the Carstairs for many generations.

The family were gathered together in the drawing room to hear the will, and once again there was a tense silence. No one wanted to catch another person's eye, let alone say anything. Frederick had been an unpredictable man and they were nervous about the contents of the will.

A small table and a chair had been positioned by the fireplace. Sidgwick, already sweating, was brought in. He shuffled across the room, plonked himself down in the chair and opened his briefcase. For a few moments he fussed around with his papers and then, after clearing his throat, he began to speak. 'Before I proceed to the reading of the will, I would just like to offer my condolences and those of everyone at the firm for your sad loss and—'

'That's very kind of you, Sidgwick,' interjected Dominic Carstairs, 'but can you just get on with it, please.' One or two people rolled their eyes with disgust at this rudeness, but no one could be bothered to rebuke him.

'Very well,' said Sidgwick, looking rather crestfallen. He picked up the document he had extracted from his briefcase. 'I won't read it out word for word, in order to save you the legal jargon; I'll give you the main points and I'll obviously leave you a copy. You are also aware, I'm sure, that due to the ongoing murder enquiry, a copy of the will has been sent to the police.

'So, in terms of the estate, comprising the house and land, this has been held in a trust, of which the sole beneficiary is Mr Alistair Carstairs. Lord Redmire was very keen that the old tradition of entailment was continued so that the estate remained whole.'

Sidgwick paused at this point and looked rather apprehensively at his audience. 'Lord Redmire intended to make financial provision for his daughter, Miss Poppy Carstairs, and for others named in the will from his personal estate, including a sum for Mr James Forsyth.

However, I have to inform you that, having been contacted by Lord Redmire's accountants, it is clear that debts had been accrued, resulting in significant financial claims on his estate, which will need to be settled prior to it being divided.'

'How much?' asked Alistair. Poppy had turned white. A number of people shook their heads.

'I cannot say at the moment. As executor, I am placing a notice for creditors. Miss Carstairs is to inherit the whole of Lord Redmire's personal financial assets, but it is from these that the creditors will have to be paid in the first instance. If this is not sufficient, other assets may have to be sold.'

'Such as what?' asked Alistair.

'Maybe some of Lord Redmire's possessions, which I'm coming to in a moment, but I think it unwise to speculate too much and I don't want to be alarmist. From my discussions with the accountants, I think it unlikely that it will come to that; but, as you were all aware, Lord Redmire was fond of, er, what is often called the, er, gaming table, and I'm afraid there was a cost.'

Poppy burst into tears and ran out of the room. Sidgwick continued with a list of items that Redmire had left to individuals: cars, one or two paintings, riding equipment, guns, bits and pieces of jewellery. Uncharacteristically, he seemed to have remembered almost everybody, as if, when considering his own demise, he was suddenly moved by a spirit of generosity.

When Sidgwick had finished, he bundled his papers back into his briefcase and left in his BMW. The meeting in the drawing room broke up. Mary Carstairs and Antonia Ramsay were left in conversation.

'It's a bit hard on Poppy, isn't it?' observed Mary sympathetically.

'I suppose so. I always expected something like this to happen. Given time, I think Freddy would have gambled all his money away. At least Alistair was partially protected from that.'

'It doesn't seem fair, does it? All the estate and the house goes to one sibling and the other gets whatever crumbs are left.'

'Well, I'm in two minds about it. On the one hand you're right: it's all part of these wretched aristocratic traditions to treat the next generation so unfairly. On the other, it's no bad idea for Poppy to have to earn a living. I can't see how it's good for young people to inherit piles of money so that they've no incentive to work for anything. At least for Alistair the wealth is all tied up in the house and grounds and he has the responsibility to maintain it. If Poppy were handed a lot of money she'd probably just spend it.'

'Me too!' laughed Mary. 'But I see what you mean.'

'Do you think Dominic was expecting anything?'

'I shouldn't imagine so, darling, given how they got on. Although I'm sure he'd have welcomed a little windfall to help him with the business.'

'Yes. I wonder why he left that money to James? Maybe he did have a conscience about leaving him in the lurch.'

'Perhaps. I think he expected the rest of us all to be happy with the little bits and pieces he's left and grateful that he remembered us at all. Come on, let's get a drink; we deserve it after that.'

Steph Johnson had found nothing of significance in Redmire's desk in the small office he shared with Andrea Jenkinson. But Oldroyd had higher hopes about what there might be in the private study, which was adjacent to Redmire's bedroom and connected by an internal door.

The study was quite small and so similar in size and layout to the locked room that Oldroyd wondered if Vivian Carstairs had used it as the model. Bookshelves above an expensive mahogany writing desk contained expensive hardback volumes on country sports, horse racing and a history of famous poker players. The desk itself was highly

polished but virtually empty apart from a curiously designed, lascivi-
ous pen holder in which the pen was held in the cleavage between a
pair of female breasts. A wastepaper bin was empty. The whole effect
of the room was ornamental; it was clear that literary concerns had not
interested Lord Redmire.

As expected, the drawers were locked, but Oldroyd was armed with
a set of keys that had been found in the pocket of the jacket Redmire
was wearing on the night of the murder. As he began his methodical
examination, Oldroyd reflected that he found Redmire a very unpleasant victim with whom it was difficult to empathise. Everything Oldroyd
had discovered about the man suggested an unsavoury character: a
lazy, arrogant, gambling waster and philanderer. Maybe there would
be something among his private things that would render him a little
more attractive.

Oldroyd always found it a poignant experience to go through a
murder victim's private possessions and find the little personal things:
a birthday card, a train ticket, an old passport, a still-wrapped sweet, a
supermarket receipt. The sad, ordinary reminders of a life being lived in
ignorance of the fact that it was about to be cut short. Oldroyd could
never comprehend how quickly a person could go from vibrancy and
animation to the inert state of a carcass. It depressed him if he thought
about it too much.

He tried to divert himself with a bit of lugubrious humour, attempting to apply one of his famous acronyms to Lord Redmire's strange
demise. None of his existing ones seemed appropriate so he invented a
new one: POM, which stood for 'Planned Own Murder'.

It was clear from the little Oldroyd found that Redmire had been
an unsentimental man and not a hoarder of any kind. The drawers contained writing paper, a collection of expensive pens, some geometrical
instruments he'd probably had since boyhood and unopened packs of
playing cards. As expected, there was no sign of any of the papers that
Richard Wilkins said had been in the estate office safe, confirming that

it was unlikely that Redmire himself had removed them. There was only one drawer in which the contents conveyed anything of the human heart.

In a small compartment near the bottom Oldroyd found a letter and a brown envelope that contained photographs. The letter was hand-written and was really not much more than a note. The address was a flat in Paddington, London. There was no date but from the contents it must have been written around Christmastime, and the faded appearance suggested some years ago.

> Dear Freddy,
> I hope this finds you well and you like the picture. Don't they grow up fast? Things have been very hard recently, as work has been hard to come by. I wonder if you could see your way to giving us a bit of help in the New Year?
>> Anyway, Merry Christmas,
>> Jane

It certainly seemed that he'd found something relating to a part of Redmire's past that he'd kept secret, but there were very few clues as to who this person was. He turned to the photographs and spread them out on the desk. It was clear that they ranged over a long period of time. There were some faded black-and-white shots of solemn-looking Victorian aristocrats, presumably Redmire's ancestors, and some early colour prints of the man himself as a boy with Dominic and his parents, posing together on a lawn with the Hall in the background. Oldroyd sorted through pictures of Poppy and Alistair as babies, along with various people who were clearly relatives, until he came to one that seemed different.

This picture showed an attractive young woman holding a tod-dler in her arms. Both were smiling into the camera. On the back was written in pencil 'Merry Christmas from us both' and two crosses. This could well be the author of the letter.

And then Oldroyd came to another; it was a small school photograph of a child of about seven, clearly the same one but a few years older. There was nothing written on the back. Oldroyd sat down deep in thought. These seemed like fragments of a story, seemingly one of abandonment. Even the cruel heart of the deserter had been affected, as he'd kept these mementoes. Oldroyd looked again at the second photograph. It somehow stirred a recognition in him, but of what? As yet, that eluded him.

It was not the most opportune moment for Steph and Jeffries to interview Poppy Carstairs for the second time, but they had their instructions from Oldroyd. They waited until the family came out of the room where the will had been read and then went to find her. In the corridor they ran into Tristram Benington.

'Mr Benington. Do you know where Miss Carstairs is, please? We need to ask her some questions on the matter I mentioned to you earlier.'

Benington looked at her with contempt. He still felt angry about their confrontation.

'She's just had a very unpleasant experience in there listening to the will, apparently, so I don't think it's appropriate for you to be asking her questions at this moment.'

'I'm sure Miss Carstairs is tougher than you think, sir.'

An exasperated Benington saw that Steph was not going to back down, so he decided that he'd better cooperate so as not to make it more difficult for Poppy.

'There's a place she used to go to when she lived here. She's there now and wants to be left alone. She won't welcome you intruding, but follow me.'

He took them outside and along a maze of paths that led through the various sections of the gardens where Oldroyd had walked earlier: rhododendrons and azaleas, fuchsias, Victorian fernery and rockery. They eventually reached the white garden, which at that moment was full of white roses, white buddleia and white agapanthus, the latter growing in large terracotta pots. Tucked away round a corner, almost concealed from view, was a small summerhouse. Benington walked up to the door.

'Poppy, darling, the police are here and want to ask you a few questions.'

'Shit, Tristram, tell them to go away; I can't talk to them now. I want to be by myself for a bit.'

'Poppy, I don't think that's wise. Just talk to them and get it over with.'

'Oh, fuck it!' came the cry, and the door crashed open. 'What the hell do you want?' She looked very dishevelled compared to her normal appearance, and had obviously been crying.

'I'm sorry, Miss Carstairs; I understand things haven't been pleasant.'

'You can say that again. It sounds as if my bloody father has gambled away half my inheritance.'

'Poppy, don't!' urged Benington. 'Look, I'll leave you with them. Come back up to the house straight away afterwards; don't stay here by yourself.'

She gave him a filthy look and then turned to Steph and Jeffries. 'Come in.'

The detectives went into the summerhouse, which was just big enough for them all. There were three chairs and they all sat down.

'Mr Benington's right. It's better if we proceed as quickly as we can and then the investigation will be over sooner.'

'OK.'

'So,' began Steph, 'we have a report that you were seen arguing with your father on the night of the murder, not long before he was killed.'

'Who told you that?'

'That's not relevant. Is it true?'

'Yes, and I wish I'd given him more shit now that I realise how bad his behaviour was. I mean, he wasn't thinking of me, his own daughter, when he was losing all that money, was he?'

No, he was thinking about himself, very much like you do, thought Steph. 'So what happened?'

'He refused to see any of us before the dinner that evening, so I sneaked out and tried to find him. I know the Hall and estate well and the ways you can get around without being seen. I found him coming into one of the back entrances. I don't know where he'd been.

'Anyway, I'd been telling Tris that I would ask Daddy to help him pay off his debts – just a loan while he earned the money. Tris could earn a lot of money if he got off his arse more and it would be a good incentive to get him to work. Daddy would have accepted instalments for the repayment. But no chance: he flatly refused me, said I wasn't going to get any more out of him. At the time I thought it was incredibly mean; now I realise he probably didn't have the money because of his own gambling debts. How ironic is that? Not only does he introduce me to someone who's a gambler like himself, but then his own gambling ruins his daughter's prospects!'

'How long had you been angry with him? Has he refused you money before?'

'Sometimes, but he's always given me plenty of, you know, spending money.'

I'll bet he has, thought Steph. 'So were you angry enough to want to harm him?' she asked, moving abruptly to the point.

Poppy looked pityingly at her. 'I feel sorry for you, having to go round making terrible accusations against people like that. No, I didn't kill my own father because he wouldn't give me enough money.'

'What did Mr Benington think about your father's refusal?'

'Tris didn't expect anything; he always said that it was some kind of code at the club that you had to pay off your own debts. He didn't want me to ask Daddy for money.'

'Did you notice anything unusual about your father when you saw him? Did he look worried or anything?'

Poppy thought about this for a moment. 'No. He looked like he always did: self-confident and suave. I might have been the last person to see him privately and it was the last time I saw him by myself. I wish we hadn't argued.' She looked away from the detectives, and Steph knew that she was crying.

'That's fine, Miss Carstairs, thank you. And I think Mr Benington was right: don't stay here by yourself.'

Poppy managed a wan smile, but she remained in the summerhouse as the two detectives returned to the house.

Late in the afternoon, the detectives were looking at their copy of the will in their office at the Hall.

'Nothing very surprising,' remarked Oldroyd. 'Except that legacy for James Forsyth. That puts him in the frame again, as he stands to gain from Redmire's death, though the amount's not massive. They won't like the erosion of Redmire's legacy through having to pay off the debts. The solicitor told me they're quite substantial.'

'It's Poppy Carstairs who stands to lose the most, isn't it? Everybody else just gets bits and pieces,' replied Steph.

'Yes.' Oldroyd looked at her with his head on one side. 'You don't sound very sorry; don't like the little rich girl, do we?' His teasing rather overlooked the fact that his own attitude to these rich aristocrats was very similar to hers.

'I can't deny it. Poor thing will have to continue to work for a living – won't do her any harm. How old is she? Twenty-three?'

'Something like that.' He looked at the will again. 'Not much help to us in terms of providing motives.'

'Maybe Poppy got him bumped off before he could lose any more of her legacy playing poker. She admitted that she rowed with her father just before he was murdered. She did seem genuinely upset about his death, though.'

'Dissembling is an important skill for criminals in a premeditated murder,' continued Oldroyd, 'and not as unlikely as you might think. Or it could have been Benington, who stood to benefit from anything Poppy inherited and had debts of his own to pay. He was in a good position to see the way things were going. Maybe he knew that Redmire was losing it at poker: losing his touch and losing his money.

'There will be other people, like Dominic Carstairs and maybe James Forsyth, who may have hoped for more, but how murdering Redmire would have helped their cause is difficult to see.' Oldroyd tossed the will aside. 'No, the documents we really need to find are the ones containing Redmire's estate plans. Someone stole those for a reason. I've got Jeffries on the job of tracking the firm of property developers that Redmire used and he should be here soon. While we're waiting, what do you think of this?'

He showed her the photographs he'd got from Redmire's desk, along with the letter.

'Who is this woman, sir? Do you think she's the author of the letter? It sounds like Redmire had a mistress somewhere, and a child.'

'I'm sure he had plenty of mistresses and maybe children too. I've no idea who she is and I don't know how relevant it is to the case, but we need to track her down and find out. Ah, here's Jeffries.'

The young detective, with his ever-bright face, entered the room.

'Well, any luck?'

'Yes, sir, I've cracked it. It's a firm called Ripon Developments. Luckily it was only the third one I tried. I spoke to one of the partners; they were very cagey about telling me anything, said it was all confidential and I would have to go to the office with a warrant, but they did confirm that Lord Redmire had discussed and agreed a development plan for Redmire Hall with them. They said he was very keen that everything remained a secret.'

'I'll bet he was,' said Oldroyd. 'I've got an idea that he may well have been going to unveil his plans to the family while they were all gathered together for the performance. It's always struck me as strange that he would make such an effort to get them all to come just for the trick. He didn't really need them for that but it was a good excuse to get them here. Right.' He got up purposefully. 'We need to get over to Ripon.'

In the part of the house that was normally open to the public, Alistair Carstairs was discussing the future with Celia Anscomb. He was still finding it difficult to register that he was now Lord Redmire and that all these wonderful buildings, grounds and works of art belonged to him. It was a sobering responsibility, and it was now his duty to preserve it all and, in his turn, hand it on. He knew that Celia Anscomb, like many of Redmire's valued workers, was anxious about the future. He also knew that, despite offering her condolences to him, she was actually pleased that his father was no longer around to run things. She was not the only one to feel this way either.

'It's just that there've been so many rumours going round about financial difficulties and we knew that Mr Frederick was . . . a bit of a . . . you know . . .'

'A gambler. It's all right, you can say it. He was; he lost a lot of money and it will have consequences.'

She looked alarmed. 'That's what I was afraid of. Will it mean that you'll be selling things off?'

'Absolutely not if I can avoid it. I'm not in the business of breaking things up. I want to keep all the art, the furniture and the other things that you look after intact as a collection.'

Her face brightened with relief. 'Oh, that's so good to hear. I couldn't bear the prospect of any of these wonderful works of art and craftsmanship being taken away from here.'

'No, well, there will be some debts to clear, but I'm sure it won't come to that.'

After further reassurances, Alistair went back to the gardener's house to get his Labrador, Lucy, and then walked with her on the path by the river. He tried to clear his mind. So many people were going to have high expectations of him: it would be his job to save Redmire from the ruin his father had inflicted. Of course, he and Katherine had been aware that these responsibilities would be coming to them, but not so soon and so suddenly. As he was reflecting on things, he heard a voice behind him.

'Hello, Alistair. I thought I might find you out here with the dog.'

His heart sank; it was Dominic. Although he had a certain respect for the way his uncle had established his own business, he'd always found him a difficult person to warm to: far too reactionary and totally lacking humour. Alistair had an idea of what Dominic might want to talk about, too.

'Do you mind if we just have a word?' Dominic was trying his best to be jovial and even smiled at his nephew. The effect was rather unnerving.

'Not at all, Uncle. What can I do for you?'

They continued along the path between the gardens and the river. On the opposite bank, anglers sat by their rods with the lines in the water. A mallard with a family of quickly growing ducklings paddled past.

'Well, first I just wanted to say congratulations on becoming the next Lord Redmire,' Dominic said.

'Thank you.'

'I think the succession has come to exactly the right person.' Alistair was finding his uncle's fawning tone very embarrassing. Dominic lowered his voice. 'I don't wish to say bad things about your father – after all, he was my brother too and a member of the family; a family must stick together – but we all know about his, er, his . . . indiscretions. With money, I'm thinking about, not the, er, the other stuff.'

'Quite.'

'Yes, well, I know that you will handle things much better, with probity and with care. You won't waste the estate's assets.'

'I shall certainly do my best, Uncle.'

'I know you will; that's exactly what I'm saying. And I know you value our family too, and if anyone was in difficulty you'd want to help them.'

'I'm sure I would.'

They'd reached the edge of the estate and turned round to head back the way they'd come.

Lucy shot off into a copse of trees in pursuit of a squirrel.

'Lucy! Come on, girl!'

The dog came bounding back, barking with excitement. Dominic struggled on with what he was trying to say. 'So what I'm saying is that things are a bit difficult for me at the moment. It's a very competitive environment we're in and I was wondering if, obviously after you've sorted everything out and it's all in order, you might see your way to giving me a little support. Just a loan, you understand. I shall pay it all back as soon as I'm able.'

Alistair tried to respond in the most judicious way he could. 'I see. Well, look, Uncle, I'll certainly bear what you've said in mind. But I'm sure you're aware, after what we've heard today, that things are going to be very tight for a while.'

'Good answer! Yes, that's exactly what I would have said. I know you can't promise anything, but I also know that the family is important to you, and the moment you—'

'Yes, Uncle. Let's leave it there for the moment, shall we?' They'd walked around the edge of the main borders and were near the gardener's house.

'Absolutely. Well, it's been good to talk to you.' He put his hand out to shake with Alistair. 'Don't get me wrong,' he said, lowering his voice again, 'but I think what's happened is going to be better for us all. Cheerio for now.'

He strode off back towards the house, leaving Alistair wondering what exactly he meant.

Alistair decided to walk through the rose garden before going home. As he crossed the little railway, he saw Ian Barden.

'Ah, Mr Alistair. I'm very pleased to see you.' He came over to the new Lord Redmire and, like Morton, almost tugged his forelock. 'It's a pleasure to see you, the new Lord Redmire, like.'

'Thank you.'

'I know it's only happened to you because of a lot of nastiness, but I want you to know that I'm working on finding the killer with the police. Well, not *with* the police, exactly, if you see what I mean, but I've got some ideas about what happened.'

'I see. And who have you been talking to about this?'

'Oh, everyone I see. I think it's important that they're warned to stay on their guard. We don't know where they could strike next.'

'Right. Well, I don't think you need to scare us all and I'm sure everyone else has told you that if you know anything you should go to the police.'

'Aye, they 'ave, but I'm just doing my bit, Mr Alistair, because, you see . . .'

'OK. Well, thank you, Ian, but I have to be off and I really do think that it would be better if you stuck to looking after and driving the train – you do it so well – and let the police get on with their work.'

'Oh, well, thank you very much for that, Mr Alistair, much appreciated. I do my best to keep the *Duchess* and *Mallard* in good working order and presentable, you know.'

'You do.'

Barden walked off grinning, seemingly having forgotten about his 'mission' for a moment. Alistair was left shaking his head.

Oldroyd contacted Ripon Developments, who had an office in Kirkgate. This ancient street led to the cathedral and always reminded Oldroyd of the many winding medieval streets in York. Oldroyd managed to park in the Market Place, and he and Steph walked across the cobblestones and past the tall obelisk.

'Someday I'm going to play a trick on Andy,' said Oldroyd with a mischievous smile. 'I'm going to bring him here for a drink in one of these pubs on the Market Place here, and then, on some pretext, I'll bring him out on to the square at nine p.m. He won't be able to believe it when the wakeman comes out in his costume and blows the horn. He'll think he's had too much beer.' Oldroyd chuckled at the prospect. 'The Ripon Hornblower. Do you know it's one of the oldest traditions in England?'

Steph smiled. Oldroyd could never resist giving you a little lecture about some aspect of Yorkshire history or culture. Some people might think him a pompous mansplainer, but it never came over like that. It was just that his enthusiasm boiled over. Besides, what he said was usually quite interesting.

'During the period of the Viking raids, after Alfred the Great had granted the city a charter in 886, the tradition started of appointing a wakeman, who would patrol at night and keep watch. The sounding of the horn signified that the watch was set and it was safe to go to sleep. They're still doing it nearly twelve hundred years later and claim not to have ever missed a night.'

'How many times is that, then, sir?'

'What?' Oldroyd appeared nonplussed by this unexpected question.

'Oh, sir, I'm really disappointed; I thought you'd know.'

'Get away with you!' cried Oldroyd, realising he was being teased.

They'd crossed the square and were heading down the beautiful old street. They saw the name Ripon Developments on a brass plate on the door of a half-timbered building.

'This is the kind of place I like to pay a visit to during my investigations, not some dreary office park on the outskirts of a town. You expect it to be Dickensian inside – the sort of place that could be the setting for a good ghost story.'

Inside, the office was surprisingly modern, with state-of-the-art workstations and contemporary décor. Oldroyd looked disappointed, as if he really had expected old clerks dressed in black and wearing spectacles to be pulling dusty volumes on to high desks from ancient shelving and scribbling away with quill pens.

'Never mind, sir,' whispered Steph. 'I'm sure you could have a ghost story with computers in it. They didn't stop with Dickens, did they?'

Oldroyd frowned at her archly. She was getting far too cheeky!

A receptionist showed them into an office, where they were met by a tall, serious-looking woman who then sat down at a desk with a portfolio in front of her. After welcoming them and introducing herself as Judith Hammond, one of the senior partners, she said, 'This is all quite irregular, Chief Inspector.'

'And this is a murder enquiry,' cut in Oldroyd quickly; he wasn't going to waste time on this confidentiality business. 'A double murder, to be precise, so I am expecting full cooperation from you. Anything less could be construed as obstructing a police investigation.'

The woman sighed. 'Very well.' She opened the portfolio. 'Lord Redmire came to us about a year ago. He was exploring the possibility of selling part of the estate to raise capital.'

Oldroyd and Steph exchanged glances. Redmire's financial difficulties must have been pretty severe.

'We discussed various options with him and he eventually decided to sell one of the estate farms to a company that builds golf courses, and other smaller areas of land to a housing contractor.'

'How advanced were these proposals?'

'Very far from completion. We had begun to put feelers out to companies that might be interested. Lord Redmire was insistent that this was done discreetly and in confidence; no adverts or anything like that. He said he would need to inform his family but he would do it in his own time.'

'I assume this would have raised a large amount of cash.'

Hammond wrinkled her nose at the use of the word 'cash', which was far too crude for this world of high-class developers.

'Yes, a great deal of capital. Of course, we understood Lord Redmire's reluctance about the whole matter. It's not the done thing for the owners of historic estates like Redmire Hall to sell off land. It usually only happens in extreme circumstances.'

And not usually because the present steward has gambled his money away, thought Oldroyd. No wonder even Redmire was embarrassed by it. And he knew he was going to have a very difficult job presenting it to the family.

'Can you show me a map indicating which parts of the estate were to be sold?'

Hammond passed a document to Oldroyd, who looked at it and then whistled.

'I see. That's very interesting. Can you photocopy this for me, please?'

'Really, Chief Inspector, is that absolutely—'

A look from Oldroyd silenced her and she took the sheet out to a photocopier.

As they were walking back to the car, Oldroyd handed the photocopy to Steph.

'That's dynamite,' was all he said.

Six

At Redmire Hall things were at last returning to normal, at least in terms of tourism. Oldroyd, in response to an urgent request from Richard Wilkins and the new Lord Redmire, Alistair Carstairs, had given permission for the Hall to reopen to the public. Certain parts remained cordoned off, to the disappointment of any visitors who had specifically come to see the 'murder room', but the grounds, gardens, café and other attractions were open.

Luckily there was pleasant weather for the reopening. A stream of cars came steadily into the estate and the gardens filled up with people ambling around, admiring the borders and comparing them favourably with their own seemingly paltry efforts. The café did a brisk business and the children's playground, complete with model steam railway and paddling pool, was a riot of laughter and enjoyment.

Richard Wilkins, out on his rounds, observed all this with satisfaction. Redmire had had a very strained atmosphere since that awful night and it was wonderful to see it back to normal. Redmire was that kind of special place that inspired affection and loyalty. The people who ran it thought of it as theirs, and in a sense it was. All the things that visitors flocked to see – the gardens, playground, café, shop – had been created and maintained by people like himself, David Morton and their predecessors. Of the owners in living memory, only Charles Carstairs had really taken a personal interest in the estate. No wonder the people who actually worked at Redmire felt a need to protect it.

Of course, Wilkins felt much more optimistic about the future now. Not only would Alistair Carstairs be a different kind of employer – much more hands-on – but he actually cared about it all too. He wouldn't fritter money away on crazy, self-indulgent whims, or lose it all at the gaming table.

Wilkins wanted to check with everyone that they were OK after the traumas of what had happened, and the enforced break. He also wanted to reassure them that they would be paid for the time off.

The one person he was hoping not to see this morning, however, was Andrea. He still fancied that they could make it up and that she would stay at Redmire. As promised, she had sent her resignation to him in writing but he hadn't yet passed it on or discussed it with Alistair Carstairs. Maybe she would change her mind if he left her alone for a while. He knew it was better not to harass her at the moment. When things had settled down he would talk to her again.

First he went to see the staff at the garden entrance and gift shop, who told him that business was brisk and coach parties were expected in the afternoon. At the café he spoke to the catering manager, who reported a few problems with food having gone past its use-by date but said that otherwise things were fine. The tables were occupied with visitors drinking coffee, and there was a delicious smell of lunches being prepared. He wandered through the children's areas and arrived at the little railway station.

Ian Barden was there in his blue overalls and cap, and the engine was steamed up ready to go. There was a queue forming at the little ticket office. Wilkins smiled as he thought about how many adults enjoyed the ride through the gardens and tunnels as much as their offspring.

Barden saw Wilkins and called him over. 'Morning, Mr Wilkins. Have you time for a quick word?'

'Aren't you busy? You've got a queue of eager customers, I see.'

'Have the police told you anything about who they suspect?' said Barden, ignoring Wilkins's comment.

'No, Ian. I don't think it works like that. They won't tell me anything.' Barden was a good mechanic, but not very bright in other ways.

'I just wondered, you know. I'm working on some ideas of my own about who killed Harry. I've seen things.'

'Have you? Well, if you know anything you should go to the police.'

'Not yet. I'm going to make sure before I accuse anybody – if I do.' He smiled in a strange way. 'It might be useful to know things about people, mightn't it?'

'I'm not sure what you mean, Ian, but you'll certainly be in trouble with the police if you withhold information from them. Anyway, I must be off.'

'OK.' Barden went over to the ticket office.

Wilkins shook his head as he walked on. Ian Barden had a reputation for being what the locals called a 'romancer'. He liked drama and the limelight; you were never sure how much to believe his stories. Wilkins continued through the gardens and again discovered Morton and his team at work, hoeing weeds in the main borders.

'Hi, David. Nice to see you here again. You probably think I don't do any work, just walk round talking to people.'

Morton laughed and leaned on his hoe. 'Well, I'll let you off as you have a desk job. I couldn't do it myself; I think everybody needs some time out in the fresh air.'

'Thanks. I take it the police have spoken to you since we met the other day?'

'Oh, yes. That chief inspector came over into the potting shed. I told him what I know, which isn't much. You know what I'm like: blunt-spoken. I made it clear that I couldn't say in all honesty that people would miss Lord Redmire as the person in charge here. Though I didn't know of anyone who'd want to kill him.'

'That's fair enough.'

'They're pretty sure poor Harry knew about that bloody trick thing and somehow he got involved and that's why he was got rid of.'

'Yes.'

'Anyway, let them get on with it, I say, and we'll get on with running this place. Things are going to be so much better with Mr Alistair.'

'I couldn't agree more. By the way, did you know Ian Barden has joined the police investigations?'

'Has he? You don't surprise me.'

'Says he has his theory about who the killer might be.'

'Well, if I were the police I wouldn't be worried that he might solve it before they do. In fact, if they listen to him, they'll get right off the track.'

The two men laughed and Wilkins continued on his rounds.

Morton returned to his work, pausing occasionally to take in the magnificent sweep of the borders, with their roses and clumps of large perennials. There was no point working to maintain these wonderful gardens if you never took time to enjoy them. He had never been an artist, but he always thought of the gardens as his painting. It was a canvas that changed continuously through the seasons as various plants in different colour combinations bloomed and then faded. Or it was like a play, where different flowers took their moment on the stage before departing and being replaced by others. Whichever way he thought about it, these gardens played a central role in his life and he was proud to be the person entrusted with the job of maintaining them.

❧

Later that day, since Oldroyd had no evidence against any of the family and friends who had been detained at the Hall, he reluctantly agreed to allow them to leave.

Douglas and Antonia Ramsay were driving back to their converted farmhouse in the lower part of Wensleydale. Douglas was his usual jovial self, but Antonia was still quietly furious with her former husband.

'I think we'll just call in to the Bedale shop, darling,' said Douglas. 'I need to have a word with Stephen about that new sofa range he's planning to stock. They sound a bit on the pricey side, even for our customers.' Ramsay's was known all over this prosperous 'county' part of Yorkshire for its luxury sofas.

'Fine,' muttered Antonia, and sighed.

Douglas glanced at her as the car glided along the country roads past herds of grazing cattle mingled with fields of ripening crops. 'Try not to let it get you down, darling. I'm sure she'll be fine. I don't think Tris is a bad character at heart, if he can master this poker-playing business.'

'But can't you see how I feel about that after the years with Freddy and his gambling? And now we've found out just how much he squandered of his children's future.'

'I know, but Alistair's OK.'

'I don't know. It's a big responsibility, running a place like that, and Freddy left him no capital. They'll make nothing out of it for themselves; it'll all have to be reinvested. Nothing for Caroline and Emily. They'll be living in that big house in genteel poverty. Alistair's too proud to work up debts; he'd rather live frugally. I can't bear to think about it.'

'Well, darling, I don't think we can really talk about poverty, can we? I mean, none of us are really badly off. I can't see Alistair and Katherine actually suffering much at Redmire Hall and, to be honest, I think it's a good thing that Poppy and Tris have to work for a living. She was far too much of a Daddy's girl.'

'Douglas!'

'She was, darling, and you know it. Even Freddy's hard heart melted, I'll bet, when she asked him for cash, though I think in the latter years he didn't have much to give her.'

They arrived in Bedale and drove up the beautiful and spacious main street with its market cross and handsome three-storey buildings. At the top, near the church, Douglas pulled in to a parking space opposite a large shopfront with big display windows full of sofas and dining-room tables.

'Well, maybe you're right,' conceded Antonia. 'But I can never forgive that man for this. Gambling away his children's – our children's – futures. Somehow it's worse than all his infidelities.' She turned to Douglas with a strange expression on her face. 'I think it was a good thing he was stopped before he could do any more damage.'

Poppy and Tristram were heading down the M1 back to London. Tristram was driving and Poppy had been silent for some time. He tried to put some music on, but she said she wasn't in the mood; she sat with her legs and arms crossed and her head resting on the passenger window.

'Oh God!' she said suddenly. 'How could he do this to me?'

'Come on, Pops; it's not that bad a deal.'

'Tris! How can you say that? And don't call me Pops! You make me sound like an old grandfather.'

'It could have been a lot worse. Think what another few years of his gambling would have done to your nice legacy.'

'Tris! That's my father you're talking about!'

He laughed rather cruelly. 'Well, to be honest, you don't seem that upset about him dying – more about not inheriting as much as you'd hoped for.'

'That's not true! Of course I'm sad about Daddy.' As if to emphasise her feelings, she started to cry gently. 'But he was selfish; he wasn't thinking about me when he was losing all that money. What if I don't get anything? That solicitor said Daddy's assets might not be enough to pay the debts.'

'He was only considering the worst-case scenario, and he said it was unlikely, so I wouldn't worry about that. No, your father wasn't thinking about anyone except himself. I'm afraid that's what gambling does to you.'

'Well, you should know,' she said, turning away from him in a sulky manner, 'and you also know what I've told you about it.'

'You haven't done that badly anyway,' Tristram said, ignoring her last comment. 'We'll be able to buy a flat somewhere with that money and you'll be able to help me make a fresh start.'

She darted a glance at him.

'And what do you mean by that? If it's what I think, you can forget it. You can pay off your debts by saving up your own money. And who is this "we" who can buy a flat? You mean "you", don't you? It's my money and it'll be my flat.'

Tristram was not surprised by this response. He was well aware of a hardness beneath her surface frivolity, especially where money was concerned.

'Come on, darling; share and share alike.'

'Huh! What have you got to share with me? Don't you mind being a kept man?'

'Not when the keeper is so attractive. It's actually quite erotic. There I am, a kind of sex slave kept for your pleasure.'

'Yes, and you're not much good for anything else, are you?'

'Hey, that's not true! I earn more than you do.'

'When you can be bothered to work at all.'

He ignored her again. 'Anyway, you should also be grateful to your poor father for bringing us together. If it hadn't been for him, we would never have met.'

He found her silence following this remark quite unsettling.

$\sim$

Dominic and Mary had decided not to return home until the following day, but they didn't want to stay any longer at Redmire. Instead they checked in for a night at an inn with a highly regarded restaurant in one of their favourite villages near Ripon. It was an old coaching inn and Dominic swung the Merc through the rather narrow gateway that led to the car park at the rear, next to the converted stable block. They'd said virtually nothing to each other on the short journey from Redmire, after Mary had stated with intense relief as they got into the car: 'Thank goodness we can get away at last.'

They were both tired after the ordeal at Redmire, so went down to dinner early. As they sat in the bar, consulting menus and drinking G&Ts, Dominic was unusually subdued and Mary was wary of what he might be thinking.

'Well, what a relief to get away! I do love this place,' she said, looking round and admiring the low wooden beams and the collections of local paraphernalia, such as horse brasses and Victorian photographs, adorning the walls.

'Yes,' replied Dominic, as if he hadn't really been listening to what she had said. 'I think I'm going to have the duck pâté, followed by the rack of lamb. How about you?'

'I'm not sure yet, darling. What did I have last time, can you remember?'

'I think you had the Portuguese salted cod for a main and maybe the prawn and avocado for starter.'

'What a memory! You never forget things to do with food, do you?' She was trying to lighten the lugubrious mood but without success. 'I'll have the wild mushroom soup and the coq au vin.'

'OK. We'll have a bottle of the Chablis for starters, then I'll move on to a burgundy.'

He signalled to a waiter, who came to take their order. After the menus had been removed, they sat in silence, Dominic sipping moodily at his gin.

'Are you all right, darling?' asked Mary.

'As well as I can be after all that ridiculous carry-on. I'm still thinking of reporting that chief inspector. A typical jumped-up official throwing his weight about and definitely a damned socialist, if not a communist.'

'I wouldn't bother, darling. Let him get on with the job of finding "whodunit", as it were.'

'I don't like his insistence that it could be one of us.'

'Well, I know, but look at it from his point of view; he has to consider everything.'

Dominic looked at her sharply. 'You don't believe it *is* one of us, do you?'

'Of course not, not really, but when the whole thing's such a puzzle you don't know what to think.'

'That's the whole point: he's done it all deliberately to make us doubt ourselves.'

The waiter announced that their table was ready and they followed him into the dining room. This also had low beams, with polished wood panelling and a deep-red carpet. Large dark-oak sideboards that looked Jacobean lined one side of the room. Lighting was very subdued and there were candles on the tables. As it was quite early there was only one other couple in the room. The waiter opened the bottle of Chablis and poured a little for Dominic to try.

'Good, but take it away and chill it a little more.'

The waiter obliged.

After a little while the soup and the pâté were brought in. Mary ate her soup daintily. 'I must say, this is excellent; you can always tell the difference between supermarket mushroom soup and the real thing.'

Dominic spread butter liberally on a piece of bread and then added a second layer of the thick pâté. The wine returned, this time to his satisfaction. He quickly drank half a glass while devouring the bread and pâté in two mouthfuls.

'What a scoundrel my brother was,' he observed as he prepared his second piece of bread. 'Not only did he never have to work for a living but he threatened to bankrupt himself and the estate with gambling debts.'

'Irresponsible.'

'Irresponsible! It was worse than that: the man was a complete disgrace. It's people like him who give our class a bad name.'

Mary kept her composure during this rant. It made her more intent than ever on keeping certain facts secret from her husband.

'Well, I suppose things will improve with my nephew in charge, but there'll be a whopping scandal when the press get hold of it. Think what that socialist rag the *Guardian* could do with a story like this – and what's more, they'd be right! They've loved all this "gambling in exclusive London clubs" business since Lord Lucan. Now there was another rogue who let the side down. It could have a bad impact on the estate.'

'Oh, I don't know. You know what they say: "There's no such thing as bad publicity." I think they'll all come flocking after everything that's happened.'

The waiter cleared away the starter plates. Dominic grunted. 'You're probably right. There's nothing Joe Public likes better than gawping at other people's misfortunes.'

The main courses arrived, along with Dominic's bottle of burgundy, which he tested to his satisfaction. He attacked his rack of lamb with gusto.

'I got nothing, of course, but I didn't expect Freddy to leave me anything. He always seemed to assume I was well off without realising it all has to be worked for. Times have been difficult recently,' he continued, taking another drink from his glass of expensive wine, 'and that detective was right: I could have done with a little support for the business. Freddy always refused but maybe Alistair will be more sympathetic when he's sorted everything out. I had a word with him. He's a man who has the well-being of the estate and the family at heart.'

'You had a word about what?'

'Well, you know, I let it be known that a little help wouldn't go amiss if he could see his way at some point and so on.'

A thought struck Mary. She hadn't realised how Dominic's prospects might improve with Freddy out of the way. Just how desperate was he for money? He would never talk about his business affairs with her.

'Not like Poppy – just like her father, that one. Mark my words, she'll work her way through that legacy in no time, or that boyfriend of hers will gamble it away if she lets him.' He shook his head and took another drink of wine. 'What I could have done with that money! I'm proud that our two are so sensible and hardworking.' Their children, Edward and Philippa, were established in steady professional jobs as a solicitor and an optician respectively.

'Sensible' is your hallmark, thought Mary. No wonder I often feel so frustrated.

Good though it was, she left some of her coq au vin, while Dominic cleared his plate completely. The waiter brought the dessert menus. Mary ordered coffee; Dominic opted for the Yorkshire cheese selection and some port.

Mary sipped her coffee and watched as Dominic loaded his plate with mature Wensleydale, Skipton Cheddar and blue Swaledale. Maybe a heart attack would finish him off in a few years' time, she found herself thinking, as he bored on about who was pulling his or her weight in the company, and who he needed to get rid of.

It wasn't until he was drinking his own coffee and finishing off the port that he returned to recent events. 'I don't know what my mother's making of it all. As far as I'm concerned she's been shown the truth about Freddy, unpalatable as it was. She refused to talk about it when I went to say goodbye, but I have to say she looked grim.'

'I think she knew what he was like. It must be awful knowledge to live with: that your son is, well, a character.'

He looked at her curiously. 'That's a rather positive way of putting it. I've never been sure what you really thought about my brother. I know all you women found him very dashing.'

'Yes, I suppose we did, but we also knew what he was like.'

'Yes, well, we've all seen it now, if we didn't already know. I wouldn't be surprised if there wasn't more to come. That detective will uncover as much dirt as he can on our family and . . .'

She let him go on and relaxed as the moment passed. It was uncomfortable for her to talk about Freddy. She didn't want to arouse any suspicions in her husband.

The MG motored smoothly down the A1. The hood was open and the occupants cut rather less glamorous figures than they had when they'd arrived at the Hall on that night, which seemed so long ago now, when Redmire had been murdered. James Forsyth was tense at the wheel of the car, and Alex Davis seemed to have lost a great deal of her style and energy. She sat with her head slumped against the window. They were driving to Cambridgeshire to stay with a business friend of James's.

'Do you think he thinks we did it? You know, that chief inspector chap,' murmured Alex.

James looked ahead at the dull road, which passed through the flat fields of eastern England. 'I think he still suspects everyone. I don't sense he thinks he's anywhere near the answer yet.'

'No.' Alex paused for a few moments. 'Were you expecting that money in the will?'

'Yes.'

She turned to face him in surprise. 'Why? You didn't think Freddy was guilt-ridden about his behaviour over the business, did you? That's not his way.'

'No, of course not, but I knew he was going to leave me something.'

'He told you? How come?'

'Let's say I'd been applying a little pressure recently. I was hoping for more, but never mind.'

'Pressure? What on earth do you mean?'

'Nothing you need to know about, my dear, but it's paid off, hasn't it? It's not a fortune, but it will help the business along a bit. Sales haven't been brilliant recently. Mind you, it's probably a good thing he popped off now before his debts got any higher, otherwise I might not have got anything.'

'James, you're being very mysterious. I hope you haven't done anything too . . . well, extreme.'

'Nice way of putting it, but "ask no questions, tell no lies" is the way. It's all in the past now, so don't worry about it.'

Alex didn't pursue it any further. The truth was that, despite what she might say, she didn't care what kind of relationship there'd been between her present and former lovers, or what they might have done to each other. Her life had been constructed around securing men who could keep her living in the style to which she had grown accustomed. Her passion for Freddy had dimmed over time and now he'd gone. James was here, and that was all that mattered.

She dozed off for the rest of the journey and only woke up when James had drawn the car up to the security gates that protected his friend's huge house just outside a Cambridgeshire village. He spoke briefly on his phone, the gates swung open and the MG crunched up the gravel drive, which curved through thick foliage towards the house.

In the former head gardener's house, Alistair and Katherine were having a difficult time. They were trying to absorb everything that had happened and deal with the reactions of their two daughters. Eight-year-old

Caroline was sitting at the large wooden kitchen table drawing pictures, while six-year-old Emily was playing with Lego on the floor.

'Are we going to live in the big house now?' asked Caroline.

'Yes, darling, but not just yet.'

'I don't want to!' cried Emily. 'I want to stay here with Daisy and Lucy,' she said, referring to the family pets. At that moment Daisy the cat slunk past and just evaded Emily's lunge towards her.

'Daisy and Lucy will be coming with us. There's plenty of room in the big house.'

'Are you Lord Redmire now Grandpa's dead?' asked Caroline.

'Grandpa's dead, poor Grandpa's dead,' sang Emily. 'He's in his coffin like this.' She lay on the floor flat and rigid with her hands on her stomach.

'Emily! That's not very nice,' said Katherine as Caroline laughed.

'Will you have to wear a crown and a long gown thing?'

'No, that's only when there's a coronation, and I'm not a king so I wouldn't have to do it.'

'Will I be a duchess when I grow up?'

'Only if you marry a duke.'

'I'm not marrying anybody when I grow up. I hate boys,' said Emily.

'No one would marry you anyway – you're too ugly.'

'Caroline! That's not very nice,' repeated Katherine.

'Am not!' shrieked Emily.

'Shh, settle down, girls,' said their father. 'It's bedtime now.'

After some protest and threats of punishment, the girls gave in. Caroline showed Alistair the picture she had drawn, which showed him sitting on a kind of throne wearing a crown. 'Lord Alistair Redmire' was scrawled underneath.

Katherine took the girls upstairs. It was her turn to put them to bed. They had always shared the childcare responsibilities and one of their many relative frugalities was their decision not to employ a nanny. Alistair preferred it that way after his experiences at boarding schools.

Katherine returned to find Alistair deep in thought. She slumped down into a chair and sighed.

'Are they settled?' he asked her.

'I think so.'

'Well, this is the first time we've had a chance to talk today. Do you fancy a glass of wine?'

'Oh, yes please.'

Alistair got up and opened a bottle of red. It was a good-quality but not top-notch supermarket wine. He handed a glass to Katherine.

'Well, cheers, Lady Redmire!'

'Oh my God; I still can't believe it! That sounds so weird but it's actually happened!'

'Yep.'

They both sipped their wine in silence for a while, each contemplating the huge change that was about to affect their lives forever.

'It's what we've been planning for and thinking about for a long time. I'm determined we're going to make a success of it.' Alistair sounded tough and single-minded.

'How bad do you think the debts are?'

'I've no idea until I've had a session with the accountant, but I expect they'll be substantial. My father never spoke to me about money and I think it was partially because he was ashamed. It wasn't just the club; I caught him once or twice in the office on online betting sites. He was pretty addicted towards the end.'

'That's awful. Why didn't he ask for help?'

'Not my father. Too proud.'

'Do you think things will have to be sold off, like the solicitor suggested?'

'Again, difficult to tell for sure, but Sidgwick seemed confident that it wouldn't come to that. I think if things are bad, I should make a bit of a sacrifice for Poppy.'

'What do you mean?'

'Well, it's not really fair that she has to take the brunt of my father's losses. The estate I inherit was protected by the trust, so if Poppy stands to lose a lot I think I'll compensate her.'

'OK, but you know she'll blow it all in no time.'

'Everyone seems to think that about Poppy, but she's shrewder with money than you think. She may not always strive very hard to earn it, and she spends a lot on clothes and stuff, but she doesn't throw it away like Father did.'

'And how will you be able to make up her losses? We're not going to have a great deal of spare money for some time if what you say about your father is true.'

'I'll find a way. There are things owned by the estate that we don't need, like stables full of horses and the vast wine cellar. We need to sell off some of these assets and Poppy can have a share.'

'As long as the girls and I can carry on riding.'

'Don't worry. It's a matter of scaling things down, not eliminating them altogether. My father and grandfather maintained a lot of this stuff because it was expected that if you had a stately home like this you would have horses and paintings and so on. My father didn't even ride, for goodness' sake, but he had to have stables. I'm going to change all that. It's time we became more pragmatic, and less concerned with status for its own sake.'

'Bravo!' laughed Katherine and clapped.

'We've got a good team here,' continued Alistair enthusiastically, 'and I can't wait to get started on it.' He drank some wine. 'Things are already kicking off, though. I've had Uncle Dominic angling for help with his business.'

'What did you say?'

'I was non-committal; I can't see that there's any chance I'll be able to help him in the near future. I think he knows that, really. Also there are my father's plans for the estate to deal with.'

'You told the police he never discussed them with you.'

'Well, it's true – he didn't. It was all top-secret; only the property developers he consulted knew anything in detail. We'll have to wait until the police have finished their investigations before we can start to take control.'

Katherine shook her head and looked around at the spacious kitchen with its Aga cooker and comfortable sofa, all soon to be replaced by much grander accommodation. 'You know, it sounds a harsh thing to say, but maybe this was the right time for your father to go. Any longer and . . . who knows?'

Alistair took another drink of wine. The steeliness was there again. 'I agree.'

While the family and friends of the former Lord Redmire were dispersing from the Hall and attempting to digest all that had happened, Oldroyd was taking a little time out at his flat in Harrogate.

When he was not at work he liked to listen to *CD Review* on Radio 3, and the 'Building a Library' slot was his favourite. The experience also stilled his mind if he was involved in a tricky case, as he was now.

He was in his armchair drinking coffee and listening to the varied interpretations of Dvořák's 'American' String Quartet when he was interrupted by a knock on the door. He opened it and was utterly astonished to find his wife, Julia, waiting outside. For a few moments he stood looking blankly at her.

'Hello, Jim. Can I come in?' she said finally.

'Yes, yes, of course. What are you doing here?' he asked lamely.

She sat in an armchair opposite his. Her skin was tanned from her recent holiday and Oldroyd's eyes were drawn towards her shapely bare legs. As he looked at her Oldroyd felt the same confusing mixture of emotions that he'd experienced every time they'd met since their separation: regret, exasperation, attraction and, yes, love. Another feeling was hope, and he wondered why she was paying him this rare visit.

'Can I get you a drink or anything?' He turned off the radio.

'No thanks. I'm meeting Susan in a little while. I just called round to tell you something that I didn't want to say over the phone.'

He didn't like the sound of this. She looked as if what she was going to say wasn't easy. 'The thing is, Jim, I've met someone else. It's only in the early stages, but if things work out I think we should get divorced.'

It was confirmation of his worst fears. He had to fight hard to take the news with dignity.

'I see. It's Peter, isn't it? Doesn't he work at the college with you?'

'Yes. I expect Louise must have said something.'

'Just that – nothing else.'

'Well, I thought you should know. I want everything to stay amicable and I don't want to drop things on you out of the blue.'

'Good, well, I appreciate it and I . . . I hope things go well for you.' He was really struggling.

'There comes a time when we all have to move on, Jim, and stop trying to recreate the past – and I mean all of us. You, too.' There was sympathy but firmness in her voice.

'I'm sure you're right,' Oldroyd said.

'What are you doing with yourself these days? Is it still just work, work, work?'

'Well, no, I hope not. I try to get out now and again, to concerts and stuff.'

It sounded pathetic. With a shock he realised how appalling his personal life had become: a lonely man living in a flat with virtually no social life. No wonder there was no desire on her side to have him back, although he'd always made it clear that that was what he hoped for. Would he want himself back?

He tried to sip his coffee, but felt he might be sick. Julia changed the subject.

'How is she, anyway? I haven't heard from her since I got back.'

'Fine, spends most of her time in Leeds.'

'Has she said when she's intending to come back home? Most of her books are at my place; I assume she's going to do some reading before next term.'

'No, but she's got another two months yet. You worry about her too much. I'm hoping she might get some kind of job for a while so she can pay off a bit of debt.'

'Huh. Well, her record on that score's not brilliant, is it?'

'Give her a chance. You're on her back all the time; that's why you're always having rows.'

'And then she comes here because you've always been a soft touch.'

It was a conversation they'd had many times. Neither of them wanted to pursue it now.

Julia stood up. 'OK, I'm off. Tell her to give me some warning when she's coming back. I stripped the beds before I went on holiday and I haven't made hers up again yet.'

'I will. Bye for now, then.'

'Bye.'

Suddenly she was gone. He felt numb. He couldn't bring himself to turn the radio back on, and sat motionless in the chair. He'd been thrust into a new world of cruel reality, in which he now saw that all his hopes of them being reconciled had been illusory. As she'd said, it had all been about trying to regain the past. The problem was that when he steeled himself to consider his future, all he saw was a terrifying void.

He was still there several hours later when Louise came in, although by then he'd drunk a bottle of red wine. He was watching horse racing on television. She threw her bag on the sofa beside him.

'Hi, Dad!' She went into the narrow kitchen and came back with a glass of water.

Oldroyd hadn't replied to her greeting.

'What're you doing? Watching racing? That's not like you.' Then she saw the empty bottle. 'Wow! You have been hitting the bottle! Are you celebrating something?'

'Nope. Quite the opposite.'

Louise sat down where her mother had sat, across from Oldroyd. She looked at his miserable face.

'What's happened? You look awful.'

Oldroyd picked up his glass and drained it.

'Your mum's been round.'

'Here?'

'Yes. She wants a divorce.'

'What? Is that what she said?'

Oldroyd switched off the television. 'If her relationship with this bloke develops.'

'OK. And how did you react?'

Oldroyd shrugged. 'I just said, "Fine." What else could I say? Then she went. She wasn't here more than twenty minutes.'

Louise sighed. Oldroyd again had the feeling of role reversal. 'So you'll just have to accept it, won't you? Did she say anything else?'

'Just something about "It's time for us all to move on" and . . .' He couldn't continue. He was perilously close to tears.

'And is she right, Dad?'

Oldroyd sighed. 'I suppose so. Somehow I never thought it would come to this. I always thought we'd, as I told you, get back together.'

'Without really changing anything.'

He shook his head.

Louise came over and put her arm around his shoulder. 'Look, you've been in all afternoon. It's a nice day. Go out and have a long walk and I'll make some tea. Do you fancy pasta bake?'

'That'll be great. Thanks. Look, before I go, I've been sitting here thinking and going through what happened and all through the past and everything. I realise I've never really spoken to you or Robert about what it was like for you when I left. You were both still at school.'

'We managed OK. It happens a lot these days. Lots of our friends had their parents split up. You and Mum weren't bitter about it all and to be honest we probably saw as much of you after it happened as we did before, because you made an effort to keep in touch with us.'

'I know. I'm sorry it was like that. I'm a work addict, always have been. It's the kind of job that really takes you over.'

'Yes. Actually Robert and I were always very proud of you, you know, all the times you were on telly and solving cases that were in the news. It impressed our friends.' She laughed. 'But it was difficult for Mum, with you not there most of the time.'

'I know. I've made a huge mess of it all. We were once all so happy together and—'

'Go for your walk now.'

He nodded, got up and went out.

He wandered across the Stray down to the Royal Pump Room, where he caught a whiff of the sulphur well beneath the building. He continued up through the Valley Gardens, past the ornamental flower-beds, the families playing crazy golf and people playing tennis. He felt strangely detached from it all, but his mood began to improve a little as he reached the Pine Woods and headed towards Harlow Carr.

Louise was right: he needed to stop deceiving himself and think more positively about some kind of future without Julia. That was still very difficult and painful to think about but he had to make a serious start. He was just in time to catch Betty's tearoom at Harlow Carr RHS Gardens and treated himself to tea and one of their famous fat rascals before walking back. He passed several couples walking their dogs.

Later, back at his flat, he sat with Louise eating the pasta she had prepared.

'This is lovely,' he said. 'I can't say how grateful I am to you for looking after your old dad.'

'Don't be silly. And I don't like that tone of self-pity!'

'OK. I haven't asked you what you've been up to today.'

She frowned. 'I've been trying to get a summer job. They were advertising for meet-and-greet people at the Imperial Hotel, where they do those conferences, and I got an interview. So I went over there this morning and there was this grinning bloke in a suit doing the introductions – fat belly and reeked of aftershave. It was all young women being interviewed and you wouldn't believe the kind of things he was saying, like: "We'd want you to wear a blouse, a formal skirt and plenty of make-up because the male clients prefer that." I'll bet they bloody do, but you won't catch me doing it. What year are some of these people living in?'

Oldroyd laughed. 'So I take it you turned them down?'

'You bet. I didn't even stay for the interview and I told them what I thought as well. I can't believe they still expect women to play that role, showing their bodies off. Dad, are you listening?'

Oldroyd had gone into one of his reveries. 'Sorry, you've just made me think of something.' He'd suddenly realised there was someone in the Redmire Hall story they'd forgotten, and he had a hunch this person might turn out to be important.

After the weekend, Oldroyd and Steph were driving through the countryside near Ripon. It was a warm but overcast day. They crossed the River Ure, now calmer and deeper after its journey from the wilds of Abbotside Common down through Wensleydale and towards the Vale of York. Steph noticed a heron on the bank, keeping a still watch over the clear water that flowed smoothly over the green weeds beneath. They were on their way to Belthorpe Manor.

Oldroyd was enjoying the drive and making a big effort not to let what had happened the previous day affect him. He knew this interview was a long shot and probably a waste of time. What could a woman who was only a child of eight at the time remember about a fleeting event on which she wasn't really concentrating? Nevertheless, it had not proved possible to track down anyone other than Lady Redmire who had witnessed the original performance of the trick and he still felt that there might be insights to be gained from finding out more about that famous night.

He turned left on to a narrow lane with high hedges and before long saw a sign pointing to 'Belthorpe Manor Walled Garden'. The house was not open to the public. It had a reputation for being a spooky old place, with staircases to hidden rooms where people had been locked up. The old kitchen garden, however, was a local attraction, with flower borders and a shop that sold fruit in season and herbaceous plants.

Oldroyd drove down a dirt road between high beech trees to a small car park near some broken cold frames. It was a weekday, and there were no other cars. The house was nearby and they approached it through an old stable yard. There was a deep quiet everywhere.

Oldroyd pressed a weathered white button near the front door, and a bell sounded in the distance. The detectives waited and Oldroyd was about to push the bell again when suddenly the door opened and a grey-haired and red-faced woman dressed in muddy cord trousers appeared.

'Ah! You must be the detectives. Oldroyd's the name, isn't it? I'm Isobel Langley, Olivia's aunt. It's all a terrible business over there. My brother was married to Rose, Lady Redmire's sister. Olivia's in the garden with her art things. She likes to paint and draw the house and garden when she comes up here. I'll take you over. I was just coming out myself; got plenty to do this afternoon.'

'So do you do quite a bit of work in the garden yourself?' asked Oldroyd.

'Oh, yes,' she continued in the same breezy, confident tone. 'I can't keep away, though I'm nearly eighty. It keeps me going. There's always so much to do and hiring staff is so expensive these days. It's not like the gardens at Redmire, of course. They're magnificent, but they have a big staff to maintain them, and David Morton in charge. That man is so devoted to those gardens and he knows every corner of them.'

'Yes, I've met him,' said Oldroyd.

'Does your niece come here a lot?' asked Steph.

'Once or twice a year. It's nice that she's kept in contact now that her parents have gone. She wasn't that old when her mother died and I think she's always looked upon me as a second mother.'

'I explained why we're here on the phone,' said Oldroyd. 'Do you remember anything about Vivian Carstairs's trick?'

She laughed. 'No, only that it was the talk of the neighbourhood for a time. We weren't there. My husband and I weren't that well in with the Redmires. Vivian was a delightful eccentric, but Johnny, that's my husband, didn't care for him. He was a much more practical man – said Vivian wasted money on his silly ideas. This way . . .' She led them through a wooden gate in the high brick wall.

'I never warmed to Ursula – always struck me as cold and rather snooty. She seemed to enjoy making little remarks about how much bigger and more important Redmire Hall was compared to here. As if I cared! I haven't seen her for years, though it's only just down the road. To be perfectly honest . . .' She looked around and lowered her voice. '. . . we never really wanted Edward – my brother, Olivia's dad – to marry into that family. I'm sure they never thought he was good enough for Rose, though they were perfectly happy together. Anyway, look, there she is. Olivia, darling, the detectives are here!'

A stylishly dressed woman in her mid-forties, with long hair tied back, looked up from where she was sitting on a garden chair. She had an easel in front of her. She waved at Oldroyd and Steph.

'Now, you go and join her and I'll get someone to bring you some tea. I'm going to do some deadheading in the rose garden,' Isobel said before she strode off.

Olivia stood up and shook hands with Oldroyd and Steph. 'Please, have a seat,' she said in a Home Counties accent, drawing up two more chairs.

'That's brilliant!' remarked Steph, who was looking at the watercolour on the easel. It was a view of the flower borders with the orangery at the top; there was a very delicate use of colour and form.

'Oh, thank you,' said Olivia. 'I love it here. It's so peaceful after London and I always bring my painting things. I find it so relaxing.'

'I can see why you're in design,' said Oldroyd. 'You have a good eye for colour.'

'You need it in my job. Anyway, how can I help you? We're all shocked at what's happened at Redmire, though I haven't been there for years. I sort of lost contact when my parents died. You want to ask me about that trick thing when I was a girl?'

'That's right.'

'It's a long time ago. I don't understand how I can really help.'

'Anything you can remember about that night; it could help us to understand what happened when Lord Redmire was murdered.'

'Freddy Carstairs – yes, he had quite a reputation.'

'For what?'

'For gambling and womanising. He was known all over. He used to get invitations to fashion shows – through people he knew, I suppose – and he'd turn up and go backstage. The models used to say it was unwise to get into a room with him. He couldn't keep his hands to himself.'

Steph grimaced at this new bit of unsavoury information.

'I never let on that my family had a connection with him. I was too embarrassed. Well, as far as that night goes, I've been thinking about it since you called. I remember Charlotte – that's my sister – and I were very excited about it, because it meant staying up. But, like kids do, we soon got bored because there was too much talking and nothing seemed to be happening. We were sitting on chairs watching while Vivian was building it all up but we started to get restless, especially Charlotte; she was only about five. So we were allowed to get down off the chairs and play marbles at the side. My mum and Auntie Ursula kept telling us to be quiet because we were scampering after marbles that we'd shot off too hard, but we got so engrossed in the game that we almost forgot what was happening.'

A young man arrived with a tray of cups and saucers and a pot of tea. There was a plate of delicious-looking scones.

'Thank you, Anton,' said Olivia, and poured out the tea. Oldroyd helped himself to a scone, liberally applying the butter.

'So you weren't really taking any notice when the room was being examined?' he asked after a while.

'No. I'm sorry. I'm not being much help, am I? We didn't really understand what was going on. It was all too slow for us.'

'Lady Redmire said you actually looked into the room at one point,' said Steph.

'Yes, I did. I remember there was a big cry of "Ooh!" That must have been when the door was opened, and he wasn't there. At that moment, Charlotte threw a marble and it went right across and into that room, so I went over to get it. No one took much notice at first. There were people in the room trying to find a hiding place and I could see my marble by the chair. I was just about to go in and get it when Mum called out to me crossly to come away immediately, so I left it.'

'OK. So at least you got a look inside. Was there anything about it that seemed odd to you? It doesn't matter that you were only a child – sometimes children notice things that adults don't.'

Olivia sighed and seemed to be thinking hard.

'No, I can't say there was. It was just a little room with a desk, chair and bookshelf.'

'What about the people? Did you notice anything unusual about them? Did they do anything strange?'

She was struggling to recall. 'I just remember a lot of grown-ups looking under the chair and knocking the walls and stuff. Charlotte and I liked the woman who was the assistant. We thought she was really glamorous. We would have liked to have been her – though with that outfit and everything, it wasn't exactly PC.' She laughed.

'Do you remember what happened next?'

'Lord Redmire reappeared and then they did it all again, I think. You see, we weren't really concentrating; the trick wasn't aimed at children. We just concentrated on our game.'

Oldroyd could barely conceal his disappointment. As he'd suspected, they'd learned nothing. He looked at Steph, who gave him a wry smile, indicating that she was thinking the same. He decided there was no point staying any longer. They had to go back and pursue another lead. He got up, shaking the crumbs off his trousers.

'Well, many thanks for your help and for the tea; we'd better be going.'

Steph and Olivia got up too.

'I'm sorry I couldn't help you more,' Olivia said.

'Never mind,' said Steph reassuringly. 'It's been interesting to talk to you. By the way, did you get your marble back?'

Olivia accompanied the officers as they walked towards the garden gate. 'No, as a matter of fact I didn't. I forgot to tell you. I waited until they opened the door again and Lord Redmire was in there and I sneaked over again, when I thought Mum wasn't watching, to get the marble. But it wasn't there.'

Oldroyd stopped and turned to her. 'It wasn't there? Are you sure?'

'Yes. I suppose it must have rolled away somewhere in the room, but it wasn't by the chair where I'd seen it before; I managed to have a good look round the floor before Mum called me out again, but I couldn't find it anywhere. Funny, isn't it?'

Oldroyd didn't reply so Steph said, 'Yes, odd – at least you had some more.'

Oldroyd remained silent as he and Steph drove back up the dirt road. From experience Steph sensed that there was something important going on in his mind.

'What did you make of all that, then, sir?' she asked after a while.

Oldroyd was thinking that it was often the last remark – the throwaway, unexpected detail – that proved to be the most significant.

'Very interesting,' he said.

Andy Carter arrived back in Leeds later that day. It was a warm evening, so he and Steph went out for a few drinks on the roof garden of one of their favourite bars. They enjoyed the thrill of being together again and looking out over the rooftops of Leeds. From the bar they went on to a pleasant little Italian restaurant by Leeds Bridge. Italian food was their favourite, maybe because their first date had been at an Italian restaurant in Harrogate. They were both eating pizza: Steph had a vegetarian one with artichokes while Andy ploughed his way through some heavy meat-feast version with spicy sausage, which to Steph seemed more American than Italian.

'It's great to be back,' he said between mouthfuls. 'God, it's so expensive down there. I don't know how anyone survives.'

'They live in garages and rabbit hutches, don't they?' Steph loved teasing Andy about his London origins.

'It seems like it; the mortgage on even a rabbit hutch is pretty high.' They laughed and Andy sat back. 'I don't know how to explain it, but

I feel I can breathe again. There's space all around me.' He lounged expansively in the chair.

'There'll need to be if you go on eating pizzas like that,' quipped Steph. She was mildly concerned about Andy's weight.

'I know, but I can't stand ones like yours with nothing on them but different types of leaves.'

Steph drank some wine, and her eyes sparkled at him mischievously. 'You're so old-fashioned, you know. You think you haven't had a meal unless you've had meat. Over-consumption of meat is one of the big problems affecting the environment, let alone the effects on health.'

He looked a little sheepish and then grinned. 'OK, but cut the guilt lecture. I'm only just back. No one down there in the family takes any of that seriously. They go to these fried-chicken shops and McDonald's and stuff all the time.'

'It's a shame; the kids are getting into the wrong eating habits.'

'I know, but tell that to my sister; she's so under pressure with work that she hasn't got time to cook properly.'

'Her and thousands of others.'

'Yeah. Anyway, talking of work, how's it going over at Murder Manor?'

'It's fascinating – makes a change from the run-of-the-mill stuff in the suburbs. You get to see how the other half lives – but they're a pretty obnoxious bunch, to be honest, with one or two exceptions. It's a puzzler, as it usually is when you're working with the boss.'

'So Lord Moneybags, whatever his name is, got bumped off in a room while he'd disappeared and then came back dead?'

'Something like that,' laughed Steph. 'You make it sound ridiculous, but actually it was pretty spine-chilling when he reappeared with the knife in his back.'

'I'll bet. And all on telly.'

Steph finished eating a mouthful of pizza. 'Then there was the second murder: of a bloke we think knew about the mechanics of the illusion thing.'

'Silenced.'

'Looks like it. We've interviewed everyone who was there who might have a motive, but nobody's stood out. It's a hotbed of sex and money and jealousy and stuff.'

'How's the boss?'

'I'm not sure. I think he knows more than he's letting on, as usual, but it's not been easy going. It's a very well-planned crime – and also someone took a shot at him.'

'What!'

'Yeah. He was coming back over the fields from a pub in the nearby village and someone shot at him with a rifle – just missed.'

'Bloody hell! That's serious stuff. You'll all have to go carefully.'

'Yeah, I know. Anyway, he's deeply into it and I think whoever shot at him knows he's going to crack it at some point so they tried to get rid of him. His mood's been a bit up and down.'

Andy and Steph had great admiration for Oldroyd and also a concern for the unhappiness they sensed in him at times.

'He was full of it the day we went to Redmire, singing in the car and stuff, but since then he's been mixed and I don't think it's to do with the case. I'm sure he's still hankering after his wife, but she's not playing.'

Andy took a swig of his lager. 'I don't know why he doesn't just forget her; move on and find someone else.'

'Hark at Mr Romantic! He's been with her a long time and I expect he still loves her. It's not that easy. I think it's quite touching – sad, but touching.'

'Maybe, but the thing is, it's not much fun living by yourself. I don't think it suits him, and I didn't like it when I first came up here.'

'Yes, and it's probably not as easy to meet people when you get to his age; not that he's that old, but you know what I mean.'

'Yes, good job I found you in time to console me in my old age. Everyone has their uses.'

She kicked him under the table. 'Yes, you have your uses too. As I'm out at work tomorrow, and you've still got another day off, you can do some cleaning – starting with the toilet and bathroom. They've not been done for a week. I've been too busy going over to Ripon nearly every day.'

'Whoa! I've only just come back; I was going to have a lie-in.'

'What for? You've been on leave. And after that, get online and see if you can find some good holiday deals: somewhere nice and hot for later in August. It would be nice to get away, assuming we've finished on this case by then. I don't think the boss will like me going away until we have.'

'OK. I suppose it's easier than trying to solve the locked-room case, or whatever you call it.'

'The Locked-Room Mystery, as the boss says. And yes, I'm afraid it's still very mysterious, but we'll get there. Anyway, come on – it's getting late. No time for any pudding.'

Andy pulled a face, but they paid the bill and walked slowly back to their flat through the lively late-evening streets of Leeds, holding hands all the way.

Seven

While Steph and Andy were enjoying being together again, Ian Barden was feeling pleased with the way his own unofficial investigations were going. It was starting to look as if he could make money out of someone, and also the police would be pleased when he finally told them what he knew. He would be a hero. It was all clear in his mind and it made him feel excited.

The estate had been shut for several hours, but he was still at work in his engine shed as the light faded behind the magnificent copper beeches that towered over the gardens. He often stayed behind doing extra work to maintain his beloved locomotives.

The *Duchess* was still steamed up after a full day taking excited children and their parents around the gardens. He was polishing the green cab of *Mallard*, a model of the famous A4 Gresley Pacific that still held the speed record for a steam engine. Outside it was very quiet. Doves cooed in the branches and there was the distant shriek of an owl. A gentle breeze rustled the leaves. Then suddenly there was a louder noise: it sounded like the branch of a tree falling. Barden stopped work and went outside to investigate.

'Hello?' he called, looking out of the door. But there was no answer.

A large branch was lying across the track out of the shed and he went to move it, looking up curiously to see where it could have come from. He was not to know that the branch had been thrown there – by someone who now scuttled silently out from behind a copper beech and hit him over the head. He slumped forward and the branch hit him again. This time he lost consciousness.

When he came round, he couldn't move his arms or legs; they were fastened to something. A gag was stuffed in his mouth. It was one of his oily rags. He opened his eyes to see that his limbs were roped to a stone pillar that supported the little railway bridge above a large pond and stream. Part of the line had been removed and his head was jammed in this gap just above the track. He heard a noise. It was the tooting of an engine.

An engine was coming down the line towards him!

He struggled against the ropes, without success. Then he saw a flash of red as the *Duchess of Hamilton* turned a corner and came down the track towards him. The pistons that he had so recently greased were pummelling away at high speed; someone had jammed the throttle lever on full. The scale model of the Coronation Class careered along, steam and smoke streaming from the funnel and valves. Barden had a final close-up view of the lovely red curved streamlining before it hit him in the face. The engine was very small compared to the full-size version, but it was heavy enough and travelling at sufficient speed to almost decapitate its unfortunate erstwhile custodian. At the collision, the engine was hurled off the track and fell into the pond. There was a roar of steam as water, some of it reddish in colour, poured into the smoke box and extinguished the fire.

Quiet and stillness returned to the night garden. An inquisitive duck paddled around the wreckage but decided that there was nothing there of interest.

~

'Well, this is becoming the Hall of Horrors, isn't it, Jim? Are you turning it into a murder theme park or something?' Tim Groves grinned at his own sardonic comment.

'Very funny,' replied Oldroyd. The detectives were grouped together at the edge of the pond, surveying the gruesome scene. Barden's head was hanging down to the side, loosely attached to his body, which was still roped to the pillar. The red funnel of the *Duchess of Hamilton* was just visible in the now blackened and oily water of the pond. The alarm had been raised by one of David Morton's team on his way to work in the nearby rockery. Yellow-and-black tape surrounded the scene and it didn't look as if there would be any more trips on the Redmire Hall railway for some time. Oldroyd had shut the Hall and grounds again following this discovery, much to Richard Wilkins's despair.

'I hardly think you need me this time for an explanation. Nearly beheaded by a model railway engine. I've never encountered that as a murder method before. I must say, whoever's behind this certainly has some very novel ideas. I'll do the tests to make sure he wasn't bumped off beforehand and placed here for effect, but it doesn't look like it. There are lacerations to the wrists consistent with him struggling to break free from the ropes. There's also a wound to the back of the head, so my guess is he was knocked out somewhere else and then placed here for the coup de grâce.'

'The engine shed's been left open, sir,' said Jeffries, who'd arrived on the scene very early. 'There are clear signs that he was working in there and was probably disturbed. His jacket, a flask of tea, some sandwiches . . .'

'Right. And you say his name was Ian Barden?'

'Yes, sir. He ran the model railway.'

'He hasn't featured in our investigation, sir,' remarked Steph.

'No. I wonder why.'

'Chief Inspector!' It was Richard Wilkins, looking extremely harassed and out of breath as he jogged over to Oldroyd. 'Chief Inspector, one of the staff has reported seeing a black BMW near the estate last night. The person lives nearby and was walking across the fields. I don't know whether it's important.'

'Thanks for the information.'

Wilkins hovered, looking uncertain. 'The other thing is,' he said, 'I know what you said about this being a crime scene, but I was wondering if you could reconsider and allow us to at least open the house today with the café and the gift shop. Celia Anscomb, who runs the house side of things, is going demented. It's nearly opening time and there's already a queue outside. Surely that's not encroaching on anything?'

Oldroyd looked at the poor man and relented. 'OK, you can open the house and the gift shop, but not the café, I'm afraid; that's too far into the gardens and near to what happened. Maybe tomorrow.'

Wilkins looked relieved. 'Good. Fair enough; I understand. That will be a big help anyway.'

'While you're here: what do you know about the victim, Ian Barden?'

Wilkins glanced at the little bridge and looked away quickly. 'God, that's awful! Whoever would do such a thing? Poor Ian. I'm sure you already know he ran the model railway. He wasn't always an easy person to deal with. One of those people who get an idea into their head and go on about it – when he wasn't going on about steam engines, that is. Often you just wanted to get away, if you know what I mean.'

'I see. Has he been getting ideas about what's been going on here, then?'

'Yes, and that must be why he's ended up like this. Ever since the first murders he's been going round warning everybody to be careful. Ironic, isn't it? And also saying he'd seen or heard things. People were telling him to go to the police, but I take it he didn't?'

'No. What sort of things?'

'He'd never say, which made me doubt whether there was anything. Sometimes people like him say things to get attention, don't they? They want to feel important.'

'As he's become the next victim himself, maybe he did know something.'

'Yes. Actually, the last time he spoke to me he was hinting about blackmail – saying it would be good to have information about people – but I didn't take it seriously.'

'Presumably that's why he never came to us. Did he mention any names?'

'No, but if he did try to blackmail someone that would be dangerous, wouldn't it?'

'Indeed it would. Thank you for that.'

Wilkins jogged back to inform his staff that at least the house would be open for visitors.

'Well, again the family must have good alibis: presumably they're all far away from the Hall by now,' observed Steph. 'Unless one of them has sneaked back.'

'Maybe, but somehow we can never pin anything on them, can we? Which means that either there is nothing to pin on them or that at least one person among them is extremely cunning and is controlling what's happening here at the Hall from a distance.' He took a deep breath. 'OK, Tim, we're going to leave you to it. Let's go back to the office, Steph; it's time we had a case review.'

Tim said, 'Before you go, Jim, I've got some news. I've been examining the knife used in the first murder and I've found a tiny amount of material on it, which I can't identify. It might not mean anything, but I've sent it off to the lab in Leeds to get a more detailed analysis. Sorry it's taking some time, but I'll let you know as soon as I have anything.'

'OK.'

The three detectives walked back to the house, where they made coffee and assembled their papers in the incident room.

'Right,' began Oldroyd. 'So, Steph, you take charge of investigating what was going on last night – who was around on the estate; did anyone see anything; who was the last person to see Barden alive – OK?'

'Yes, sir.'

'Now, where are we up to with the rest of it?'

'As far as that locked room goes, sir,' said Jeffries, 'we've had teams of people looking outside at the walls and roof, and double-checking every part of the interior for moving panels, hiding places and everything you could think of. Nothing, I'm afraid. There doesn't seem to be any way a person could either hide in there or get out.'

'OK. I'm starting to think we need to approach the whole thing differently.'

'How, sir?'

'I'm not sure, but the assumptions we're making about that room are wrong. I'm not sure how, but I've got some ideas.'

Jeffries listened for more, but Steph knew that Oldroyd would often refuse to share his ideas until he knew his theories were correct.

'As for this latest murder, the victim may have known something or he may have just been a crank, but it confirms the ruthless nature of the people we're pursuing.'

'Do you think anyone else is in danger, sir?'

'Who knows? I don't think so, unless they know something and fail to tell us, which may have been the case with Ian Barden. Are we any further on with our list of suspects? Have we any further evidence? Is anyone starting to stand out?'

'Forsyth and Benington weren't very cooperative,' said Steph. 'I think they had some of the strongest motives in terms of money and revenge, especially as we've now discovered that they've both benefitted from the will.'

'Yes. It's strange that Redmire left that money to Forsyth. It seems out of character.'

'Also, both Benington and Poppy Carstairs were definitely seen arguing with Redmire regarding Benington's debts.'

'The person who had most to gain from Lord Redmire's death was actually his son, Alistair, wasn't it, sir?' suggested Jeffries.

'You're right. Especially as we now know from our meeting with the property consultants that Redmire was planning to sell off sections of the estate to raise cash. I think Alistair would have strongly disapproved of that, as would his mother and grandmother.'

'He claimed not to have known anything about his father's plans, didn't he?'

'He did, but we don't know if that was the truth. If he *had* found out then he may have wanted to get his father out of the way before the plans were put into action.'

'Of course,' said Steph. 'That story of the person breaking into the office to steal the plans may have been made up to conceal the fact that he and his wife took the plans themselves. They may have staged the burglary.'

'I looked at the report of that break-in at Ripon station, sir,' said Jeffries. 'It was all routine stuff: no suspicious fingerprints anywhere, including the window itself, and nothing stolen. That was the odd thing at the time. But we now know that the plans were most likely taken, but not missed until you spoke to Wilkins.'

'Exactly, so we need to go back to Alistair with what we know and see how he reacts. What about any of the others?'

'Dominic Carstairs obviously felt he had a better chance of getting some financial help from Alistair – and that's aside from his general resentment of his brother,' replied Steph. 'Also, if there was anything between his wife and Redmire and Dominic had found out, there's another motive.'

'Yes. And then there's Redmire's ex-wife and his mother: they both wanted Alistair to succeed his father as soon as possible, so there could have been some sort of alliance there, unlikely as it sounds. There's something else that came to me the other night,' continued Oldroyd. 'Someone we've forgotten about, and it might prove important. I'm going to pursue this myself and . . .'

At that moment a police constable burst into the room. 'Sir, we're tracking an armed individual out there. I think you'll want to see this.'

'Oh my God. Not another!' Antonia Ramsay gasped and put her hand up to her mouth. She was standing in the large kitchen of their house above the village of Wensley. From the window she could see the flat bottom of the dale, with sheep and cows grazing in the fields divided by drystone walls. In the distance was Castle Bolton, the medieval home of the Scropes, and beyond that the fells of Askrigg Common separating Wensleydale from Swaledale.

The majestic beauty of the view contrasted with the horrible news she had just received in a phone call from Redmire Hall. Alistair had rung to tell her about the murder of Ian Barden, though he'd spared her the gruesome details.

'Oh, the poor man!' said Antonia. 'But what did he have to do with anything? He just drove the little train, didn't he? He always seemed harmless to me.'

'No one knows, Mummy. He was going round saying he knew things about what's been going on and presumably that's what did for him. Whether or not he actually knew something's another matter.'

'For goodness' sake, take care of yourself and Katherine and the girls. Who knows who might be next? I don't like to think of you in that place. It's like a haunted house to me now.'

'Don't worry, Mummy. I still think this is all about getting rid of Father for some reason. I think whoever's behind it doesn't mind me inheriting the estate. Anyway, it'll all settle down when the police find the culprits.'

'And when's that going to be?'

'I don't know, but I think that chief inspector is a clever chap. Where's Douglas, by the way?'

'He's gone to the York shop – left early this morning.'

'Right, but he was there last night?'

'Last night? Of course he was. Why?'

'Oh, nothing; it's just that someone reported to Richard Wilkins that they'd seen a black BMW near the estate late yesterday evening. I wondered if Douglas had driven over here for something. The police will no doubt get on to it, so you'd better warn him.'

'But Alistair, you surely don't mean . . .'

'Of course not, Mummy. Look, I have to go, so I'll speak to you later. Bye.'

Antonia closed her eyes as she put her phone down. This whole thing seemed to be getting worse, expanding to engulf the whole family. She thought for a moment: no, she wouldn't even consider it. Nevertheless, she found herself going upstairs. She and Douglas had separate bedrooms at the moment because his loud snoring kept her awake. She went into his room in a panic, and was relieved to see that his bed had been slept in the previous night. She sat on the bed feeling weak. What was she thinking of? This terrible business had so completely unsettled her that she didn't know what to think anymore.

Treading very carefully, a muffled figure moved through the outer part of the Redmire Hall estate. The person appeared to have a keen sense of purpose and was carrying a rifle. They cleverly evaded all the official entrances, and instead made for the Hall while staying under cover in the woods.

Security at Redmire Hall had been increased since Oldroyd had been shot at. There were now low-key armed patrols around the grounds. While the detectives were in their case meeting, two officers had spotted someone crouched in the undergrowth at the edge of the woods, not far from the main entrance to the Hall. When they edged closer under cover and used binoculars, they could see the figure had its head covered with a hoodie and they could see a rifle. It was important not to scare the person away. DCI Oldroyd would want an arrest. They spoke on their radios to the commanding officer.

Oldroyd arrived quietly at a second surveillance point that had been quickly established on the second floor of the house. He looked through the binoculars.

'They certainly seem to mean business,' he said.

'Yes, sir,' replied the commanding officer. 'We were particularly concerned that from the position they're in they could take a shot at the entrance to the Hall, which is where your car is parked and the detective sergeant's too.'

Oldroyd looked from the woods to where he could see his car and Steph's, and then back at the armed intruder. 'I see; you're right. OK. Well, I'll leave it to you to organise a move in. Obviously try to avoid any exchange of fire. If they are after me, I want to question them. It might mean a breakthrough in this case.'

'Sir.'

The officer spoke into his radio. Oldroyd stayed in position and monitored what happened next. Slowly and quietly the armed figure was surrounded by police officers. The person had been still for a while, but just as Oldroyd was expecting the officers to move in, they raised their rifle and fired straight ahead, apparently at nothing in particular.

This triggered an immediate response. Police officers jumped up from their hiding places and aimed their pistols at the figure.

'We're armed officers; put down your weapon!'

As Oldroyd left his position and ran out of the building towards the scene, the figure stood up, glanced around and dropped the rifle. When Oldroyd arrived, the shooter was being bundled out of the woods. An officer pulled off the hoodie to reveal a very startled Scott Handley. Oldroyd didn't know whether to feel relieved or frustrated.

'OK, OK; I know this person and I think I also know what's going on. You were firing at a rabbit, weren't you, Scott?'

Scott scowled at the officers who held him. 'Yeah, I was, and I got it, too. Tell them to let me go back to collect it. What's goin' on? It's a bit heavy, in't it, for killing a rabbit?'

Oldroyd had to smile. 'I suppose so. What you don't realise is that after we spoke that night at the pub, someone took a shot at me when I was coming over the fields back to here.'

'Well, it wa'n't me!'

'No, I never said it was, but you can see we're a bit jumpy if we see someone sneaking around here with a rifle. OK?'

Scott looked sullen. Oldroyd spoke to the officer who'd pulled off the hood.

'He's a poacher; let him off with a caution. He's helped us with the case and I don't think he's any danger.' He turned to Scott. 'Look, just keep away from here. There's a murder enquiry going on. Do you want to get mixed up in that? There must be other places you can shoot rabbits.' He gestured to one of the officers, who came forward.

'Right, come with me.'

As Scott was being marched off, Steph appeared. 'Who was it, then, sir?'

'False alarm – just a poacher silly enough to trespass here at a time like this. It was the bloke who told me about the hidden car. We're all getting very nervous, unsurprisingly. Anyway, come on. I think it's time we paid another visit to Alistair Carstairs, see how he responds to the plans his father had for the estate.'

Alex and James lived in an apartment in an immaculate Georgian terrace in St John's Wood. This was within walking distance of James's sports-car showroom, which was discreetly situated at the corner of a street, with its windows and doors designed in art-deco style.

While the false alarm with Scott Handley was being played out at Redmire, Alex, stylishly dressed as ever, in three-quarter-length trousers and a white silk blouse, was about to leave the house. It was ten thirty in the morning.

'Are you going to the office, darling?' she called to James, who was in the high-ceilinged living room, which looked out upon the street.

'In a while, although I'd rather go to the cricket.'

There was a Test match about to start at nearby Lord's, where James was a member.

'I'm sure you would, but you need to keep an eye on Graham and the team, don't you? You've always made a big thing about working for your living compared to your aristocratic friends and customers, so off you go. See you later.'

The door closed, and seconds later James heard the sound of a sports car revving up and moving off sharply. Alex had gone off to meet her friends for coffee in a swanky new café that had recently opened in Knightsbridge.

Lucky for some, thought James as he stretched, yawned and tossed the *Times* he'd been reading to one side. He tried to summon up the energy to pop into work, but was seriously drawn to the cricket. He had a manager, Graham Sturridge, and a sales team working for him, so there was not a great deal for him to do. Nevertheless, having been away for a time, it would be prudent to go in and check that all was well. First, however, he needed to make a call. He pulled his phone out of his pocket and dialled a number.

'Hi, yes, it's James Forsyth . . . Yes, we're back. It's been bloody awful, I can tell you. We were holed up for days in that place . . . Yes. I got your text, but it doesn't matter now; it's all over, isn't it? . . . Goodness knows – no, of course not . . . Yes, don't worry: I got my legacy and you'll be paid. That will be the last time, I'm afraid . . . Soon, yes. Bye for now.'

He ended the call, got up, put on an Irish-linen jacket and left the house. Unfortunately he failed to notice that, when he'd pulled the phone from the pocket of his chinos, he'd also pulled out a business card, which was now lying on the chair.

Over coffee, Alex regaled her friends with her account of the gruesome events at Redmire Hall.

'Poor Freddy,' remarked one rather languidly between mouthfuls of croissant. 'And even more poor you, seeing your old amour murdered like that.'

'Nothing ever surprised me with Freddy.'

'It must have been sort of thrilling, though, being there when it was all on television,' giggled another.

'Arabella! That's not very nice,' remarked a third.

'Oh, I know what she means, but actually it wasn't; it was ghastly.' Alex closed her eyes and shook her head.

'I'm sure it was – dreadful,' observed a fourth vaguely as she stifled a yawn. 'By the way, shall we try Carabini's for lunch? Marie went there and she said it was excellent.'

Alex considered telling them about the silver lining of James's legacy but, having observed the yawn, decided against it.

'Well, you haven't missed much here. It's been a dull month; there are so many people away. The only thing that's happened is we know that Cordelia's definitely having an affair with that man from the publishing company. They were seen together in a restaurant in Kensington and she . . .'

Gossip and chatter continued for a while and the group progressed to a saunter around some exclusive boutiques, and lunch at the recommended Carabini's.

Alex returned home in the late afternoon to find James still out. She dropped her bags, made a cup of tea and went to sit down in the living room. Almost immediately she noticed the card that had dropped out of James's pocket. She picked it up, began to read it and froze.

James had made a brief visit to the office, but had then found the lure of the Test match irresistible. He stayed until close of play in an exciting encounter between England and the West Indies.

'Hi, darling!' he called breezily as he took off his jacket in the hall. There was no reply. He wondered if she was still out, but then was surprised to discover her sitting silently in an armchair in the living room.

'What are you doing in here?'

She turned a withering glance at him and held up the card.

'I'm sitting and wondering why my partner might need the services of a woman like this.'

The new Lord Redmire was occupying his father's seat in the office with Andrea Jenkinson for the first time. So far it had been another terrible day at Redmire Hall. Richard Wilkins had rung him early to tell him about Barden's murder, and mentioned the black BMW seen near the estate. Alistair was glad Wilkins had done this, as it had given him time to tell his mother before the information got to the police. How paranoid they were all becoming! There must be hundreds of black BMWs around but he knew this might throw suspicion on Douglas. Douglas, of all people! The mild-mannered man who had made his mother happy. The atmosphere was electric with tension and suspicion.

Andrea had not yet said anything about handing in her notice. The plan had been for her to brief him about his new role but the terrible news about Ian Barden had overwhelmed this task for the moment.

'Did you know him well?' asked Alistair.

'No. He was one of those people you tended to avoid, unless you wanted to know about valves and steam pistons, but he always seemed harmless.'

'Yes, I know. I spoke to him recently; he had these ideas about knowing something about my father's murder and he was going on about warning people. I told him not to scare them.'

'He said the same to me. I think he was saying the same thing to everybody, but I don't think anyone took it seriously.'

'No. I take it Richard is handling the fallout with the police. We'll have to close again, no doubt.'

'They've allowed him to open the house and the gift shop but not the gardens or café.'

'OK. Well, at least that's something. We might as well get on with what we were going to do.'

Andrea moved her chair next to his at his desk and opened some files on the computer to show him. 'Your father's day-to-day role in relation to the estate was very light-touch. He oversaw the work of Richard Wilkins and his team, but spent most of his time talking to business people, the media and other stately-home owners trying to drum up money and support. He'd agree to something like the vintage-car weekend and then hand it over to Richard to arrange the details. It was my job to look after his diary and make appointments, arrange transport, accommodation and so on.'

'He spent a lot of time in London, didn't he?'

'Increasingly so in the last year. It was often difficult for people to get to see him. We lost a few opportunities because he wasn't around.'

'Such as?'

'Well, there was a company that wanted to mount an exhibition of their camping equipment in the show area of the grounds. They were prepared to pay a good price, but your father kept putting them off and eventually they went elsewhere.'

'Damn,' said Alistair. 'Well, it won't happen again, I can assure you.'

At that moment Oldroyd and Steph arrived.

'Good afternoon, Chief Inspector, Sergeant,' said Alistair. 'Dreadful news again. I can't believe it; you'll continue to have our full cooperation.'

'Thank you,' replied Oldroyd. 'Can we have a word in private?'

Andrea left the office. Oldroyd took out his copy of the plans from the property developers and placed them on the desk.

'I'd like you to take a look at these, sir.'

Alistair looked solemnly at the documents. 'I presume these are my father's plans for the estate?'

'They are.' Oldroyd watched Alistair very carefully as he looked at the documents.

'So I take it these shaded areas are the parts he was preparing to sell off?'

'Correct.'

Alistair whistled. 'Good Lord, that would have been terrible; it would have significantly diminished Redmire. What was he thinking of? Do you know how far advanced these plans were?'

'I don't think anything had been finalised, but you're free to contact them now and discuss it. So this is the first time you've seen these proposals?'

'Yes. I told you: my father wouldn't discuss them with me. All he did was hint that there were going to be changes to the estate – although I have an idea he might have been intending to reveal things after the performance of the trick, while everyone was together. That didn't happen very often.'

'Wasn't it rather odd to keep it all to himself like that?'

'He could be very secretive and I'm not surprised he didn't tell me about these plans; he knew what I would have said. And not just me: I can't think of anyone who would have supported him over this.'

'So I suppose we could say that it's a good thing they were stopped?'

Alistair looked sharply at Oldroyd. 'Yes, Chief Inspector, I'm glad these plans were never implemented; but I think your implication is that they gave me a motive to get rid of my father, and that's not true. I repeat: I knew nothing about what his intentions were.'

'But is it true to say that any major "changes", as he put it, would have antagonised you even if you didn't know the details?'

Alistair seemed a little nonplussed. 'Well, yes, I suppose so, up to a point. I mean, I'd never have used any violence to stop him – obviously.'

'That story that you and your wife told us about the break-in at the office. Are you sure that wasn't a cover for you breaking in yourself? Because we know that your father's copy of these plans was stolen, most probably that night. Did you take them from that safe, sir? Maybe you managed to get your father's key. And when you saw what he was proposing . . .'

'Hold on, Chief Inspector! None of that is true. Katherine and I told you the truth – and I'm not the kind of person who would kill their own father, whatever he was planning for the estate.'

Oldroyd was unrelenting. 'And what about your grandmother? I imagine she would have felt the same way as you if you'd told her. Maybe she knew more than she's told us about how the trick works, and you and she planned it together, with more help.'

Alistair laughed. 'This is getting ridiculous, Chief Inspector.'

Oldroyd looked at Steph. 'Maybe, but we can't discount you, sir. After all, you had the most to gain from Lord Redmire's death.'

'I can see that, but you're wasting your time. It wasn't me.'

'Very well, we'll leave it there.'

The detectives left, and Alistair sank back exhausted into his chair. There was another knock at the door. Bloody hell! What a day! He badly needed a break. Who was this?

'Come in.'

The shabby figure of David Morton pushed his head around the door. 'Sorry to disturb you, Mr Alistair; I just wondered if I might have a word.'

'Yes, of course, David. Come right in.'

Morton shuffled uneasily into the room. In his boots and dirty trousers, he looked completely out of place in the office. He wore soil-encrusted gardening gloves.

'I just wanted to say that, well, I know these are bad times, Mr Alistair – bad times for your family – but I hope that nothing is going to happen to the estate. We're all so keen to keep everything as it is.'

Alistair couldn't stop himself smiling. It was Celia Anscomb all over again. It was quite touching to see how many people cared about the integrity and wholeness of Redmire.

'Don't worry, David. Whatever my father might have had in mind, I can assure you that the estate will not be broken up. I care deeply about this place, as I think you know.'

Morton grinned from ear to ear. 'I do, Mr Alistair, but it's still good to hear you say it. And all the precious plants will be safe. It would have been a terrible shame if there'd been any damage done.'

'It would. Now, if you don't mind, it's been a difficult day and I'm busy, so off you go to tend to your charges.'

'I will, Mr Alistair, and thank you.'

He turned round and lumbered out, leaving Alistair to reflect that it wasn't difficult to get the staff on your side if they felt you shared a common purpose with them. It gave him a lot of hope for the future.

At the flat in Chelsea, Poppy was taking a call. Her black-and-white cat, Rosie, was asleep on her lap and through the window the leaves of the plane tree in the street outside were visible. Tristram was at a photo shoot for Crazy Pants fashion house.

'No, there was no alternative. It had to be done . . . OK, keep me informed.'

She ended the call and gazed abstractedly at the window, watching the movement of the leaves for a while as she stroked Rosie. Then she called another number.

'Hi. Yeah, it's me . . . Not too bad, thanks . . . Yeah, I got it. Not as much as I'd hoped for, and I was pissed off about it to begin with, but actually it's not bad as long as my father's debts don't start eating into it . . . I'm going to start my own photography business . . . Yeah, I'm sure Tris can get me some contracts with some of the fashion houses . . . Thanks. Yeah, it's been bloody awful; I'd never go to that place again if it wasn't for Granny – and she was pretty bad too, to be honest . . . Oh, she goes on about Tris all the time; basically she doesn't like him . . . I know. What can you do? Mum's up there too, plus my darling brother and his family, no doubt revelling in their new wealth . . . No, I'm not really jealous. I couldn't stand it, hidden away in a place like that, look-ing after mouldy old furniture and paintings and trying to keep the tourists happy . . . I know, can you imagine me doing that? I'd tell the first person who complained about anything to piss off somewhere else if they didn't like it! Anyway, how are you and Jack? . . . Good. That's great; I bet that was fantastic! . . . I don't know when Tris and I'll be able to get away – the police say we've got to stay in the country until

they've solved the case. I know that means we're still all suspects . . .
Terrifying, isn't it? Yeah, anyway, we must meet up at the weekend. I'll
talk to Tris and get back to you. He's got a busy schedule now because
I gave him the hard word about work . . . Yeah, I did. I'm not keeping
him, whatever he thinks . . . Oh, he's been OK, I think, but he needs
watching and I've given him a warning about that too . . . Yeah, I did.
I'm working on it. I'll tell you all about it sometime . . . OK. Bye.' She
put the phone down.

'Now then, madam, down you go.' She lifted Rosie off her lap,
much to the cat's meowing disgust, and brushed some black hairs off
her jeans. She stood up and began to get ready to go out. She felt a
spring in her step. She was taking control and things could only get
better, as the old line went.

Later that day Oldroyd, sitting alone in the makeshift office at Redmire
and trying desperately to get some new angle on the locked-room
conundrum, was conducting some obscure research. He was exploring
the internet for information about magicians and their tricks to see if he
could find anything about an illusion similar to the locked room or anything about Count Mazarini himself. The man must have been famous
in his time, but that was back in the sixties and seventies. There would
probably be little on the internet unless things had been archived and
digitised. As Oldroyd formulated various searches, he thought about
the eccentricity of Vivian Carstairs, bringing a whole team of Italian
craftsmen over to England, presumably at great expense. However, it
had proved a success in that the trick remained unexplained. Two of the
people who knew how it worked had been murdered. The murderers
might well be the last people alive to know the secret.

His doggedness was eventually rewarded when he found an obscure
site devoted to 'Great European Magicians of the Twentieth Century'.

The home page consisted of a clunky cartoon figure of a magician in a cloak holding a glowing wand. The introduction explained: 'Here we celebrate the now vanished era of great illusionists. No longer are they mesmerising audiences; they have hung up their cloaks and magic wands . . .' The material was arranged alphabetically, so Oldroyd scrolled down to the 'M's and, yes, there was an entry for Mazarini:

> *Mazarini, Count (actual name: Roberto Mazzola), 1920–1995. Born in Turin; father and uncle were also magicians. Mazarini first performed on stage at the age of fifteen, at a Fiat car workers' social club in Turin; he came to prominence in the post-war years and toured Italy extensively with a wide repertoire of tricks and illusions. He became renowned for a locked-room illusion in which he disappeared from a small room and then reappeared, despite there being no apparent exit. This illusion was never explained or duplicated by any other illusionist and remains one of the most mysterious tricks ever performed. Mazarini would only perform the trick after extensive preparations in highly secret conditions, which gives a clue as to the complexity of the mechanisms involved. He died in Turin in 1995. He had no family.*

Interesting, but not particularly useful – although it confirmed that there was a considerable amount of engineering involved in the illusion. Why? And what did this mechanism do? Did the room come apart somehow and reveal an exit? If so it was bafflingly well concealed as no one could find a crack or a hinge anywhere. The website entry was, of course, wrong. The trick had been performed by two other people: Vivian and Frederick Carstairs. What a price Vivian must have paid for Mazarini to part with his secret and send a team to construct it in Yorkshire! It was probably because Lord Redmire was not a professional magician, and would thus not be a rival to Mazarini, that the latter consented to sell the trick to Redmire for him to entertain his friends with in private. No wonder that, even in those days, the estate had always been short of money.

Oldroyd sighed. He would get someone else to do further research and contact the Italian authorities, but he wasn't optimistic about it. Count Mazarini and Vivian and Frederick Carstairs were dead and had gone to their graves without revealing the secret; the answer wasn't going to come from them. Oldroyd and his team were going to have to work it out themselves.

He turned his attention to the other research project he'd set himself, and this proved much more fruitful. Officers at Harrogate station had been doing the legwork, but when he saw their reports he was pleased. In this case, he reflected, many things were not what they appeared to be. He reached for the file containing the letters and the photographs again and examined them very closely.

Something attracted his attention and he took up a magnifying glass he'd brought from Harrogate for this very purpose. He sat very still, looked through the glass carefully and then smiled. At last things were starting to move forward.

Mary and Dominic lived in a large, ugly, 1960s detached house in the Fulford area of York. The contrast between this residence and Redmire Hall was sharp and Dominic felt it keenly every time he returned from the ancestral home.

It was the evening after their return from Redmire. He and Mary were out on the wooden decking outside their French windows facing the garden, Dominic in a cushioned metal seat and Mary with her legs stretched out on a lounger. A bottle of wine, two glasses and a bowl of pistachios stood on a matching round metal table that supported a green sunshade. The garden consisted of a huge square of lawn edged with bedding plants and a scattering of ornamental trees and bushes. Neither Mary nor Dominic had much interest in gardening, and relied instead on the basic services of a gardening contractor.

Mary drank her wine with gusto. She knew she was drinking too much, but the boredom she was suffering was intense. For years she'd been in the role of a stay-at-home mum. Their children, Edward and Philippa, had gone to an independent day school, which they could hardly afford, but Dominic's pride and snobbery had not admitted to the possibility of them attending a state school. Now the nest was empty, as the offspring had fled to university and then to jobs in other places, and she was left with Dominic. The prospect of the dull years ahead with a grumpy, negative husband was too bleak to consider.

'How was the office, darling?' she asked through partially gritted teeth. There was no reply. 'Dominic?'

He was dozing, and woke with a jolt. 'Oh! Did you say something?'

'Yes. I asked you how it was at the office.'

'Don't talk about it.' He shook his head and fiddled with his wine glass. 'We're not getting the clients at the moment. Mind you, we're in the summer – holiday period and all that. Recruitment always slackens off a bit.'

'Will it pick up in the autumn, then?'

'I certainly hope so. We've got a few . . . a few cash-flow problems, but we'll come through.'

'I could go back to work. I'd like to.' She'd worked as a legal secretary for a large firm of solicitors in York and risen to be office manager before she'd had the children.

'There's no need for that, my dear.'

'Why not? Why do you think I'm happy just to stay here all day and follow the tedious social round of coffee mornings and meeting people for lunch?'

'Well, you could always do some voluntary work at one of the charity shops.'

'Oh, wonderful! I don't want to join the grey-haired brigade yet, thank you very much.' She looked at him defiantly. 'The problem is, you don't really want me to go out to work because I might prove to be more successful than you. You're so 1950s, aren't you? Keep the little wife at home.'

Dominic was shocked by her outspokenness. 'Don't be ridiculous. It's not that at all, I just . . .'

'Don't want to have to rely on your wife for money?'

'No, well, what's wrong with that? What man would? Anyway, it won't come to that. I'm sure Alistair will come to our aid if need be.'

'But I've been thinking about that. Surely you can't ask Alistair for money? He's got enough problems running Redmire, especially after the state Freddy's left it in. Anyway, aren't you ashamed, asking your own nephew for support?'

'Why should I be? Alistair understands the importance of family. I knew things would be better when Freddy was out of the way. Why shouldn't I have some of the family money anyway? I'll do a lot more good with it than Freddy ever did. I deserve it.'

'I see.' Mary drank her wine thoughtfully. 'You didn't feel anything for your brother, did you, except jealousy?'

Dominic frowned at her. 'What's got into you this evening? Why should I feel anything for him? He never did anything but deride and belittle me. I expect a lot of older brothers are the same, but that doesn't make it easier to bear.'

'You're actually glad he's dead.'

'So what if I am?' Dominic replied angrily. 'He was not only vile to me, but his behaviour let the family down – and our class, for that matter. Good riddance, is what I say!' He glared at her in a strangely defiant way that made her wonder again about what exactly he knew, or at least suspected.

~

On the same warm evening in Kirkby Underside, the hilltop village between Harrogate and Leeds where Oldroyd's sister, Alison, was vicar, the two of them were sitting in the sprawling but unkempt garden of the vicarage. Swifts were hurtling and shrieking around the old house. There was a wide, panoramic view over the fields of Lower Wharfedale, with Otley Chevin and Ilkley Moor rising in the distance to the west, illuminated by the slanting evening light. Further east Oldroyd could just make out Harewood Bridge over the river and the ruins of Harewood Castle at the top of Harewood Hill. It was one of those views of a sweeping landscape that made you understand why Yorkshire was known as the 'Broad Acres'.

The remains of a tennis court, greenhouses and a broken-down summerhouse were testimony to the comfortable lifestyle enjoyed by the Anglican clergy in an earlier age. Alison, recently returned from her retreat, filled up their glasses with red wine and relaxed back into her chair.

'Well, what a lovely evening, Jim! We didn't get many like this in Scotland, but never mind. Iona is one of the most spiritual places I know: those white sands and that ancient abbey church. When the sun is out, the sea is Caribbean blue and crystal-clear. You can see right across to the Cuillin Hills on Skye.'

'What was the retreat like?'

'Wonderful! Just what I needed – lots of sessions on prayer and meditation led by people from different traditions in Christianity and Buddhism. It gets deep into you and puts everything into perspective.'

'Right.' Oldroyd was rather sceptical himself. He'd never found any kind of prayer or meditation helpful, preferring music and walking on the fells.

'You would have enjoyed some of it,' said Alison, as if reading his thoughts. 'There was a woman recommending late Beethoven string quartets for their serene, unworldly quality.'

'Now you're talking.'

'Yes.' Alison looked at her brother. 'You look as if you would have benefitted, Jim. You seem tired.'

'Do you wonder?'

Oldroyd had told his sister about Julia asking about a divorce.

'No, it's not easy for you; I understand. But I can't say I'm surprised. You've not really done much since your separation to persuade Julia that anything's changed, so you can't blame her if she's started to look elsewhere. Most of us prefer to have a partner; we don't like living alone.' Alison had always had the elder sibling's authority to tell her brother off.

'I could change, given time,' said Oldroyd sulkily, sipping his wine.

'That's what you always say. How many times have we had this conversation about overworking and what it does to you? But nothing happens; you carry on in the same way. We're none of us getting any younger, Jim. Julia's thinking about her future. Why should she face old age alone if she doesn't have to?'

'What about me facing old age alone?'

'Well, that's up to you, isn't it? No one, Julia included, wants to have an absent partner. You can't neglect people and then expect them to be there when you want them.'

'She said something about moving on and not trying to recreate the past.'

'Well, perhaps she's right.'

'Louise said the same.'

'I'll bet she did. That daughter of yours has a wise head on her young shoulders.'

Oldroyd looked into the distance. As it got darker, he could see the lights of cars on the A61 in the dale bottom approaching Harewood Hill.

'Trouble is, I don't go anywhere to meet anybody. It doesn't seem the same when you're older. I thought Julia and I would always be together. Isn't that what the Church believes anyway? Marriage for life?'

'Ideally. But things are often far from ideal, aren't they? Many of us would now teach that marriages should not continue if they are truly unhappy. I'm sure you don't want to hide behind the Church's teaching anyway.'

'No. I suppose I've just got to bite the bullet, whatever that involves.'

'It'll definitely involve putting yourself before work; if you don't, it will consume you and then when you finally have to retire you'll be hollowed out and you'll have nothing.'

Oldroyd winced. It was a terrifying prospect. 'Then maybe you can help me with this locked-room case. If I can solve it more quickly, I can start to do other things. You know how I value your comments.' Oldroyd knew that Alison was always intrigued by his work, particularly its human and moral dimensions. She often made some perceptive observations.

'You mean this case at Redmire Hall?'

'Yes. Three people have been murdered now. I've got some ideas, but we've got a way to go yet.' He outlined the key points.

Alison drank her wine and thought for a while.

'There are two things that strike me,' she said at last. 'The first is the ruthlessness of the people involved: they don't hesitate to kill anyone who they think might be a threat to them. There's something strange about their psychology; it suggests they're damaged in some way. They believe that what they're doing is justified and that they have a right to get away with it. It makes me wonder whether the money motive, strong though that can be, is enough to explain things.

'The second point is the method of the first murder, which is clearly the main one. I've no idea how this illusion business might work, but what puzzles me is: why bother in the first place? Why go to all that trouble to kill someone when there must have been easier methods? Very strange.'

'You've "harped my fear aright", as Macbeth says,' replied Oldroyd. 'The third murder was particularly brutal and cruelly cynical. What kind of a mind would devise that as a method for killing someone? I told Stephanie Johnson that we need to approach it all differently. Nothing is what it appears to be on the surface.'

'Which is also a very Shakespearean theme,' remarked Alison.

They continued to drink their wine as the warm darkness fell and a few bats fluttered around. Oldroyd reflected that, however difficult this case was, it might turn out to be more easily solved than the problems of his private life.

'It's not what you think, darling. I . . .'

'Well, what am I supposed to think? "Astrid Belanov. Discreet Personal Services. Men Only." You've got the card of a bloody call girl! Are you telling me she comes to wash your socks and shirts when your partner's too busy?'

'No! Look, OK, OK . . . I wasn't going to tell you, but . . .'

'Not going to tell me what, for God's sake?'

'I don't go to her – of course I don't – but Freddy did.'

'Freddy!'

'Yes. He had a number of these women that he saw when he was in London.'

'Freddy?' she repeated, and shook her head. 'Why am I surprised? He was a bigger bastard than we all realised, wasn't he? Even those of us who thought we knew him well. But what's it got to do with you?'

James looked very sheepish. 'I was blackmailing him.'

'What?'

'I was getting money out of him to help with the business and I forced him to leave me that legacy in his will in case he suddenly popped off, which in fact he did.'

Alex got up and walked to the French windows. She opened them, walked out, lit a cigarette and looked down into the street below. Forsyth joined her, but she didn't look at him.

'Bloody hell, James. I can't believe it.'

He tried to put his arm around her but she shrank away.

'I'm sorry; I didn't want you to get involved. I didn't want that man to figure in any way in our relationship. It was just between me and him.'

She looked at him with a mixture of curiosity and distaste. 'How did you find out about it?'

'I had him followed.'

'What?'

'I suspected what was going on and I hired a private detective. When I was certain what he was up to, I went to see this woman and got her involved in my scheme. I paid her to continue seeing Freddy, report back to me each time and be prepared to testify against him. When I thought I'd got enough evidence, I confronted Freddy.'

'But so what? He's not in a relationship with anybody.'

'That didn't matter. Freddy didn't want the scandal of being the Lord Who Visited Call Girls. It wouldn't have made the national news these days, but it would have been enough to damage his social standing, especially at his clubs. He could have faced being thrown out of some of them. It wouldn't have done Redmire Hall's tourist reputation much good either: "Come to Redmire Hall, the home of sleazebag Frederick Carstairs."'

'How long has he been giving you money?'

'Just over a year – and it's come in very useful, I can tell you.' He looked at her. 'I don't feel sorry about it. He ruined our business venture and I lost a lot of money. This was payback, as far as I was concerned.'

'But blackmail, James. It's such a nasty thing.'

'That's as may be, but it's the only way you can get through to a man like Freddy. He had no conscience, as far as I could see. He didn't care who he damaged with his thoughtless career of gambling money away and womanising.'

'I see. So that money he left you was not some kind of goodwill gesture?'

'I'm afraid not.'

She took a drag on her cigarette and looked down on the street, where cars and people were moving past. At the end of the block, there was a pub with tables outside and people drinking and laughing.

'That must have put extra financial pressure on Freddy, given that he was also in debt through his gambling.'

'No doubt it did.'

'How convenient, then, that he "popped off", as you put it. It's made sure that his financial help continues.'

'It has.'

'What will the police think if this gets out?'

'We've got to keep it from them.'

'It already looks suspicious, doesn't it? That you benefitted from the will.'

'Perhaps.'

'And what am I supposed to think? Maybe it seems suspicious because it is.'

'What do you mean by that? You don't think . . .'

'Maybe Freddy wasn't the only man I didn't really know.'

'Do you feel better after talking to Auntie Alison?'

'Yes. Have you been talking to her too?'

'She called me for a chat. She's worried about you.'

'Yes, everyone seems to be.'

'That's because they care about you, Dad.'

Oldroyd and Louise were having breakfast together. She'd asked her father to call her early to make sure she got up and did some work instead of lying in bed all morning. Toast popped out of the toaster and she went over to get it.

'I always thought I could look after myself. I've always been success-ful at work and good in charge of others,' said Oldroyd glumly.

'That's the problem, though, isn't it? How many successful people have rubbish private lives? You haven't really been taking care of your-self, have you?'

'I suppose not.'

'You really need to think about where your life might go from here.' She yawned. The effort of getting up so early was already taking its toll. 'Anyway, I'd better get started.' There was a pile of weighty tomes on the table next to the marmalade. She must have called in at her mother's to get them.

'What are you doing next Michaelmas?'

'It's sixteenth and seventeenth century: good old Tudors and Stuarts. I'm looking forward to it. There were a lot of strong women around then, you know: Mary Tudor, Mary Queen of Scots, Elizabeth herself. No wonder that John Knox talked about a "monstrous regiment of women". I'll bet he was a fun guy to have around!'

'I don't think you'd have got on together. I don't think he frequented bars much, for one thing.'

'No,' she laughed. 'By the way, I've got some good news: I finally managed to get a job. It's bar work and only part-time, but it'll be fine. I really need to be doing some reading anyway and this'll give me the chance during the day. That's why I wanted you to get me up.'

'Which pub is it?'

'It's that one with the funny name in High Harrogate: The Orphan Girl.'

'Yes, it's curious, isn't it? I've often meant to research that name and . . .' Oldroyd trailed off, looking distracted.

'Dad?'

'Sorry, that just made me think of something.'

'What did? The pub? Dad, you're so funny.'

'Yes, I'm sure I am, but I'd better be off.' He drank the last of his tea and put on his jacket. 'Have a good day. Concentrate; turn your phone off – no distractions.'

'Yes, if only.'

'Well, I'll help you, then.'

He made a lunge, grabbed her phone from the table and ran to the door with it.

'You'll be better off without it.' He waved it teasingly in the air.

'Dad! No way! Bring it back!'

She pursued him, laughing, and managed to prise it out of his grasp before he shut the door behind him.

Eight

Andrea Jenkinson felt that the moment had come to tell Alistair Carstairs about her resignation. She had agonised about it for several days, but as she was on her early-morning drive to Redmire from Ripon she came to a decision. She'd spent quite a bit of time with the new Lord Redmire, bringing him up to speed on a variety of matters, and he was now able to function on his own until a new PA was appointed. She would also be there for the duration of her notice, so her conscience was clear that she wasn't letting her employer down. She didn't want to do that: she was fond of Redmire Hall and respected the new lord.

Alistair Carstairs was already there when she arrived at the office. 'Good morning, Andrea.'

'Good morning.' This was the awkward moment. 'Before we start work, I have something I want to say.'

He turned to face her. 'Yes?'

'I'm resigning; I want to leave Redmire. In fact, I've already handed in my notice to Richard, as he's my line manager. I told him not to say anything until I'd spoken to you.'

'What? Really? You don't need to worry about your job here long-term: it's absolutely secure.'

'Yes, I know; you've been very kind, but I think I've been here long enough. I need a new challenge and the fact is, I've realised that I'm not really a country person. I'm going to go back to the city.'

'I see. Do you have a job lined up?'

'No, but I've started a job search and I'm hoping to get something in Leeds so I can commute to begin with.'

'Well, this is bad news, for me at any rate. I was hoping to keep you as a continuity person; it would have been useful at a time like this.'

'I know, but I think the time is right for a change and you can start afresh with a new PA. I'm probably too used to the old ways of doing things. I'll be forever saying to you, "Oh, we used to do it this way" and so on.' She laughed to try to lighten the mood.

'Well, you may be right, but I don't think it would have been a problem for me. Are you sure I can't get you to change your mind?'

'No, it's made up. Also, to be honest, after all that's happened, I don't find it pleasant to work here anymore. I don't think I'll ever be able to feel the same again about the place, though I've enjoyed working here and . . . I'll be sad to leave in many ways . . . It's just that . . .'

'It's OK. I see what you mean, and I can't blame you, especially as you worked so closely with my father. It must have been a terrible shock.'

'It was.'

'Of course, it's bad for us too, but we've no choice; we have to battle on here. But you can make a new start elsewhere. I quite understand.'

'Thanks.'

Andrea settled down to work, feeling very relieved.

Alistair, however, was not only disappointed to lose a good worker but also found himself reflecting on how many other employees might be feeling the same way. There was a hard core of loyalists like David

Morton, but what about the rest? Who would actually want to work at a place where three people had recently been murdered?

After work, Tristram had to relax. He was worn out. People thought that being a model was easy: just stand or sit in nice clothes while photographers click away. They didn't realise the effort of standing around for hours and having to keep up the smile. Your jaw felt paralysed after a while and the boredom was crippling.

Unfortunately for Tristram, 'relaxing' meant going to the club for a spot of poker-playing. For money, of course. He had considered resigning from the Red Hot Poker, as the subscription was quite weighty, but the opulent gentlemen's-club atmosphere allowed him to indulge himself in the illusion that his activities there had a certain gravity about them – which in reality they didn't. It was a gambling den like any other on the street corner, despite the attendants dressed like butlers. And where players won and lost (mostly the latter) large sums of money.

He walked down the street to the tube station but didn't notice that he was being followed by a sinister-looking character in dark glasses. When he took the tube to Soho, the man sat near him on the train. When he emerged into the warm London evening, he headed through a series of narrow streets towards the club, still followed by this man. His pursuer took out a phone. Tristram arrived at the club entrance feeling a sense of excitement as he saw the old-fashioned club sign in red lights on the side of the building. He approached the steps but suddenly his way was barred by a burly individual.

'I don't think you want to go in there, sir.'

Tristram was astonished. 'What do you mean? Who are you?'

'Just come with us, please, sir.' This came from the man who'd followed him from the studio and was now standing right behind him.

'What are you talking about? Where?'

'Nothing to worry about; just come with us.'

They stood at either side of him and frogmarched him away, holding him firmly with their muscular arms. Tristram struggled to no avail.

'Are you police officers or what? What's going on?' There was no reply.

Just round the corner was a bar and Tristram was hustled inside, where Poppy was waiting for him at a table, drinking a cocktail.

'Thanks, boys. I'll be in touch.'

Without a word, the two men manipulated Tristram into a seat at the table and left. Tristram was relieved but irritated. 'Poppy, what the hell's going on?'

She leaned back in the chair, crossed her legs and smiled.

'I told you that you had to kick the habit, Tris, and I meant it.'

'Who the hell were they?'

'Private detectives I've hired to follow you.'

'What?'

'You should be pleased that I care enough to try to save you and our relationship. I could just dump you, like I said at the Hall. I can afford to hire these people now in order to help you stop gambling. I'm not going to allow you to squander money like my father did. You promised me you'd stop but I know you've been coming to the club since we got back to London. They called me about it. This club, of all places, where my father lost a big part of his fortune – *my* fortune, I should say. It's a good job it came to me when it did, isn't it? Even if poor Daddy had to die.'

'Yes. But . . . I'm . . .'

'There are no "buts", Tris. This is happening my way. You're going to be followed until I'm convinced that you've genuinely broken the habit.'

'But I'll recognise them.'

'It's an agency; they send out different people each time. They're not going to allow you to enter any gambling establishment and I'll be informed if you try to.'

'I can go online.'

'I've taken your laptop and your smartphone.'

'Bloody hell. I thought I'd lost it!'

'Here, take this: it's a phone without internet access.' She put a small, old-fashioned-looking phone on the table. 'Of course, if you're really determined to carry on I can't stop you, but that will be the end, Tris, after I've done all this to help. You'll be showing that you value the gambling more than me.'

Tristram shook his head. He was speechless and completely out-manoeuvred, but he was moved by the fact that she was doing all this for him. Her hardness both impressed and shocked him. He shrugged his shoulders and smiled at her. 'Well, there's no doubt who's in control here. I'll have to take my nasty medicine, won't I?'

'You will.' She smiled back, and drank some more of her cocktail.

Richard Wilkins was restless and miserable. The house and estate were slowly getting back to normal, but he was still struggling with the shock of Andrea's rejection and there was no sign that she was having any kind of rethink. He and his wife were not happy and he'd tried to play a double game in order to keep some stability for his children while enjoying an illicit affair. It had been very convenient for him, neatly separated between home and work. But now everything was unravelling and maybe this was all he deserved.

He was sitting in the café near the white garden. It was lunchtime, and he knew that Andrea often came over to eat here. It was a pleasant spot away from the office. He sat waiting with a mug of coffee and an uneaten sandwich and saw her arrive at the little cafeteria-style servery.

She took a tray and chatted with the staff before someone handed her a bowl of soup with bread and a cup of tea. She still hadn't noticed him and took her tray out on to the terrace, which overlooked the white hydrangeas, buddleias and roses. He scooped his food on to a tray, followed her out and came up behind her at a table.

'Mind if I join you?'

She put her tray down, turned to him and frowned. 'Richard. I'm not sure this is a good idea.'

Ignoring her, he placed his tray down and sat at the table. 'Please, I just want to talk to you.'

'There's nothing more to say. It's over. I've handed in my resignation and I've spoken to Alistair. I'll be away from here soon.'

'Where to? Where are you going?'

'I told you, I want to get back to the city. I'm looking for a job in Leeds to start with.'

'So you'll commute to that?'

'Yes.'

'So couldn't we still see each other? You know you want to really. It's been good, hasn't it?'

She looked at him quizzically, shook her head and continued to eat her lunch.

'You don't get it, do you? You expect me to continue to be your old-fashioned mistress, your bit on the side, and off you go back to the wife.'

'It'll be a lot better here now that Alistair's taking over. You won't have to work with that old roué anymore. It's going to be different, exciting.'

'You're wasting your time. I'm just not cut out for working on a country estate. I've done everything I can here and now I want to do something different. I know you're only thinking of me,' she added sarcastically.

'But surely . . .'

'OK, I've had enough of this.'

She picked up her tray and left the table, leaving him to contemplate his still-uneaten sandwich.

Oldroyd was in the office at Redmire when his phone rang.

'Hello. Are you that detective chap who was talking to us in t'Pear Tree t'other night?'

It was the voice of an old person with a strong accent. Oldroyd was momentarily puzzled and then he recognised it as belonging to Bill Mason, the friend of Harry Robinson's whom he'd interviewed in the pub that night he'd been shot at. 'Ah, it's Mr Mason, isn't it?'

'Aye, that's right, Bill Mason.'

'What can I do for you?'

'You were asking about poor old Harry and that locked-room carry-on.'

'Yes.'

'Well, I've remembered something that Harry once said to me. It's a while back now, but it was when we'd had a few pints one night, at Christmas I think it was, and we got talking about that locked room and how people got out of it; I can't remember why. Anyway, Harry was laughing and he said, "Bill, the point is, they don't get out." Well, I'd no idea what he meant and he wouldn't say any more. He never wanted to get on t'wrong side o' t'family up there at th'ouse and he probably shouldn't even have said that to me. Anyway, afterwards he never mentioned it again; I think he'd forgotten he'd told me and I thought he was just drunk and talking rubbish, you know, because surely t'thing about that locked room is that people do get out, so what he was saying seemed daft. Anyway, it just came back to me last night so I found your card and I thought, I'll just give him a ring and let him know.'

Oldroyd had listened intently. 'Thank you very much, Mr Mason. So, just to be clear, he said "They don't get out" and he meant that room?'

'Aye, that's right, but it still doesn't make any sense to me.'

'Well, it's starting to make a bit of sense to me, at last. Thank you very much.'

Steph had been busy organising the investigation into the circumstances of Barden's murder. Questioning witnesses had so far revealed very little: no one had seen anything. The crime had occurred so late that the estate had been almost deserted when it occurred. There had still been some officers performing a night patrol following the attack on Oldroyd, but they had stayed around the house and were too far away from the train track to have heard anything.

Barden appeared to have had no enemies, but was universally thought to have been a fantasiser and often a nuisance. He didn't appear to have told anyone any details about what he allegedly knew about the case, although he'd hinted at something to a number of people.

Steph was by the entrance to the house on her way back to the office to report these matters to Oldroyd when she was surprised to see her boss running towards her.

'Sir?'

'Come on: follow me back to the locked room. I think I've got it.'

'Got what, sir?'

'The answer, I hope.'

She followed him down the corridor towards the locked room. He stopped halfway to send her back for the key, which he'd completely forgotten in his excitement. When they finally made it, she unlocked the room and they went in. It was all eerily the same as ever.

'Now,' announced Oldroyd, enjoying the sense of drama, 'we've been looking at all these things for clues – the chair, table, windows, bookshelf, walls, floor, ceiling and all – without success. What we really needed to do was this.'

To Steph's astonishment, her boss stood in the middle of the floor and started to jump up and down.

'Sir? What . . . ?'

'Yes!' shouted Oldroyd. 'I can just feel it. Get Jeffries over here and between you organise another search, but this time I'll tell you what you're looking for. And when you've organised that, come back to the office; I've got something to show you. Things are really moving at last.'

Before Jeffries received the call from Steph he took an unexpected call at Ripon station.

'You're a private detective in London? I see . . . The Red Hot Poker Club? . . . Did they? . . . Yes, I'm involved in investigating the murders at Redmire Hall. And what do you wish to report?'

Jeffries was silent for some time, listening to some very interesting information.

'Yes, I can see why you thought that; definitely a suspect, yes . . . Don't worry, you did the right thing . . . Yes, I'll take your number. And thank you.'

When Jeffries eventually ended the call, he reflected on the shady life of a private detective: following adulterers, wayward offspring and crooks. But they did often prove useful.

Steph and Oldroyd were in the office, feeling much more relaxed about the investigation. A second, more focused search of the locked room had taken place, finally making the discoveries that Oldroyd had expected. At last they were reaching the point where everything was coming together. One person had been identified as needing further investigation and Jeffries was undertaking the task at that very moment.

'I can't believe we've finally discovered the secret of that locked room – at least, you did, sir.'

Oldroyd was on his laptop as he talked. He looked up. 'Not without clues and a bit of luck. But if you stay rational and think hard, eventually you'll get there. It's made me think about Arthur Conan Doyle.'

'The man who wrote the Sherlock Holmes stories?'

'Yes. Holmes was famous for his rational powers of deduction; everything was based on evidence. Ironically, though, his creator could be a very credulous man who allowed his beliefs to affect his thinking.'

'How?'

'He was a Spiritualist, and he believed in mediums, psychic powers, ectoplasm and all that. He even believed in fairies. Do you know the story of the Cottingley Fairies?'

'No.'

'It was near Bingley. Some children took some photographs of themselves with fairies and it caused a sensation. Conan Doyle thought they were genuine, though when you look at the pictures they seem obviously fake, and years later it was revealed that the girls cut the figures out of a children's book and supported them with hatpins.'

'How come he believed them?'

'He wanted to. And he wasn't the only one. People look for evidence to support their beliefs. He also knew the escapologist Houdini and this is even more interesting. Doyle claimed that Houdini had psychic powers that enabled him to perform illusions. Houdini, who was a rationalist and often exposed the fakery of mediums, denied this and told Doyle that all his illusions were just tricks. He warned him not to believe in supernatural accounts for things just because he couldn't explain them. They fell out about it.'

'So the moral is: don't allow anything to interfere with your reason. Magic doesn't exist and if we persist we can find the rational explanation,' said Steph.

'Exactly.'

'What will happen to it – you know, that room – now that we're going to reveal its secret?'

'Good question; never thought about it. I expect it'll just go back to being forgotten about again.'

'That's a shame, in a way, isn't it? After all the skill and effort that went into it.'

'Maybe the new Lord Redmire could sell the idea to someone. Or I suppose it could become a visitor attraction. It has a ghoulish fame now, doesn't it?' He looked at his laptop again. 'Ah! At last. Tim Groves has sent me something.'

He opened the files and quickly read through the forensic reports on the murder weapons.

'Well, have a look at these – I'll forward them to you. They make very interesting reading. In fact, I think they confirm another of our suspicions.'

Steph was going through the files when Jeffries arrived.

'Yes, sir, we've found them. You were right.' He proceeded to tell Oldroyd about his earlier conversation with the private detective.

Oldroyd beamed. 'Good Lord, we are making great strides today! Well done, everybody.' He sat back in his chair. 'Just a few more things to clear up and then it's time we brought all this to a conclusion. I've got an idea about how to end it on a triumphant note.'

'What do you mean, sir?'

'Call all the family and friends back to the Hall and say we've got some important announcements. This is what we're going to do . . .'

There was a gleam in his eye that Steph knew meant he was planning some mischief or other.

~

It was a sultry, overcast day threatening rain as the Carstairs family and friends travelled again to Redmire Hall just as they had on the day of the murder. This time they knew they were coming to learn The Truth. But what exactly would that be? And what was going to happen when they got there?

As the various cars headed towards the Hall, there was little conversation between the tense occupants.

Dominic Carstairs grumbled all the way from York as he sat frowning behind the wheel of the Mercedes. 'I don't know what that chief inspector thinks he's playing at. This is highly irregular.'

'I'm sure he knows what he's doing,' said Mary. 'I think he's very good.'

'Do you? Well, if he knows who's guilty then why not just arrest them?'

'Who knows? Anyway, what are you getting so jumpy about?'

'Me? I'm not jumpy, I'm just . . . Watch what you're doing!' he shouted at a car that had cut in front of him.

'I'm actually quite looking forward to it. I want to know how it was done as well as who's behind it. I think everyone should feel the same, if their conscience is clear.'

'What on earth do you mean by that?'

'Draw your own conclusions, darling,' she said, and glanced at him archly.

Antonia and Douglas drove slowly along the beautiful winding roads of Lower Wensleydale.

'At last we'll get to the bottom of this dreadful business,' said Douglas.

'Yes, but what will we find? I've just got this awful feeling that there's a lot more ugly stuff to come out.'

'What sort of stuff?'

'I don't know. But why are we being called back to the Hall? I think there might be some terrible things that detective wants to tell us and he thinks it's better if we're all together.'

'That's very dark and mysterious. You mean like skeletons in the cupboard?'

'Maybe. I just think there's a lot more to it than we've been told so far. After all, three people have been murdered. There's been something sinister at work.'

'Has there? Well, you seem to know a lot about it.'

She turned to him. 'Douglas? Whatever do you mean?'

'Only joking, darling.'

Poppy sulked her way north from London, driven by the newly subordinated Tristram in the powerful little Mini.

'We could just do without all this again,' she moaned. 'I've got too much to do. I need to start looking for some new equipment. This time I'm really going to make it in photography.'

'Not to worry; that'll wait – and while we're up here I can't be tempted by the gambling dens.'

'Very funny.' She sighed. 'Oh God! I don't want to go back there again to see where Daddy was murdered!'

'You've seemed quite OK about it recently.'

'About what?'

'About Daddy dying and all that.'

'Tristram!'

He laughed. 'You seem quite happy now you've got your hands on his money.'

'What! How dare you? If you weren't driving I'd punch you.'

'Steady on; I'm only joking. I'm sure he'd be pleased, anyway, to see his daughter set herself up using his money, even though you didn't get all you wanted when he was alive.'

She started to hit him on the shoulder.

'Hey! Steady on, I'll crash!'

'You're a pig! It's completely different now and I'm going to show people that I can make a go of things.'

'Good, I'm glad to hear it. Anyway, it's not just about your father. Two other people got murdered so we owe it to them to cooperate with the police.'

'Yes, well, if you want my opinion, I think the police think that you did it.'

'Why would they think that?'

'Because you argued with him about borrowing to pay your debts and you also knew that I would inherit money from him.'

'I see. Well, what's it like to be driven by a murderer?'

'Get lost!'

'What's it like to have sex with a murderer?'

'Tris!' She punched him lightly on the shoulder 'again. 'You're just the worst!'

After this they were quiet for a while and then suddenly she said, 'You didn't do them, did you, Tris?'

'What?'

'The murders. You and your accomplices could have organised it all. I wonder who helped you? Who did the dirty work?'

'I beg your—'

'Only joking! Got you!'

'Very funny.'

∼

Alex and James decided to travel first class on the train to Leeds and take a taxi to Redmire.

They were comfortably established in their wide seats with a generous table as the train pulled out of King's Cross. Alex fiddled with her phone and James read a copy of the *Times*. A waiter brought them complimentary drinks.

'This is much more relaxing,' remarked James. 'I couldn't have faced the M1 again so soon after we've just driven up there and back, even in the MG.'

'I agree. I've always loved train travel. Talking of which, are you still going to treat me to a trip on the *Orient Express* to Venice?'

'Yes, some day, when business has picked up a bit.'

'Well, we're enduring "Murder at the Manor" so we should be well prepared for *Murder on the Orient Express*.'

'Very funny. And thinking of Christie's famous novel, I wonder if the chief inspector thinks we all did it? You know, we planned and executed it together – the whole family. There are so many motives around among us I wouldn't be surprised.'

'Well, he'd be wrong, wouldn't he? At least as far as I'm concerned.'

'What do you mean by that?'

'I don't think the police regard me as a serious suspect, but you: falling out over the business; refusing you money; your partner's former lover . . . There's plenty to go on there – and that's without your blackmailing and the knowledge that he was probably worth more to you dead than alive.'

'Good Lord, you're still thinking about that?'

'Just a little.' She smiled mischievously.

'Those motives came up when they interviewed me, apart from the blackmailing, so there's nothing new there. What about you, darling? The rejected lover. "Hell hath no fury", remember.'

'Yes. Maybe they think you and I did it together – with help, of course.'

He laughed again. 'What an idea! You little devil.'

James took up the newspaper again as they sped past Stevenage and Alex returned to her phone.

Alistair walked across to his grandmother's flat and found her sitting on the patio. Her face lit up when she saw him.

'Ah, Alistair, come here; it's so good to see you.'

He leaned over and kissed her. 'How are you, Granny?'

'I'm very well today, thank you. It's very hot and humid, isn't it? Sit down.'

'Yes, it is.' He sat on a chair beside her. 'I can't stay long, Granny. I've come to tell you that the police want to speak to us all again, and this time together. Chief Inspector Oldroyd wants us to meet by that room, you know, the one used in the trick.'

'Oh, that one.'

'Yes, but I'm sure if I asked them they would allow you to stay here. I think it's going to be stressful and dramatic, as it were. I assume he's going to tell us about that trick business and who killed Father and the others. I don't know why he's doing it like this but there must be a reason.'

'I see. Of course I'm going to be there. I want to hear it all. I want to know everything.'

Alistair was a little taken aback. 'Are you sure, Granny? It's going to be awfully grisly, finding out who the murderer is. I can hardly bear to think about it. I could come and tell you everything later.'

'But what if it's you?'

'Granny!'

She chuckled. 'Don't worry, dear; just my little joke. You have to admit, though, you did have a lot to gain from your father's death.'

'You sound like the police looking for motives.'

She leaned over to whisper to him in a way that made him draw back. 'I could tell the police everything they already know about all the suspects and more. People think I'm too old to notice things but I'm not.'

'Very well. If you're sure you want to come I'll be across later to help you over.'

She ignored this. 'I believe that there's always justice in the end, however long it takes.'

'Quite. Bye for now.'

Alistair got up from his chair and left. It had been a very disconcerting encounter.

It was late in the afternoon when people started to arrive. The sky had been darkening all day and the air was hot and sticky.

Alistair was at the main door to welcome them. Douglas and Antonia were the first to arrive, looking grave but stoical. 'Hello, Mummy. Douglas.'

'Hello, darling. How is everyone? Are Caroline and Emily OK? Remember they've lost their grandfather. I know they never saw much of him, but still . . .'

'Don't worry, Mummy. Katherine's doing a wonderful job with them. I'm very busy, as I'm sure you understand.'

'I don't doubt it; she's a wonderful mother.'

'Any idea what's going on, old boy?' asked Douglas affably.

'I'm afraid not.'

'Never mind, eh? We'll find out soon enough.'

Dominic slammed the door of the Mercedes and walked up to the door tight-lipped and grim. Mary followed behind, looked at Alistair and raised her eyes.

'Do you know what this is all about, Alistair?' asked Dominic.

'I don't, Uncle.'

'Well, it's completely unacceptable and I shall make it clear that . . .' He disappeared through the door.

'How are you, darling? Just ignore him. He thinks the world should be run for his own convenience.'

'I think we all do at times, Auntie,' said Alistair as he gave Mary a hug.

A taxi drew up and Alex and James got out. Alex looked up at the imposing frontage of the Hall while James paid the driver.

'Welcome back again,' said Alistair.

'Nice to see you, Alistair, but we must stop meeting in circumstances like this.'

'I know.'

'How are you doing with the new responsibilities?' asked James. 'I take it you've reopened properly.'

'Yes, but only just. Richard Wilkins and I had a deal of persuading to do to get the police to agree.'

'That's great. Just keep at it. I'm sure you'll be a better businessman than your father.'

'James! Now's not the time to bring that up,' said Alex.

'It's OK, don't worry. We all know my father was not famous for his business acumen. I'm pretty sure I'll do better. We're all meeting just in there.' Alistair pointed at the door.

Poppy and Tristram were the last to arrive. The sporty Mini roared up the drive and the occupants strode stylishly up to the door.

Alistair, sensing Poppy's mood, moved in pre-emptively. 'Before you say anything, Poppy: I can't tell you what all this is about. Everyone's asking me the same questions but I don't know any more than you.'

'Fine. It's a bloody waste of time, I can tell you that.' She flounced in followed by Tristram, who winked at Alistair. Before he joined them all, Alistair looked up at the sky, which was now menacingly black in the distance. Clearly there was soon going to be an almighty thunderstorm.

Inside, everyone gathered in the entrance hall. There was no sign of the police.

'Can you tell us anything, then, Alistair?' asked James.

Alistair shrugged his shoulders. 'Not much. The chief inspector asked me to inform you that he wants us all to gather in that lobby by the locked room at six o'clock and "everything will be revealed". Those were his exact words.'

'Not that bloody room again!' said James. 'He's not going to perform that trick, is he?'

'If he does,' growled Dominic, 'I hope he disappears and fails to reappear. It'll serve him right.'

'Well, I think it sounds rather fun,' said Mary. 'I like that chief inspector; he's got a fine mind and a sense of drama – much better than some boring procedural type who does everything by the book.'

'Fun! This is a serious business, Mary!' exclaimed Dominic.

'And I'm sure he's got some serious answers. I'm looking forward to hearing them.'

'There must be some reason why he's chosen to do it like this,' observed Douglas.

'I certainly can't think of one,' replied Dominic sharply.

'There's no point arguing about it,' said Antonia. 'He's the police officer in charge and we've no choice other than to do what he says.'

'I agree with Antonia,' said James. 'However strange we think it is, we'll just have to go along with it.'

That statement had a feeling of finality about it and everyone, however reluctantly, seemed to accept it. Everything went quiet as the group dispersed, looking for ways to pass the time before six o'clock.

Nine

Oldroyd stood once again in front of the door to the locked room and faced his tense and perplexed audience.

Comfortable furniture had been brought in and assembled in a half-circle. Oldroyd had insisted that this denouement took place by the locked room. He knew he was really stretching the rules of how to conduct an investigation, but the wonderful opportunity to indulge his sense of drama was irresistible and the literary resonances were exquisite. All the family including the dowager were assembled before him. He had put his tuxedo on and was revelling in the chance to play a part so reminiscent of one of his fictional heroes. Outside, there was the first rumble of thunder.

'Ladies and gentlemen,' he announced portentously, 'this case has been one of the most intriguing in which I have ever been involved.'

This was too much for Dominic Carstairs. 'What on earth do you think you're playing at, Chief Inspector? Who the bloody hell do you think you are? Hercule Poirot? Where's your little moustache and your Belgian accent? I'm going to put in a formal complaint about you, make no mistake. I'm absolutely—'

'Oh, for goodness' sake, Uncle, be quiet!' said Alistair. 'Let the man do his job. If this is how he wants to explain everything, then why not? At least he's solved the case and we'll know who murdered Father, Harry Robinson and Ian Barden, and how it was done. I've just about had enough of the agony of not knowing and I'm sure everybody else feels the same.'

Dominic was surprised at Alistair's assertiveness. This new Lord Redmire was clearly taking control as the head of the family. He realised everyone was looking at him and his cantankerousness subsided into a grumbling mutter.

'At the beginning of this affair,' said Oldroyd, looking pointedly at Dominic, 'I was exposed on television without being consulted, so I hope you will not begrudge me the right to present my findings in a similarly dramatic and public manner.'

No one felt able to make any further objections as Oldroyd, after his little prologue, embarked upon the main act of his performance. Steph turned on the spotlights that illuminated the door area, and turned off the other lights.

'There were, of course, two mysteries in the first murder. Who killed Lord Redmire? And how did this illusion work? It was clear from the outset that the two were linked, that whoever the murderers were, they'd discovered the perplexing secret of this famous locked-room trick and most likely told Lord Redmire about it. We discounted the idea that Redmire knew the secret of the trick all along because it was unlikely that he would not have used it to his advantage earlier. No: someone came to him quite recently with the knowledge of how his father's illusion worked – the secret that had remained hidden for so long. This information may not in itself have meant much to Lord Redmire, but when it was suggested to him that this was an enormous opportunity in terms of money-making publicity, his interest was immediately aroused.

'Of course, he didn't know that these people, whoever they were, had seen the potential of this trick to commit an extraordinary murder, one in which the corpse was left for all to see, but in which the act of murder and the murderer were rendered invisible, concealed within the illusion. And the whole thing was more audacious because it was carried out before a live television audience. Nevertheless, you may be thinking, as did we, that it was quite a risky and unnecessarily complicated way of killing someone. However, there was a particular motive for doing it this way, which I will come to later.'

'Get on with it,' muttered Dominic to himself.

'The financial potential of the illusion, in terms of the publicity and consequent stimulation to tourism, blinded Lord Redmire – a man in constant and serious debt and in need of money to satisfy his gambling addiction – to any sign of danger; and anyway he had no reason to suspect that these people were planning his death. So, in a somewhat macabre manner, he became an unwitting accomplice in his own murder and its concealment by keeping the identity of his killers a secret. He had to do this because they had a practical part to play in this performance and the decision would have been taken early on that it was much safer if this secret remained between them. Just as Vivian Carstairs, in his time, had made sure that the number of people who knew anything about the illusion was small. Conspiracies work best with small numbers of people, which is why I find some of the outlandish ones around, such as the faked moon landings, ridiculous. And we suspect it was for this same reason that, after the trick, Harry Robinson was killed. Robinson was the only person who we knew from the beginning must have been involved in this plot in some way, because his murder was most likely the result of the other plotters wanting to limit the number of people who knew the truth of what had happened.

'The planning was very careful and discreet and on the night it was a great success.'

'Really, Chief Inspector,' said Douglas Ramsay. 'That's rather an inappropriate way of putting it, don't you think?'

'I mean, of course, from the murderers' point of view,' continued Oldroyd. 'But' – here he smiled rather wickedly – 'Lord Redmire did at least have the satisfaction of seeing his father's trick bamboozle an audience for a second time before he died.'

Some winced at this but there was silence.

'Harry Robinson followed shortly after, and then the unfortunate Ian Barden. I will return to them later.' Oldroyd took a drink from a glass of water. 'And so we come to the resolution of these mysteries and to the revelations.'

Poppy hid her face against Tristram's shoulder. A number of people shifted very uneasily in their places. The thunder, which had until this point been far off, now sounded much closer and there was a flicker of light from distant lightning. Outside it seemed almost dark, though it was still only early evening.

'First of all, the Locked-Room Mystery. It has now been performed twice in this country without explanation, and we don't know how many times it was performed in Italy long ago. Making people or objects vanish and reappear is, of course, one of the foundations of magic. It seems to defy the laws of physics: how can a person disappear from a sealed room like this and then reappear?'

'I take my hat off to you if you can explain it, Chief Inspector,' said Douglas Ramsay.

'Well, we know that there isn't really such a thing as magic, so we have to think about what the so-called magician is actually doing. As with all illusions and conjuring, one of the secrets lies in misdirection. Sometimes the magician draws people's attention to something and then, while they are looking away, performs his trick with a coin or card. In this case we are encouraged to concentrate on the wrong idea: that the person disappears from the room.'

'But surely they do, Chief Inspector,' said a puzzled Mary Carstairs. 'Everyone saw Freddy go into that room and then when the door was opened again he'd gone.'

'Exactly,' replied Oldroyd archly. 'That's what you were meant to think, but in fact Lord Redmire never left that room.'

There were mutterings of 'No' and 'That's impossible'. James Forsyth laughed, shook his head and said, 'You've completely lost me, Chief Inspector.'

'You mean he was hiding in there?' said Alistair Carstairs. 'But that's incredible. You yourself couldn't find any hiding places. There were no mirrors or anything.'

Oldroyd shook his head. 'No, he wasn't hiding and nor did he leave the room. There is a third alternative, which took me, slow-witted as I am, a long time to realise. I needed a number of prompts to help me to start thinking along the right lines.

'The first thing that gave me a clue was a present my daughter bought for me. It was a Russian doll, and the concept of one thing fitting inside another somehow resonated in a way I couldn't define. Obviously there wasn't another room that fitted inside the first, but it made me consider that somehow, maybe, there was more to the whole thing than the room we were seeing.

'Secondly, when we interviewed Lady Redmire's niece, Olivia Pendleton, I at last began to form an outline of the answer. Olivia had attended the first performance of the trick, as a little girl of eight, and initially it seemed that she'd been too young at the time to remember anything significant, but she did tell us the apparently inconsequential story of her marble . . .'

'Her what?' muttered Dominic incredulously.

'This marble, unnoticed by all the grown-ups around her, rolled into the locked room after it had been opened and Lord Redmire was not there. She had not been able to retrieve it then, so she went back to get it when the door was opened for the second time to reveal that Lord Redmire had returned. He was there but the marble wasn't. She looked all over the floor but couldn't find it.

'Finally, Bill Mason, one of Harry Robinson's friends, called me to say he remembered Harry saying in a drunken moment that in the illusion people didn't leave the room. My first reaction was similar to yours: surely that is exactly what people did? They weren't in the room when it was reopened, and also the first Lord Redmire actually walked to where we're standing now after he'd disappeared for the second time. So what Harry said seemed to make no sense at all at that point, but it made me think. And I suddenly realised: yes, as with all the apparently insoluble mysteries of magic, the answer is simple – so simple, in fact, as to be almost disappointing. I came down here with my detective sergeant, went into the room and jumped up and down.'

Dominic Carstairs's mouth dropped open, and he looked at Oldroyd as though the man was raving bonkers.

'And what I found made me pretty sure. All we had to do was find the mechanism – and I had a fair idea of where to look.'

Oldroyd, adopting the heightened manner of the stage announcer, raised his voice, threw up his arms and struck a pose.

'So now, ladies and gentlemen: the Locked-Room Mystery revealed!'

He pulled back the curtain to expose the door, which he opened.

'Detective Sergeant Johnson, please.'

Steph came forward and entered the room. Oldroyd shut the door but left the curtain back.

'OK, Jeffries!' he called out.

Suddenly there was the sound of some kind of mechanism whirring and then, with a faint rumbling noise, the door moved away to the left. A small section of plasterboard moved across and then another door appeared and came to rest exactly where the first door had been. There were gasps of astonishment.

'Now, if I open this door, you'll see that my colleague is not inside.' He opened the door to confirm this fact. 'Because, of course, this is a different room, identical in every way to the first. This is an illusion about two rooms, not one; and so we can see what Harry Robinson meant when he said that people don't leave the room. The person who disappears doesn't leave the room they entered: that one moves away and is replaced by this. Little Olivia couldn't find her marble because it was in a different room.'

Everyone was paying rapt attention now. Oldroyd seemed to command his audience like a charismatic performer of magic tricks himself, except that he was the anti-magician, the one bursting the bubble of illusion. Thunder sounded nearer still.

'But how on earth does it work?' asked Alex.

'Quite a complicated mechanism, which is why it took so long to construct. The two rooms are mounted on a track like a railway line and they move across on metal wheels. It had to be superbly well built to feel solid. When I jumped up and down hard on the floor, I could just feel a slight movement, which told me that the room was suspended and not on solid foundations.

'Two things that they could never eliminate completely were the noise of the electric motor that propels the mechanism, and the noise of the wheels on the track.'

'Which is why the loud music was played each time!' said Douglas Ramsay.

'Exactly, and it was just the same nearly forty years ago. This rigid curtain conceals the moving doors and I was suspicious about that from the beginning. Whenever a magician covers things over with cloths, drapes or whatever, you can be sure that something's going on beneath or behind them.

'The fact that there are two rooms is also cunningly concealed outside. If you look at the extension that was built, it only looks big enough to contain one room. There are very wide stone pillars at each end, but these are false, so that in fact there is just enough space for two narrow rooms and to allow for the movement. The mechanism is operated by a switch in the wall just round the corner in that small corridor. That part was sealed off on the night that we were all here, and would have been on the first occasion too. Whoever is operating the mechanism can hear what is being said here by the locked room and will know when to start the music and to flick the switch to move the rooms.'

'Well done, Chief Inspector,' said Antonia Ramsay. 'But you haven't explained how someone can actually get out, which Vivian clearly did. The murderer must have used the same method to murder Freddy.'

'You're absolutely right. Maybe Detective Sergeant Johnson can explain this. Here she is . . .' He pointed behind them.

In a curious echo of that evening many years ago, everyone turned and was amazed to see not a triumphant Vivian Carstairs this time, but a smiling Stephanie Johnson.

'Again, it's quite simple,' she said, taking her cue from Oldroyd. 'You remember there is a trapdoor in the floor of the room, which leads to a cavity where there's wiring and stuff and a concrete base. When the room moves across to its other position, this hole in the floor is no longer over the concrete base and it is possible to get out, down beneath the room, and exit through a small door concealed in the wooden panelling of the wall in that corridor where the control switch is.'

Oldroyd took up the story once more. 'So, on the night Lord Redmire met his end, the murderer waited underneath and climbed quickly up into the room when it had moved across. As he or she was part of the team behind this performance, Redmire might have been puzzled by this, but he wouldn't have sensed danger until it was too late and the knife was in his back.'

'Oh, Daddy!' exclaimed Poppy, and burst into tears.

'The murderer would have acted very swiftly and as quietly as possible, though I'm pretty sure the walls of those rooms will have been sound-proofed. Even if Lord Redmire had cried out, he wouldn't have been heard. The murderer exited by the same route before the room shifted back. So, instead of appearing to great acclaim, Lord Redmire, I'm afraid, returned to view as we and the startled TV audience saw him.'

Oldroyd paused and again raised his arms melodramatically, signalling the end of part one of this extraordinary exposé.

'So now, ladies and gentlemen, having finally explained the locked room and how it was used for murder, we come to the second question in this incredible case: who was responsible for the murders of Lord Redmire, Harry Robinson and Ian Barden?'

He felt more like Hercule Poirot than ever as he looked around at each person with his penetrating grey eyes. Everyone was now totally transfixed, but Dominic Carstairs made a last desperate attempt to slow Oldroyd's terrifying momentum. How dare this upstart play such games with the Redmire family? It was outrageous!

'Oh, so it's *Cluedo* now, is it?' he said contemptuously. 'We know the crime was committed in that bloody room with the knife, so who was it? Maybe it was the Reverend Green or Colonel Mustard? Do we all have to make a guess? Can't you just tell us who it was without all this ridiculous pantomime? You are putting a lot of stress on my mother, who is—'

'Shut up, Dominic; I'm finding all this fascinating.' The dowager Lady Redmire raised an arthritic hand, silencing her son.

Before Oldroyd could continue, there was a flash of light and a crash of thunder that shook the house. The drumming of torrential rain could be heard outside and on the roof. It was the perfect atmosphere for the next revelations.

'We were already pretty sure that Harry Robinson's technical knowledge was vital and that he was disposed of as soon as his usefulness was over. He knew too much. But the interesting question then was why he got involved in the first place. The answer was money. Harry Robinson had given indispensable help to Vivian Carstairs when the illusion was initially constructed, and for those services, and to buy his silence, he was paid a handsome salary and a generous pension when he retired. It was clear when my colleague and I visited his cottage and saw the expensive furniture and artwork there that he had financial resources beyond those normally available to a retired jobbing mechanic. Harry Robinson lived well. The problem was that his old employer was dead, while the incumbent Lord Redmire was under financial pressure and probably regarded Robinson's pension as excessive. Neither did he share his father's sense of gratitude to his old employee. I suspect that Robinson didn't know what was really being planned and that was why he was got rid of so quickly after the first murder. I think he was probably told that if he shared what he knew about the trick, Lord Redmire would be pleased with him and would leave his pension untouched. And I think that was agreed. Anyway, no need to speculate. We can shortly ask the other people involved – the people who devised this fiendish piece of theatre and who cleverly persuaded Lord Redmire and Harry Robinson to play their parts before murdering them. We know, of course, that no one here committed the actual murder because we all watched it together, but that doesn't mean that no one here was involved.'

He stopped and stared menacingly at the people before him. The spotlights cast shadows on his face, giving him a devilish appearance. Poppy clung on to Tristram and refused to look at Oldroyd. Tristram was very pale. Dominic was on the far left with Mary and returned Oldroyd's menacing look. Mary tried to look calm but was frantically twiddling with her necklace. The dowager Lady Redmire sat forward in an armchair near to Oldroyd, utterly still and slightly bent over. Alex Davis and James Forsyth sat on the far right, Alex looking at the floor and James frowning with his arms tightly folded. Antonia sat in the centre with Douglas, who was shaking his head slowly while she looked calmly and with some defiance at Oldroyd. Alistair also looked tight-lipped at the detective, who seemed to have morphed yet again into the family nemesis. Katherine seemed to be near to tears. The suspense was overwhelming.

'So, Miss Carstairs,' said Oldroyd.

Poppy swung round. 'No!' she cried. 'It wasn't me. Why would I kill my own father?'

'Maybe because he wouldn't give you what you wanted and you also knew his gambling was steadily eroding your inheritance. You had to stop it going any further. You were also overheard having a furious row with your father just before he was murdered.'

'That doesn't mean I . . . No!' shouted Poppy.

Tristram had noticed the twinkle in Oldroyd's eye. 'Calm down, darling. I don't think he's serious. This is the bit at the end when he goes through all the suspects.'

'You're right, Mr Benington, although you are also a suspect. Lord Redmire refused to help you with your gambling debts but you knew that if he was out of the way your girlfriend would inherit a lot of money, which would be extremely useful. We also have witnesses to a furious row that you had with Lord Redmire at the Red Hot Poker Club.'

Benington shrugged his shoulders. 'True,' he said. 'But I didn't kill him.'

Oldroyd sniffed and walked on slowly, stopping at Alex Davis and James Forsyth. He nodded his head.

'Well, Ms Davis and Mr Forsyth, you are a very likely partnership in this crime. Both of you were badly treated by the victim, one in love and the other in money. How strange that you ended up as partners while both being, as it were, the ex-partners of Lord Redmire. Or maybe it wasn't so fortuitous after all. Maybe the purpose from the beginning was to plan your revenge together.'

Alex looked away from Oldroyd in disgust, and Forsyth laughed. 'Well, you're still stuck on that scenario. You make it sound like a third-rate romantic thriller, Chief Inspector. You've certainly got imagination.'

'Maybe, but if that "scenario", as you put it, is not accurate, Mr Forsyth, then perhaps you planned Redmire's death alone. What a useful legacy he left you in his will, which could have been a motive in itself! But I did find myself wondering why Redmire had left you that money, given that your friendship had long since foundered on the ruins of your joint business venture. I think we know the answer, and her name is Astrid – although that is unlikely to be her real name.'

Forsyth went pale as people turned round to gaze at him. Oldroyd pushed on relentlessly.

'We know all about how you blackmailed Lord Redmire after you'd discovered his link with a London call girl.'

There were some gasps at this.

'James?' said Antonia.

'It's true,' he said. 'How did you find out?'

'The most likely explanation for why Redmire left you that money was that he was forced to, and then we discovered a series of payments to an account that we traced to you. The question then was: what hold did you have over Redmire? This is when we had a stroke of luck, which you often get in this line of work as a reward for your effort. The private detective you used got very suspicious when he read about Redmire's death, so he called us and explained how you'd employed him to track Redmire to the call girl.'

'Well done.'

'That's routine hard-graft policing. It's what the police do every day to earn their money.'

'However, no matter how bad it looks, I didn't kill him,' insisted Forsyth. 'Why would I if I was getting money out of him?'

'Maybe because you knew his money was running out so you "cashed him in", as it were, for your legacy in the will.'

Forsyth shook his head.

Oldroyd turned to fix his gaze on Dominic Carstairs, who drew back as if a poisonous snake was approaching him.

'Be careful what you say or I'll be calling my solicitor.'

'The disappointed younger brother,' continued Oldroyd, undeterred and enjoying this more and more. 'You never forgave your older brother for being your older brother, did you? It was so unfair that such a lazy, irresponsible man should inherit this estate and the title that went with it. What a much better job of it you could have made! As it was, you've had to work for your living and things have not been going too well, have they?'

'You've made these preposterous remarks about me before and if you think I intend to discuss my business affairs with you, you are entirely mistaken. They are completely irrelevant to this case.'

'I don't think so,' insisted Oldroyd. 'We believe you'd asked your brother for help with your struggling business recently and he'd refused. Was that the final humiliation, Mr Carstairs? The one that really tipped you over the edge? The brother who'd had everything given to him refusing to help his less fortunate brother.'

Carstairs went red in the face and looked as if he might explode. He was so angry he couldn't get any words out.

Mary Carstairs grabbed his arm. 'Dominic, pull yourself together; he's just winding you up.'

Oldroyd, however, was intent on continuing the process and savouring his power over these people. He turned to Mary. 'And Mrs Carstairs . . . maybe you assisted your husband, though it seems you didn't feel the same as he did about Lord Redmire.'

'What on earth do you mean?' She looked very uncomfortable.

'You were seen by a member of the estate staff coming out of the stables on the evening of the crime, and Lord Redmire followed soon after. It seems that a little tryst had taken place. After we received this information we considered that you were well and truly on the list of suspects – another potentially jealous conquest.'

'Mary, is it true?' For the first time, Dominic's voice lost its loud arrogance. He faltered and sounded distraught.

Mary was looking with great hostility at Oldroyd and then she turned to her husband. For a moment she looked as if she might be considering telling a lie or making an excuse. Then she simply said: 'Yes.'

Dominic looked away and seemed to be on the edge of tears.

Oldroyd, having inflicted the damage, moved on. 'And what about the long-suffering wife and her new husband?'

He turned to the Ramsays. 'The dignified couple who have conducted themselves impeccably throughout. Often the guilty parties are the ones you least expect. What a terrible force of anger and resentment must have built up over the years due to your former husband's infidelities! And you, Mr Ramsay, must have despised Redmire too and been only too ready to assist your wife in attaining her revenge. Plus, of course – as we've pointed out already – the money and the estate have now come to your wife's children before Redmire could squander any more of them.'

The Ramsays remained impassive. Douglas spoke for them both. 'Yes, Chief Inspector, if I were you I'd have us down as suspects too – but it's a no-go, I'm afraid; Antonia and I are not murderers.'

Oldroyd moved on again and then paused dramatically. 'And now the people who stood to gain most from Lord Redmire's death, the new Lord and Lady Redmire.' He gestured with his arm as if introducing them. Alistair and Katherine sat together silently. He addressed Alistair. 'Was it too painful to watch your father make a mess of running the estate and using it to finance his gambling? He was even planning to sell off parts of it, wasn't he? Did you think it was better to act now rather than see him break up the estate or reduce it to bankruptcy – maybe even entertain the unthinkable prospect of having to sell up? No more Carstairs at Redmire Hall after how many hundreds of years? That scenario must have haunted you when you considered your children's future and their inheritance. Of course, it was patricide, but sometimes you have to think of the greater good. I'm sure your wife understood and was very supportive, and your grandmother.' He gestured towards the dowager.

'Steady on,' said Douglas Ramsay.

Alistair turned sharply to Oldroyd. 'That is really very offensive, Chief Inspector. Unless you have any proof I suggest you withdraw that. How dare you accuse a woman in her eighties of conspiring to kill her own son!'

'A son she didn't have much time for and who she, like many others, thought was making a terrible mess of things. Tradition is very important to you people, isn't it? If the line of succession is threatened I think you'd be capable of a great deal.'

'You're right, Chief Inspector.' The dowager spoke in an icy voice. 'Freddy was a poor custodian of Redmire. And, although it might seem a horrible thing to say, I'm glad things have passed to Alistair and Katherine. However, much as I disapproved of and disliked my son, I would never have contemplated having him killed. Good heavens, you're making me sound like some monstrous figure from a Greek tragedy.'

Oldroyd did not reply. He walked back up to the now *un*locked room and stood looking at them all. He had delivered his thoughts on each one of them in turn. His expression was at its most commanding and hawkish. The suspense was now beyond unbearable as they waited for his pronouncement. There was another great spark of lightning and a tremendous crash of thunder.

'Well,' he said at last in his portentous voice again. 'You will be pleased to know that, unlike in many Agatha Christie stories, the culprits are not here. The family and friends are not guilty.'

Only Steph saw the little glint in his eye that suggested he would like to have added 'unfortunately'.

The tension in the room collapsed like a burst balloon.

'Oh, thank God!' murmured Antonia and gripped Douglas's hand. All around people were breathing out and shaking their heads.

'What the—?' spluttered a rejuvenated Dominic, who got up from his chair. 'Do you mean to say that you've brought us here and submitted us to all this for nothing? How dare you! I shall complain to . . .'

'Sit down, sir,' insisted Oldroyd. 'Unless you don't want to know who killed your brother.'

'But . . .' Dominic turned to the others, looking for support. There was none, so he sat down again.

'All right, bring them in,' called Oldroyd. There was a short, agonising wait until police officers appeared escorting two figures: David Morton and Andrea Jenkinson. They were brought briskly over to two chairs placed symbolically at either side of the room they had used to commit murder. At the edge of the room Richard Wilkins crept in looking devastated.

'Morton! What on earth?' said Alistair.

'I'm sorry, Mr Alistair,' said the gardener, who sat down on the chair looking tired and stared sullenly at the floor. Andrea Jenkinson glowered at everyone with defiance and contempt.

Oldroyd continued with his explanation. 'Tim Groves, the forensic pathologist I work with, started me thinking very early on about the possibility of someone here not being who they appeared to be. When we'd been through all the possible motives of the original suspects, I wasn't happy that any of them amounted to enough to lead someone to murder a family member or an old friend, never mind people who worked on the estate. And then there were means and opportunity. It didn't seem plausible that somehow one of you had stumbled upon the secret of the locked room. You were all present in the audience that night, which was consistent with the fact that you would have to have had accomplices, but it would have made the whole thing more difficult and risky. And we kept coming back to the point that we couldn't really see why any of you would want to use this elaborate method to get rid of Lord Redmire; there were much easier and simpler ways of doing it.

'No. I decided we had to look deeper and wider to get the answer. What was it that compelled the murderers to use this outlandish method to dispatch their victim? This search took us all the way back to the beginning of this long and tragic story, to a person of little consequence who has long been forgotten. A young woman called Esmeralda.'

'Who?' asked a bemused Douglas Ramsay. Everyone was looking puzzled.

'My mother!' snapped Jenkinson, wiping tears from her eyes with a shaking hand. She was clearly struggling hard to stay composed.

'Yes, but not yet on that night in 1980, when the illusion was first performed and she played the part of the glamorous assistant to Vivian Carstairs. Maybe you'd like to continue the story?'

Jenkinson looked at Oldroyd with surprise. She hadn't expected this, but Oldroyd knew she would be keen to tell her story to the people before her and wanted to give her the opportunity.

She turned to the assembled members of the family. 'Yes, my mother was Esmeralda, or Liliana, or Natalia, or any of the other cheap, exotic names they gave her – the men who exploited her. Her real name was Jane Dawson, an ordinary girl from a poor family. She was desperate to make it into showbiz, as people called it then, but she had no money and no connections. She wanted to be a dancer, but she got no breaks. She couldn't afford to go to dancing school; the only asset she had was her looks.

'Vivian Carstairs hired her from an agency. She came here to rehearse her part, which, of course, was all about showing her body and her smile, and it was here that she met Frederick Carstairs. My father!'

There were gasps from everyone in the room.

'What?' shouted Dominic.

'No!' wailed Antonia and put her head in her hands. Others were shocked by the terrible look of hatred on Jenkinson's face when she spat out the name of the man she claimed was her father.

'He used his seductive charms on her, as he did on so many vulnerable women. She was young. She'd been looking to establish herself, and he promised her things. Said he would get her on to the stage in the London shows. Their affair continued when she returned to London but then it all went wrong. She became pregnant and he was the father. The bastard couldn't get rid of her quickly enough. He couldn't afford to have any connection with a cheap showgirl. That would have been a scandal. I think he sent her some derisory sums of money and told her he couldn't marry her because he was expected to marry someone in his own class, and that was you.' She pointed at Antonia.

'How does that make you feel? When he married you, he'd already had a child with a poor, weak young woman whom he'd just cast off like a petty nuisance.' She was shouting now and Antonia Ramsay was sobbing.

'OK,' said Oldroyd. 'Stop there. Just tell us what happened.'

'My mother never recovered. I think she loved him, poor thing. She tried to get him back, writing letters, sending photographs of me and her together when I was a little girl. But he refused all contact. I'd never even seen him before I came here. She got some small parts in variety shows in choruses and stuff, but it never came to anything – partly because she started drinking. We were always poor, living in tiny cold flats. No one helped us; I think her family had disowned her when she got pregnant. I was only in my early teens but I had to cope with a mother who was cracking up. She became delusional; she told me she was convinced that "Freddy", as she always called him, would come back to help us some day. He probably hadn't been getting her letters or he was too busy at the moment. It was pathetic. I got her to see the doctor, but it didn't help.'

Jenkinson stopped talking. Tears were running down her face. 'One day I got home from school and found her dead.'

'Oh God!' cried Mary Carstairs.

Jenkinson was really struggling now. 'She'd slit her wrists in the bath. The water was red, and her face was white and cold. I was sixteen years old. I never blamed her, though.' She wiped her face and glared at everyone. 'No, I reserved my anger for the man who'd destroyed her life: Lord Redmire; Frederick Carstairs, an honourable member of the British Establishment,' she continued with vicious sarcasm, and then stabbed her finger at various people. 'Your husband, your lover, your father and your son was a bastard through and through.'

'I already knew that,' said the dowager in a deadly voice that added to the visceral intensity of the terrible reckoning now being enacted. Her aged body was almost completely doubled over, as if with an enormous weight.

'Continue,' said Oldroyd, the dark orchestrator of these terrible revelations.

Outside, the storm raged on.

'It's simple,' Jenkinson said. 'I vowed to avenge her, however long it took. I had to go into care for a while, but I attended college and trained in office skills. I spent years planning how I might take revenge. I tracked him in every way I could without appearing to be a stalker. I knew about his business, his clubs in London, his friends and contacts, his family, his gambling and his womanising. I thought at first it might be possible to sabotage him in some way or damage his reputation, but nothing worked. I couldn't get near him. It affected my whole life, of course. I had jobs and short-lived relationships. I tried to live as normal a life as possible, but there was always this dark secret within me and I remained alone.'

'But finally you got your big opportunity?'

She smiled grimly. 'Yes. After years of frustration, I saw he was advertising for a PA. I couldn't believe it. I was perfectly qualified and he called me for an interview. I knew how to handle it, how he would like women who seemed to admire him. I was very flattering in a subtle way. And I got it.'

'Wasn't it weird, being interviewed by your father, and even having to work for him?'

'I never looked upon that man as my father. I never felt the slightest connection with him. The only emotion I felt was hatred.' She laughed scornfully. 'And when I met him he confirmed my image of him. He was arrogant, leered over women and was utterly self-centred. I had wondered whether there would be something about him I might be drawn to, something that might make me pause.'

She closed her eyes and shook her head. 'But no. The more I saw of him, the more I was determined to rid the world of him.'

'Using the locked room was perfect for you, wasn't it?'

She smiled with a chilling expression of satisfaction. 'There may well have been other ways of killing him, but I couldn't resist the wonderful poetic justice of it. It was that trick that brought Mum and him together, so how appropriate that it should end him. I imagined Mum closing that door and drawing the curtain on him.

'Over the years, Mum had told me the little she knew about the trick. She had been under strict instructions not to look behind the curtain, which is very tight-fitting against the wall and covers a big area, as you've seen, so she didn't know about the two rooms. She knew there was a mechanism, but not what it did. The crucial thing was that she identified Harry Robinson as someone who was involved. This was my way in. I had to cultivate a friendship with him and find out how the thing worked. At first it all seemed a long shot, but I was lucky and it all came together.

'My father was constantly in debt, of course, and he let slip that he had plans to make economies on the estate and even to sell part of it off. He didn't tell me any details, but I'd seen him in the office with some documents that he'd sealed up and taken to the estate safe in Richard Wilkins's office. They were clearly highly secret.'

'So that was your motivation for starting the affair with Wilkins?'

She glanced in surprise at Oldroyd. Richard Wilkins looked down. 'You seem to have discovered everything, Chief Inspector. Yes, I thought that through him I'd get access to the safe and see what I could find out.'

'So you stole his set of keys from him, got into the office one night and took the envelope with those documents in it.'

'It was easy. Men are always off their guard when they're getting sex. I got the keys from his jacket pocket and returned them the next day. He never missed them. I broke a window and opened it so that it looked as if someone had got in that way.'

'Andrea, how could . . . ?' Wilkins cried out and then put his head in his hands.

'Unfortunately for you, you were seen,' continued Oldroyd. 'Although for some time we had no idea who it was who'd been in there. We later found all those stolen documents hidden inside other papers in the desk in your office. I imagine you couldn't believe your luck when you saw the contents.'

'No. There was a sheet containing a list of the economies he was considering and Harry Robinson's pension was listed with a comment in red: "Far too generous, needs to be cut."'

'But there was more in those documents that you could use, wasn't there? Let's have Mr Morton continue.'

The gardener, who had remained silent throughout, looked up sullenly as if he had no intention of saying anything. Oldroyd spoke first, to prompt him.

'You told me you'd always been too busy in the garden to get married – and that was true, wasn't it? The gardens here have been your life: your father and grandfather worked here; the great and rare specimens you've nurtured all these years have been so important to you. You're married to this garden, aren't you? So what did Ms Jenkinson show you?'

Morton had become animated as Oldroyd spoke about the gardens. His face was full of anger and disgust. 'She showed me the plans that Lord Redmire had agreed with the developers. The whole of the old kitchen garden was going to be sold off for housing. That part of the gardens is one of the oldest and most beautiful. It would have meant demolishing the old brick walls. The magnolia wilsonii, those abutilons you were looking at and lots of other wonderful plants. They've been there for generations and they'd have been killed.'

His eyes gleamed with a fanatical devotion. 'I couldn't let him do that. It would have been murder. I've known them all my life. Granddad planted some of them there.'

'They're your family, aren't they? And who wouldn't kill to protect their family?'

Morton looked at Oldroyd with a strange, twisted smile. 'Yes, Chief Inspector, exactly; you understand why I had to do it.'

'Andrea Jenkinson knew you'd be horrified and so you started to plan together. The first thing was to get Harry Robinson on your side.'

'It was easy,' continued Andrea. 'I told him about Lord Redmire's plans and showed him a photocopy of the document. He was terrified about losing his pension.'

'So you devised a plan?'

'Yes. Robinson went to Redmire and said that he wanted to tell him about the locked room before he died and the secret went with him. He suggested that it might be useful to him in these days when money was tight. He also asked in a careful way for reassurance that his pension would be safe.

'I don't think Redmire suspected anything. Of course, he told Robinson his pension would be safe after he'd given this very important information. We had to keep my involvement in revealing Redmire's plans a secret, so Robinson suggested that, if he wanted to re-enact the trick, Redmire would need an assistant he could trust. I knew he would come to me and he did. I had so ingratiated myself during my time with him that he thought me reliable, maybe even indispensable. I enjoyed that power over him. So, although it was all risky, he took the bait as we planned.

'I had to tell David who I was, and my mother's story, in order to explain my motives. But he was sympathetic. I told Redmire that Robinson needed help in restoring the mechanism and that David Morton was the right person to approach. He was capable and reliable. Redmire trusted us all; it was wonderful.'

'Where did you get the key?'

'Luckily Robinson had kept one hidden away in his cottage. It was the only one left.'

'It must have taken a long time to get the whole thing back into working order.'

'It did,' said Morton. 'It took months of greasing and oiling, but it was so well made that it hadn't deteriorated that much. It was just a bit rusty and some of the wiring needed replacing.'

'The rooms themselves were in perfect order, just as they'd been left,' said Jenkinson. 'We only needed to dust and polish. Redmire himself, of course, did nothing; he would never get his hands dirty. But it was soon completed to his satisfaction and we started to rehearse.'

'How did you prevent anyone from finding out about both the plans and who was involved?'

'Redmire closed that whole area off and we were very careful to meet at unusual times. Often I would return to the Hall when people thought I was at home.'

'And you came in your second car, so as not to be recognised – the VW Polo, which you also used on the night you broke into the office. Your parking place hidden by the trees was spotted and we traced the car to you.'

Jenkinson looked at Oldroyd with a mixture of animosity and admiration.

'If only you hadn't been here. I didn't want Redmire to invite the police to take part in the trick, but he was so insistent that it would be wonderful publicity. Actually I began to warm to the challenge of carrying out a murder right under the noses of the police. We did. And we nearly got away with it.'

'And how was it done?'

'I ran things from the side corridor. I turned on the music and operated the switches. He didn't have much to do, apart from the build-up on the television. He just had to be locked up. He thought he was going to get out through the trapdoor in the second part of the trick, like his father had done, but David was waiting to climb in, finish him off and get out before the rooms moved over again.'

'I killed him to save my trees and plants. Rather him than them.' Morton seemed almost proud of what he'd done and showed little emotion about having killed a human being. 'I knew that when Mr Alistair took over those plans would be abandoned and they'd all be safe.'

Oldroyd looked at Morton's tough, weather-beaten face and saw no trace of remorse. In his eyes there was no warmth. Only a terrible vacancy.

Alistair Carstairs shook his head in disbelief at the mad loyalty and devotion of the man.

'So what happened about Harry Robinson? I suspect you kept the real reason for the plan from him?' asked Oldroyd.

'You're right,' said Jenkinson, also without emotion. 'The poor man thought we were doing it for him, and to help Lord Redmire make money for the estate, so it must have been a huge shock when Redmire was murdered. We knew we had to get rid of him straight away. I left quickly, so as not to be seen, and David dealt with Robinson.'

'I went round straight from the Hall,' said Morton. 'Strangled him with a length of rope. It was a shame, really. He was a nice chap.' The matter-of-fact manner of his account was chilling.

'We found traces of unusual plant residue on the knife, which suggested it had been used in a garden.'

'I use it to divide iris rhizomes. Blast it. I wanted to get the knife out, but it was lodged in his body and I had to get out of that room quickly.'

'There was fertiliser on Harry Robinson's neck, which again suggested a garden origin for the murder weapon.'

'It was a piece of old rope lying around on the floor – must have picked up the fertiliser there. Well done, Chief Inspector. You don't miss much, do you?'

'Well, I'm pleased you missed me,' replied Oldroyd. 'It was you, wasn't it, who took a potshot at me?'

'Yes. We decided you were asking too many questions and getting too near the answers, so I followed you that night over to the Pear Tree. I was in the other bar when you were talking to Bill Mason and Frank Bridges. I knew they might be telling you dangerous stuff. I knew I had a chance because you'd be walking across the fields alone. I came back to the Hall and got a gun from the gunroom by the stables. I've had a key for that cupboard for years. I went back to the field where the footpath goes across and waited for you. But I missed . . . and here we are.'

'And finally, what about Ian Barden? The poor man who went round telling everyone he'd seen things and maybe knew who the killers were. He never told anyone what he knew and he never spoke to us. Did he know anything?'

Morton answered this question. 'Probably not, but we couldn't take any risks. I think he was just a fantasiser, but he did it once too often. I was so irritated by him that I decided to finish him off with one of his precious engines.'

'So, ironically, although he was warning everyone else, he was the one in danger because he drew attention to himself; a hapless victim who knew nothing.'

Morton shrugged, as if the sadistic killing of Ian Barden had been of no more significance than swatting a pesky fly.

'You tried a little to incriminate other people where you could, didn't you?' continued Oldroyd.

'Yes,' replied Jenkinson. 'I did see Poppy arguing with her father and I thought it wouldn't do any harm to tell you about it. I tried to direct you towards the people who'd asked Redmire for money.' She shrugged her shoulders. 'To no avail, unfortunately.'

Oldroyd looked at her solemnly. 'I hate to have to tell you this, but in the end it was your mother who gave us a clue as to who you really were.'

Jenkinson frowned at him. 'How? That's impossible.'

'You were right that in her desperation she sent photographs of you and her to Redmire. He kept them and we found them in his study. Of course, you were very small at the time; but when I looked closely at the photograph, I could see that birthmark you have under your ear.'

Her hand went up instinctively to the patch of discolouration.

'It was only a small detail, but it was another piece of information that enabled us to eventually track you down and to discover that your real name is Andrea Dawson.'

'It is and I'm proud of it.'

She and Morton remained defiant and unrepentant.

'So . . .' said Oldroyd. He was reaching the end of his orchestrated unravelling of the mysteries at Redmire Hall. 'We've seen what an audacious and cunningly contrived plan it was, and also how deadly. I'm sure you both still believe your actions were justified, but the law, I'm afraid, thinks otherwise. Take them away.'

The officers led Jenkinson and Morton swiftly out of the room and to waiting police cars. Morton called to Alistair Carstairs as he was bundled out.

'Look after them, Mr Alistair. I know you will.'

Alistair looked away and said nothing. He felt sick. With the exception of Wilkins, who had already left, everyone was slumped and unresponsive in their chairs. The multiple stresses that had afflicted them since the night of the murder, coupled with the intense emotions they'd experienced and witnessed this evening, had left them exhausted. Slowly and without a word, even from Dominic Carstairs, they got up and left, with Antonia helping the dowager.

The thunder had passed and the sound of the rain had died down.

Oldroyd was drained. He was familiar with the feeling of anticlimax that he usually felt at the end of an investigation. The adrenalin flowed during the chase, and then it was a huge let-down when the case was solved. This time it felt even worse after the intense high he'd just experienced in handling the great denouement.

He and Steph returned to their makeshift office for the last time. Oldroyd poured out coffee, but could have done with something stronger.

'You shouldn't really have done that, you know, sir.'

Oldroyd glanced up to see Steph looking at him rather sorrowfully. He felt a fleeting anger – she'd no right to reprimand him – but this soon passed because he knew she was right. He also knew that it was a sign of the real strength in their relationship that she felt able to confront him, her senior officer, with uncomfortable facts.

'Why do you say that?'

'You deliberately put them through a lot of unnecessary emotional turmoil and you did it because you don't like them and because . . . I don't know what else.'

Oldroyd sighed and looked very sheepish. He drank his coffee in silence for a few minutes, sighed again and then said, 'You're right – right about what I did and right to say it to me. The truth is I've always disliked people like that: the idle rich with their arrogant sense of entitlement.'

'But they weren't all like that, sir. The Ramsays and Alistair Carstairs and his wife seemed like decent people to me.'

'I know. You're right, you're right. I just couldn't resist making them squirm a bit. I suppose I enjoyed the power it gave me over them. And you know I'm a sucker for a bit of theatre. The whole idea of ending the case as we began it, in a dramatic way, was too much, especially in this big-house setting and . . . Oh, you know what I mean.'

Steph laughed. 'I do, sir, and although it was a bit malicious to reveal to Dominic Carstairs that his wife had had an affair, I must admit it was all worth it to see him outmanoeuvred the way you did it. He was up and down like a jack-in-the-box and utterly speechless by the end.'

Oldroyd had to laugh. 'I know. Anyway, we'd better get our stuff together and get back to Harrogate.'

He looked round their little office and felt quite sad to be leaving. He could get used to working in a stately home.

As they were packing up, Jeffries came into the room. He was elated that they'd solved the case but also disappointed that his time working with Oldroyd was coming to an end.

'Sir,' he said, looking embarrassed, 'I just wanted to say . . . it's been a . . . privilege to work with you and . . .'

'OK, Jeffries. I appreciate that – and thank you for your good work. I shall be sending a report to your inspector and I'll mention you.'

Jeffries glowed. 'Thank you, sir.'

Steph suppressed a laugh. 'He'll be telling his grandchildren that he once worked with the great Detective Chief Inspector Oldroyd,' she said when Jeffries had left.

'Or at least that he was there when the great Locked-Room Mystery was solved!'

Still chuckling, Oldroyd and Steph got all their stuff together and went to the Saab.

Before he started the engine, Oldroyd turned to Steph. 'I'm proud of you. You were right to say what you did. Never be afraid to state truth to those in authority, whoever they are.'

'Well, I learned everything I know from you, sir – so, following my boss, I'm not likely to sit there and take it, am I?'

'I suppose not.' He sighed. 'You also said there was another reason why I behaved like that, and you're right.' He paused. 'My wife wants a divorce, or at least she might, and I'm . . . I'm angry about it and . . . sad . . . and I'm by myself, you know.'

Steph gave him a sympathetic smile. 'I understand, sir.'

The journey back to Harrogate passed in near silence.

∽

When Steph got back to HQ she went to see DCS Walker, as Oldroyd had asked her to report back on the case. She returned to find an envelope by her computer. Inside was a printed message, which read:

> It's lovely having you around, but not so nice when
> we have harsh words. Remember what I said about
> being friendlier.

Clearly there was going to be more trouble from that direction.

Next morning, Oldroyd came in rather late to Harrogate HQ, just in time for Tom Walker to call him into his office.

'Well done for cracking that one, Jim; I've already spoken to Stephanie. So you worked out how they used that bloody conjuring trick to commit the first murder?'

'I did, Tom, and it took a bit o' doin', I can tell thi.' They enjoyed heightening their accents and sometimes using a bit of Yorkshire dialect in these private conversations.

'I can imagine, but then you did have a front-row seat when . . .' Tom stopped for a moment and looked away. Oldroyd could see he was finding it difficult not to break into laughter again at the memory of seeing him on television that night. Walker coughed and calmed himself. 'There's just one thing. I've had a complaint from a Mr Dominic Carstairs – brother of the first victim, I understand.'

'Yes, I know him. He was difficult all the way through.'

'Was he? Thought he sounded a snooty bastard. Well' – he took up a piece of paper – 'he says you put them "through unnecessary stress because of the way you revealed your findings about the case". What's he on about?'

Oldroyd shook his head. 'I went over the top; you know what I'm like with a bit of drama. I gathered them all together and explained everything, but I delayed telling them who the murderer was – and in fact it wasn't any of them anyway. I suppose it was a bit . . . cruel, but I have to admit they got to me. All those rich, arrogant . . .' He shrugged his shoulders. Walker looked at him.

'I see. That was a bit naughty, I have to admit, but don't worry. I had a call not long after that one.'

'Oh?'

'Yes, from the bloke's wife. Mary Carstairs, was it?'

'Yes.'

'She said not to take any notice of her husband, who is a boring old fart – those were her very words. She said you'd done a magnificent job and the way you ended it was splendid entertainment. What's more, she was absolutely sure that the other members of the family would agree with her. They were pleased to get it over with and I was to congratulate you on a first-rate effort all round.'

Oldroyd looked at Walker, who, he realised, was trying to suppress a smile.

'Tom! You've been leading me on, you old bugger!'

Walker could no longer contain himself and burst into laughter. 'Oh, I'm sorry, Jim, but your face again! That's the second time you thought I was going to have a go at you! Anyway, what can I say, except well done? I'd like to have seen it!' He laughed some more, dried his eyes on a white handkerchief and then tried to be serious for a moment. 'Just try not to get carried away. I know things haven't been too good for you recently, so we'll say no more about it, eh?'

'Thanks, Tom,' said Oldroyd as he realised that Steph had not just been reporting on the case to Walker the night before.

The end of the day was turning into another warm and pleasant evening as Oldroyd left Harrogate HQ and went home. After he'd eaten, he felt restless. He didn't want to be in the flat by himself, especially when it was so inviting outside. Why not walk over to High Harrogate and see how Louise was doing in The Orphan Girl? He would enjoy embarrassing her, and what fun to be served in a pub by your own daughter!

He walked around the long arc of the Stray from his flat to the Skipton Road. The pub was a low early-Victorian building with the door opening on to the road. It was busy, with drinkers spilling out of the door. Oldroyd made his way to one end of the bar and saw Louise talking to someone at the other end, with her back to him.

'Service!' he called out. She looked startled in his direction until she saw who it was and then frowned. She came over.

'Dad! What are you doing here?' she said quietly, but she wasn't angry, as she would have been in her teenage years.

'I'd like a drink; pint of Nidderdale bitter, please.'

She smiled sardonically at him as she pulled a pint.

Oldroyd passed over the money and took a sip from the glass. 'Excellent. Very good service; I'll have to come here again.'

'Don't make a habit of it while I'm working here,' Louise said. 'What brings you out here anyway? I thought you didn't have any time to enjoy yourself. Have you finished things off at the big house?'

'We have indeed, at last – absolutely fascinating. It turned out not to be any of the obvious suspects after all. It was a woman who worked as Lord Redmire's PA, who was actually his love child and in cahoots with the gardener.'

'What's a "love child", for God's sake? You're so quaint sometimes, Dad.'

'His daughter by one of his lovers, who he disowned; left her to bring up the child by herself.'

'The bastard! Isn't that just typical of men? And the wealthier they are, the more arrogant they are and the more they think women are just there for their own amusement.'

'Yes, well, this woman got her revenge in the end; at least, her daughter did on her behalf.' He took another drink and looked around at the pub. 'You coming to work here gave me a bit of a clue about all that.'

'How?'

'Just the name of the place: The Orphan Girl. We had evidence that Lord Redmire had an unacknowledged daughter and the mother had tried to get him to support them. The girl wasn't an orphan at that stage, of course, but it set me wondering. What if the mother had died, leaving the daughter with a terrible bitterness against the father who'd abandoned her and treated her mother badly? She would blame that man for her mother's death and rightly so. And that turned out to be exactly what had happened.'

'Wow! Well, glad to be of help.'

'I looked up the pub name, by the way; it's named after the wife of the first owner, who was an orphan. She was working as a maidservant at the house of someone he knew and they fell in love and got married, much against his family's wishes, not surprisingly in those times. Anyway, there's a nice Victorian romantic story for you.'

'Yes, and what you uncovered was the shadow side of that, wasn't it? Lord whatever-his-name as the Victorian blackguard deserting the seduced girl.'

'Yes. All he needed was the black twirling moustache.'

He finished his beer and put the empty glass on the bar.

'I'll be off, then. Enjoy yourself, but remember you're serving, not consuming: no one wants to be served by drunken bar staff.'

'Get out!' she laughed, and threw a beer mat at him.

It was still quite early in the evening as Oldroyd walked back across the town on a different route. The Harrogate Festival was under way and there were street entertainers: little theatre and music groups per-forming short pieces of drama and playing folk music up and down the town. As he walked down the pedestrianised Cambridge Street, he saw a group of adults and children gathered around a performer. As he got closer he saw that it was a magician dressed in a black cloak and a hat decorated with stars. He was wielding a wand.

Oldroyd stopped for a while and watched as the man made play-ing cards disappear, produced bunches of flowers from his sleeves and reconstituted a torn-up piece of paper magically into a whole sheet. The audience was 'spellbound' even though they – or at least the adults – knew that it was all trickery. The magic of magic was that you couldn't explain it, even if you knew it wasn't magic!

Oldroyd applauded after each trick and again when the magician took a bow at the end of his little show. Then he continued his solitary walk back to his flat on the Stray.

Acknowledgments

I would like to thank my family and friends for all their support and encouragement over the years, particularly those who read drafts and made comments.

The Otley Courthouse Writers' Group, led by James Nash, has helped me to develop as a writer and given me the extra impetus to get things completed.

Some readers will recognise Newby Hall near Ripon as the model for Redmire Hall. I have spent many happy times with my family exploring the wonderful gardens there and riding on the train! I would like to thank the owners for their care in maintaining one of the finest estates in England.

The West Riding Police is a fictional force based on the old riding boundary. Harrogate was part of the old West Riding, although it is in today's North Yorkshire.

J. R. Ellis

About the Author

John R. Ellis has lived in Yorkshire for most of his life and has spent many years exploring Yorkshire's diverse landscapes, history, language and communities. He recently retired after a career in teaching, mostly in further education in the Leeds area. In addition to the Yorkshire Murder Mystery series he writes poetry, ghost stories and biography. He has completed a screenplay about the last years of the poet Edward Thomas and a work of faction about the extraordinary life of his Irish mother-in-law. He is currently working on his memoirs of growing up in a working-class area of Huddersfield in the 1950s and 1960s.